THE CROOKED MAID

THE
CROOKED
MAID

· A NOVEL ·

DAN VYLETA

BLOOMSBURY

NEW YORK · LONDON · NEW DELHI · SYDNEY

Copyright © 2013 by Dan Vyleta

Published by Bloomsbury USA, New York

All papers used by Bloomsbury USA are natural, recyclable products made
from wood grown in well-managed forests. The manufacturing processes
conform to the environmental regulations of the country of origin.

LIBRARY OF CONGRESS CATALOGING-IN-
PUBLICATION DATA HAS BEEN APPLIED FOR

ISBN: 978-1-60819-809-2

First U.S. Edition 2013

1 3 5 7 9 10 8 6 4 2

Typeset by Hewer Text UK Ltd, Edinburgh
Printed and bound in the U.S.A. by Thomson-
Shore Inc., Dexter, Michigan

In memory of my father, Michal.
This is a story about angry sons, written by a grateful one.

I am afraid of houses in which one grows comfortable and allows oneself to be taken in by the banal truth that life goes on and time heals all wounds.
—HEINRICH BÖLL, *Billiards at Half-Past Nine*

In answering them he said, among other things, that he had indeed been away from Russia for a long time, more than four years, that he had been sent abroad on account of illness, . . . Listening to him, the swarthy man grinned several times; he laughed particularly when, to his question: "And did they cure you?" the blond man answered: "No, they didn't."
—FYODOR DOSTOEVSKY, *The Idiot*, trans. R. Pevear and L. Volokhonsky

BOOK ONE

Part One

The names were strange to those who came to conquer. They said "Ti-moh-schen-ko," "Tschuj-kov," and "Kat-ju-scha," rolled them in their mouths like rough-edged pebbles they could neither chew nor spit. "Red October" was a steelworks; "Red Barricades" an arms factory: chimneys rife with soldiers taking aim. There was a factory that made tractors named for Dser-schin-ski, the founder of the Soviet secret police: Felix by first name, son of Edmond the Pole. The city itself used to be called Tsaritsyn, for the river that had dug a gorge south of the city before pouring its waters into the Volga. If not for the name change, it might not have pricked Hitler's pride. Stalingrad: 48 degrees north, 44 degrees east. One hundred and sixty-three days of battle.

They fought in streets, in sewers and factory hallways; amongst the silo's concrete walls. Artillery bombardment and air raids had levelled the city. What was left was debris—and men. On the eleventh of October the Axis soldiers in the city launched their final assault. By noon of the next day, in a section of town southeast of the "Barricades" plant, they got within seventy yards of the riverbank before the Soviets managed to dig in. Seventy yards. The width of a football pitch. They never got any further.

News travelled erratically, traversing the air as radio waves or crawling through the network of gullies that housed the civilian population; through leaflets raining from the sky. There was no single message that prepared them for defeat.

On Christmas Eve 1942 they listened to a broadcast purporting to capture their voices. They heard themselves sing carols: hale and hearty voices rising from the field radio without the customary plume of exhalation. At night the rats made off with frozen toes. Men shitting on shovels, flinging their filth out of the trench. Stalingrad. Both sides set off fireworks to welcome 1943.

Close to 700,000 soldiers died at Stalingrad; more than 90,000 Axis soldiers were taken prisoner. In one of the photos that document the surrender, taken by a Soviet journalist working for the news and propaganda division of the Soviet Ministry of Defence, a figure draws the eye. It is a German medical officer, recognizable by his armband and staff-and-snake insignia, guiding a wounded comrade by the elbow. He looks older than one might expect; a ragged figure, his face made harsh by hunger. But there is something to his gesture—to the angle of his arm, and the spread of fingers on the muddy sleeve—that leaves no doubt about the softness of his touch. As for his charge, he does not have a face. Where one looks to find his features, one finds a bandage, speckled with dirt and photographic grain.

One

The train was running late.

It had been running late since before Nancy and had made several unscheduled stops between Basel and Zurich. Near Innsbruck it broke down altogether, or rather it stopped, and men could be seen running around outside, inspecting the tracks and wheels and shouting at one another. Then it gathered velocity once more, tore along a long, narrow valley before once again coming to a screeching halt. The sun was setting, and a fine, dreary rain was running down the windowpane. Despite the season—it was July already—the compartment grew drafty and cold whenever the train was in motion, then turned close and somehow oppressive when it shuddered to a halt.

She had been on the train now for close to fourteen hours.

During the first hours of their journey the conductor had made a point of stopping by the compartment with great regularity, to offer his services, ply her with a peculiarly sweet yet bitter tea which he dispensed from a blue enamel pot, and to keep her abreast of the reasons for their delay. He was a fat man, doughy, and as though held together by his ill-fitting uniform. Whenever he leaned over to arrange the cushion behind her head or to fuss over the luggage that was hanging in a net above her seat, he left behind the sweaty mark of his plump little hands. Above all he liked to talk. His explanations were as inconstant as his crablike gait. At first he had told "mademoiselle" (as he insisted on calling her, even though she

5

was no longer young, and even though they spoke in German, he in an accent that was broadly Viennese, she with the crisp formality of someone no longer used to the tongue) that the train's delay was due to the circumstance, "and a rather odd one at that," that the company had been unable to locate the engine driver in Paris, from where the train hailed. They had found him at last, dead drunk, at a public pissoir not far from the station, sitting on the ground, that is, with his arms wrapped around a plucked and broken-necked goose. All attempts at revival had failed, and at long last it was decided that a replacement had to be found.

An hour later the conductor seemed to have forgotten about the engine driver whose goose he had taken such pains to describe. Now he insisted that a tree had been found lying across the tracks in circumstances that were nothing short of suspicious. To wit, the trees were considered to be located too far from the tracks for it to have been a matter of chance, and besides, the trunk had been cut rather than broken, "and with a proper saw at that." Twenty miles on, it was the activities of the Swiss officials that were holding up the train. Some papers had been filled in incorrectly and they—"that is, the Swiss"—had called ahead to the next station with instructions to stop the train "whatever the cost."

Through each of the conductor's lengthy explanations the woman listened with an air of evident boredom, nonetheless smiling at him and accepting his cups of sweet-yet-bitter tea. Whenever the conductor left the compartment, the woman let lapse this sugary smile and turned her attention back to the boarding school boy who was sitting across from her. He, in turn, never left off staring at her with open curiosity. They had been alone in the compartment for some six hours now and had yet to exchange so much as a word.

There was little about him that was remarkable: a young man dressed in black, with a stiff white shirt and dark, patterned tie, holding a book closed upon his lap. He was perhaps eighteen years of age; too slender yet to be thought of as a man; rich (how else would he be able to afford the first-class ticket?); a boy very pale, with a mask of freckles sitting lightly on his face; the hair nearly black, thick, and falling low into his forehead; the brows long and straight, sloping gently to the temples. There was something wrong with his eye, the one that faced the window and found its own reflection in the darkness of the pane. It looked as though it had been beaten, broken, reassembled. Its white was discoloured and it drooped within its socket, giving a new note to his face, of belligerent reproach. His shoes were made of a shiny black leather and looked as though they had never been worn.

In fact, there was nothing about his person or his clothes that would have marked him as a boarding school boy—he might have been a clerk, or an apprentice undertaker—had not the satchel and cap that were stowed in the netting above his head proclaimed him as precisely that, the student or recent graduate of an institution that thought highly enough of itself to affect a crest with lions and a motto in Ciceronian Latin. He also owned a knapsack and what looked to be a lady's hat box. At intervals he would stand up on his seat and pull a wrapped sandwich out of the former, then sit eating it with obvious relish. He was tidy and handsome and really quite short.

Darkness fell and the train rattled on. The boy seemed eager to start into conversation but uncertain where to begin. From time to time he would flash her a smile, red-lipped, innocent, and watch her form a smile of her own: grown-up, guarded, graceful, and quick. Once he pulled a sketchbook and pencil from his knapsack and sat as though he wanted to draw her, then flushed and tore out the page. The pencil he wedged behind his ear, where it hung for some minutes before coming loose and falling on the seat next to him. He grabbed it, smiled, put it in his pocket, then found it made a bulge in his pressed trousers, produced it again, and balanced it on the half inch of ledge beneath the window, from where it was sure to fall when they reached the next bend. His fingernails, she noticed, were freshly pared, and he had not undone a single button on his collar. There was a callus on his middle finger such as is formed by the routine use of a pen; and a small red pimple where nose tucked into cheek.

That, and his eye was broken at the socket; bled its iris into the white.

The woman found it hard to stop looking at this eye. It was much older than the rest of him, a mark of violence on his pretty, lively face; did not spoil it, nor yet set off its beauty, but sat instead like a fragment of some other face that had risen to the surface. He seemed to have no control over the lid. It would slide shut from time to time, droop across the waking eye like the line of the horizon, and he would raise one hand, making no effort to hide the motion, grab hold of his thick lashes, pull back the lid and stuff it into its fold under the bone. He'd smile then, and she'd grow conscious of her staring, so obvious under the boy's observant gaze; would catch herself and make an effort to look away. But within minutes her eyes had returned to his, the broken eye, and she found herself wondering whether it had any life.

"I got into a tussle."

He spoke abruptly, without introduction, the voice high and quiet, pink tongue tapping against teeth.

"Excuse me?"

"A tussle," he repeated, leaning forward, his hands spread on his knees. "Almost a fight, actually, with a boy in my class. That's why it looks so funny. There's something about it. Nerve damage. The doctors say it will never really heal. But all the same I see just fine."

He leaned back, pleased to have broken the ice, so much so that he even laughed out loud, a quick, high chuckle, good-humoured and young.

"Did you win?" she asked, after a pause.

"Win?"

"Your tussle."

He shook his head and smiled: ruefully, cheerfully, unperturbed in his good humour. "You know, I very nearly did. I was surprised myself. The boy was much bigger than I. But then, I've always been good at games."

"Good at games. Football, I suppose."

"Tennis," he smiled, and pointed to the handle of a racket sticking out of his knapsack. "School champion three years running. And you?"

"I?" She laughed. "I'm nearly forty—too old for games. But what a queer little fellow you are!"

Not in the least offended by this appraisal, the boy quickly joined her in her laughter, held out his palm and introduced himself as "Robert, Robert Seidel."

She shook his hand and offered no name of her own.

2.

The boarding school boy might have continued the conversation—indeed he seemed eager to—had not a group of men pushed into the compartment at precisely this point, bringing with them the noise of their banter. There were four of them. They were dressed in French uniforms, and for a moment she thought they had come once again to inspect their passports and travelling papers, though there had been two such inspections already since they had crossed the border into the French-controlled parts of Austria. Then she was hit by the smell of alcohol and tobacco that clung to the men, and their air of awkward bravado as they jostled for position between the two rows of seats. They stood, brushing her knees with their legs, taking up space and looking to one another for someone to make a start of it; rubbed shoulders, dug elbows into one another's sides and exchanged coarse little whispers—in short, they performed all the myriad gestures that expressed their soldiers' camaraderie as they got in line to flirt with her. It was a blond lad who seized the initiative at last and stepped closer yet to loom directly over her, his head tucked into his shoulders to avoid the overhang of the luggage rack. He addressed her in French, speaking as much with his eyes as with his tongue.

"*Bonsoir, madame.* But we weren't told that such a beauty shared the train with us. You travel with your son?"

She looked up at him, studied his bluffly handsome features, then turned her head away to stare into the darkness of the window. She was not wearing a hat. In her reflection she was struck by how red her lipstick looked, how pale and delicate the long powdered plains of her cheeks. The soldier bowed down to her so that his own reflection loomed next to hers, blue eyes growing out of the undulations of her auburn hair. His lips were very close to her ear.

"*Madame*," he tried again, switching to German."*Ich Sie kompliment auf Ihrs—*" He stopped, struggled for the word.

"*Schönheit—beauté,*" the schoolboy piped up, then added in rapid schoolboy French: "*Mais je ne suis pas son fils.*"

The soldier straightened, turned around. His comrades likewise shifted their attention from one side of the compartment to the other. It was like the sea-heave of the ocean. Pretty soon they would all swing back.

"So you speak French, boy?"

"Yes. *Je m'appelle Robert Seidel. Je suis de Vienne.* I speak quite well, don't you think? I can understand you quite clearly."

"And *madame*? Does she not speak it?"

"I suppose not."

The soldier took this in, stood pondering, lit a cigarette, blew smoke into the air.

"And she really isn't your mother?"

"Not a bit," the schoolboy answered, still in his quick if clumsy French. "We have only just met. I don't even know her name."

"Then perhaps you can translate." The Frenchman turned his back on the boy, leaned a hand onto the expanse of window to his side, and stooped down once again to the woman with the made-up lips. "Tell her she is very beautiful."

"I can't tell her that!"

"Tell her, boy, or I'll box your ears."

The boy seemed undaunted by the threat, and inclined to argue, but a different thought took hold of him just then, and he licked his lips as he sat looking for the right phrase.

"He says," he said at last, speaking at the back of the man, who stood blocking his view, and craning his neck around the man's buttocks to watch her reaction, "he says to tell you that you are very beautiful." He paused, flashed her a smile unspoiled by irony. "I suppose he doesn't mean anything by it."

"Doesn't he?" the woman answered. She looked up at the soldier's face, first with annoyance then with something like warmth, and spoke her words softly, a half smile playing on her lips. "Tell him I am married. Tell him my husband was in the war."

The boy did as he was bidden, and almost immediately the Frenchman's expression changed and turned from smile to frown. He turned around to consult with his comrades in rapid whispers, then swung back towards the woman.

"Where did he serve? Which front? In the east or in the west?"

Again the schoolboy translated his words, more boldly this time, his dark eyes shining with his own curiosity.

She took her time with the answer, played with the gloves she had placed on the seat next to her, hooded eyes studying the man. "In the east," she said at last. "But that's just a matter of chance. He would have gone west, had he been asked. All the way to the Eiffel Tower."

The boy translated as best he could, stumbling a little over the conditional. Despite the woman's assertion, the soldiers relaxed as soon as they heard that her husband had been shooting at Russians, not Frenchmen.

"Tell her," said their leader, raising a hand to his lips and kissing his fingertips in a quick and habitual motion, "that she has the most beautiful eyes. It is foolish of her husband to have her travel alone."

The boy launched himself into the sentence, but all of a sudden the woman seemed to tire of the game.

"Enough," she said in perfect French. "You have paid your compliments. You are very gallant and no doubt a formidable lover. I am flattered, but married. And rich enough to buy my own stockings, or chocolate, or whatever it is you wish to trade." Her voice was quiet, though not without a certain force. "It would be tiresome if this grew into an incident involving your commanding officer, don't you think?"

She flapped her gloves in front of her face, dismissing them. The blond soldier blanched and straightened up. He seemed to wish to say something more, but was lost for words; whipped around and pushed one of his comrades in the direction of the door into the corridor; threw his cigarette down at their feet. In the doorway he took a moment to turn around, blow a line of spit past his chin onto the floor.

"*Putain*," he mouthed. "German whore."

The schoolboy heard it and jumped to his feet.

"You mustn't call her names!" he shouted, more in reproach than anger, then stumbled forward as the train entered upon a curve. He fell to one knee and collided head to groin with the soldier at the door. The man took hold of a fist-load of his hair and shoved him back contemptuously into his seat. He spat once more, turned, and left the door open as he followed his comrades back down the corridor towards the second-class section of the train.

"Gentlemen, he's led you on," the woman called after them, her voice gently mocking. "*Il est bien possible qu'il soit mon fils.*—Perhaps he is my son after all."

She blocked with a stare the boy's attempt to run and give chase. The next instant they entered a tunnel. Darkness swallowed them, sang back the screech of the train's rapid journey. When they emerged, the boy had shed his anger. He was laughing.

"You speak French," he laughed, "and so much better than I. *Mais vous n'avez rien dit!*"

She felt it would be churlish not to join him in his laughter. It took them some minutes to calm down.

"Is it true, though?" the boy asked at last. "Your husband is a soldier?"

"Was," she said, and smoothed her skirt over her thighs. "An officer in the medical corps."

"He wasn't killed, was he?"

"No. He lived. He was taken prisoner."

"By the Russians."

"Yes."

"And now?"

"And now?" She paused, smiled, studied the face of this strange boy across. There was no malice there, just good-natured curiosity, and a guileless wonder at the world. One had to search out his eye—the one that lay broken in its socket—to remind oneself that he too must have some knowledge of pain, however vague.

"As a matter of fact he's just been released. I'm on my way to meet him."

The boy made to ask more, leaning forward in his eagerness to learn, but she quickly interrupted him.

"Does it hurt?" she asked. "Your eye, I mean. It looks like the bones weren't set properly."

She reached out and touched him, to the left of his brow. He blushed under her touch. It pleased her to see it. He really was a very pretty young man. She allowed her fingers to linger, then settled herself back in her seat. It took him some moments to recover and answer her question.

"It doesn't hurt," he said. "Only sometimes   "

"Yes?"

All at once his voice took on the urgency of confidence. It was as though he thought himself back in the dormitory, swapping secrets across a linen sheet.

"It's stupid. But when I look in the mirror sometimes, in the morning you see, when I'm still sleepy (I'm not a good riser—not that I'm lazy, mind, I try not to be, but in the morning I find it hard to find my feet, I even get dizzy sometimes), I catch sight of the eye, hanging there in the mirror, and, well, for a moment I myself don't know what to do with it. I mean, it doesn't look right."

He gesticulated, bit his lip in frustration at his inability to explain himself.

"It's even a bit spooky. I stare in the mirror, and the eye stares right back. It's as though it belongs to someone else.

"My father is dead," he added after a pause, carried away by a chain of associations she found hard to reconstruct. "He died when I was still a little boy. I wonder sometimes—but it's too stupid to say it out loud." He looked up then, stared at her shyly past his coal-black lashes. "Is it very ugly?"

She laughed, brushed away the question with a wave of her hand. "Your mother remarried?"

"Yes. A Herr Seidel. He insisted that I take his name. To be honest, I hardly know him at all. We'd only lived with him for a short while when I was sent away to school. And with the war and all . . . In short, I've not seen him in years. Nor mother."

"What was your father's name?"

"Teuben," the boy said, gratified that she had asked. "Maybe you have heard of him. He was a famous detective."

The woman nodded blankly. The name was unknown to her.

She stood up and excused herself, went to the toilet.

3.

When she returned, the boy was standing on his seat, digging around in his knapsack. He produced a bottle of milk that had evidently leaked: the top inch of liquid was missing and the bottle sticky with its spilled contents. He took a swig, then offered it to her like a workman passing around a cigarette. She declined. The milk clung to the down on his upper lip. She laughed, and he looked at her confused until she raised her finger to her own mouth and ran it lightly along its curve. His hand mirrored the gesture, shook loose some pearls of milk. Embarrassed, yet smiling all the same, he began to wipe at his lips with his sleeve and the back of his hand. She offered him a handkerchief and he took it, then decided it was too precious or too clean to be put to the profane use of wiping his mug. He sat there with the silk hanky in one fist and the milk bottle in the other, a sheepish smile upon his face.

The train hissed, rolled to a stop. All at once the electricity failed both in the corridor and in the compartment itself. They sat in total darkness. She could hear the boy's breathing. A cone of light lit up the corridor outside the compartment, ran shakily along the carpet, the windows, the ceiling. She expected the conductor to show, torch in hand, and explain the latest breakdown, but the light flickered and disappeared without anyone entering the compartment. The rain grew stronger, beat patterns on the windowpane. The boy across kept shifting in his seat: the creak of leather underneath his skinny bum. She reached out into the darkness, found his knee, then his hand. They linked fingers, very lightly. Minutes slipped past. She raised her left wrist to her eyes but could not make out her watch. It must have been gone midnight. In her right hand the boy's fingers beat an urgent pulse into her own.

She broke the silence.

"Before," she said, "when we weren't yet talking. You took out a sketchpad, then put it away again. You wanted to draw me."

"Yes," he answered, though it hadn't been a question. "But it seemed rude, drawing a stranger. And besides—you would have asked to see the picture."

In the darkness she could hear him lean his face against the pane.

"I'm not very good, you see."

"What is it about me you wanted to draw?"

He answered her without the slightest hesitation, as though he had waited for her to ask him precisely this. As before, when he'd told her about his eye, his voice took on a special sort of quality, at once secretive and earnest. A child might make its confession in a voice like this: shuffling its feet, slyly proud at the wit of its new sin.

"I wanted to draw your face," he said. "Your lips, actually. You have a long upper lip. It curves, a little lopsided, and there's almost no dip at the centre. Under the nose, I mean. I've read about it in novels but have never really seen one. 'A cruel upper lip.' That, and your hands are very large."

"That doesn't sound very appealing."

15

"But it is!" he protested, almost yanking free of her grasp. "It's true, you know. What the soldier said before."

"That I am beautiful."

"Yes."

"I'm old," she sighed, gratified, and let go of his hand.

For a half-hour or so neither of them spoke. She pulled her legs up onto the seat next to her and willed herself asleep. In her head an image formed, of her husband's face with sunken cheeks. His eye was broken, and he hadn't shaved. In his mouth there stuck a cigarette. The smoke kept stinging her eyes.

A sudden tremor ran through the train, tossed her out of her half-formed dream. It was followed by first a screech, then a long and rasping whinny. She sat up, alarmed, still enveloped in darkness. The train jerked, struggled, lay silent; raindrops pelting the windowpane with the force of a proper storm. A flash of lightning off in the distance gave them a mo-ment's illumination. She saw the boy's face, artless and smiling, glad to be trapped in the storm with his milk bottle, his knapsack, and her. Then, in the renewed darkness, a thought must have come to him. He soon put it into words.

"How long has it been?" he asked. "Since you last saw your husband?"

She yawned then stretched, took her time with the answer. "Nine years."

He whistled in his schoolboy manner, did the maths. "But that's longer than—I mean, unless he was in the army even before—Or perhaps it's been eight and a half—"

"Nine years," she repeated. "Since the spring of '39. He wasn't con-scripted until March 1940."

She paused, gave the boy time to formulate a theory.

"He left you," he said at last. "And now he wants you back."

She laughed out loud, listened to herself. *A cruel laugh*, she thought, *to go with my cruel upper lip.*

"I left him," she said. "He was having an affair."

"Oh no!" said the boarding school boy.

"Oh yes," she said, her voice gently mocking. "And you? How long has it been since you saw your good mother?"

"Five years, ten months. I wanted to go after the war finished, but there was a problem with the paperwork. And then Herr Seidel wrote to say I should stay and finish school."

"Let me guess." She lowered her voice to lend authority to the phrase. "*A young man is nothing without a good education.*"

"Yes, something like that. He even wanted me to stay the rest of the summer, saying that it was hard to get proper food in Vienna, and that the streets were full of riff-raff. But then I got another letter. This one came from Mother."

He paused for effect. She obliged him. "What did it say?"

"That Herr Seidel had fallen out the window. He almost broke his neck."

"He fell?" She tried not to laugh. "Just like that?"

"Yes. Only maybe he was pushed."

In the darkness she heard him lean forward, until she could feel his breath upon her face. The thought occurred to her that he had decided to kiss her. But he continued to talk instead.

"There's a family secret," he whispered, playfully and yet in earnest, clearly tickled by the thought. "It all started when my stepbrother disappeared. After the war. And now Herr Seidel! Mother thinks the maid . . . But she never spelled it out, you see."

"The maid? Your family is rich."

"Very." He said it with enthusiasm but no pride, as though it were a remarkable item of trivia that in no way affected his life. "Herr Seidel owns a factory."

"Then I'm sure everything will turn out just fine."

He was about to reply when all of a sudden the overhead lamp came alive and flooded the compartment with its bright yellow light. It found them in an odd position, him leaning forward, with his arms thrown out for balance, his bottom perched on the very edge of his seat; his face so close to hers that she could count his freckles. As for herself, she was sprawled awkwardly across a seat and a half; sat broad-lapped, her thighs spread, her silk shift showing at the hem of her skirt. The boy recoiled as though stung and pressed himself back into his seat, fingers busy straightening his tie. His eyes followed her legs as they crossed themselves in front of her. The milk bottle, she noticed, lay discarded on the floor. He had drained it, and only a white film clung to the inside of the glass, trembling now, as slowly, by increments, life returned to the engine. It was as though one could feel it will itself into a state of deep inner tension: a bass line throbbing underneath their feet and buttocks and their thighs. Tentatively, unsure of its own strength, the train eased into motion, inched forward along the tracks. She checked her watch and was surprised to find it was no later than two. There was still time to make it to Vienna by dawn.

4.

They did not speak again until they were almost at the station. For much of the time she drifted in and out of sleep. Her mouth was parched and she found herself wishing the conductor would stop by with his kettle of tea. The boy too dozed off, murmured gently in his dreams; once he kicked her as he pushed his legs out in front of him. At four-thirty a sudden hunger overcame him, and he fetched an apple down from his knapsack and sat chewing it with great noise. When the conductor came to advise them that they should arrive within the hour, he was a different man and did not carry tea. She accepted a swig from the boy's hiking flask and was amused to discover it contained some sort of cordial diluted with water. They each reached up to their bags, made sure everything was packed. The boy sat with satchel and hat box piled upon his lap. At the city limits there was another inspection of their papers: a whole committee of men in rumpled uniforms. When the border guards had left them, the boy stood up, stretched, rubbed his shoulders, neck, and face.

"Almost home," he said.

"Almost."

"How will it be, you think? Seeing your husband after all this time?"

He asked with great simplicity, from curiosity, and compassion, and because he felt he was her friend. She remembered holding his hand in the course of the night. It was hard now to reconstruct what had brought them to that juncture. She flashed him that fleeting, empty smile that she knew men found so beguiling.

"Nice," she said. "I'm sure it will be nice."

"You'll take him back? Despite the—you know."

"Yes. Despite. Though we'll have to wait and see, of course." Her voice turned mocking. "You think I shouldn't?"

The boy did not answer. He was busy with a different thought.

"How did you find out?" he asked. "Did you find a letter? Or perhaps you came home one afternoon and they—"

He flushed, gestured, fell silent: a boy like a puppy, clumsy, foolish, a constant quiver to his tail. It was an effort to summon the anger required by propriety.

"You're being a boor," she said. "You would do well to remember that you are no longer in the schoolyard, or the dormitory."

He bit his lip and launched into apology. She cut him short. She had told the story before, always with the same omissions.

"I followed him. I suspected, and I followed him. He entered a building and went up to a flat. I waited twenty minutes then rang at the door." She paused, mimed the gesture, one slender finger pressing down on the bell.

"You saw her?"

"Yes."

He stared at her, gaily, simply, without malice, yearning to learn and not to judge, the down on his lip twitching with excitement.

"Was she very beautiful?"

In her mind's eye she relived the scene, saw the door swing open and a young man standing there, dressed in his shirt sleeves and trousers, a silver

19

cross around his neck. He wasn't painted or perfumed or even particularly clean. One of his buttons was undone.

She'd pretended she had mistaken the door.

"Beautiful?" she answered at last. "It's hard for me to judge. I should not have thought so, no. It wasn't how I expected. A woman in garters. That's what I had pictured. Someone who'd thrown on a dressing gown just before she opened the door. Charming, pretty, a sort of gentleman's whore. But I see that I shock you."

The boy had indeed blushed a deep crimson, but he quickly composed himself and shook his head.

"No. It's how I pictured her myself just now. I mean, something like that. Not that I know about . . ."

"Garters? Or whores?"

"Neither," the boy managed, and fell silent.

Outside, dawn broke as they rolled into the station.

He carried her bags for her. Once on the platform she was surprised by the crowd of men, women, and children that spilled out of the second- and third-class compartments. It was as though, all of a sudden, they had entered the bustle of the city. Some tired relatives stood freezing near the barrier gates. They had waited all night to greet the husbands, wives, sons, and daughters now threading down the platform. Above them gaped the bombed-out roof.

A porter approached her, loaded her things onto a cart. The boy walked by her side, scanning the faces in the crowd. There was nobody there to welcome either one of them, just the morning light and the broken cobbles of Vienna. Out on the street a taxi driver accosted them and the boy insisted she should take it. They pressed hands briefly, and the boy bowed as though he wished to kiss the back of her hand (the tennis racket that stuck out of his knapsack nearly whacked her on the head). In the end his courage left him and he let go of her, mumbling that it had been a "deep pleasure."

Through the rear window of the taxi she watched him turn away from her to gather up his luggage. Behind the boy a vagrant shuffled, restless in his Wehrmacht coat, and a child sat selling nuts and berries from a hand-drawn cart. At length the woman too turned, ahead to where her husband would be waiting in whatever might be left of their apartment.

"You come from abroad?" the driver asked, studying her clothes across one burly shoulder.

"Just drive," she said, and dug in her handbag for makeup and mirror, intending to paint new life upon her fading lips.

Two

1.

As they disembarked from the train and left the station, there stood amongst the crowd a man neither tall nor particularly short, and self-effacing of manner, if wrapped somewhat conspicuously in a dyed army coat and a red woollen scarf of better quality than the rest of his appearance would lead one to expect. He scanned the emerging crowd with the curiosity of someone who hoped to find a familiar face. It was not long before his eyes settled on the woman in something more than homage to her beauty. In fact he crossed himself and muttered some few silent words; started forward then stopped, and was soon pushed aside in the press of the crowd.

Some years previously, at school, Robert Seidel had read a story by an American writer in which the protagonist, his nerves still strained from recent illness, was able to discern the profession and indeed the biography of passersby simply by studying their dress, their gait, the lines inscribed by life upon their faces, and who was distraught to find amongst the evening crowd a man who resisted his attempts at interpretation and was, in fact, *illegible*. Had Robert noticed the stranger, it might have struck him that the man posed a similar riddle to observers: his face obscured by scarf and low-drawn cap; his old man's gait ill matched by his still-youthful hands; his gestures acquired both in drawing room and barracks. All that could be said with any certainty was that there clung to the man—as he pushed through the crowd with a slinking kind of grace, never quite touching those who surrounded them—an anxious, timid quality, as though he were awaiting the answer to some fateful question that he himself had asked.

Outside, beyond the station doors, the stranger raised a finger to his mouth, tore with strong teeth at the ruin of a fingernail; and though his hands were cleaner than his coat and fraying cuffs, he found his cuticles encrusted in dark blood. This simple fact seemed to recall him to his purpose. He looked up sharply, fresh urgency grown into his gaze. In the early morning bustle it took the man a few moments to catch sight again of the woman and her young companion, who was helping stow her luggage in a taxi. For a second, through the car's back window, she seemed to look at him, and he stared back, entranced, as though tracing a softer, younger face through the coolness of her features. Then she turned towards her driver and soon was lost from sight.

The man seemed inclined to shift his attention over to the boy, who stood gathering his things, and in his hesitant way had taken a step towards him, when a policeman started walking in their general direction, drawn perhaps by the stranger's shabbiness and eager to forestall any pickpocketing. The stranger started, spun, and walked away in subdued haste. He did not slow until he had crossed the street and disappeared into the shadow of a gateway. There he stopped, rewrapped his scarf, and waited to see whether the boy too would climb into a taxi or join the ragged crowd that stood waiting for the tram.

Across from the gateway, in a house thrown open to the public eye by a bombed-away wall, a woman woke to her doll's house existence. She stretched, sang a snatch of Wehrmacht song, put a pot of water on the cooker; and, in the coarsest of Viennese dialects, tilting the "a" in arse into a drawn-out, listing *oh-ah-rse*, she cursed in lazy succession first the Germans, then the Allies, then the Jews, all of whom stood invited to insert into their backsides some unidentified object she seemed to think was clinging to her palm as she thrice performed a shoving motion in front of her broad hips.

The stranger saw her, tipped his cap. Just then the boy made up his mind and set off on foot. Almost at once the man too set off, walking in the same direction as the boy, although he moved too timidly, perhaps, to bring to mind the notion of pursuit. Within minutes they were lost from sight.

Behind them, the morning sun sought out the woman, set alight her reddish hair. Thus favoured by celestial attention, she laughed, dropped a pile of potato peels into her pot, and began to cook herself a starchy soup.

2.

It took Robert more than an hour to get home. He stood gazing after the woman's taxi for another moment, then shouldered his knapsack, picked up his satchel by its worn leather handle, wedged the hat box between his elbow and his hip, and—ignoring the cabbies who accosted him within twenty steps of the station (though he had plenty of money and could have afforded the ride)—started walking. He walked north at first, following the long bend of the Gürtel, then west towards Vienna's more affluent suburbs, keeping in sight a stretch of tram tracks but making no move to climb aboard a tram.

Throughout his long march, the boy paid little attention to his surroundings but rather walked with a fast, driving, almost mechanical step. What absorbed his attention so thoroughly, displacing all his pent-up curiosity for a city that, only yesterday, he had been impatient to see, was the thought of the woman who had shared his compartment, cruel mouth screwed into a smile. He thought of the things he might have said to her; invented touches, brushes, a chaste kiss in the darkness of the shorted-out train. Her name was Beer, Gudrun Anna. He'd found a name tag on her luggage when she'd left the compartment to use the lavatory; had pulled out a scrap of paper and made a note of her address. He thought about her husband too, whom he pictured as somehow very tall; witnessed their first handshake across the dusty threshold of their stagnant flat, tentative and awkward, until the husband grabbed her waist and crushed her into the double fold of his embrace. So vivid was this vision of the estranged couple's reunion that, if challenged to do so, Robert could have described the shade of the husband's eye (a flinty blue) and the crease made by his hand in the silken blouse at his wife's slender back.

And then his thoughts abandoned husband and wife, still locked in their embrace, and raced ahead instead, to Herr Seidel's accident and his mother's letter, her dark hints of "conspiracy," the long lists of all her ailments, the blandly tender phrases with which she had instructed him to "stay away" even as she complained about her isolation and the family's ruin. There was something in the letter's tone, in its omissions and sudden shifts of topic, that had fed a feeling—long grown into conviction—that there was something odd, fishy, and, so to speak, out of joint going on at the house, and that his mother was, if not precisely suffering, then at any rate besieged, and consequently in need of his help. "The important thing," he told himself, repeating a maxim he had culled from an English spy novel, "is to keep one's eyes peeled and one's powder dry." But despite this—as he called it—"detective resolution" and the attendant weight of responsibility, he found himself humming, alive with the expectation of "pressing Mother to his breast" (he'd written just such a phrase into his diary). It would have taken a good ear—and imagination—to pick out from these distracted notes the opening bars of "Cherokee."

So absorbed was Robert in these thoughts that he did not notice entering the old neighbourhood, nor passing the familiar park in which he had played as a child and which now lay denuded of trees. It was only in his own street, walking up the hill past the densely clustered villas, that he finally came to his senses. Robert looked up and, heedless still of the weight of his knapsack that was cutting into his shoulders and of the awkward ridge of the hat box that was biting into his hip, he ran the final few yards to the house.

It might have been six-thirty or seven in the morning: a warm and humid summer's day, sparrows chirping in the garden pine. The ornate metal gate opened under his probing hand, revealed a short flight of steps overgrown by moss and weeds. At their top, a pair of marble pillars flanked the villa's double doors, the brass knocker green and stiff. He knocked tentatively at first, then with some force; turned, found the doorbell, sent a buzzing through the house.

It took three or four further rings to produce a response. He heard the clatter of feet descending the hallway staircase, too light and fast to be his mother's. The door swung open and there stood a girl, hardly older than himself. Her face was sleep-creased, her expression sour, the hem of her blouse spilling from the waistband of her skirt as though she had dressed in great haste. Robert whistled in surprise. It wasn't how he had pictured her.

The girl was pretty, and also—a cripple; had "shot up tall" (as they said in novels) and, it seemed, very recently, especially from feet to girlish waist, her short, rigid torso perching on two stilt-like legs and threatening to topple. She was slender, quick in her gestures; the chest very high, the complexion good, of puckish features, with hair that might have darkened from a childhood blond to its current hue of burnished copper. There were short, sharply angled eyebrows and a plump lower lip; the arms spilling thin and naked from the elastic of her half-length sleeves.

It was her back that was twisted: not hunched, but spun like a twist of hair around a finger. It was as though she'd been caught in a perpetual pirouette, one hip higher than the other, the right shoulder leading, an odd sideways prancing to her ever-shuffling feet. If she could but unscrew herself: throw her chest out, gain some range of movement in that stiff and leaning neck; tuck in the shoulder blade that stuck out like a broken flipper.

The boy stared at her in wonder, a hat box growing from his hip. She returned his gaze with a studied rudeness that wrinkled her nose and put a tidy little crease into the bony flesh between her brows. She raised one hand and scratched herself at the height of the navel where blouse rose out of checkered skirt. It shook her breasts. He lowered his eyes and she adjusted her stance. Her shins were scraped like a tomboy's.

"You are the son," she said at last, proved unresponsive to his winning smile. "Just like the letters: meek as a lamb. Though they forgot to say about the eye." She gestured, rudely, stabbed a finger in his face.

"Robert," he said.

"Eva Frey." Her gaze was defiant: cloudy, grey-blue eyes, the iris rimmed as though by crystals. "The maid."

She turned without another word, moved away from him, down the hallway and onto the stairs. He remained where he was, on the threshold, the morning sun hot on his back.

She stopped, halfway up, where the staircase swung at a right angle.

"So, here you are," she called down, the same defiant dismissal still in her voice. "At the scene of the crime."

Robert felt neither shock nor surprise. "It really was a crime, then? Herr Seidel was pushed?"

"Your mother didn't tell you?"

"Only hints. She said something about the police coming to question her." He paused, searched her face. "She also wrote that you were there when it happened, and saw . . ." He gestured and succeeded only in dropping the hat box at his feet. "But where is Mother?"

"Asleep."

"Didn't she get my telegram?"

"Oh, she got it all right. Went to the station last night. You didn't show."

"The train was running late."

She shrugged and continued on her way. Soon only her legs were visible, sticking out of her too-short skirt. She wore socks rather than stockings.

"What do I do now?" he called after her.

She neither slowed nor bothered to turn, her voice loud and ringing in the stairwell. "What do I care? Go wake her up. Or wait for her here. Just as you please."

Three more steps carried her out of sight. Upstairs, on the lush carpet, her step became inaudible. All at once a great silence settled. There had, in the past, been a cook, a secretary, and a gardener, along with a maid: the steady bustle of busy feet. Now the great villa stood as though empty.

Robert put down knapsack and satchel, closed the door, and made his way into the house.

3.

He went into the kitchen first, found it in a clutter of open tins and dirty dishes, a cloud of flies rising as he stepped into the room. Everything—the sink and cabinets, the heavy painted dresser, the kitchen table with its coarse, much-spotted cloth—was familiar to him from childhood, and yet everything seemed subtly distorted in size, as though the intervening years had shrunk one wall and elongated the other, straightened the frame of the dark electric stove and shrunk into a midget's portal the bent old door that led into the larder. A jar of jam stood open on the windowsill, its mouldy top alive with buzzing movement.

Confused, intrigued, Robert walked to the drawing room next door. Here too, neglect and flies prevailed. Used wineglasses and dirty coffee cups littered the many tables, the ornate mantelpiece and heavy carpets. There hung in the air the smell of cold ashes.

Robert stepped further into the room, swallowed dust motes dancing in the air between the walls and dirty window. Peering out, it was a shock to see the garden, the ground dug up and shaped into black rectangles of soil. Arranged within these patches he made out carrot tops and marrow plants; tomato vines clinging to a length of chicken wire. Ahead, past the hedge that served to bound the property, the neighbour's house stood reduced to a black shell. A flock of birds patrolled its charred perimeter.

Robert turned, picked his way through dirty cups and overflowing ashtrays back across the room. As he reached the door, his gaze fell on a pair of boots that flanked an ottoman: worn, mud-caked, calf-high boots, their long tongues lolling, as though someone had only just stepped out of them. These boots gave Robert pause. They were army issue, made for marching onto enemy soil. But Herr Seidel had never been conscripted.

Quickly, impatient now to get to the bottom of the mystery, he charged up the stairs and on towards his mother's room. Upstairs, the corridor stood empty, the maid long gone. He found his mother's door wide open, drifted shyly through, then past the garments littering the floor. His mother was asleep, not on the unmade bed with its embroidered drapes, but on a wicker armchair by the window. A pang of tenderness rushed through him, along with a reverent kind of shyness, the solemn hush of church. He paused, glanced briefly at the dressing table, where a dozen little bottles crowded the picture of his father, the policeman, his uniformed chest cut in half by the frame. Two more strides carried Robert to his mother's side.

He did not wake her right away; stood, gazing down at her small figure. She had aged, grown plump, or rather puffy; was dressed in an old dressing gown, fraying at the cuffs. A knitted blanket, no bigger than a shawl, lay crumpled on her chest; her features cast in caked-in powder, faded lipstick on her mouth. At long last his hand reached down to touch his mother's; stroked it, recalled her gently from her sleep.

She woke, sat up, threw off the blanket: alarm, then malice, spreading through her features. The next moment she was on her feet, raised her hand as though to strike him, and in this manner chased him halfway across the room. There, from one second to the other, recognition lit within her eyes. Without a word, and without interrupting her movement, she stepped over to him and wrapped him in her arms.

Mother and son were of the same height.

"Robert," she breathed, and squeezed him, reached up and gently cradled his face. "But will you look at that eye!" She bent his head to one side and kissed it. "And how cold your face is! You must have caught a chill."

Again and again she bent forward to kiss his cheeks, his brow, the hands she lifted up towards her lips. Robert accepted her caresses with perfect passivity, at once touched and embarrassed by her show of affection, and too moved himself to easily find words.

"Mother," he managed at last, laughed, and freed himself enough to take a breath. "But what a mess the house is in! I took a turn downstairs, and everywhere it's dirt and flies."

She did not seem to hear him, but rather closed the distance he had opened between them with two rapid steps; took him back into her arms. Up close she smelled a little musty, as though her clothes had been neither washed nor aired. Perfume overlaid this, rosewater and honey, hung heavy around her wrists and throat. Again he freed himself, stepped back some dozen inches, held on to her hands.

"You must tell me about Herr Seidel." He flushed, bit his lip, took hold of his duty to learn the truth. "The maid says he was pushed."

At the mention of the maid, his mother's face darkened and a hardness crept into her mouth. She let go of her son's hands, stepped close again, put her fingers to his cheek.

"He sent everyone away," she whispered. "All the servants. Everyone but *her*. And now she walks around as though she owns the place.

"That creature," she continued. "Would you believe I picked her myself? Out of charity. And look how she repays me!"

She flew into a sudden frenzy, grabbed his sleeve, and tugged him out into the hallway. "She steals like a Gypsy," she hissed, still dragging him along, then stopped in front of an empty patch of wall near the stairs. "Look! Right there."

After a moment's incomprehension Robert made out the faint outline of a rectangle, no bigger than a magazine cover, upon the stripy plain of wallpapered wall. The rectangle was a shade lighter than the wall surrounding it; a picture must have hung there until recently. Now that he looked for it, he found the little hole left by the nail.

"*She* took it. That and the candlesticks. Sold the lot, she did. She steals like a Gypsy. She, she, she—"

He was startled to see that his mother was literally spitting with each word. Her face was flushed, its loose skin shaking with her anger.

"And now she says she *saw*, and she will testify. The dirty little bitch." She choked on the word, shook her tiny, puffy fists. Her voice descended to a whisper. "She says that if he dies, they'll call it murder. And here he's left me without a penny. Cut me off, he has, even *before*. He's so tight you'd think he was a—" She paused there, waved him over to the corner, put her finger to her brow, and drew a hook nose into her face, her heavy lids rising over manic, tear-filled eyes.

They stood like that for three or four breaths, their heads together in an empty corner, her bosom heaving as though poisoned by the air. And then, the very next moment, the anger lifted from her features and the tenderness with which she had greeted him stole over her again. She grabbed his neck, his head, his cheeks.

"How big you have grown!" she cooed (though he knew very well that he was short). "And you were such a sickly child. Almost died of the croup. But how cold your face is. You must have caught a chill."

He tried to say something—reassure her, ask her was she feeling well—but she had already turned away and had taken some steps down the staircase when her eyes fell over the banister and onto his belongings, which lay where he'd dropped them near the front door.

"Just look at what a mess she's made," his mother muttered, full of hate, and cut him off when he tried to protest. "She does it to spite me."

"Those are my things, Mother."

"Your things?"

"Yes. My knapsack and satchel. And a present for you."

A thought stole through her, almost comically obvious, ran through her eyes and tugged at her lips. "You have the money we sent you?"

"What's left of it."

"Give it to me."

Her voice was strained, and somehow artificially sweet. She lowered her lids and watched him closely as he descended the stairs to search his satchel.

"Yes, there it is, I can see it from here. And what a nice little wallet you have. You won't need it now, will you? You are home."

He returned to the top of the stairs, offered her the leather wallet. She took it quickly, furtively, all but snatched it from his hand.

"But I'm tired and have to lie down. You will find the way to your room, won't you? I expected you last night."

There was, in her voice, hardly a hint of reproach.

She kissed him one last time, pressing his wallet into his back as she embraced him, then turned away from him and slowly walked back down the corridor towards her room.

"You have changed," he called after her, but received no answer; then added, remembering the boots he had found on the drawing room floor, "Has Wolfgang come home?"

She nodded absently without looking back.

"Where is he?"

"Jail," she said, disappearing into her room and drawing the door shut behind her. "Wolfgang is a martyr."

Robert sighed, ran down to pick up his belongings, then quickly remounted the stairs.

4.

He stopped at the door to his stepfather's study.

Robert had been heading for his childhood room, thinking he would drop off his things, then go find the maid and press her for answers. But when he passed the study, he stopped in his tracks and stood outside the door, trying to account for his nagging sense that something was out of place. It took him a moment to interpret the feeling.

The door should not have been closed.

Throughout the year and a half Robert had spent in this house, the door had always been open, if no more than an inch, creating the illusion that Herr Seidel was always inside, alert to the volume of Robert's play. Every evening Robert had approached that never-closed door dressed in his pyjamas. He had knocked and presented himself, reported on his school work. To this day, the scent of a certain cologne, spread by a stranger on the tram or bus, or in the queue for the pictures, never failed to return him to the memory of Herr Seidel bending forward to kiss his forehead before sending him to bed. On the way out he'd pass Wolfgang, awaiting his turn by the door; and once outside, Robert would linger in the corridor, twisting with nervous fingers the shrimply tip of his foreskin through the flannel of his pyjamas, and eavesdrop on the report of Wolfgang's latest outrage and the boy's sulky promise of reform. Robert had, to the best of his memory, never once been in the room alone.

Now the handle gave under his probing elbow and—satchel, knapsack, and hat box still stacked before his chest—he slipped inside. What drew him had little to do with childhood memories. Though his mother had not said so in her letter, he had long formed the opinion that it was here, from one of the windows in the study, that Herr Seidel had had his fall. Quietly, Robert set his things on the floor, rounded the big desk that had frightened him as a boy, both by its bulk and by the authority it represented, and drew to the windows. There were on them no marks of violence. On the sill stood a geranium in vivid bloom.

Robert peered past it, saw the front garden with its tiled path and, with quiet horror, pictured his stepfather's trajectory. A drizzle had started that seemed to confirm the heat rather than dispel it. It would take a determined leap to fall afoul of the metal fence with its row of ornamental spikes; a dead drop of five yards to drive one's shins into the mound of bricks that awaited builders near the basement window. Beyond the fence, on the bucking cobbles of the narrow street, a man in a worn soldier's coat stood looking up at him, his face muffled by a scarf. For an instant their eyes locked. Then the vagrant quickly shuffled on. His furtive speed struck a chord with Robert and he looked after him for some moments before turning his attention back to the room.

How well he remembered all its details! There had always been something bare and monkish about Herr Seidel's study. The desk, a bookshelf, and a heavy carved chair were its only furnishings; the walls panelled chest-high in dark oak. Only a wooden cross broke the monotony of the walls above, Christ's body hanging thin and mangled from its nails. As

33

he took a step towards the desk, Robert noticed that its main drawer had been broken open. Inside, a pile of documents had been rifled and then carelessly replaced. Herr Seidel's telephone was missing from the desk, its cable cut and snaking across the floorboards.

While he stood trying to reconstruct the sequence of events that would account for these details, a sound reached Robert's ears, faint yet urgent, and cut up by sudden skips and crackles. Intrigued, he walked to the door, then on down the corridor and up the stairs to the next floor. The music, though quiet, seemed to grow more frantic with every step of his approach. A woman was singing in German, Wagner he supposed, the orchestra rising with her mounting agitation. As he reached the room from which her singing issued, the record jumped and tossed her back to where she'd started, calmer, easing slowly to the edge of her abyss.

"Hello!" he called through the half-open door.

The music wasn't loud enough to drown out his voice, and yet he received no answer. He knocked against the door frame, stepped slowly into the darkened room. The gramophone was by the open window; summer drizzle weighing down the half-drawn curtains. At the far wall stood a bed, its mattress hidden by a heavy footboard. A hand rose up beyond its edge and waved him over.

He took a step, kicked something small yet solid, heard the slosh of liquid near his toe. He bent down, found a brass chamber pot covered by a wooden lid, in a house that had three toilets. The hand kept on waving, impatient, imperious, slack at the wrist. A cough sounded, phlegm spat into cotton, and a hanky dropped from the side of the bed like a discarded flag of surrender.

Robert approached.

He found a woman, very thin, coughing, grinning, purple bags slung under her eyes. She was young and yet had lost the bloom of youth, along with half her teeth; thin, dirty hair spread like a halo on her pillow. The nightdress piled ruffles onto her bony breast. She spoke coarsely, in some accent he didn't know. From Germany, he supposed, somewhere to the east. It was clear to him that she was drunk.

"Who are you, then?" she asked.

"Robert."

"Robert who?"

"Robert Seidel."

"Wolfi's brother?"

"Yes. Stepbrother, I suppose." He smiled at her and added shyly, "And you?"

She cackled, flashed him a smile, half bashful, half proud, and marred by missing teeth. "I'm the wife, en't I? Got the papers and all."

"His wife? I had no idea. *Mazel tov!*"

She stared at him uncomprehendingly, coughed, spat phlegm in one hand. "Muzzle what?"

"It's what a friend of mine says, when somebody gets lucky. To congratulate them, I mean. In school, in Switzerland—" He broke off, dressed his confusion in another smile.

"Well," she said, a little pouty, "they don't say that here."

Into the silence that fell between them, Brünnhilde wailed, or Freia, or Isolde, then was silenced by a sea of strings. The woman snickered, mimed the crescendo's climax with an elongation of her narrow throat, and threw open her jaws as though she were about to bite into an apple. In the next movement, she had wrapped a hand around his tie and was pulling him closer.

"I'm Poldi," she said.

"Poldi," he repeated, quietly struggling. "It's a pleasure."

She looked him over, her face inches from his own. "Handsome," she decided at last. "Only, someone knocked out yer eye."

She coughed again and let go of his tie, which crumpled back against his breast. His head jerked back too, and he almost lost his balance, swayed over her like a midnight suitor worse for drink. Nervously, on guard against her movements, he tried to explain himself.

"I haven't heard from Wolfgang in years. He never wrote, you see, not even a postcard, in all the years I was away. And then, last thing I heard, he had vanished. Gone into hiding. Because of the war, I suppose. And now Mother says he is in jail."

She nodded, scratched under her blankets, licked some spit from off her lip. "The coppers took him. After yer father—" She paused, made a falling motion with one hand, slapped it flat onto the bedding. "He used to be hisself, you know. Police. It's how we met."

"You worked for the police?"

She laughed, shook her head. "Don't be daft now. I was a singer, wasn't I? Some dancin' too."

She lifted the thin blanket and pushed out a leg. It was thin, bony, covered in fine golden hair. She lay bared to the upper thigh, hip and pubic bone sketched by threadbare wool.

He turned away quickly, found his face in a dirty mirror by the side of the bed, the pale, bashful features of a boy with a wonky eye. It vexed him for a moment, precisely this boyishness, and the pallor of his cheeks. But when Robert turned back to Poldi and found her leg still out and folded across the lip of the blanket, his thoughts nonetheless turned to retreat.

"I should go," he said, eyes glued to her white flesh. "You must be tired."

"Tired? Oo, I don't know." She sat up, waggled her toes. "The thing is," she said, "there's sod all left to drink. Got a drop?"

"No."

"Ciggies?"

He shook his head.

"Money?"

"Mother took it."

"Be a pet and turn the record. I'm sick of this side."

"Of course," he said, and did as he was bidden. Brass began to rumble as he stepped away from the gramophone. On the way out, he once again ran into the chamber pot and, gripped by a solemn sense of duty, picked it up to dispose of its contents in the bathroom downstairs. His task completed, he collected his belongings in his stepfather's study, entered his room, and, feeling soiled and exhausted and afraid he might crease, he took off his coat and trousers and lay down for a moment on the bed in which he had slept as a child.

Three

1.

It was less than two miles from the station to the apartment building. At Anna's request, the taxi left the ring road and headed north through the Neubau district. It took longer this way, but she wanted to become reacquainted with the city and defer the moment when she would stand face to face with her husband. After their initial exchange, the driver made no further attempt at conversation. She, in turn, remained silent and stared fixedly ahead.

Before long they turned into ——gasse. Another few blocks and she would be home. The car passed their bakery, and the corner *Tabak*: a queue for hot rolls, and the ring of the bell as the tram pulled out of its stop. Their street, as they entered it, seemed unchanged to her. It had been spared by the bombs. Only Pollak's Auto Repair Shop had changed owners—a painted sign hung low above the gate. It was no longer a garage. They were now mending stoves.

The driver stopped by the side of her building, got out, and unloaded her luggage onto the pavement. Anna produced her wallet. All she had were hundred-shilling bills. He looked at her sourly, rummaged through his pockets, but was unable to produce the full change; shrugged, picked through his pockets one more time, then gave her all he had. It was three shillings short. Without listening to her protests that it didn't matter and that she would be "quite all right" without his help, he picked up her luggage and walked over to the entrance, then turned around, waiting for her to take the lead. He was a big man, burly, a roll of fat sitting in the nape of his neck; wore his tie loose around the open collar. Yesterday's sweat had left a yellow patch on the linen of his shirt. The face was ruddy, sulking. He carried her bags like a personal affront.

They entered the building. The front door was unlocked, gave way to a hallway that connected it to the inner courtyard. The building's main staircase rose on their right, its stuccoed ceiling spotted with dirt. The old wooden banister with its elegant curves was gone; perhaps it had been chopped up for firewood. She mounted the first dozen steps, aware of the driver's movements behind her; looked back once and found him staring fixedly at her legs and rump.

On the first-floor landing they came upon a commotion. The police were at the door of the flat that used to belong to a retired professor of gynecology. A woman, short and slender, and wearing the sort of suit whose very plainness pointed to its expense, was talking at the two policemen in broken German. Her accent sounded American. A group of neighbours had gathered, as was customary in the event of ill fortune, but for some reason they had collected not on the landing but in the flat itself, adding their own comments and observations in muted but excited voices. A fat woman in a housecoat kept repeating the phrase "how shameful it is, how shameful," but what it was that had her so agitated and what indeed was the nature of the foreigner's complaint, Anna was unable to discern. She slipped past the group without stopping, the taxi driver two steps behind, still watching her rump. One of the policemen noticed her passing: their eyes met, she flashed him a smile, sweet, playful, and alluring, and he inclined his head to wish her a good day. By the time she reached the next bend of the stairs, she had dismissed him from her mind.

"Here?" the taxi driver asked as they approached the next landing. He was sweating, sullen, hostile; a suitcase in each meaty fist.

"One more flight."

"Let's move it, then."

They carried on. His rudeness did not upset her. He was right: she had been tarrying. The door to their flat came into sight, her husband's name was on the bell. Dr. Anton Beer. The taxi driver read it with interest.

She pulled the keys out of her handbag and wondered if they would still fit. It was a mystery how she had not lost them through a dozen moves and a series of lovers, but when she had set about looking for them, in the storage closet of her Paris flat, she had found them at once, looking rusty, it was true, and somehow foreign in their shape.

"You can put the luggage down here," she instructed the driver, and pointed at the floor outside the door. He stood stolidly, ignoring her, holding on to her bags. It was as though he had not heard.

In a hurry now, wishing to "get things over with," and a little amused, too, at the absurd note provided by the driver's presence, she slipped the key into the lock. It turned without resistance. She swung open the door, stepped over the threshold, listened for a sound. The driver pushed in behind her. He looked around the spacious hallway, pursed his lips into a whistle. Beside them, in the windowless space that had once been her husband's waiting room, a dozen chairs stood in an orderly square.

"You live here alone?"

She understood the question. Vienna was overpopulated and had been for as long as she remembered. After the war, with whole parts of the city in rubble, the situation had only become worse. When she had first received news of her husband's being taken prisoner, she made inquiries about the apartment and learned that the city had seized it and was about to pass it over to some Party functionary. Furious, moved by an odd loyalty to a set of rooms that had been furnished with her misery, she had written to an old school friend who had since become a prominent lawyer and instructed him to reverse the seizure. She'd wired money to cover the rent from then on. Thus, in the middle of the overcrowded city, the apartment had stood empty for the better part of seven years.

"Yes, alone," she answered, speaking louder than was necessary, still listening into the flat. "Just my husband and I."

The cabbie nodded, put down the bags, walked past her and deeper into the hallway; scratched his chest and looked around. "But he isn't here now, is he?"

The face was blank, impassive. One had to look to his hips to form the notion of a leer.

"Go," she said.

"No need to get gruff, Frau Doktor."

"Go!"

He yawned and stretched, filled up her hallway; stood lumbering, neither amiable nor threatening but *simply so*, yet all the same somehow expectant, as though she must treat him to a beer, or kiss him, take him by the hand and pet his ugly mug.

"Get out of my sight."

He winced at the sharpness of the phrase, then nodded, turned sulkily, took two steps, and stopped once more, inches from her, as though way-laid by a thought too momentous to ignore.

"I owe you," he said, scratched his chest through his shirt, brushed her with his elbow on the side of her left breast. "Three shillings. For the fare."

"Just leave," she said, more gently this time, and pointed with a finger to the door.

Still he hesitated, considered doing something foolish, his right hand shaping itself into a heavy, five-pronged scoop.

She followed the gesture with her eyes. "I met a boy last night who was just like you. Very different, naturally, but just like you all the same." She paused, smiled, never lost sight of his hand. "An oaf."

He flushed, grew confused. The scoop, already half raised between them, unbent itself and drooped. "No need to get gruff," he repeated, but his courage was spent.

"There are police in the house. Better just go."

And he did: hung his head, picked a path through her scattered lug-gage, and ran down the stairs in his rubber-soled boots.

She locked the door behind him.

"Anton?" she called into the flat.

There was no answer other than the burp of plumbing chasing water through the walls.

2.

He wasn't there.

She stayed in the hallway a moment longer, stood, shoulders squared, chin raised, calling her husband's name; then quickly walked around the flat and opened all the doors. Vexation rose in her that Anton wasn't there to greet her, followed immediately by the sudden conviction that he had never returned at all. All she had received, since the news of his imprisonment, were two cards that had been posted through the Red Cross, of twenty-five words each ("Fully recovered from dysentery. Conditions good. I am putting on weight." Et cetera.), then a letter, postmarked in Berlin for some reason, informing her that he had been released and was on his way "home." It had reached her five days ago: she'd returned to Paris from a trip to the coast and had been handed the envelope by her building's concierge, whose smile mixed mockery and commiseration.

"*De votre mari. En Allemagne.*"

The letter had been dated the twelfth of June. On the second of July she had sent him her reply by telegram and booked her ticket for the train. It had not occurred to her that he might not have made it home.

Caught by this unexpected thought (and feeling annoyed, too, that it should trouble her: her husband's absence), she walked through the flat again, more carefully this time, studying the rooms for any sign of his return. That *somebody* had been there recently was beyond any doubt. Both kitchen counter and sink were littered with empty bottles, some of beer and some of schnapps; a broken glass lay shattered in the bin. The antique clock in the dining room had been wound, set, and dusted, though this care, she noticed, did not extend to the table and chairs. Both her and Anton's clothes were hanging in the wardrobe; smelled musty, moth holes in her camel hair coat. The sofa in the living room had been made up as a bed: a pair of boots stood at its end, dirty socks stuffed in their shafts. A rumpled blanket had been flung over the backrest, was spotted with filth. Their bed, by contrast, was neatly made and looked unused; a layer of dust on the lip of her sheet and on the pert, downy curve of the pillows. A toothbrush, new and dry, stood in a water glass on the bathroom sink; the mirror hung splattered, encrusted with soap. There was no toilet paper. A ripped-up newspaper lay stacked by the bowl.

She noticed other things. There was a photo, for instance, above their marital bed, of a young woman in a negligee, lying propped up on cushions. The photo was not framed, but had been pinned to the wall with two nails. She drew closer, staring at it with a stir of jealousy and hope, and saw that it had been taken in this very room, and that the nightgown in question, rather plain and made of ordinary linen, was one of her own. Then too, on the wall of the study, some inches below the light switch, hung a palm-sized smudge, more black than red. Five steps from it, on her husband's desk, there stood an upturned glass, under which, as though in a bell jar, sat a curiously orange spider: not large, but with a meaty, triangular body ringed by hairy legs. It did not react when she stepped close and shook the glass, then it scampered off as soon as she removed the glass altogether. Underneath was a torn typewritten letter to a Bregenz orphanage pertaining to one of their charges. The final line and signature were missing. Judging by the size of the missing patch and the fag ends that littered the nearby ashtray, it had been used to roll a cigarette. Specks of ashes lay scattered across much of the large wooden desk. She opened a drawer and found a roll of *Reichsmark*, now defunct. A bottle of ink stood open amongst broken pens and had long since dried out.

None of these findings was entirely able to settle the question of whether her husband had returned. Anton did not drink, or in any case not to excess. The only time he had been known to sleep on the sofa was on the last night she had spent in the flat, when she had already packed her bags and announced her departure (he'd come to the station with her and offered his handkerchief when she needed to blow her nose). He might, it was true, be the kind of man who would dust the clock but forget about the chairs and table; imprison a spider that had caught his attention under an upturned glass; compose a letter that "begged" the reader's pardon for the whole of the first paragraph, then "kindly urged" him to address himself to the inquiry contained within. But it wasn't enough. She needed to be sure of his return.

Hastily, casting a glance in the hallway mirror and noticing how tired she looked, how wrinkled her clothing, she left the flat and pulled the door shut behind her. There was a flat across from theirs: she would ask the neighbour. Just then—she was still reaching for the bell—she heard voices travel through the stairwell and was reminded of the commotion two floors below. She hesitated, pressed the bell, received no answer. She rang once more, then turned on her heel and quickly walked down the stairs.

The scene was much as she had left it. Most of the bystanders had dispersed by now, satisfied in their curiosity, but the small woman in the expensive clothes was still standing there, arguing with the police in her broken German. She was very animated, explaining some point with great emphasis and counting off her arguments on the tips of her fingers. The two policemen, by contrast, were quite openly bored with her and in a hurry to leave. When the woman caught sight of Anna (who, like her, was expensively dressed), she flashed her a despairing smile and inquired, "*Guten Tag, lieb Frau*—you wouldn't speak English by any chance?"

"Good morning, my dear," Anna responded at once, calling to mind the lessons she had taken as a girl. "How do you do?"

No sooner had the policemen heard her use an English phrase than they turned to her and themselves began beseeching her to intervene.

"*Sie sprechen Englisch, gnädige Frau? Aber san's keine Ausländerin? Kommen's aus Wien? Wie fein. Man sieht's aber sofort. Meine Verehrung die Dame!*"

Anna quickly interrupted their chatter and confirmed that she was indeed Viennese but spoke some little English ("albeit badly") and that, yes, she would be delighted to stay a moment and translate, provided it did not take too long.

The situation was this: the woman was renting a room in this apartment and had been burgled the previous night while she was out ("my typewriter, my camera, all my best clothes—in short, everything that has any value"), most likely by one of the other lodgers, of whom there seemed to be a great many. The policemen wanted her to come to the station and fill out the paperwork before they took any further steps.

"Please tell them that if they would but come inside and talk to all the lodgers, there won't be any need for a complaint. If I leave now, the thief will simply hide my things elsewhere and we will all be wasting our time. I am much obliged to you."

Anna related the argument, but it was evident that it was pointless. The problem was not that the policemen did not understand the woman's reasoning, but simply that they did not wish to go to the trouble of questioning half a dozen people one by one.

"Explain to her," the younger of the two told Anna, holding on to her elbow for greater emphasis, "that it isn't safe to lodge with so many strangers. Things are bound to be stolen. Surely she can afford a room in a hotel?"

At long last it was agreed that the woman would come by the police station later and bring along a male friend of hers who was "well acquainted with the law" and would act as her interpreter. The policemen left and, a flight down, could be heard joking about the woman's accent and discussing where best to have lunch (there was a butcher's nearby that smoked its own meats). Anna and the foreigner were left behind, still standing on the landing.

"Thank you very much for your help," the woman began. She had short, wavy, mouse-brown hair; thin lips, a sharp chin, large dewy eyes; good features, but somehow as though put together in a hurry, without proportion or harmony, and given to twitches. "I saw you arrive. You must be here on a visit. My name is Coburn. Sophie Coburn, Mrs."

"Anna Beer."

"The doctor's wife!"

"You've met my husband?"

"Only in passing, on the stairs. You need to feed him up! He looks frightfully thin. I heard he's been a prisoner—though he didn't say so himself. I—"

"When?" Anna interrupted, not bothering to hide her irritation.

The woman reacted at once; stemmed her prattle; grew serious. "Two days ago, or maybe three. You—" She interrupted herself, wet her lips, pushed ahead with her train of thought. "You have not seen him yet? Since he came back? It's been many years—"

"Nine," said Anna, nodded her head in parting.

"I'm a journalist," the woman called after her, obviously embarrassed by the situation. "Forgive the many questions. I did not mean to pry."

"How does he look?" Anna asked without turning.

"Handsome," the woman said with a special sort of warmth. "Thin, careworn, but handsome. We hardly exchanged a word."

"And your own husband, Frau Coburn?"

"Dead."

"My condolences," said Anna, and returned to her flat, on one of whose walls there hung a smudge she had yet to verify was blood.

3.

She decided to ignore the stain; ran a bath, cleaned up. It was somehow very important to her that she look good for her husband's return, and this despite all that divided them, his infidelity and perversity, the long years of estrangement—but how sick she was of this *despite*. At the same time she did not want to be surprised by him, and sat in the water listening for the door, then hurriedly towelled off, put on first one set of underwear and then decided on another (it was older, less frilly) and got dressed in a fresh if rumpled suit. Before long she had applied fresh makeup, brushed out her hair (there had not been time to wash it), and composed herself in one of the living room armchairs, wiping off its dust before she sat. It was going on nine o'clock. Anton might return at any moment.

At ten she felt her stomach grumble. There was very little food in the house, but she found some stale rolls in the kitchen basket and sat dunking them into a cup of malt coffee that she'd brewed for herself. On the way back to the armchair she stepped into the study, wet a fingertip, and ran it through the stain's black crust. The colour turned and she left behind a crimson print.

Back in the living room Anna scanned the shelves for something to read. She fetched down a volume of *The Complete Chekhov* that she'd bought for her husband one Christmas and started reading the first story she chanced upon, a nasty little anecdote about a man who froze both his arms as he tried to ferry his sick wife to the hospital in the middle of a storm (the wife died, naturally). Annoyed, she threw down the book, aware it would rumple its pages, walked over to the window, stared out onto the street below. Twice she saw a man who she thought might be her husband, though what led her to the supposition it was hard to say: she was high above and they were all wearing hats, so that not even the hair could be seen with any clarity. The first passed by the building altogether; the second entered the front door—her heart skipped a beat, and she composed her lips into a winning smile—but somehow failed to arrive at the flat and had to be given up for a stranger.

By noon she had returned to the smudge, stood scrubbing it with a wet rag that stained pink a yard-wide section of wallpaper. There was no rip or bullet hole beneath; no bandage or soiled handkerchief amongst the refuse in the bin. A noise roused her, sent her running to the door and out onto the landing, empty but for the echo of a neighbour's shuffling step. Retreating once again into the living room, she trod upon the crumpled Chekhov lying prostrate on the floor. Anna picked it up and read. She read of peasants picking bugs from out their bowls of tepid soup. A village bum caught fish and slept with someone else's wife. A doctor settled, prospered, and grew fat, all because he'd failed to marry in his youth.

At two she rushed out to the butcher's, then on to the baker's; ran back expectant but found the apartment just as empty on her return. She ate in the armchair hunched over a plate of cold cuts, bread, and gherkins, then at once fell asleep; woke up ten minutes later and hurried to the mirror, worried that her hair might be dishevelled; laughed at her own vanity but grew angry, too, at her useless, tardy husband, whom she had rushed to join from Paris after a decade spent apart. Some cigarettes calmed her, then a bottle of beer she picked from a crate in the kitchen. She sat drinking, smoking on the windowsill. Three o'clock passed, four-thirty, five; she nodded off, spilled ash on her blouse and skirt, dabbed at the specks with a spit-moistened cloth. Weary now, she shifted to the couch, stretched out upon the dirty sheet, and decided just to "rest her eyes."

Within minutes she was fast asleep.

4.

She woke to the sound of a key in the front door lock. At first, disoriented, she could not make sense of where it was that she was lying. It had been a long time since she had slept this soundly. The light was on in the corridor but not in the living room, where she lay in darkness on a sofa, a pillow spread under her head. She registered dimly that it was night; was raining by the sound of it, a faint patter on the pane. Then the latch snapped back within the lock and summoned all her senses out into the hall. She heard the front door being swung wide open; heard it thrown shut again, crash into its frame. Footsteps sounded in the breath of time between, more like a soldier's charge than a doctor's measured step, ringing loudly on the hallway parquet. She stirred, sat up, fell back onto the sheet, lay motionless, eyes fastened on the living room door. It had been left half open when she'd decided to lie down for a moment's rest. A column of light cut across the swirling patterns of her husband's Turkish

carpet and stopped just short of the sofa's feet. She lay and listened, followed his progress through the flat.

There wasn't much noise now after that initial, startling charge. His
movements were shuffling, searching, full of doubt. She could hear him
walk down the corridor and push open doors, much as she had done
some hours earlier; heard his quick, hoarse whisper calling through the
empty rooms, using some word or name she failed to understand. Somehow (with his hand, she imagined, or the crown of his hat) he must have
brushed the hallway lamp, sent dancing the bulb, and forced an eerie sense
of movement on the ceiling, walls, and floor. She listened and waited and
struggled with vertigo.

When he stepped into the doorway of the room, pushing open the
door with a quick slap of his hand, the bulb at his back made him look
impossibly large: a backlit giant who stood swaying, framed by wood and
light. He was wearing a greatcoat; mud-caked boots upon his feet. It was
impossible to see his face.

Still she did not move. The rectangle of light that fell from the open
door (twitching, quaking, taking orders from an agitated bulb) reached
all the way over to the sofa: caught her hair, she hoped, the slender curve
of her silk blouse. Indeed he seemed to make her out at once: gave a cry,
or maybe coughed, and staggered forward. His movements were alien to
her, and it flashed in her that he must have been wounded and robbed of
his gait.

At the edge of the sofa he fell to his knees; reached forward with both
hands (but how different they seemed to her than those that she remembered: enormous, calloused hands, thick and knotty at the knuckles);
cupped her cheeks, her throat, her neck, and pushed his face right into hers.
His breath was poison, catarrh and vodka, the features coarse, and sheer, and
bony, with a sloping forehead and enormous brows. He held her, tilted her
head into the light, and studied her with open disappointment.

"*Schaaßdreck*—shit," he said, and lost his balance, fell against the sofa's
armrest, then slid in a heap onto the floor. A moment later he had started

snoring, arms spread, head drooping, one hand dug into the cushion by her knee.

It wasn't Anton. Even now—sitting there, staring at his sprawling limbs and picking through his coarse, broad features (*"as though dug with a spoon from out a lump of rotten wood"*)—she could not accept this simple fact. Perhaps, she thought, he had been beaten, the face reset by army surgeons who cared too little for his noble brow; had his fingers broken one by one, then pulled them straight in some dark prison and tied them to some sprigs of kindling in the hope that they might heal.

Distraught, not daring to wake him, she slipped down next to him; sat on the floor, with her back leaning against the sofa, and measured herself out against his long and sprawling legs. The man was enormous, a full foot taller than herself. Something gave in her, physically gave, a sense of tension that had run from rib cage to the dimple at the base of her throat; snapped, recoiled onto itself, pushed out a hoarse, impatient grunt. Her husband could not have grown this much: there wasn't a rack (not even in Russia!) that would account for the extra height. All at once she grew angry, jumped up, and started kicking him awake. She wore no shoes, bruised her toes upon his greatcoat's buttons; put a heel into his face and pushed it over, startled him awake.

"What?" he asked, shook himself, tried to focus, eyes gone bleary with the booze.

"Who the hell are you?"

She had to say it twice until he understood, grinned, shook his finger at her, mumbled something, fell asleep. Again she kicked him, again he came awake, swung out with one arm as though with a cudgel, hit her knees, and nearly slapped her to the ground.

"*Ticho!*" he yelled, in Russian, Polish, God knows what; crawled his way face down onto the couch and threw forward one arm in the manner of a swimmer. His snore was heartfelt, rumbling, rich in bass; head, chest, buttocks rising up like a bellows with every slurp of cushion-thickened air.

"I will call the police," she yelled, but wasn't heeded. He snorted, shifted, and slept on.

5.

Anna Beer calmed herself. She was not, by nature, easily frightened. Just to see whether it worked, she picked up the phone on the little table in the hallway alcove. There was no signal, just the tinfoil rattle of the static, feigning interest in her lot.

Pensive, her hand still holding the receiver to her chin and ear, she stared back into the study, at the snoring, sprawling sleeper on the couch. Water might wake him, a glass poured over the face, or, better yet, a bucket. But water would not sober him: he would wake, grow violent; lash out at her with those enormous hands. Who was he? She replaced the receiver and had a look at the apartment door, wondering whether he had somehow forced his entry; found his key still stuck into the lock. Mechanically, considering its implications, she pulled it out and slipped it in one pocket. She left the hallway, went first into the kitchen, where she searched the drawer for the carving knife, then back to the living room, where she drew up a chair next to the sleeper and sat there with the blade across her skirt-clad thighs.

The clock struck one, a single bleating running solemnly through the flat. Outside, the rain had stopped. The yard was dark and quiet; cloud chasing cloud in the city's ambient glow. As she sat there, waiting, there came through the ceiling the strains of a muted argument. It was the woman's voice that carried, high-pitched and insistent, interrupted only by her cough. She kept repeating her phrases, "What a pig you are" and "It cannot be borne," over and over, in a tear-choked falsetto that seemed to whistle through the building's brick.

Within half an hour Anna could not listen to it any longer, stood up and shifted to another chair, closer to the bookshelf and the door, where the voice was less audible. The chair was large and cushioned, upholstered in blood-red velour. She pulled up her feet, slipped out of her jacket, and hugged it like a blanket to her chest. But what if she should chance to fall asleep again? The man might wake first, might approach her: curled up, sleeping, one stockinged heel tucked under her rump. The thought unsettled her.

She picked up the knife, walked over to the sleeper, stared blankly at those giant hands. The palms were nearly square, the backs thick-veined and bony, the fingers broad and flattened at the tips. And everywhere there was a terrible angularity about the man, his giant back and yard-wide shoulders, the unbending stiffness of his neck. It was as though a too-modest wrap of skin had been stretched across an outsized frame of bones: he contrived to be both massive and at the same time very thin. He was not the sort of man she wanted creeping up on her.

Standing there, listening to his snore, the neighbour's whine still seeping through the ceiling, she came to a decision; turned around at once, left the study, and locked the apartment door from the inside (it could not be opened without a key). Then she picked up a dining room chair and, wedging it under the handle, barricaded herself in the bedroom as best she could.

Anna Beer lit a cigarette, smoked about one-half of it, pacing the room with measured steps, then sat down on the dusty covers of her marital bed, underneath the picture of a pretty girl in a linen nightdress. Ever since leaving Vienna, she had got into the habit of sleeping no more than five or six hours a night, lying in the dark in a state of angry boredom, then waking the next morning feeling drained and restless, unrefreshed. But now she again fell asleep, almost at once, her breathing shallow and even, her features happy, smiling, one hand curved around the handle of the knife.

Four

He slept, not having expected to; slept soundly, the brow smooth but for that wrinkle round his broken eye. When he woke, she was standing in the room, halfway between door and bed, a model airplane hanging from a thread an inch above her head. She smelled of food. It wasn't anything that she was holding; she herself smelled of it, smoked pork and sauerkraut, the sour tang of pickles. The bedside lamp he stretched to light found a spot of grease still moist upon that puckish chin. From his perspective, belly down, face half burrowed in his pillow, there was no way to see her hump. He noticed other things. The rigid structure of her bra made poignant those gentler protrusions of her body, and for a moment he marvelled at her, at her slimness and her leggy grace, the buttoned tightness of her blouse. But then, as though on purpose, she turned and made a show of her deformity: bent over the corner desk, where tin soldiers, corralled in distant boyhood, still huddled in a circle at the centre of the oaken plane, and went through its drawers one by one. What she was looking for was in the bottom left. She retrieved it, blew off the dust, threw it over to him (tousle-haired, sitting up, fumbling witless for his wits), onto the rustic tartan bedding, the smell of childhood seeping from its down.

"I didn't steal it," she said brusquely, took his measure with her sullen gaze. "She put it here herself."

It took him a moment to realize it was a frame, a picture, he was hold-ing, and another to connect it to the empty square on the wall that had pushed his mother to such fury. A wipe of his sleeve was unable to erase what proved to be not dirt but a crack in the glass that ran from bottom left towards the centre, forked lightning leaping from the lacquered frame. The picture, a portrait, was familiar, not just in outline but in its lighting and pose. It was one of a handful that had been in constant circulation even in Switzerland, a publicity shot taken early in the war. Robert had never cared for the moustache. It sat on the lip like a rectangle of tar; hid the furrow; drained all rhythm from the hard line of the mouth. Adolf Hitler looked sullen in the picture, masterly; a little heavy in the jowls. The hairline crack made incisions in his collared throat. Robert studied the picture, then dropped it on his lap; turned his attention over to the girl. He was wearing nothing but his shirt: buttons gaping at the chest. All at once he worried what sort of bulges his body might have cut into the bedding in his sleep.

"How long have you been here?"

"Some minutes. Your eye moved under the lid. The good one."

A memory returned to him, of a long valley overgrown with summer wheat; bent stalks swaying to the breath of breeze. Somewhere in that porous sky, where dream had given to reality, he'd been troubled by the ardent caw of crows.

"I was dreaming," he smiled.

She shrugged, one shoulder leading on her crooked trunk, then peeled a finger from her long-boned fist and pushed it near his face.

"That eye was moving. The other one was dead." She bent closer, breathed sauerkraut onto his mouth. "Is it blind?"

"No," he answered, aware that the lid had fallen shut, and pulling it up now with his thumb. In his confusion he edged away from her and drew the bedding closer around him. The movement dislodged the picture on his lap and sent it crashing to the ground. Neither of them moved to pick it up.

The girl turned away again, resumed her survey of the desk. She pulled the topmost drawer out of its compartment then dropped it on the table-top, spilling soldiers left and right.

"It's full of her stuff," she said, sifting through the contents with both hands. "Photos, magazine clippings. Letters of congratulations, thank-you notes, commendations. Her Party correspondence. Nice stationery, some of it. She even has a set of napkins somewhere with swastikas stitched on. Your letters are here too." (She pulled out a tied bundle.) "What rubbish you write! Do you think you are a poet or something?"

While her back was turned, Robert reached to retrieve his trousers from the floor. He looked to the window, found the heavy curtains drawn. It was hard to say how late it was.

"I met Poldi," he said abruptly, and struggled to pull on the trousers under the bedding. A corner of the shirt got stuck on the buttons. He lay flat on his back and wrestled with his fly. "She said that Wolfgang was arrested."

"What else did she say?"

"Not much. I think she was tipsy."

The maid smirked at that, watched his struggle underneath the blanket. At last he threw back the bedding and sat there, with his shirttails hanging out.

"Please," he said. "I beg you. Just tell me what is going on."

She seemed about to refuse him, turn away, then stopped short and forced her shoulders into that peculiarly lopsided shrug of hers.

"There isn't much to tell," she said. "Wolfgang came home six weeks ago, Poldi in tow. Your parents kept it quiet, of course: no registration papers, no ration cards, all the while hoping the neighbours hadn't noticed. They were worried he'd be arrested. Wolfgang's never been denazified." She paused, wet her lip, the down on her chin catching the lamplight. "And then, ten days ago, Herr Seidel was pushed out the window. He and Wolfgang, they had a fight."

He looked up at her, found one half of her face eroded by shadow, the other lit up starkly, like the waning moon.

"And it really was Wolfgang who . . . ?" He paused, and she waited him out until he found himself enacting it, making a shoving motion with both his arms.

Again the girl shrugged. "He confessed."

"You saw it, didn't you?" he told her softly. "Mother said you saw and you will testify. She's angry with you."

He expected a response, perhaps a denial, but she just stared back at him, wrinkling her nose at the last phrase. There was something about her face that moved him to pity; it mingled vulnerability with spite. All at once he wanted to be friends with the crooked girl.

"You come from an orphanage. It's where Mother found you."

"And what if she did?"

"How long were you there?"

"Seven."

"Seven years?"

"Yes."

"And I was in boarding school for almost six!"

"So?"

"So we have something in common." He reached out his hand, hoping she would shake it. "And I'm not even angry you read my letters."

She stared at his hand, first with bafflement, then anger, reached into her blouse, and retrieved a cigarette and matches. It wasn't until she'd lit up that she seemed to trust herself to speak. "Asshole," was all she said. She sat down on the desk, spat smoke across the room, kicked her heels into the wood.

But she didn't leave.

"What's that?" she pointed, shot a finger at the hat box. It was resting on a chair near the door, where it shared the space with a button-eyed teddy and a cutlass made of wood. The box's lid was decorated with a glued-on bow.

"A present for Mother. I'll give it to her after dinner. There was this hat maker's in Zurich. I had to write away and have it sent."

Robert had yet to drop the hand he had extended in friendship. The "asshole" did not trouble him. Her name, he recalled, was Eva. He itched to try it out loud.

"Go on, take a peek. They wrapped it up beautifully."

She jumped down from her perch, snatched up the box, shook it, pulled off the lid. Inside sat a bright red hat with a soft felt crown and delicately moulded brim, cushioned on all sides by little balls of crumpled paper and wrapped protectively in a square of translucent silk. She stared at it with an expression the boy found hard to read: a tender shyness spreading through her features. Slowly, gently, her hands reached in and touched the fabric.

"Better leave it where it is, Eva. I'm not sure I can wrap it up as nice."

At the mention of her name she flinched, cast off the tenderness. Her hands grabbed the hat, yanked it out by crown and brim, spilled the wrapping to the ground. She snapped it onto her head as though it were a bathing cap, pulled it low on her brow; stood in front of him, planting her hands on those uneven hips, daring him to tell her off.

"So?" she asked. "How do I look?"

"You're not wearing it right."

He got up, stepped over to her, reached with outstretched fingers for her head. She recoiled despite herself, then forced her face back into range. He pulled up the hat, set it down again, more lightly and further back upon her head; arranged the brim at some slight angle; reached for a strand of hair that he sought to tuck behind her ear. She slapped away his hand then let him do it, her stare belligerent, flinching every time he touched her skin. Another tuck and she pushed him away, stood scowling, waiting for his verdict.

He struggled for a phrase. "Not bad," he said at last. "It's just that it's not your colour. It asks for darker hair." And then, moved by a sudden recollection: "There was a woman on the train who could have worn it. Thick auburn curls." He caught himself smiling, bit his lip. "Do you think Mama will like it?"

"She's too old for it."

"We better put it back."

Eva took off the hat and seemed prepared to surrender it, then replaced it on her head, trying to imitate the adjustments he had taught her. He opened his mouth to protest, but a noise cut him short. It was the front door bell. The ringing was continuous and shrill.

"That'll be the taxi," said the girl. "You better go down."

"A taxi going where?"

"The clinic. It's gone four. Visiting hours will be over by five. I thought you would like to see your father." There was something nasty to her smile.

"Gone four? I slept through the whole day!" Robert's stomach grumbled. "And I haven't even had lunch."

He cast around, collected his waistcoat, his jacket, his socks and shoes. It did not even occur to him to resist her will and refuse the taxi. All he wanted to know was: "What time is dinner?"

"Do you think I will cook it for you? You think your mama will?"

Robert looked over to her, standing at the centre of his room, with her arms locked wrist to elbow, wringing cleavage from her lean and narrow chest; the toy plane gunning for the crimson crown of captured hat. Robert found it easy to forgive her manners; he had never learned to hold a grudge.

"You're angry," he said. "Life's been—"

"Fuck you," she cut him short, and slammed the door on her way out.

2.

Her name was Dorfer. The boy walked into the clinic a little after four and asked her if she could lend him the money for his taxi. He asked her shyly, explaining it all with a good deal of detail, how his mother had taken his wallet and how "Eva" had called the taxi, and in any case the fare was not much.

"Please," he said. "I'll come by tomorrow and pay you back."

What struck her most was the pale, freckled agitation of his face: he did not want to be thought a cheat. When he wrote down his address and named the paltry sum, she acquiesced at last, went outside and paid the surly driver. She did not tip and watched the man drive off: shallow puddles standing in the cobbled courtyard, the smell of pine trees blowing in the wind.

Back inside, the boy had peeled out of his coat and stood rubbing his wet footprints into the hallway rug. He stopped at once when she approached him and made a beeline for her chair. It was her thirty-second year of nursing. She was overweight and tired and fifty-one years old.

"It's so quiet here," said the boy, looking past the reception desk, down the corridor that led to the patients' rooms.

"We are a private clinic. Eighteen beds. Not like the bustle of the hospital."

She did not say that they only had five patients. Half the staff had been laid off.

"Who are you here for?"

"Herr Magister Seidel."

"You are the son?"

They both noted the surprise in her voice. She had read in the newspapers that he was older. And in jail.

"Stepson."

"I see. Come, then, visiting time is almost up."

They walked down the empty corridor together, the boy curious, catching glimpses through half-open doors. There wasn't much to see: a handful of pale faces made paler yet by the starched radiance of their bedclothes.

"Here."

She opened the door and stepped out of his way. He entered—hastily it seemed to her, a boy afraid to be thought a coward— then stopped dead in his tracks at the centre of the room. From where she stood, all she could see of the patient was the outline of his calves and feet. The boy, she noted, did not approach the bed. He stood breathing for some moments, his hands forgotten in his trouser pockets.

"Is he always like this?" he chanced at last.

"From the day he came. Once in a while it sounds like he is talking. But all it is is a sort of groan."

The boy tilted his head to one side, as though he could hear it now, his eyes turned inward, to the half-remembered past. "He used to sing in church," he said distractedly. "A beautiful voice. Tenor, I think. *Gloria in excelsis Deo.* Afterwards people would line up outside to shake his hand. Or, you know . . ." He raised his arm briefly and indicated the Nazi salute, unselfconscious, still lost in memory. It was surprising how once so common a gesture now made her wince.

The next moment the boy had shrugged off the past and moved on to questions of logistics. What he was puzzling over was: "How do you feed him?"

"Sugar water. It goes in through that tube." She pointed. "Thankfully, he can breathe by himself."

"He'll die, won't he?" The voice was quiet but firm.

"It's in God's hands."

She was amused to find his hand mark a cross on chin, chest, and shoulders in response to her words. He kept facing her, unembarrassed under her gaze.

"I've been away for several years. At school. I only returned today. My mother—" He paused, rephrased his thought. "They say my brother did it. But nobody told me a thing."

One of his eyes had been injured and retained a hardness quite at odds with the other. It was as though one half of him was grown up.

"Come," said the nurse. "We can talk in the tea kitchen."

It was a room hardly bigger than a closet. Her girth filled it, consigned him to a corner stool. She caught him staring at half a slice of buttered bread sitting on the table but ignored his silent appeal. There was an immersion heater plugged into the outlet. Turning her bulk away from him, she boiled a pot of water and made a flask of rosehip tea. He accepted a cup, drank, burned his tongue, then cooled it in the pocket of his cheek.

It took him a minute to retrieve it and speak. "They told me—that is, Poldi did, his wife—that Wolfgang was arrested. Herr Seidel's son."

She nodded, hid behind her cup. "All I know is gossip."

"Please," he said again. "I must know."

"Well, then. What I heard is that he beat your stepfather and threw him out the window. And then your brother went running into town. Never even put on his shoes. Ran his feet bloody, telling everyone he'd killed his father. So they arrested him. The papers say he was SS."

"Poldi said police."

"Not what I heard."

The boy nodded as though he was unconcerned by her correction. "Why?" he asked at length. "Why did he do it?"

She bristled. "How should I know? I wasn't there."

He put a hand on her sleeve. It was so young and white and slender, it did not feel like an imposition.

"There must be gossip," he said, repeating her word, the grown eye flashing boldly in his boyish face. "It's better I hear it from you."

Again she acquiesced; drank tea; spoke through its steam. "You have a maid."

He nodded.

"They say the two of them, your father and your brother, they both—" She broke off. "It happens in the best families, you know."

He thought this over, neither incredulous nor outraged, his brow creased, as though working on his homework. Halfway through his thought his eyes once again found the half slice of buttered bread. He noticed her noticing, and blushed.

"Well, now," she said, reached out a chubby hand. "I suppose we can share."

They ate in silence.

Ten minutes later she led him out past the front desk, where the telephone was ringing.

"I'm Robert," he said in parting, and as though suddenly grown shy. "You've been very kind—"

"Sissi," she said. "Like the empress."

She picked up the receiver and through the lead-shot pattern of the clinic's windows watched him leave: his head bowed, his collar turned up against the early evening air, the white face thoughtful under the mop of dark hair. Then he turned up the driveway and was lost from sight.

When Robert approached his parents' villa some twenty minutes later, he for a second time that day exchanged glances with the vagrant in the red scarf.

3.

The man was gone before Robert could place him. The boy had walked as he had earlier, on his way from the station: his attention turned inward, placing foot before foot. It was only the man's movement that alerted Robert to the stranger's presence, the furtive haste with which he turned tail. He had been standing in the shadow of a mound of cobbles piled up on the side of the street across from the villa's garden gate, or rather had squatted, the skirts of his greatcoat trailing in the street. His shoulders and hair were wet from the day's rain. When he heard Robert approach, he rose and turned, stared timidly across the space dividing them, then quickly slipped through a gap in their neighbour's garden wall. Robert was left with the impression of a thin man, eyes still as buttons sewn onto his face. It occurred to him to follow, but when he stuck his head through the garden wall across, he caught no trace of the stranger and reluctantly turned back towards the house. What stayed with him as he climbed the steps to the front door were the soft, rich coils of the man's lambswool scarf.

Robert had no key, but he found the door ajar, leaned shut upon its bolt, either from oversight or in anticipation of his return. As he closed it behind himself, his mother's head emerged in the doorway to the drawing room at the other end of the hall. He saw nothing of her but the sagging, bloated chin and the dark wave of her loosened hair. A black lace collar cut in half her throat; beneath it she was lost in shadow.

Robert ran over to her, wishing to tell her about his visit, the grimy, dark windings of the clinic. But what came out instead was this, somehow too lightly, like schoolyard gossip traded in the dorm:

"There is a man watching the house."

She started, stared at him, the face puffy and devoid of any definite expression.

"I went to the hospital, Mother. Herr Seidel isn't well."

Again she started, as though frightened by a noise, and again her face failed to register emotion. Slowly, thoughtfully, she trained her dull eyes on his face and at the same time withdrew into the room.

"Robert," she said, faintly yet warmly. "You've come home!"

Into the silence that followed, his stomach ejected a long, low grumble, grieving over its missed lunch.

Robert mounted the stairs and returned to his room.

4.

She was still wearing the hat. There it perched, upon her crown, its crimson clashing with the spark of copper the lamplight teased from her thick hair. The angle was getting more rakish by the hour, the left eye in the shadow of its down-turned brim. She sat on his windowsill, her nose stuck in the pages of a book. On top of the desk, amongst the fallen soldiers, she had placed an open tin of English beans and some gammon on a painted china plate.

"Took you a while," she said, looking up. "Long talk with your father, I suppose."

The book she was reading was his school edition of Schiller's *The Robbers*. His satchel lay upended on his bed. On the bedside table lay his diary, on top of the scrap of paper on which he had scribbled down Frau Beer's address. Both looked as though they had been moved.

Robert repeated the phrase he had used with his mother. "Herr Seidel isn't well."

The girl made a sound, more cackle than laugh. "Was he—?" She rolled back her eyes and let her jaw go slack, mimed the gaping blankness of Herr Seidel's coma with surprising accuracy. He felt he should tell her off, but sat down on his desk instead, tucked into the tin of beans with the spoon she had provided. The beans were quite cold.

"You should have warned me," he complained between spoonfuls.

"I thought you better see for yourself." She stretched, dangled her legs. "He fell three yards, maybe three and a half, and managed to land on his head. Clumsy, eh?" Her eyes found his, a smile playing on her lips. "You have a good thing coming. If he dies, I mean."

"You shouldn't do that," he told her. "Speak ill of the sick." Robert sampled the gammon, found it salty and tough. All the same, he kept on eating.

"Did you like him?" she asked abruptly. "When you were a child?"

He took refuge in his usual platitude. "I hardly knew him."

"Oh, go on. You can tell me. Your big secret. That you hate Seidel's guts."

He began to protest, swallowed beans. "You hate him too?" he asked her shyly.

"Me? Oh, no." She flushed, not quite in anger. "He's my benefactor." She paused, leaned back against the window, drew a knee up to her chin. "Did he send you nice things? When you were at school."

He nodded and chewed, baffled by her change of topic. "For Christmas. And on my birthday. A knife once, and a leather folder. Only . . ."

"Only?"

He thought about it, constrained by his habitual sincerity, and struggling to formulate his thought. "It's just that everything he sent—it was never more than it should have been. Though nice all the same."

"Nice," she repeated. "Yes. Within reason." She bent forward now, put her hands on her knees, and spoke animatedly, distinctly, one eye in shadow under the brim of the hat. "It's like this. He rations it, weighs it out. Just the right amount for each occasion. Warmth, I mean. It's like he learned kindness from a book."

"You are very clever. They way you say things"

She almost smiled when she realized he meant it in earnest; pointed to his bedding, where his report card peeked out from underneath the satchel. "And you are terrible at maths."

"Not terrible," he grinned. "'Satisfactory.' Dr. Schweizer said that all I lack is 'application.'"

He laughed then and hoped that she might join him. Perhaps she did, because she hid her face behind a yawn. A sound rose above them, barely muffled by the ceiling, Wagner paced by skips and crackle, and haunted by a thin, light voice. They both kept silent and listened for some moments, wincing when Poldi failed to rise to the high C.

"The tart loves her opera," said Eva. "It goes with her new station in life. Did she show you the certificate? For the wedding, I mean. She keeps it handy under the bed. It looks like even the registrar was drunk."

"Is that what they fought about? Wolfgang and Seidel?"

The girl threw down *The Robbers* and climbed down from the window-sill. The movement was awkward, neck and shoulders stiff upon her trunk. She straightened her blouse before she answered.

"Why don't you ask Wolfgang yourself? I am sure they'll let you see him. You are brothers, after all."

"Has Mother gone?"

"Once." She smiled. "Came back spitting bile. He kicked her out, I think."

"What's wrong with her, Eva? She's not herself."

"Nothing much. All it is, she's in mourning. For that." She tapped with a foot on the picture of Hitler lying face down on the floor. "Taking powders to soothe her soul." Eva shrugged, smiled, began walking to the door. "Some family you have, Robert Seidel."

"You seem nice," he said quietly, talking at her hump.

"I'm not family," she answered brusquely, but when she turned he could see that she was pleased. As she stood there, in the doorway, one of her hands reached out, plucked the toy plane from the sky. "How did you get that address?" she asked, pointing to the table by his bed. "The one you scribbled on a piece of paper."

"There was this woman I met on the train. Frau Gudrun Anna Beer. A pretty name, don't you think? Her husband just got out from a camp. Prisoner of war. Just imagine, she hasn't seen him in nine years! And before, she ran off because she'd caught him having an affair."

Something inside Eva seemed to flinch at this, a current running through her crooked frame. She dropped the plane. It fell nose first.

"You met her by chance?"

"Yes. We talked all night. She was very beautiful."

"Auburn locks," said the maid. "The one you think the hat would suit."

"Yes. I'll need it back, you know. The hat."

She walked out, turned one more time, looked long and thoughtfully into his eyes. "The whole world is your friend. Isn't it, Robert Seidel?"

He smiled, took it as a compliment. "I got into a fight once," he said. "Someone said something, about my father, you see, and I—"

"Oh, shut up, you spoiled, ugly brat."

She seemed hell-bent on always leaving him with an insult.

Five

1.

She woke to blood. Her feet were wrapped in it, a knot of scarlet top sheet, not wet but as though dyed along the outlines of her shins and ankles, the graceful hollow of one arch. She reached down, confused, still drunk with sleep, searched with her hand in the bedding and had her fingers nipped by metal: new blood forming in a bead upon her thumb. It broke before she had time to stick it in her mouth.

Slowly, licking the wound, she began to pull her legs from out of the bedsheet. As her red feet emerged, so did the wooden handle of the knife. In the course of the night it must have slipped out of her hands and made its way towards the ankles. She wasn't badly cut, but both her feet and the lower parts of her shins and calves were covered in a dozen nicks, shallow like paper cuts. They had dried and now broke open under her probing fingers; stung when she wet a corner of the sheet with spit and tried to wipe away the blood. It was a mystery she had not woken. The knife tip scarred the parquet floor when she pushed it out of bed.

She got up, rushed for the door, intent on scrubbing off the dried-in blood. It was only when she found it barricaded with a chair that she remembered the stranger in her flat. Taken aback, she reversed her movement, turned back into the room; smoothed down her crumpled blouse and cast around for her stockings, the only item of clothing she had taken off when she had gone to bed. She found them flung over the top of the radiator; but when she tried to pull them on, a scab on her heel broke and bled an angry smear into the stocking's silk. It was barefoot, then, that she took to the corridor, the knife back in her fist. She held it hidden behind the long curve of her hip.

Quietly—taming her pulse, her lungs, the nervous need to force her pace—she walked to the doorway of the living room, a brisk, light sting-ing in her calves and feet; stopped on the threshold, peeking in. The sofa was empty, the cushions scattered, a wet spot where his mouth had drooled into the armrest's leather crook. She swallowed and tasted smoke upon her tongue, found the stub of a cigarette crushed halfway between desk and door. It was tempting to stamp and shout and go tearing through the rooms, the knife blade flat against one haunch. She mastered the impulse; turned soundlessly and tiptoed on. Her feet were sweating: the itch of salt along her wounds. When she passed the hallway mirror, she was surprised by the mask of courage she saw etched into her face; pearl earrings glowing in both lobes.

She found him shaving in front of the bathroom mirror. The door stood wide open. He had taken off his coat and shirt and was standing there in a cotton vest, threadbare and filthy, lather on his cheeks and throat. On his feet were his soldier's boots, enormous, muddy, spreading dirt upon the patterned tiles. A cigarette lay balanced on the edge of the sink, the ash long and curling, its thread of smoke alert to the shaver's every move. The cigarette's smell mingled with the aroma of his lather. The whole bathroom reeked of man.

She could see his face quite clearly in the mirror, the giant jaw and bony cheekbones, a dark ring of lashes around each eye. As for him, he appeared not to notice her at all: his attention was poured into his task. She stood undecided for a moment, watched him shave. Just then he was working the cutthroat's blade along a length of leather strap that he had suspended from a hook. Perhaps it was his belt. His forearms were enormous, so muscular as to look swollen, with a thick cord of vein running from elbow to wrist. Beneath the vest his ribs wrote great wide arches into its much-boiled cotton. Tufts of hair collected on the tops of his shoulders, charged up the sunburned line of his strong neck. He was like a man carved from a block of wood: coarse, unyielding, riddled with knots. Each time the blade touched his skin, the sound of scraping carried through the room.

It occurred to her that it might be better to conduct their interview through a closed door. All it would take was for her to pull the key out of the keyhole; slam shut the heavy door; insert the key back from the outside, lock him in. She gauged the distance between them, wondered how fast he would move. Then she caught his eye in one corner of the soap-flecked mirror. He was watching her. Perhaps he had been watching all along.

It was he who spoke first. "What's that, then?" he asked. "You step on glass or something?"

His voice was deep and playful, hard to place. There was something odd about his intonation. She waited until she was sure of her own voice, watched him raise the blade and cut a path of skin into the soap and bristle of his throat.

"Who are you?" she asked.

He turned his waist and shoulders, not the feet, gave the ghost of a bow. "Neumann, Karel, pleased to meet."

His cutthroat rose in the space between them, its handle lost in one enormous fist.

Alarmed, unthinking, she too revealed her knife, then let it droop from her thin wrist. He followed the gesture with a laugh.

"No question about it. Yours is bigger than mine." His eyes sank down, from knife to thigh, on to her naked feet. "Or did you cut yourself shaving?"

"Who are you?" she repeated. "What are you doing here?"

He shrugged, turned back to the mirror. "Looking for Beer."

Again she noted his accent, faint and playful, the open vowels of a Slav.

"You are his wife." He opened his eyes comically, made a whistle from his soap-framed lips. "Enchanting."

"Talk, before I kick you out."

"In my undershirt?" He grinned, winked, went on with his shaving. "We are friends. Beer and I. We met out there." He tilted his head, indicating a direction, as likely east as any other. "Five years in Russian spa. Lots of fresh air."

"And you were what?" she asked, grateful for her anger. "His camp guard?"

He looked up, puzzled, then laughed. "His camp guard! Very funny. You mean because of accent. No, no, we were prisoners together."

"You are Austrian?"

"Czech," he answered. "Ethnic German. With Austrian passport." He made a gesture indicating that he could be many things if the circumstances required: an odd little flutter of his spread-out hand. "Austro-Hungarian at heart."

She refused to be charmed. "Who gave you the key?" she demanded. "To the flat?"

"Beer did. We are comrades. Army buddies. Thick as thieves."

"Where is he? Where is my husband?"

He shook his head. "I thought he'd be here. I need a place to kip. My landlord—" He paused and smiled, ruefully she supposed, curled a finger to scratch within his beard of lather. "We had disagreement about rent, you see. That and his wife, she is crazy for men. Completely shameless. Nobody is safe."

"Listen to me. I want to know where I can find my husband, and then I want you to leave."

He considered this, ignored the first part of her request. "Perhaps I can finish shaving first? I also need—" He pointed down the hallway, where the door to the toilet stood open near the front door. "Something I ate. Regret to be so frank. With a lady, what is more."

His German seemed to grow worse the more he grew into his role. She was not ready yet to choose for it a name.

2.

The doorbell rang. It had a peculiar sound she had forgotten, high-pitched, urgent, threaded with a darker buzzing as of an insect caught between two windowpanes. She turned automatically, started for the door. It was clear to her it must be Anton. She raised her fingers to her messy hair, realized she was still holding the knife; dropped it on the table near the phone, smoothed down her blouse, got blood from her thumb onto its fabric.

The spy hole disabused her of her mounting hope. She opened the door and found the woman journalist there, looking small and tidy in a light grey summer suit. Her hands were hung with shopping bags.

"I'm bringing rolls," she smiled. "For breakfast, Frau Beer. I wanted to thank you for your help."

She spoke slowly so that Anna could follow her English. Her eyes were roaming, on her, past her, up and down her crumpled clothes.

"But what's happened to you? Your feet are bloody!"

"It is nothing," said Anna stiffly. "I stepped on glass."

"You need to clean the wound. Here, let me help." She pushed in, leading with the shopping, half ducking under Anna's arm. "Alcohol is best, for disinfection. Is your husband in? Ah, here he is himself—"

The sight of the half-dressed giant cut her short. He had stepped out of the bathroom, one cheek still painted white with lather, the cotton of his vest struggling to contain his chest. Its straps looked flimsy on his bony shoulders. The fabric finished level with his hairy navel.

"Goot day," he said in terrible English, wiped the cutthroat on his wrist. "Brakefast? Goot, Goot."

"Rolls." The woman gave a nervous smile, looked from him to Anna and back at the man, trying to decipher their relation. "And some rye bread."

"Mrs. Coburn," said Anna sourly, "meet Karel Neumann. Karel Neumann, Frau Coburn. Herr Neumann is friend with my husband. They were *Kriegsgefangene*, prisoners, together."

"A pleasure," said the journalist.

"*Ja*," said the giant. "Bik pleasure. Brink caffee?" He aimed his razor at her shopping bags.

"No, I'm afraid I didn't. I thought there would be—"

"No caffee, no ham, no preserve," said the giant. "No egg." He made a face, at once mournful and hungry. "Like camp."

The journalist laughed at his expression, then stopped when he bent his brow into a frown. "I'll go get them. I have coffee in my room. Butter, eggs, some cheese. I'll just be a minute."

"It isn't—" Anna struggled for the English word. "—required."

"I'll only be a minute." Mrs. Coburn shoved her bags into Anna's hands, turned on her squat-heeled leather pumps, and clattered down the stairs.

Once again Anna was alone with Neumann. She switched back into German. "What a colossal swine you are."

He grinned at *colossal*. "At least we'll get breakfast. I bet you she's got real coffee."

He winked, ran the razor down the final rectangle of foam, then walked in even steps over to the toilet and locked himself in. A whistle sounded, then the clang of his belt buckle hitting the tiles. She stood outside the door as though waiting in line. He seemed to take an age.

"Suppose," she said into the passing of the minutes, afraid that Mrs. Coburn would return. "Suppose you are lying to me. Suppose you don't know my husband at all and only stole his key. His name is on the books, the stationery. You had all morning to figure it out."

The door stood mute, then opened a crack, his head poking out, the rest of him still sitting on the toilet. "Your name is Gudrun. Gudrun Anna."

"So?"

"You left him. Before the war. He was working at a hospital but then he quit."

"Did he tell you why I left him?"

He hesitated, sought out her eyes, his face a study of calculation. "There was a man—" he said, then broke off, stared at her through the gap in the door.

"You are guessing."

"A lover."

"Get out of here. Before she comes back." She started pulling open the door. He let her, sat unabashed in the light of the hallway, his trousers piled around his ankles.

"There was a man," he repeated. "But he wasn't *your* lover."

She froze. His German, when he put his mind to it, was perfect, with barely a trace of an accent. Only occasionally, from clownishness she supposed, or from some strange caprice, did he drop an article or mangle an ending; stretch a vowel to some comic Slavic length.

"He was *his*," he finished, then smiled, as though absolving her from all fault. "Life's a fucker, eh?"

She refused to be cowed. "And you?" she asked. "Are you and Anton—"

His smile vanished, the cheeks colouring in sudden fury. "Nothing like that. We are comrades—"

"Take your shit," she said, banged shut the door. "Breakfast is coming. And you better wash your hands."

3.

They had breakfast together. Frau Coburn ("Sophie," she whispered while they were setting the table, "please!") had brought butter, eggs, cheese, and what passed in those days for honey; a half pound of real coffee, some slices of Hungarian salami, an earthenware jar of jam. The Czech sat down first, still in his vest, watched them arrange the tablecloth and plates. He held his cup out when the coffee was brought through from the kitchen and smacked his lips as he sipped at the hot brew. They put the bread into a wicker basket and he tore open a fresh roll, then plucked and ate the dough from its centre before slapping butter on both halves.

"Is shame," he complained between bites, "no ham, no smoke *Zunge*."

"*Zunge?*"

"Tongue," Anna explained. "He eats like a pig."

"Yes," said Sophie, not without admiration. "What an appetite he has! A big man like that, he could probably eat a horse. *Mehr Kaffee, ja?* Wait, I'll run and put on the kettle."

For all her admiration for the former soldier's frame and masculine relish, the journalist proved adept at pumping him for information. Within a few minutes, using Anna as an interpreter when her faulty German could no longer be rescued by his threadbare English, she had established that Neumann had been a junior officer in the infantry and met Beer only in the camp; that he was single, from the Bohemian town of Liberec, also known as Reichenberg, "depending who talk, you see," but had spent some years in Vienna before the war; and that he had last seen the doctor "the day before yesterday," when they had gone drinking together and might have had "one glass too *viel.*" At Anna's brisk correction that her husband did not drink, he merely raised his eyebrows, then reached out a giant paw and laid it on the journalist's hand, as though it was she who needed comforting.

"The war," he said. "We drink, we forget. Leningrad, Stalingrad, the camps." The next moment he had returned his hands to the task of scooping artificial honey onto a slice of dark rye bread.

Slowly, using the same careful, leading questions, the journalist turned her attention to Anna Beer; learned the date when she had left Austria and probed the cause of her and her husband's pre-war rift ("a marital misunderstanding"); then pressed for some facts about the source of Anna's income through the years in Switzerland and France. Throughout this questioning the journalist would repeat every answer she received in a crisp, abbreviated form, as though she were mentally composing a dispatch. She looked small and scrawny at the table, her thin arms stretching to assemble food upon her plate which she then forgot to eat. Her lipstick was a deep carmine red, a shade too dark for her wan skin.

About herself, Sophie Coburn told them only that she was American, from New York, and that her husband had been a Canadian RCAF officer who'd been shot down during the war. She was working for a Toronto paper, strictly on a freelance basis. She did not explain why she was living in a shared apartment with a half-dozen lodgers rather than a private flat or a hotel. There was no reason to believe it was for want of money. Her wristwatch was of solid gold.

"I've been here for six months," she said. "When all the pictures came out"—she left it to them to decide which pictures she was referring to—"well, I just had to go see for myself. I write lifestyle pieces, and I take photographs. Only now my camera has been stolen." She sighed dramatically, laughed, proposed a course of action. "We need to find your husband, Anna. We should call the hospitals first, I suppose. Does your phone work? No? Then you must come down and use mine. The landlady will snoop around, but never mind, I'll chase her away. If he's not taken ill, then I'm afraid you'll have to go to the police. Domestic, I suppose, since he is an Austrian subject."

Anna heard it, studied her in wonder: that ill-assembled, mobile face, whose expression so often seemed at odds with the substance of her words. The woman's hands were groomed and nervous; there was always one more query tripping from her carmine lips. It used to be one had to crush insects to produce that shade.

"How was it," Frau Coburn asked, and tapped Neumann's wrist with one small finger, "your life in the camps? Difficult, I suppose. *Schwierig in Lager, Herr Neumann?*"

He took a bite before he answered, washed it down with coffee, held his arm out for another cup. "*Schwierig?* Yes, at first. *Ruhr, Fleckfieber.*"

He looked to Anna, who obliged with a translation. "Dysentery and typhus." It was strange, the words one learned, listening to the BBC.

Neumann carried on. "Later," he said, "thing not so bad. Beer likes guards."

"What he means is, the guards liked B—my husband," Anna explained. "I suppose he would have treated them."

"What was he, a surgeon?

"A psychiatrist." A note of pride crept into Anna's voice. "He was highly

respected in the field. But then he left the hospital to start a general practice. He worked right in this flat."

"That's unusual, isn't it? A specialist withdrawing into general practice?"

Anna took a moment before she answered. Her face was smiling, bland.
"There was a disagreement about policy. After the *Anschluss*. The annex-
ment, or however you say it." She rose from the table. "If you will excuse
me. I need to take a bath and change."

Sophie Coburn left shortly afterwards; rushed the dishes to the
kitchen, then began packing up the food before she decided against it
and simply placed it all in the kitchen cupboard "in case you get hungry
later on."

"You will come and use the telephone," she told Anna as she saw her
off at the door.

"After my bath."

"I'll see you later then. Goodbye. A pleasure meeting you, Herr Neumann."

"Yes, yes, goot-bye."

They stood next to each other, the Czech in his vest and Anna in her
still-bloody blouse, and watched the journalist descend. Neumann turned
to Anna after she had closed the door. His hips swung out, first right then
left, as he mimed Mrs. Coburn's walk.

"A bit of a crumpet, eh? Pint-sized, no chest, but a crumpet all the
same."

Anna suppressed a smile. "Time for you to leave, Herr Neumann."

He looked disappointed, stared down at her from his great height. "Do
you have cigarettes? Money?"

She cast around for her purse, found it on the bedroom floor, gave him
a pack of Gauloises and twenty shillings in coins. He flipped one into the
air, caught it in his giant palm. Two steps brought him to the front door.
He'd laced his boots and put on a dirty shirt; the woollen greatcoat slung
over one arm.

"I'll make inquiries," he said grandiosely. "About Anton."

She heard the words and realized that chances were she would not see him again. He'd drink up the shillings, sleep it off under a bridge. And after that: the road. It was clear to her he had no home.

"What did you do before the war?" she asked him. "For work, I mean?"

"Tram driver. Plumber. Trapeze artist."

She laughed. "That's quite a list."

He joined in her laugh, then stopped; raised some thoughtful fingers, scratched his head. "Or maybe I was physicist. Working on bomb. In secret lab in Kutná Hora." He painted a mushroom into the air between them, his hands parting to make space for its rich bloom.

"You're a buffoon, Karel Neumann."

"Yes," he nodded. "That's what it was. Buffoon. Was all right, only now it's back to being a bum."

He took a bow as they shook hands. She locked the door once he had left. Two hours later, with lunchtime approaching, she descended the stairs to avail herself of the telephone in what used to be an old professor's flat and which now housed amongst its many lodgers an American widow hunting for copy amongst the city's broken brick.

4.

"Baer, with an *ae*?"

"With a double *e*. Anton."

"Anton. Any middle names?"

"Leopold Joseph."

"Leopold Joseph. Very good. Denomination? Catholic, I suppose."

"Yes, of course."

"Catholic, then. And he was last seen when?"

"I've already told you: I'm not entirely sure. Two or three days ago. I only returned to Vienna yesterday. But I met a friend of my husband's, a fellow prisoner of war, who—"

"I'm afraid that doesn't fit on the form. There is only enough space for a number, see. Two days, then, or three?"

"Three."

"There we go: three days. I suppose I could have written 'seventy-two hours.' But never mind, it's too late for that; three days it is. It's not very long, is it?"

"Are you telling me that I shouldn't worry?"

"Worry? I wouldn't like to say. I suppose you never know."

"How will you find him? Once you are finished with the form, I mean. What's the procedure?"

"Procedure? Well. I suppose I will check in with the morgue. Most of them turn up, you know. In the end."

"Dead?"

"No, no. Drunk."

The man was exasperating: slow, colourless, and stupid, with the insolent habit of passivity; accustomed to complaint; long-suffering, long-suffered, his hands and face a yellowed grey, nicotine stained deep into his teeth. They were sitting in the cramped little police station responsible for her part of the district; he, boxed in behind a table and typewriter, an ashtray overflowing by his elbow; she, across from him, catching the draft from the window, on a narrow stool long worn of its varnish. She had answered the sergeant's flow of questions twice now, once at the front desk, where he had greeted her with gloomy indifference and asked her to kindly state her business, then here at the table, where each of her answers found an echo in the clatter of the typewriter at whose keys he stabbed with rigid fingers as though poking out a row of eyes. Occasionally he'd stop and swear, re-prime the paper, cross out some letters, and correct the word. Whenever he completed an entry, he would look up and grin at her, retrieve his cigarette, indulge in a long, much-savoured drag. They had been at it for some twenty minutes. There was no end in sight.

Throughout this long stutter of an interrogation Anna was distracted by a sound drifting through the propped-open door at the back of the office: the quiet drone of a voice, strangely muffled, as though coming through a pillow, and at the same time slow, methodical, and patient, the speaker first offering consolation, then asking precise, gently worded questions and pausing to listen with a strange air of solemnity. As the man in front of her kept stabbing away at his typewriter, Anna found herself increasingly drawn to the sound of this voice, even bending forward a little on her stool the better to make out the words. Slowly an image formed in her mind of a man sitting in an office, or else leaning, half perched, on his desk, and speaking with that quiet assurance, never correcting himself or finding himself lost for words, as though he were reading a part from a script. Anna could not hear the other half of the conversation and concluded that the man must be on the telephone. But this too struck her as peculiar, because the more she heard of the man's voice, the more she became convinced that he was speaking to a child, perhaps even quite a young child; that this child was in pain, or at any rate weepy; and that the man's aim was to draw the child into a conversation about ordinary things and thus distract its attention from its hurt or fear. Just now he was asking the child what it thought about police horses (were they better than cars? what colour was best?), then quickly moved on to dogs. "German shepherds?" the voice said thoughtfully. "Why, yes, they are good dogs. How about schnauzers, though? The large kind? Yes, you may be right, they tend to be naughty. Though I knew a schnauzer once that dragged a man out of the river. He was drowning, you see—Oh, no, he didn't jump. I suppose he just slipped and fell. The dog, in any case. . . ." And so on, telling the whole of the little story in that quiet, solemn, droning voice that would have suited a lecture hall, or a pulpit.

At long last the man wished the child a good day and hung the receiver on its cradle (she could hear the telltale click). A moment later he emerged, walked up behind the sergeant, read the form over his shoulder. He was a plump man of middling height; wore his trousers high upon his waist, had white, soft hands. The hair was neatly parted, the face dominated by a pair of steel-framed glasses that gave an eerie prominence to his watery eyes and light, soft lashes. It was hard to guess his age. He might have been no more than thirty-five or forty but had the movements of an older man.

A watch chain hung in a fastidious arc between waistcoat pocket and but-tonhole. He was not wearing a uniform.

"You misspelled 'prisoner of war,'" he said laconically. Again she noted his voice, pedantic and muffled. Perhaps he had a cold. "Never mind, Haselböck, just cross it out by hand."

He shifted his eyes to Anna. His lenses were so thick they gave the im-pression his eyes had been worked into the glass: when he took off the spectacles, she mused, the eyes too would peel off and leave behind the long blank of his face. His words were polite, even gentle, but he wasted no time on a greeting.

"Your husband is missing, Frau Beer. Have you called the hospitals?"

"Yes. This morning."

"Can you name them? The hospitals you called."

"I suppose."

"Please do."

She counted them off, watched him blink with every mention of a name and commit them to his memory.

"Very good," he said, though it was unclear to her what exactly he was lauding, her thoroughness in calling all the major infirmaries or her ability to recall them all at will. "How about his family?"

"His parents are dead. His brother moved abroad. Before the war. I don't know whether he's alive. They weren't close."

"Friends?"

Anna shrugged, licked her lips. "How would I know? I have not seen him in—" She stopped, embarrassed, grew angry at her embarrassment. "He expected me back. I sent him a wire. Surely he would have left a note if he was going to be away."

The detective nodded, ran a palm over his hair along the path of his neat parting. "So he has no reason to be out of town." He bent forward again, studied the form. "He's a doctor, I see. What specialization?"

"Psychiatry and neurology. But he ran a general practice the past few years. Before he was conscripted."

"Quite. He wasn't a member of the SS by any chance?" His smile was innocent, avuncular; the eyes bloated, drowning in their seas of glass.

Anna frowned. "Why do you ask?"

"It's routine, really. Certain people—people with qualifications, scientists, experts—they are being 'requisitioned,' if you see what I mean. Largely in the Soviet sector. People who have special knowledge, or have conducted research of a classified nature." He paused, slipped his hands into his pockets. "In one of the camps, say. Or at some special facility. Others make themselves scarce of their own accord. There are trials going on for war crimes, you see, and—"

"It isn't like that," she interrupted, gratified by the flush of loyalty that rose to her throat and cheeks. "Anton is . . . a good man. And now your sergeant tells me I will find him in the morgue."

The detective merely nodded. He had the good grace not to ask her why they had been living apart, she and this good man of hers.

"Anything else we should know? People he might have socialized with, places he liked? Any personal habits we should be aware of?"

The question startled her. She shook her head, rose to leave. "There was blood on the wall," she said abruptly. "A little patch."

"Blood?"

"In the study." She described the size and position of the stain.

"It's probably nothing. He tripped and bumped his head. All the same, I should like to take a look."

"Too late," she said. "I washed it off."

The detective looked at her quizzically, then nodded. "Very well, Frau Beer. We will be in touch if we hear anything."

She pressed his hand—dry, weightless, without pressure—and left with the vague impression that it was she who was under investigation, or, in any case, had been disbelieved. Anna had boarded a tram by the time it occurred to her that she had not even learned the detective's name.

5.

She headed east, into the inner city rather than back to the apartment, crossed without incident into the international zone, and was amused when, stepping off the tram, she saw her first patrol roll past in a military jeep, four men in the respective uniforms of their nations, the Russian blond and ruddy, the Frenchman with a pencil moustache, the American and the Brit both smoking, laughing, distinguishable above all by the differing quality of their teeth. They were so perfect, so unhurried, they might have been heading to a photo shoot for *Life* magazine. The Russian even had the good grace to turn and stare after her with his hungry peasant's eyes; had it been the Frenchman, he might have blown her a kiss. She smiled despite herself, straightened her hat, and headed into the warren of streets behind the Stock Exchange.

Within ten steps the city absorbed her. She had been born here, knew the streets and intersections, the flights of steps that connected the different levels of the city. As she walked and stared, familiarity began to wrestle with suspicion. It was as though her childhood city had been snatched and then replaced by its near copy: at every corner the relish of homecoming soured by the sudden fear she had been duped.

For all that, the changes were less dramatic than she had imagined, the bombs' incisions more precise. The northern part of the inner city had not been subject to direct attack and had only been hit by strays. Most of the rubble had been cleared. There were buildings, upper storeys, that were missing. Her eyes stared up at gaps into which her mind would paint a row of windows; a stuccoed gable perched atop a brass-shod door. Here and there torn walls had been patched: dull, artless plaster clinging like a canker to ornate facades. Men and women walked the streets, hungry, threadbare, dressed in shabby clothes; blind to the pockmarked beauty of a capital whose empire had been mislaid.

She hurried on, aware of the stares of passersby who looked with envy at her well-cut clothes and Parisian boots; lit a cigarette, smiled at some more soldiers; approached the street she had sought out. The house, she saw, was still standing; was untouched, in fact, save for some bullet holes that marked the plaster, the front door open and letting in the air. Inside, in the entrance hall that connected the door to the inner courtyard, there stooped a cleaner dragging her mop along the floor. Anna nodded in greeting, ran her eyes over the names on the postboxes, then walked up the main staircase to the second floor. She had been here only once, agitated, angry, bent on confronting the subject of her husband's indiscretion, then had balked when faced with his young lover, whose gestures had been oh so subtly fey. His name was Kis, Gustav Kis: a handwritten sign above the bell. The sign was old and dirty, a pre-war stopgap that had never been replaced. Anna wondered whether the same could be said of her husband's relation to the man.

She lingered on the landing; didn't reach for the bell and kept her distance from the door, soaking in the noises of the house. Anna had not planned to come here. It was only when the detective had asked about her husband's friends and habits that the thought had risen in her and at once transformed into a necessary duty. All the same it sickened her: the thought of confronting again that pudgy, youthful face, the cheeks still flushed from her husband's kisses. She had only the vaguest sense of the nature of Anton's attachment to this man and to his circles, and a vital need not to delve into its details.

A cough sounded in the stairwell below, the cleaner spitting phlegm into her hanky. As though in response, the door swung open at the far end of the landing. A head poked through, stared at her with a pre-emptive hostility much favoured by the Viennese. It was a young woman in a housecoat, a dozen curlers in her hair. She took in Anna's clothing with derision and actually snorted when her gaze reached her boots. It occurred to Anna that she had been standing at her spy hole for some time.

"What do you want?" the woman asked, in the overly loud, overly emphatic German reserved for use on foreigners.

Anna forced her lips into a smile. "Nothing."

"So what are you standing around for?"

"I used to live here. That is to say, a relative of mine. Some time ago."

The lie did not appease the woman. Instead her mouth formed a scowl. "Oh yes? Who?"

Anna too dropped her smile. "What does it matter to you?"

At the first sign that Anna might approach her, the woman slammed the door. A moment later she opened it again, no wider than a crack, shook her fist through the gap and yelled at her in red-faced fury: "There's nothing for you here. All over and done with. Legal, too. So don't come knocking here, from America or wherever. Don't think I won't call the police." She slammed the door again, sent its bang ringing through the stairwell.

Perplexed, a little embarrassed, and in no mood now to speak to Kis, Anna abandoned the landing and walked down the stairs. In the front hallway the cleaning lady stood leaning against the wall, the mop thrown headfirst into its bucket, her haggard face wrapped in a dirty head scarf, exhausted, malnourished; the eyes meek and wet. Anna stopped, dug in her handbag, offered her a cigarette. The woman took it but refused to have it lit; slipped it in a pocket instead.

"You heard us?" Anna asked.

The woman nodded, blew her nose. "She thought you were . . . you know."

"What?"

The cleaner dropped her voice. "A Jew, I suppose. Some of the flats here"—she pointed up with her chin—"changed hands after the *Anschluss*."

Anna considered this. "Is that what's happening? Are the Jews coming back?"

This time the cleaner shook her head: the knot of her head scarf wagging under the haggard chin. "Not really. They're all dead."

"Yes, of course."

Anna turned to leave, then felt the woman's hand upon her elbow.

"What did you want up there?"

"Herr Kis," Anna said, slipped her fingers into her bag to fish for another cigarette. "Does he still live here?"

"His name is on the door, isn't it?"

"Does he live alone?"

"He has some lodgers. To make rent, I suppose."

Anna handed over three more cigarettes, then pulled a photo out of her wallet. She had meant to leave it at the police station, then forgotten all about it when she'd met with the sergeant's litany of questions. "This man," she said now. "Have you seen him here? Mind, he is a little older now."

The cleaner looked at her suspiciously. "Can't say. Who's he?"

"My husband."

"Ah," she said, reassured. "Ran away, eh?"

"Yes. He ran away. He used to know Kis. Before the war."

"Go up and ask him, then. He may be in. I don't think he has steady work."

"Some other time," said Anna.

Outside, a jeep rolled past, four soldiers smoking, scowling, shielding their eyes against the sun.

6.

Anna Beer did not notice the girl who was sitting on the stairs above her apartment when she returned home that evening, having walked for some hours in the inner city before dining in the restaurant of one of the hotels. She was a young girl, unremarkable if rather pretty, save for a cramped and painful twist that held in lock the shoulders, neck and spine. On her head there perched a red, outlandish hat that did no favours to her complexion.

Had Anna been less tired from her long walk in the city, and less preoccupied with the sense of anticipation that rose in her every time she approached the apartment door (for was it not possible that this time, at long last, she should find her husband home and they would finally go through with their long-deferred greeting and be free to explore what remained of their marriage?), she might have noticed that the girl kept her face averted as she stepped into her line of sight, then stared after her with ill-masked curiosity. Indeed there was something impatient, unsettled, about the girl. She had been sitting on the stairs for more than an hour, rising periodically to stare out the window at the sagging ruin of the building's back wing and starting at every step that sounded in the stairwell, and at every voice that carried from below. Periodically she had lit a cigarette and calmed herself by blowing rings into the air above her head before crushing the fag end into the stone of the stairs. There were three such shreds of paper and tobacco dotting the space between her feet.

As soon as Anna had locked up behind herself, the crooked girl crept down from her perch, approached the Beers' door, and pressed an ear against the wood. She heard muffled steps and, some minutes later, the rush of water from the toilet; no talk, no greeting, nothing that would have pointed to the presence of another person in the flat. Quickly, her face annoyed and hostile, the girl reclaimed her place upon the steps, then dug a book from one of her pockets, a school edition of a classic play. As soon as she started reading, her brow smoothed and an excited, girlish look stole across her features. She looked younger then, unguarded, the lips mouthing scraps of Schiller too ardent not to be picked off the page.

A man's steps interrupted her. They sounded from below, near the building's entrance, and threaded their way up; shuffled, then charged, the unsteady zigzag of the drunk. Soon the stairwell spat him out onto the landing beneath her, a scarecrow figure, tall, broad-shouldered, very thin. He pulled out a hand that had lain buried in a pocket, bunched it up into a massive fist; leaned his weight into the door and began to hammer on it with great force. It was only now, with him measured against the door frame, that she realized how big he was, his large head stooping to avoid the lintel. And still the fist went on hammering, driving his drunken agitation into the varnished panel of the door.

The woman answered. She did not open the door but simply called from the other side, telling the man to stop making a racket. She had to repeat it a number of times before her message sank in. The man lowered his arm.

"Let me in," he bawled.

"Piss off."

"Let me in. I need a bed."

"Go find a hotel. I gave you money."

"All gone," he yelled, dropped to his knees all of a sudden, then sank onto his bum. He resumed his knocking but received no answer. After some minutes he gave it up.

He fell asleep then, for no more than a minute, woke up with a start, and pushed himself to his feet; lost his balance, charged forward, half ran, half fell into the wall across, then slipped onto the bottom step of the upward flight of stairs. His eyes rose, found Eva. He stared at her with the quizzical look of someone urging his brain to help him make sense of the world. The face was big-chinned, bony, the brow a ridge of coarse brown hair.

"Is Dr. Beer back?" the girl asked him as he struggled to get up. He teetered, threatened to topple into the stairwell. There was no banister there, just a sheer oblong hole. The girl slipped the Schiller back into her pocket, stood up, and grabbed him by one flailing hand. He regained his footing, stumbled back onto the landing, dragging her along. Again his eyes found her, discovered her hump.

"*Křivá*," he said, the language unknown to her. "Bent like a—" He stopped, considered his simile, stuck out a pinky, and laid it in a curve. "Ah, to hell with it."

"Dr. Beer," she repeated. "Is he back?"

The man shook his massive head and began his descent, dragging her down with him, his hand locked now on her wrist. "No, no, no. The wife. *Madame Beer.* From Paris." He pushed up his chin, pursed his lips, flashed her a study of self-importance. "Nice legs, though. And an arse on her—" He stopped, found a wall to lean against, threw his head back to consider Eva's rump as a point of comparison. "You have bed for me, sweetheart?"

The girl was undeterred. "Where is her husband?"

At this the man opened his eyes comically, waved her closer, spat, and whispered in her ear. "Nobody knows."

"He's still a prisoner, then?"

"No, no, no. He came back. And then . . ." He paused, leered, slapped a palm against the wall. " . . . whoosh, he disappeared."

They passed the apartments on the second floor, carried on.

"What about the bed, kid?"

"Forget it."

The girl broke loose and prepared herself for the giant's anger but was met instead by drunken equanimity.

"In that case," he said, "goodbye and *na shledanou!*"; said it, charged down towards the first-floor landing and the door of the apartment ahead; applied his fist before he found his balance, leaning hard into the wall. "Sophie!" he pleaded with the spy hole. "Sophie, Sophičko, darling, open up.

"Coffee," he yelled. "Eggs and bacon, little widow. Come on, be a good girl, open up. It's Karel, Karel Neumann, come to show you a good time."

Eva stayed until the door flew open, a commotion of tenants shouting questions at the drunk. Then she ran down the last flight of stairs and out into the summer night.

Part Two

More numbers. Of the 91,000 German, Austrian, Romanian, Italian, Hun-garian, and Croatian soldiers taken prisoner at Stalingrad, fewer than 6,000 returned home. The majority died in the first year, on the foot march to Beke-tovka, or on the train to Frolovo (or Yelabuga, or Saratov), where half the bar-racks had been bombed away by German raids. Picture these barracks, count the lice. In the mornings they stacked the dead outside the doors. Dysentery is an infection of the colon. Typhus, scabies, diphtheria spreading through the ranks. A whole barrack itching, sweating side by side; the brotherhood and anger of a thousand shared excretions. It may be impossible to write a stench.

Capitulation had carried with it hopes of food. In a propaganda leaflet dropped over Wehrmacht lines in the fall of 1941, prisoners were promised a daily ration of 600 grams of rye bread, 10 grams of wheat; 70 grams of groats; 10 grams of pasta; 30 grams of meat; 50 grams of fish; 10 grams of tallow fat; 10 grams of oil; 10 grams of tomato paste; 17 grams of sugar; 2 grams of fruit tea; 10 grams of salt; 0.1 grams of bay leaves; 0.1 grams of pepper, 0.7 grams of vinegar; 400 grams of potato flour; 100 grams of cabbage (pickled or fresh); 30 grams of carrots; 50 grams of beets; 10 grams of leek; 10 grams of roots, cucumbers, or herbs. In the accompanying photo a smiling prisoner held aloft a gleaming ladle; in another an injured man, half stripped, enjoyed the ministrations of a feisty nurse.

Supply problems dogged the Soviet army, and fighting men took precedence over captured enemies. More often than not the captors starved alongside their captives. Each kilo of body fat holds 7,000 calories. The brain needs sugar to stay alive. In the absence of sufficient food intake, the physiological adjustments made by the body to convert fat into sugar-substitutes lead to the gradual souring of the blood. Acetone builds up and is released in urine and breath. Within a week starvation starts to smell, each exhalation laced with the scent of ripe fruit: entire camps suffused in the sweet reek of the body's self-cannibalization.

One

1.

The boys shared a room. There used to be a girl too, their sister, and the boys had been forced to share a bed, but Rosi had died a year ago, of pneumonia and flu, and they'd each had their own ever since. Karlchen, the younger of the brothers, was ten; was slight, sandy-haired, and timid by disposition, with a small, solemn voice. He worshipped his brother, who consequently treated him with despotic disdain. Franzl was thirteen, bold-chinned, gap-toothed, a "daredevil" and a "bruiser." Both boys were dirty, tanned, and underfed. They were also very happy. It was summer. School had been out for almost a week.

The boys had been sent to bed at eight. It was nine o'clock now, the window open to the yard. Neither of them was asleep. The situation was as follows: Karlchen was waiting for Franzl to come over and climb into his bed. Some nights he came as late as nine-thirty or ten, and other nights he did not come at all. If Franzl found Karlchen asleep, he'd almost always do something nasty: yank a hair from the back of his head, or tie his feet together with a sock so he'd trip when getting up to pee. Once he had placed a dead frog under the covers, right on Karlchen's naked chest, then held his mouth shut so Karlchen could not scream. He remembered the feeling, the still, clammy weight at the centre of his chest where the ribs flared out from the flat shovel of the central bone. He had endured the trial as he endured all of Franzl's humiliations, in the full acceptance of their justice. A sentry must not fall asleep. Karlchen was on duty seven nights a week.

Karlchen heard his brother move and did not dare to draw another breath. Any sound now and Franz would crawl back into his bed, make him wait another quarter of an hour, or more. Karlchen lay still with his eyes screwed shut until he could feel Franzl's breathing on his skin.

"Password?" his brother asked.

"Ithaca." Ithaca was an island in Greece. Oddisses had lived there, a hundred years ago, and had owned a horse that knew how to fly.

"Wrong," whispered his brother.

"But you said—"

"Password?"

Karlchen bit his lip. "I thought it was Ithaca."

"You mustn't think."

For a moment Franz hesitated, trying to decide whether it behoved him to punish the infraction. In the end he opted for leniency. He had news to convey.

"Never mind, make space."

He crawled into bed. Karlchen rolled onto his side, stuck out his bum, felt his brother mould himself around his form. The bed was so narrow there was no other way for both of them to fit. Franz reached out a hand, put it on Karlchen's biceps, asked him to flex. He did so, awkwardly, trying to find space between his body and the wall.

"Not bad," said Franzl. "You've been doing your exercises." Then added: "Steinbeisser found a body today. Dead. Not a soldier, mind; a fresh corpse. He says he saw an arm sticking out from under a newspaper."

Karlchen pictured it. "What if it's only an arm?"

Franzl did not answer at once, which meant that he was thinking. Karlchen hoped he hadn't said anything to make his brother mad. Franz did not like to see his authority questioned.

"Well," he pronounced, "we'll just have to go and see. We are meeting Steinbeisser after breakfast. He'll take us to the place."

Franz broke wind noisily under the linen sheet, and they lay, shoulder pressed to shoulder, evaluating the aroma.

"A real stinker," Karlchen said at last.

"We had eggs today," Franzl reminded him. It would have been immodest not to acknowledge he'd had help.

He left the bed a few minutes later and crawled back into his own. As he got settled, Karlchen asked him, "What was the password?"

"Ikkerus."

"Ikkerus? Another island?"

"No, stupid. It's a bloke who could fly."

"Like Oddisses' horse."

"Yes."

"Did they fly together?"

"Yes."

"They were friends?"

"You can't be friends with a horse."

"Oddisses and Ikkerus then. Were they friends?"

"Yes. They flew together and killed many Russians."

"Russians! That's marvellous. A hundred years ago. In Greece."

He would have liked to continue the discussion, but it seemed that Franzl had fallen asleep.

2.

Steinbeisser was a fat child. Or rather he was skinny like the rest of them, but he had sloping shoulders and a moon face, which made him look fat all the same. He did not like to play football and was always out of breath. Despite this handicap he enjoyed a certain status at school. His father was a tram driver, which was almost as good as driving a lorry. That, and he claimed he had flown in a balloon once, and knew all of Russia's rivers by heart. Franzl treated him with respect. "He's full of shit about the balloon," he had explained to Karlchen, "but it's true about the rivers. I tested him myself."

"Are there a lot of rivers in Russia?"

"Fifty-seven. There's a map in the science classroom. Me and Gernot, we counted them up."

Karlchen had looked up to Steinbeisser ever since.

He met them in front of the *Tabak* and greeted them by sticking out his chin and spitting from one corner of his mouth. Inside the *Tabak* a woman in a tatty housecoat was trying to sell the vendor some embroidered shirts. When the man steadfastly refused, she started yelling at him. The boys listened as the argument escalated. In the end the woman hurried off in tears while the vendor shouted abuse at her. The range of his vocabulary was impressive.

Franzl whistled in appreciation. "Did you hear that? He called her a stinkin' tart."

"You think she was?" Steinbeisser asked, looking after her.

"No idea."

They walked a few steps, with Steinbeisser taking the lead.

"So you want to see the dead guy," he said nonchalantly, as though offering them a round of fizzy sodas.

Franzl shrugged and pretended indifference. "I found a cat the other day. Dead in a drain."

"This isn't a cat. It might even be a woman. We could take off her blouse, look at her titties." Steinbeisser spent considerable time these days hatching plans for how to get a look at titties. Neither Franz nor Karlchen could quite see the point.

"Where are we going?"

"Better save your breath. It's quite a hike. Last time I went by tram. For free, mind. I never pay."

It took them a good forty minutes to reach their destination. Gradually the character of the city transformed around them as they entered one of Vienna's more industrial areas. The bomb damage in these parts remained extensive. Hole-pitted work yards sat amongst the ruins of residential buildings, their walls blackened and crumbling. In some streets whole blocks of houses had disappeared, leaving behind nothing but the gaping mazes of their raided cellars.

They came to a stop at last in front of a bombed-out block of flats: from the outside it seemed in good-enough nick, but once they had stepped through the entrance it became obvious that the entire back of the building had been blown away. Even at the front none of the flats seemed inhabited. A crew of workmen were putting gas pipes into a gutted room at ground level; a crate of beer stood on the threshold. The boys peered inside but were soon shooed away. Across the hall a space that might become either a bakery or a butcher's shop was taking shape. Shop tables and shelving had already been put into place, and the walls were freshly painted. An electrician was wrestling with a tangle of wires that hung from the ceiling. He too shouted at them to be on their way.

Steinbeisser led them into what would have been the inner courtyard; turned and found the door that led into the building's cellar. A hand-painted sign identified it as an air-raid shelter, with a capacity of sixty-nine. The door had warped within its frame and stood ajar; they had trouble squeezing through the gap. Inside, a steep flight of concrete stairs led down into darkness.

"This is grand. How did you find it?"

"I had Rüdiger with me," Steinbeisser said. Rüdiger was his dog, some sort of terrier mix with a salt-and-pepper coat. "I was walking around, exploring, and he sniffed it out." He reached into his trouser pocket, brought out a candle and a match. "I came prepared this time."

They lit the candle huddling on the topmost stair. An odd smell rose from below, at once stale and biting, of rotting wood and worse. A sudden hesitation seemed to take hold of Steinbeisser: he fussed with the candle, pretended the wick had not quite caught. Behind him Karlchen kept his back pressed against the door, as though afraid of losing his footing.

"Let's go," Franz urged them on. A peculiar calm came over him in moments of grave danger, along with a sort of prickling in the loins. Steinbeisser did not resist when he wrested the candle from his hand. At the foot of the stairs the corridor split into a T.

"Right or left?"

"Left. Rüdiger went nuts when we got here, kept pulling at the lead."

The corridor widened after a few steps into what seemed to be a cavernous room some fifty feet across. The light of the candle jumped, recoiled before this expanse of space. Decay hung heavy in the room, was cut by something chemical and sharp; piles of litter strewn amongst the wooden posts that supported the ceiling. A patch of sun found its way in through the broken pane of a barred cellar window (the pane itself was caked in dirt). It was followed by a sudden draft: shadows spinning in the flame. Franzl turned to shield the candle, felt Karlchen crash into his arm. He had no memory later of dropping the candle, could not say whether it was the collision or the fall that extinguished the light. All he knew was that all of a sudden it was dark, save for that shaft of sunlight etched into the flying dust. Amongst the rustle of their breathing there was one louder, more ragged, than the rest. Karlchen screamed and Steinbeisser whimpered; it was left to Franz to shut them up. He ordered them to hold their breath, held their mouths shut for good measure, dirty fingers smeared across their dirty mouths. And still there came that ragged breathing, rising, falling in the room ahead.

"Who's there?" Franz turned and called, releasing the others from his hold. He heard one of the boys run down the corridor, stumble, fall upon the stairs. The other reached and took his hand. He was surprised to find that it was Karlchen. Together they stepped deeper into the room.

"Who's there?" he called again, willed his eyes to penetrate the gloom. They crossed the shaft of light and for a moment he saw his brother's face, two lines of quiet tears falling from his scrunched-up eyes, his left fist pushed deep into his open mouth.

Another step took them into renewed darkness, the stranger's breathing growing louder to their right. The stink grew stronger too, the sticky smell of rot overlaid with antiseptic. Again their eyes adjusted to the dark and shadow peeled itself from shadow. A mound of newspapers rose before them, piled on top of a coal sack, or a corpse. At its side sat a man, his back against the wall. The boys saw the boots first, coarse soles gaping from the leather uppers: a grin of nails bridging the dark gap. The face came next, was a pale smear amongst shadows, then grew features, mouth and chin lost beneath a double coil of scarf. The scarf, Franz saw, was red and new; the man himself not old but spent, sunken temples pressing in against the hot, dark eyes.

They stopped two yards from him. He rose, stood stooped under the sagging ceiling, his lips shaping words too soft to hear; then a bony wringing of his hands. One step towards them was all it took to panic Karlchen: he spat out his fist and, screaming, dragged his brother through the room. Franz allowed himself to be led; stopped at the entrance to collect the fallen candle off the floor. He turned and marvelled how light the room seemed to him now; a bright, high singing spreading through his abdomen and boyish prick. The man was standing in the middle of the room, haggard, lonely, his body lost within his dirty Wehrmacht coat. His hands kept moving, along with his lips, shaping greetings, pleadings, swallowed by the sound of running feet.

3.

It wasn't until the brothers were outside, blinded by light, that they realized how bad the air had been down in the cellar. They found Steinbeisser six blocks away at the tram stop. Pale and sulky, he did not speak when Franz returned his candle to him, and though his moon face betrayed the most intense curiosity, he forbade himself all questions. Franz, for his part, started prattling about nonsense and compelled Karlchen's silence with a series of stern looks. It was only when they saw the tram approach that Steinbeisser cracked. Too loudly, his voice hoarse as though from shouting, he asked whether they'd found the dead man.

"Dead man, my arse," Franz told him. "Just a scarecrow chasing off the sparrows."

"A scarecrow?"

"A bum, you idiot! All your stupid dog found was a drunk asleep under some papers."

"But the smell!"

"So he shat his pants. Looks like you did too."

Steinbeisser's moon face rose, cast around for bluster to dismiss the taunt. There was none that could be summoned. "Don't tell anyone," was all he managed as the approaching tram screeched to a halt. He held out his hand. Franz paused, then shook it. Steinbeisser climbed aboard and immediately began explaining to the conductor why it was he needn't pay.

The two brothers turned and made their back way on foot. They did not speak, Karlchen quiet, busy with his thoughts. That night he gave the password listlessly and waited impatiently for a jesting Franz to leave his bed.

For the first time in his life he held a secret from his brother, and it placed a weight upon his heart. Nor did he see a way to shift it. If he were to say what he had seen, Franz would want to return. Karlchen's eyes, down in the cellar, had adjusted more quickly to the darkness than his brother's, and when he'd stood before the stranger, they had fastened on the pile of papers by his side, where a heavy hand, half pale, half livid, lay unwrapped amongst the newsprint, its fingers long and fanned and broken, and sprinkled with a fine red dust.

Karlchen slept badly that night and by morning had developed a light fever. Franz went out to play alone.

Two

1.

It took him four days to arrange his visit to Wolfgang. Robert might have
been able to see him sooner, but when he went to the police station to
inquire how to proceed, it was noticed that he no longer held valid registration papers for Vienna and had, in fact, failed to deregister upon leaving his school in Switzerland. It took visits to four separate offices until
this oversight had been cleared up and Robert was not only registered but
had been issued a ration book and received official permission to visit his
stepbrother.

Robert experienced, in these encounters with Viennese bureaucracy, an
impatience that went beyond the natural annoyance of waiting in line only
to be sent on, with well-rehearsed rudeness, to some other office in some
other building with its own queue of shuffling petitioners. Whenever he
emerged from the last of his day's errands, he found himself running, first
to the clinic to inquire after Herr Seidel's health, then on home, slowing his
step only when he approached the villa's front door.

He felt he roamed the great house like a ghost—or a detective. All
evening he'd be on his feet, drifting through its corridors and rooms, looking for conversation; for answers, explanations, some magic phrase that
would allow him to reconstruct the events of the past weeks. But neither
his mother, nor Poldi, nor Eva seemed to notice him on these wanderings;
were wrapped up in lives he struggled in vain to understand. He who hungered after conversation—some "true and fateful word"—had to contend

with the dross of pleasantry and small talk. His mother petted and ignored him; Poldi sang and drank and offered glimpses of her tired skin; Eva went out, returned to scold him for unspecified ineptitudes, then left again on errands of her own devising. Only now and then would something more be said, some shard of talk that dropped out of the rest of the words and urged the study of its meaning. At night he dreamt of screaming crows. Home was a riddle to Robert. He was looking to Wolfgang to provide the key.

The visit was scheduled for the mid-afternoon. Robert spent the morning first taking a bath, then ironing his underwear and shirts. Four days into his stay his clothes remained stuffy and wrinkled from being packed in a bag. Initially he had hoped that his mother might pick them up if he left them draped over a chair in a corner of his room, or perhaps Eva, the maid. Growing familiarity with the house had disabused him of the notion. His mother was not interested in his linen. Neither was Eva. At long last Robert had decided to see to it himself.

It was no later than ten o'clock in the morning. Robert stood, stripped to the waist, in front of his desk, where he had spread a towel to stand in for the ironing board he had been unable to locate. In his left hand he held a brass watering can, intended for the care of household plants, which he used to moisten the cotton; in his right, a flatiron whose handle was so badly insulated that he had to wrap it in a sock. Two shirts hung freshly ironed from the doorknob behind him. He was seeing to the cuffs of a third.

A bird walked into his line of vision. It did not fly, or hop, but precisely walked, one funereal step after the other: sparse, toe-splayed, brittle feet, their talons snagging in the much-washed flannel of his towel as it walked along its seam. A black bird, its black eye cold and oily like spit-moistened tar. When it reached the towel's edge, it flapped its wings and gave a caw, thin tongue flicking at the centre of its open beak. Robert recoiled, iron in hand; then drew close again, shooing the bird with the hot wedge of metal without discommoding it in the slightest. When the bird reversed direction and hopped from towel to shirt, the movement shifted the angle of a button: it caught the sun and blinked. The bird saw it, pounced, and cut the button from its moorings, the shirt front rising in a ghostly wave until the thread snapped against the knife edge of the horn-black beak.

Next Robert knew, the bird had leapt onto the windowsill then flung itself into the air: the button, a double-punctured pearl, twinkling on each corkscrew turn as the bird rose towards roof and sun. Above them a hoarse chorus greeted its ascent and roof-tile landing, a sound both resonant and hollow, as though rising from the house itself. Robert recognized it at once. Without the slightest hesitation, throwing a shirt over his naked shoulders, he ran out of the room and up the stairs.

At night he dreamt of screaming crows.

He had not known his dreams would summon a live murder.

2.

She found him amongst birds.

He had hit upon her hideout in the attic and was curled into her armchair by the window, in his hands one of the books she had stolen from his satchel. The sun that fell in through the open pane lay on his face and chest. He did not notice her at once. Her entrance had been masked by bird call.

They were everywhere, a dozen crows lining the rafters, discussed his presence with wild chatter, watched him with their flat black eyes. At times Robert stirred: drew up a leg, or turned the pages, shifted his weight from one slim buttock to the other. Each movement was greeted by fresh catcalls, the subtle rearrangement of his watchers' constellation; a hop, a flutter, the quick ingestion of a woodlouse pecked from a crack within the wood. It was different for Eva. Her entrance drew no comment from the birds. She was a member of their tribe.

For another minute or two she stayed where she was, halfway through the trap door up between the top floor and the attic, her feet on the sixth rung of the ladder. She stood and watched him, her face shielded by the brim of her hat. Eva liked watching Robert. It was not often that one got to see a perfect fool. One of his lids had slipped, hung like a flap over the orb of his eye, a vein snaking through it like a piece of black thread.

Ever since his arrival the whole house had been alive with Robert, its many rooms resounding with his bumbling footstep, his every movement marked by a benevolent sort of haste. Always he seemed to be looking for her, and, through her, for answers. She avoided him, gave hints not answers, rationed the truth as she rationed the household's butter, the lion's share for herself. It helped at times to trace in his features those of his mother: remind herself that he was her son.

She climbed two more rungs of the ladder and he noticed her at last.

"Eva!" he called, and sent the birds into a chorus. "I've been dreaming of crows all week." He smiled, unstuck the lid from his eyeball with a finger. "And here you shelter a whole roost."

He made to get up, but a warning gesture stopped him. "Watch!"

Her right arm rose in a slow and ritual gesture until it was level with her shoulder. Immediately one of the crows detached itself from the rafters and swooped down onto her wrist. She scratched its head, fed it a crumb of *Speck* she dug from a pocket.

Robert broke into applause. "What's his name? He's quite in love with you!"

"Yussuf," she answered tartly. "All it is, I'm feeding him *Speck*."

The phrase drew an angry blush from Robert, as though she had caught him in some foolish supposition. In his white shirt and black trousers he looked as neat as a button.

She let go of the bird, walked over to her chair. He gave it up without a murmur, from courtesy, or pity, she'd have liked to know which. The seat was still warm. The window claimed his interest, while she pretended to read.

He spoke abruptly. "I've seen him again. The man watching the house." He pointed outside, as though the man were there even now, standing sentry in the noonday sun. "I've seen him four times now. Once outside the clinic, and otherwise right here. Whenever I try and approach him, he runs away from me. There is this look on his face: expectant. Like he is waiting for something. I thought at first he was police. Undercover or something. But it doesn't go with that look."

"So?"

"So Mother asked me about him. Last night. She came to my room and showed me a photo. Is this the man? she asked. Only she asked more slyly than that, the way a child thinks it is being sly. Is this the man? Is this the man? Petting me, waving the photo at my face."

"And was it?"

He shook his head. "The man in the picture was fat."

"That can change."

"That's just what Mother said."

He paused, watched her, hoped for information. At length she obliged him.

"Your father was waiting for someone. Someone other than your brother. Sometimes he'd send me out when he saw a stranger pass the house. He never told me what to say."

"So who is he?"

"Ask your father."

"He's dying. And besides, he's not my father."

"Ah, the policeman. I forgot."

Silence fell between them, was broken by an avian squabble. Robert waited until the dispute had been settled before returning the conversation to the subject of his mother. She feigned a lack of interest, sat leafing through the book.

"I can't figure it out," he said. "Last night, when she came to my room, it was like she was in a fever. All of a sudden she was there, hugging me, kissing me, never standing still. And today she can hardly turn her head. She lies on the couch and stares at the wall." He frowned, bent down to her. "You told me she's taking powders. You mean drugs."

"Veronal," she said. "And morphine. And last night it was flying lessons."

"Flying lessons?"

"Pilot's chocolate. Pervitin. During the war they mixed it into chocolate. For the troops. It kept them alert. It also—" She wedged a limp arm between her thighs, the elbow dug into her pelvis; formed a tight, hard fist, then slowly stiffened, raised it, curling the forearm lightly at the wrist. "I suppose that part doesn't happen to a woman. Funny thing to give to soldiers."

She laughed at his embarrassment, and he turned away from her, cast around for a change of topic. In each of his gestures it seemed possible to read the sequence of his thought. Deceit was unknown to him. Habit helped transmute her envy into scorn. He mistook her smile for an invitation to resume their conversation.

"I'm seeing Wolfgang today."

"Yes," she smiled. "The family celebrity. A Nazi hood turned parricide."

She said it lightly, turning pages in her book. And still he flinched.

"What exactly did he do?" he asked. "During the war, I mean, so that he had to hide all these years?"

She did not know. "He was Gestapo," she said.

"Gestapo?" The word carried its own indictment. "And I had hoped that he was innocent."

"Like you, you mean."

Her eyes found his, the first direct look they had exchanged throughout their talk. It should have sufficed to chase him but helped encourage him instead. He drew closer, sat down across from her on the crate that served her as a table, their knees almost touching. His eyes stayed on her face then slipped downwards, to her body. Her skirt remained crumpled where she had placed her elbow. It marked the outline of her inner thighs.

"You have to help me, Eva," he said. "Help me understand. All these days I've been walking around like a ghost. Everywhere I go, people look at me funny. At the police station, when I was trying to register, the clerk asked me where I had been. And when I said Switzerland, and that when I left it was still war and I'd been in the Jungvolk and had only just been given the shirt and badges, well, he just started laughing at me, but he was angry, too, I could tell by the way he filled in the form. He couldn't wait to get rid of me. It's like everybody knows something I don't."

She shrugged, offered no help. Her silence burdened him, egged him on. Afterwards, looking back to this moment, she came to realize that it was she who had wakened him to spite.

"There is another thing Mother told me," he said. "Last night, when she came into my room. About the orphanage, and how she picked you.

"Your name isn't Eva," he said. "It's Anneliese. Anneliese Grotter."

She slapped him then, hit him square on one cheek, and they sat across from each other breathless, as though they had been fighting, kissing, making love. After some moments she retrieved her book and started reading. He watched her, rose, and walked away; crows cawing, laughing at his back.

3.

She came to his room and picked him up. A little more than an hour had passed. Robert had lost patience with the ironing; sat idly at his desk. Neither of them made reference to the slap. She simply asked, "So you want to understand? How things work around here?"

"Yes."

"Then come."

Outside, on the pavement, she slipped an arm through his, mischief dancing on her face. "You don't mind, do you?"

"Where are we going?"

"To buy fruit. Here, let's run and catch that tram."

For the first time since he'd known her, she seemed young; weightless. They ran, and she held on to the side of her skirt so it did not fly and reveal her legs. Robert had no money and she paid the fare for both of them.

They sat down on the hard wooden seat, buttock to buttock, laughing. He looked at her sideways and wondered did he dare. The impulse took hold of him. He did not resist it.

"Anneliese," he said, his lips not far from her ear. "Liese, Lieschen. It's a pretty name."

She held herself still, did not respond.

"Who is Eva?"

This time a smile formed, grudging, wistful, her fingers drumming on her thighs. "It's just a name."

"What's wrong with Anneliese?"

She turned, flushed, grew angry. "Have you never wanted to be someone else?"

He shook his head and was surprised to find a look of envy in her eyes.

"Wait," she said, "I'll show you," then fell silent for the rest of the ride.

They got off in the ninth district, then walked a few blocks until they came upon a little shop selling groceries. An Austrian flag hung in the window above a display of tinned goods. In front of the shop the owner stood amongst some meagre crates of summer fruit and vegetables. He smiled when he realized they were customers, his mouth a hole with no front teeth. He might have been forty-five or fifty, jovial, fat-faced, born to chat. While Eva stood picking out a little basket of raspberries, she and the shopkeeper engaged in idle prattle: praised the weather, touched lightly on the Berlin blockade, cursed all politicians for their stupidity and graft: all in the same playful, conversational tone that was as much a part of commercial transactions in Vienna as was the exchange of money. She picked a basket at last, haggled, paid, and led Robert off to the low wall of a schoolyard, where they sat and ate the berries.

She waited until the basket was half empty, then asked him casually, "What did you make of him?"

Robert looked at her in surprise, then back at the shop. "The vendor? He was nice, I suppose. Bad teeth."

"That happened in prison. He was a resistance fighter."

"What did he do?"

"Oh, he was a real hero: sold produce on the sly, rationing be damned. But then one of his customers denounced him, and they pulled him in for questioning. The story goes, he just sat there, grinning at them." She whacked the flat of her hand against the stretch of wall between them, startling him. "They lost patience, I suppose."

"So?"

"Another story I heard. Back in '38, when the Germans marched in and everyone was cheering. They were rounding up Jews then, to clean the streets, perhaps you remember. Lawyers, doctors, old ladies, crouching on their knees, and a ring of people around, jeering. Well, he walked past one of those little parties and one of the women there spilled some water on his nice new boots. So he shoved her, with the knee I suppose, and she falls right into the puddle by her side. Nothing happens to her, mind, she's only lost her balance, but the crowd's cheering him, like he's a hero or something, and he looks up, embarrassed at first, and then, as though to test it, he gives the woman another little kick." She paused, scratched her nose. "They say the police had to drag him off her in the end, he was kicking her to death. Stomped on her face like a madman, his fat mug flushed with his success." She ate another berry. "And the beauty is it happened right here, in this street, so everybody here knows about it, and he knows that everybody knows. But they come to his shop and listen and nod when he tells them about the Gestapo and how they bashed in his teeth."

They were silent for a moment, Robert mulling over her story.

"Did you see it happen?" he asked at last. "With your own eyes?"

She shook her head.

"Maybe it isn't true."

"Robert Seidel," she said, "you're just like everybody else."

He chewed on that, along with his lip, searched her words for meaning. "You're saying he's an antisemite," he tried to summarize. "He's friendly, he jokes about politicians, but he hates Jews all the same."

She laughed, hugged her crooked frame, something wicked running through her features. "Ah, the Jews, the Jews," she started singing to herself. "There was a boy in school—" She paused, lost track of her thought. "And, of course, they made them into soap." She mimed washing her armpits.

"You're evil."

"I'm a hunchback. What do you expect?"

She jumped down from the wall, turned around, and pushed her hips between his knees. They were face to face, close enough for him to see white down curl on her cheeks; copper hair burning in the sun. The brim of her hat threw a shadow on one eye.

"We are a people," she intoned, playful and serious all at once, "who have already forgiven themselves."

"Not you."

She wrinkled her nose and snorted.

He looked at her in wonder. "How did you get so smart?"

She smiled, pleased, leaned forward and blew a mouthful of air up his nose. "If you were smarter, you'd have kissed me."

She stepped away, spun, one twisted shoulder leading the way.

"Your brother told me once that only a cripple cares about the past. Next thing you know, Herr Seidel falls out of a window." Again she laughed. He could not tell whether her merriment was forced. "It's what I love about Vienna," she continued, relentless, laughing, raising her voice. "Everyone knows everyone, and what they did. You meet a strange lady on the train and next you know—"

"What?" he asked, remembering Anna Beer.

"Was she really very pretty, your brunette?"

He did not hesitate. Perhaps he should have. "Beautiful."

She danced away, left him.

"Where are you going?" he called after her.

But she only turned her head around, stuck out her tongue over one sloping shoulder, and ran away.

4.

"Look at you! Like a dog waiting to play fetch. Frisky. And look at the shirt you put on, it's literally stiff with starch. Well, sit down then, little brother. No, stand, let me hug you. There, you even get a kiss. Don't look at me so surprised. It's the bloody prison—makes you sentimental. That, and you are pretty like the Virgin, never you mind about the eye! There, you even blush like her.

"But go on, say something. Though I already know all about it. The guard told me—Bastel, the fat one with the pockmarks and the beard. Says you came here last night, 'just to make sure you knew where to come,' and then sat chattering away for a good half-hour, though you were in a 'terrible hurry' and got up every three minutes in order to head home. Oh, they had a good laugh once you left. But don't be angry! They rather liked you. They laughed at you, but they fell in love with you all the same. You were like that even as a little boy.

"But tell me, Robert, what is it you want? To see me? Well, here I am. What do you think? I'm growing stout. There's a Magyar here, in the kitchen, I mean, a cook, and he makes a goulash, let me tell you—There is no meat in it, naturally, just bones and gristle, but it's not bad all the same. I'll miss it when I get out.

"But speak, speak, and stop creasing your brow. I can see it from here: you've come with a plan. Well, then, out with it! Only sit, make yourself comfortable, and don't mind the guards. They are listening, naturally, it's not from malice or anything, but *a matter of policy* (they are awfully fond of that little phrase). The truth is, they're bored, terribly bored, and there's no drinking here on duty, they are very strict about that, and one of them even got suspended over a little glass. So it's no wonder they all come out to nose around a little. After all, it's an occasion, you have even washed and combed your hair!"

Robert sat and watched his brother without saying a word. Wolfgang looked much as he remembered; not at all "stout" but rather trim, with a loose-jointed athleticism that had marked him even as a youth. If anything he had grown more handsome as he passed into manhood: a broad-shouldered man with long limbs and a square chin, and soft hazel eyes it was said he had inherited from his mother. The swooping "cavalry" moustaches made him look like a dashing officer from some historical portrait, an appearance not at all lessened by the dirty state of his clothing and the scratch that was healing on his forehead. It was only the voice that betrayed something morbid and unhealthy in the state of his soul. It struck Robert that it had been a long time since Wolfgang had spoken to anyone, and that now, all of a sudden, he was terribly greedy to speak, though there was something artificial, too, about this greed, something nervous and forced, and that some part of him was listening to his chatter with angry disdain. Wolfgang's hair had been shorn close to the scalp but was already growing back with peculiar vigour.

Despite Wolfgang's comments about the boredom of the guards, there was only a single guard present, along with some sort of representative of the court, sitting in one corner of the room and listening to them with lazy equanimity. The room, incidentally, was not a cell but a larger furnished room reserved for visits. It had been a special favour to Robert to arrange a visit outside regular hours. They had the room all to themselves.

Robert turned his attention back to his stepbrother. His eyes wandered from Wolfgang's face down to his hands, surprisingly small for a man of his frame and even somewhat plump. A crescent of dirt was wedged under each of his nails.

"I met a man today," Robert found himself saying, "a greengrocer. He had half his teeth knocked out by the Gestapo."

His brother pulled a face. "So that's why you are here," he said sulkily. "You want an answer to that nagging question: is he a good man or bad? Well, Robert, I don't remember any greengrocers. Though perhaps, who knows—" He grimaced, leaned back on his chair, folded his hands behind his neck. "You know what the guard said to me? Yesterday it was, right after lunch. He puts his hand on my shoulder, friendly like, and says, 'No chance of bail, eh? Never you mind. At least you're safe in here.' Real touching it was. I suppose he pictures him, that greengrocer of yours, honing his paring knife in my honour. Or maybe he thinks they are out there somewhere, a whole cabal of hook-nosed little vagrants on the lookout for my kind." He laughed, then spat. "The rubbish people will believe! My kind, indeed. And what about his, eh? It never occurs to him there may be a little pack of them out there for him too!" He paused abruptly, leaned forward across the width of the whole table, and added somehow nastily, "You haven't asked me yet whether I threw Father out the window."

"They told me you confessed. Walked around with bleeding feet and confessed to everyone in earshot."

Wolfgang shook his head. "I only told one little boy. And then the police at the station, but that doesn't count. Besides, it's nonsense. They—" He caught himself, smiled a sour little smile. "But look, the court official is getting nervous. I'm not supposed to talk about the 'evidence.' Not even one little word.

"I have a lawyer now," he added. "Herr Doktor Ratenkolb. And what a sly dog he is."

Robert nodded. "I know. I went to get his signature. For the visits. He is a dreadful little man."

He paused, dug in his pocket, and passed over the bar of American chocolate he had found hidden at the back of a kitchen cupboard. There had been a whole stash. Wolfgang took it greedily, unwrapped the chocolate, and ate it at once. It was only when he had eaten most of the bar that he remembered Robert and passed him a little square.

"Here, take it. For coming to this valley of the lepers." He licked chocolate off his fingers and crumpled up the paper. "You know, in all this time you are the first to come and visit."

"Eva says Poldi is afraid to. She thinks it'll hurt your reputation. She also says you turned away Mother."

Wolfgang flushed with anger. "So you've discussed it all, *Eva* and you." He pulled a face, ran a hand through his stubble. "Poldi may be right at that. About my 'reputation.' Father used to say, 'Where did you find her, this twopenny tart of yours?' If she does visit, they'll never let me hear the end of it." He nodded his head at the door in the direction of the guards. "As for your mother, all she was worried about was how I would testify."

"She says you are a martyr."

"A martyr? For the cause, eh?" Wolfgang chuckled and shook his head. "Still holding out for the *Endsieg,* is she? Funny how things turn out. When she came to us—"

"Yes?" said Robert, aware of the catch in his voice. "Tell me."

"Well, you were there yourself. She started working at the factory at first. A pretty little widow. Packing goods or something, right on the shop floor. Then Mother got ill and we needed a housekeeper. She came as a maid, same as the hunchback. God, what a mouse she was then! Afraid of her own shadow. And every time anyone mentioned her dead husband, you would have thought she'd get on her knees and cross herself. I think Father married her out of pity."

"And then?"

"She bought into it. The speeches, the newspaper, all that stuff on the radio. I did too. Joined everything I could, shouted all the slogans, hoping I'd dodge the draft somehow, especially once they'd flunked me out of school. It all made sense, you know: the more I shouted, the more everyone praised me. I remember sitting over dinner with your mother, swapping the latest stories from the *Stürmer,* Father looking on confused, like it was all very well to go on like that in public but wasn't it time for dessert?"

He chuckled, stroked his chin and moustache. "And then, when it all went to shit, well—I dropped the slogans, same as everyone else. Only your mother didn't. She still had Hitler hanging in the hallway when I came home six weeks ago."

He cleared his throat and spat on the floor next to his chair, looked up and continued in an offhand manner. "You know, Robert, it is good talking to you. Like putting on clean underwear or something. I feel—what's the word? *Resurrected.* And it's all because you have such a sweet little face. And now, tell me, little brother. Did you bring any cigarettes? You did!

Well, bless you, my little angel, I swear to God I want to kiss you again, only the guards, they wouldn't approve."

He grinned, leaned back, and lit up a smoke.

5.

Silence fell between them as they shifted nervously in their chairs. Wolfgang looked over to the two men on the far side of the room and Robert half expected him to ask to be walked back to his cell. But instead he pulled a face and sat smoking his cigarette in quiet, methodical drags. When he had finished with it, he stubbed it out on the scarred surface of the table, reached across, and took hold of Robert's hand.

"Look here, little brother," he said, his voice quite changed from the jeering note that had coloured it before and taking on a solemn tenderness that went straight to Robert's heart. "In a few short weeks I will be in court. Don't imagine for a second that it will just be about Father. They will put me under the microscope, mull over every little sin, and by the end I'll have turned into a monster. No, no, don't contradict me, it's how it'll be, and who knows, perhaps I even deserve it. But for now—while you still love me—let's talk, even if it's just for one little hour." He reached over and tousled Robert's hair. "Tell me about yourself. We are brothers after all."

"That's just how I'd imagined it," Robert answered, half embarrassed by the eagerness in his voice. "That we would sit here and talk about God and the world."

Gott und die Welt. Wolfgang smiled at the expression and lit another cigarette.

"Go on, then, tell me a secret. What, no secrets? Surely there must be at least one. Let me guess, you are in love. No? Not even a little bit? Something else, then. You're running off to be a sailor. No, better yet, a monk!"

Robert blushed and shook his head, and began to talk about his years in the boarding school, the teachers and his schoolmates and their boyish little pranks. The brothers spoke for another twenty minutes, until the guard stood up from his bench and escorted Robert outside.

Three

On the fourth morning after her return to Vienna, at eight-thirty in the morning, Karel Neumann rang the bell to Anna Beer's flat. She was not entirely surprised to see him. For the past two days she had, on various occasions, been privy to the neighbourhood gossip which held that a young widow, "an American, and some sort of journalist," who was lodging in Anna's apartment building, had taken to receiving a man at all hours of the day and night, disregarding all rules of propriety. What was more, the man was not registered at this address and often arrived in a state of advanced inebriation, waking up the other lodgers with his knocking and outbursts. The neighbours, and especially the landlady, were deliberating on what was to be done. The issue was far from simple. On the one hand such criminal behaviour could hardly be tolerated and there was little choice but to call the police and have both of them turned out. On the other hand the woman was a foreigner and as such subject to "quite a different code of law," as the shopgirl at the bakery explained to Anna, taking obvious pride in her polished turn of phrase. Besides, it was rumoured that the widow paid more than twice the rent of the other lodgers. Thus far, in any case, neither Frau Coburn nor her visitor had been asked to leave, and there was even some evidence that the other lodgers had started taking a liking to her beau, who was described to Anna as "very presentable, if not exactly handsome," and "in any case tall"; a man of some humour, whose drinking habit could be excused with reference to the privations he had experienced as a prisoner of war.

Despite all this talk about "Herr Neumann," Anna had not actually seen him these past few days. After her aborted visit to Herr Kis, she had spent her time looking up friends and acquaintances of old and inquiring whether they had seen her husband. The results were meagre. An old colleague of Anton's, a neurologist who was working at the hospital, reported that they had passed one another in the street about a week ago. The two men had tipped their hats in greeting, but—walking on opposite sides, and both of them evidently in a hurry—they had not actually stopped to talk. The old doctor had been sufficiently struck by this chance encounter to call Beer on the telephone that same afternoon, only to learn that the number had been disconnected.

Other than him, only the bank manager had seen Anton. He had come into the branch ten days previously, to withdraw money from his account. The bank had been crowded just then, and the two men had no opportunity to speak or even shake hands; a clerk had handled the transaction. Beer had looked well enough, if thin and dressed "a little below his usual standards." When Anna asked if it had seemed to the manager that Anton had been drinking, she was met with a professional smile. "Out of the question," the man had said, brushing lint off his jacket sleeve. He'd served her an apple brandy and stared at her bottom when she got up to leave.

None of her other visits uncovered anything further. It seemed that Anton had talked to nobody at all.

Unless, that is, he'd talked to Kis.

She'd gone to bed the previous night wondering whether she must, after all, take upon herself the tiresome chore of paying a visit to her husband's lover. Now her doorbell was ringing, the spy hole showing Karel Neumann slouching on the other side.

She opened the door just as he'd abandoned the bell and started knocking. He was dressed in his cotton vest and trousers, held a bundle tucked under his arm.

"Can I wash here?" he asked.

Anna looked him up and down. "Did she kick you out already? Three nights. Not much to shout about."

He grinned. "No, no, things are just fine. But there's a queue for the bathroom as long as my arm."

"This is not a hostel," she said, but she let him in all the same. He threw down his bundle and locked himself in the toilet; emerged a few minutes later, walked over to the bathroom, and started running the hot water. Anna lingered in the hallway, wrapped her dressing gown closer around her frame. She heard him climb out of his clothes and test the temperature of the water. After a few minutes there sounded a deep sigh as he lowered himself into the bath.

"Come in," he hollered, "it's boring all alone."

She stuck her head through the door, saw he was sitting in the bath with his head, shoulders, and knees sticking up above the rim. The water was milky; he had taken liberties with her Parisian soap.

"I'll make some coffee," she said, and disappeared.

When she returned, he was running more hot water, then settled back into its warmth. She set a cup down on the rim for him, cleared the bathroom stool of his clothes, and sat down. Neumann's big shoulders stuck out a full foot beyond the edge of the tub. His massive hands were resting on his knees. She pictured his bulk alongside Sophie Coburn's tiny frame. It wasn't an easy thing to do.

"So, how did you charm her?" she asked, sipping her coffee. "I hear you went down to her flat and hammered on the door. The same night I told you to get lost."

He grinned, scooped up some water, and poured it over his hair. "Do you remember how drunk I was? Four sheets to the wind. Barely made it down the stairs. Some lass had to help me, a young thing with a hump on her shoulder. I was trying to talk my way into her bed, but she had other takers I suppose."

He chuckled, fished with his hand for her washcloth. His accent grew stronger as he launched himself into the story. "So there I am, banging on door. It isn't late, mind, eight, maybe nine o'clock. One of the lodgers opens, a little old man, stares up at me, and I shout that I want to see 'widow journalist' and something stupid about jam and eggs. Before I know it, all the lodgers come out their rooms and are crowding in corridor. The landlady's there too, some nasty old crone with dyed yellow hair, getting ready to tell me off.

"Who are you? she yells, and I tell her—why wouldn't I? I've got nothing to hide—I'm Karel Neumann, I tell her, here to see my Sophička. Sophička? she says. Who is this Sophička? I have never heard of such a person. And I say, You don't know Sophička? She lives here with you, they shot down her husband, the pilot, now she's lonely and rich, and all sorts of nonsense in the same vein. We don't make any progress one way or the other, the landlady and I, until Sophie herself comes out her room, dressed in a little silk dressing gown. Christ almighty, it's the kind of thing you see at a good brothel, and she's covered her bosom with a shawl. I know this man, she says, real prim, like she's learned sentence from a language book, which I suppose she has. She takes me by the hand and leads me to her room, puts me in bed, takes my boots off, and tucks me in, like I'm five years old. The landlady's after her, shouting at her back, the two have conference right in the doorway, with all the neighbours craning over both their shoulders. It's all the same to me. I'm tired, I fall asleep; pass out, as a matter of fact, it's like someone's slipped coal sack over my head. The last thing I remember is finding her nightie, it's crumpled up next to the pillow, something frilly and smooth, so I press it to my face and off I am.

"When I wake, everything's quiet; moonlight in window, Sophie sleeping on a wicker armchair she's pushed into one corner. It's a tiny room, packed with bed, desk, mirror, and dresser, you can hardly turn around in it, and she's found for herself the corner that is furthest from the bed. I get up and she wakes, holds her blanket tight against her chin. I pick her up like a child, she weighs nothing at all, and I carry her to bed. And then, well . . ." Neumann smiled, scratched himself beneath the waterline. "I'm afraid we woke neighbours. She's a widow, you see. Grateful."

Anna watched him rearrange his hips in the water. Amongst the soap bubbles floated his penis, large and flaccid, in proportion with the rest of him. She turned her eyes back to his face. "Is the landlady still giving you trouble?"

He shook his head. "Sophie told her I was her brother-in-law. She's agreed to making an exception for a relative. Not a cheap exception, mind, but an exception all the same."

"You're a pig."

"Yes, yes, naturally," he said. "But then again, one has to live."

He reached forward, turned the tap, let in some more hot water. His indolence and sense of ease were not without charm to Anna. Her husband, Anton, was a creature of discretion and duty. It had tired her sometimes, back in the days when they'd been young and were courting.

"So now that you've become acquainted—what do you make of Frau Coburn?"

"Ah," said Karel. "Sophička. She's a lost soul. Came here because this is where her husband died; shot down by flak. Left the hotel and rented herself a room so that she'd meet the natives. And now she has no idea what there is for her to do. Write stories, naturally—but what about, God only knows."

He stood up all of a sudden, stood naked and dripping, gestured for a towel. She gave him the one hanging from the hook on the wall. His nakedness did not frighten her. She had seen her share of naked men. He dried his hair and shoulders first, then wrapped the towel around his hips.

"You know what she says to me last night?" he went on. "We were talking with our hands, you understand, her jabbering in English, and me making sense of it best I can. Vienna is finished, is what she says. *Finito.* For journalists, she means. No more stories here. She even heard they are going to do a movie. In the fall. With Orson Welles. She was really quite upset."

He bent over, prised a pack of cigarettes from the trousers on the floor, lit up.

"All the same, she has some interesting ideas. About Beer. She says a lot of people are being picked up by the Russkies at the moment. It's piqued her curiosity. The Cold War, she calls it, the Soviets taking on the West. 'Vienna is turning into an Intelligence playground.' She liked the phrase so much, she found a pencil and wrote it down."

Anna frowned and shook her head. "It's exactly what the detective said to me, that Anton might have been 'requisitioned.' But the very idea is ridiculous! They only just released him. And besides, what does Anton know that would be of interest to them?"

"Ridiculous," Karel mused. "Is it really? Well, listen, in the camp Beer spent a lot of time with this officer. Oh, no, not like you think. He was, you know, curing him. Head-shrinker stuff."

"So?"

"So I don't know. Sophie thinks it's *relevant.*" He chuckled at the word, spat smoke. "It's just an idea anyway. I'll ask around. See what I can find out. Of course, I'll need some money—"

He smiled at her, clutching his towel, smoked his cigarette in even drags. All at once she was annoyed by his brazenness. She turned away from him.

"You're clean," she said. "Now get dressed and get out." Then a thought occurred to her. "There's one thing you can do for me," she said. "To pay for your bath."

"Go on."

"I'm going to see someone. I need a chaperone."

"Who is it?"

"Kis," she said. "My husband's—friend."

"I'd be delighted." Karel Neumann yawned, stepped into his under-wear. "But first, do you have any more coffee? No? Well, I'll just pop down and drink one with Sophie. She gets lonely when I'm not around. And then, later, we can go and see this Kis."

2.

Anna had arranged to visit an old school friend for lunch and felt it was too late to cancel. Karel agreed to meet her mid-afternoon in front of Kis's apartment building. Lunch was uneventful. Her friend, Gerlinde, had lost her husband in the war and had reverted to living with her parents. They sat across from each other eating the poor fare while her mother fussed over them like a servant. She actually winced when Anna started cutting the gristle out of the morsel of pork she had served up. Both mother and daughter praised Anna's attire in a manner that ill concealed their envy. They might have accepted a gift of money, but Anna decided against it, not from delicacy, but from some incoherent feeling that she must uphold a sense of pride that they themselves had long abandoned. All she left them with was a box of French chocolates that they took care not to unwrap. There was no telling what price it might fetch on Vienna's streets.

Anna arrived at Kis's house with time to spare and found a bench not far from it, sat down to rearrange her makeup. Neumann was some minutes late. He strode up with his loafer's walk, kissed her hand in smirking imitation of a ballroom cavalier. His cheek was dark with afternoon stubble, the smell of beer tart on his breath. Here he was, the only person in the world with whom she shared her husband's secret: a drunk buffoon with hands as big as hocks of ham. Still, it was better than seeing Kis on her own. She accepted Karel's arm and they strolled over to the open door.

"Have you met him before?" Karel asked.

"Once. You be quiet now. I'll do the talking."

This time there was no cleaning lady mopping the floor. Instead the house was alive with the shouts of children playing in the yard. They mounted the stairs, found Kis's door. She hesitated, gathered her thoughts. Beside her a mighty fist reached out, hammered boldly on the door.

"There's a bell, you know."

"Yes," he said, "but I like the noise."

He knocked again, then stepped back when Gustav Kis opened the door. Anna recognized him at once; later, she would be surprised that she had done so. The man who had opened the door to this flat nine years ago had been young and gently plump; had owned a clean, fine-pored, almost luminous skin, and a thinning crown of lightly oiled hair, worn neatly parted to one side. The one who stood in front of her now was fat around his thighs and midriff but had seen the weight fall off his cheeks; was bald on top, with only a sparse island of hair plastered to his forehead. The skin had coarsened, a rash of pimples clinging to his chin. What remained was the speed and harmony of his gestures, the hint of femininity as his hands rose in surprise.

"*Grüss Gott*," he said, looking first at Anna then at the bulk of Neumann looming behind her. "How can I be of service?"

"I'm Anna Beer. Dr. Beer's wife."

He smiled, a little nervously perhaps. Behind him, in his hallway, the face of a man emerged at one of the apartment's doors, looked over at them, then disappeared. He might have been one of Kis's lodgers.

"I am afraid," he said, "I do not recall a Dr. Beer."

"Please, if we could just have a moment of your time."

"If you must," he said, stood aside, then led them into the hallway and on to the second door on his right. The room was large, well-appointed, and clearly served as both his living room and bedroom. A little table stood by the window, on it the remnants of his cold lunch. The large bed was half hidden behind an Asian folding screen, ornate dragons writhing in black lacquer. Two bookshelves were entirely crammed with records. On the wall a large pale rectangle indicated a space where a wardrobe had once stood. There was a blotchy mirror but no pictures.

Kis pointed them towards the sofa and drew up an armchair to sit across from them. "I remember now. Dr. Anton Beer. He treated me for hives. But that's half a lifetime ago."

"Herr Kis," she said, sat stiffly on the edge of her cushion. "I have quite an accurate picture of the nature of your relationship with my husband. You will believe me that I have no desire to spell out the details. My husband and I have been living apart these past years."

The fat man smiled at her, slid quietly from buttock to buttock. He interlaced his stubby fingers, looked over to Karel. "And who is this gentleman?"

"Never mind him. He is here to assist in what is to me an unpleasant duty. The fact is, Herr Kis, my husband has disappeared. Or rather, he has not been seen in several days, and he hasn't come home. I would like to know whether you know his present whereabouts."

Kis shook his head with almost comical emphasis, the chin swivelling from shoulder to shoulder. "No," he said, "I do not."

"But he has come to see you, has he not?"

"No."

"Please, Herr Kis. Tell me the truth. When did you last see him?"

"Not for—" He stopped, gave an affected little cough, then started coughing in earnest, one hand searching his pockets for a hanky. "Not since the war, Frau Doktor. Thirty-nine, maybe '40. He had me over for dinner one evening. Yes, I believe that's the last time I saw him. The fall of 1939. We'd just taken Warsaw." He smiled, coughed again, tucked away the handkerchief. The reference to dinner stung her, conjured pictures of dessert.

"You are quite sure?"

"Quite, quite sure." Kis rose to dismiss them. "I'm afraid I have some pressing business to attend to."

Anna stood, allowed herself to be walked to the front door, Karel Neumann by her side.

"My compliments," Kis said in parting, happy now, bending his neck to suggest a bow.

They heard him lock the door behind them and quietly descended the stairs. Outside, in front of the building, her eyes found Karel's. The big man was smirking.

"He's lying, you know."

Anna was inclined to agree. "What do you want me to do?" she asked. "Beat it out of him?"

His smirk grew wider. "Wait here," he said. "It appears I forgot my cap upstairs. I won't be a minute."

He turned, but she stopped him, put a hand upon his arm. "Don't—" she said. "You'll get arrested."

Playfully he cupped her face, the palm so large she felt herself disappear into its curve. "Is kind of you to worry, *Pani Beerová*," he said in his broadest Czech accent. "But I'm just fetching hat."

She watched him re-enter the building and charge gamely up the stairs.

3.

Kis opened the door, listened to Neumann's explanations, and announced he would look for the cap himself. Unperturbed, the big Czech strolled after him into the flat then closed the door of Kis's room, where its owner was crouching on one knee, searching the worn carpet.

"I cannot find it," he said, flustered to find his visitor had followed him.

"Kis," said Karel. "That's Hungarian, isn't it?"

Kis looked up at Karel as though he required reappraisal. "My grandfather," he said at last. "Are you—"

"No, no," said Karel, pushed past him, sat down on the couch where he had sat before. "Sudeten-Bohemian, with splash of Gypsy. Which is to say, Viennese." He made an expansive gesture with his bony hands. "So when did you last see Beer?"

"I already told you—" Kis flushed, finally understanding the situation. Almost instantly a sheen of sweat settled on his pimply face. He took a step back, raised a finger in his guest's direction. "I will call the police."

"No, you won't."

Karel stood up with no particular hurry, crossed the distance separating them with a single step, caught Kis by the florid tie hanging from his ruddy throat, and hit him. It wasn't an angry gesture, or even particularly threatening. He hit him with the flat of his hand, not hard but repeatedly.

And with every blow Kis gave a soft little cry, as though of surprise. And no matter how often Karel hit him, Kis answered every blow with precisely this cry of surprise until, at last, Karel relented and watched the pale cheek fill with blood.

"Come now," he said, no more angry than before. "When did you last see Beer?"

A tug at the tie manoeuvred Kis over to the couch. En route Karel scooped up a decanter of brandy. Before he sat down, he returned to the little coffee table on which it had stood, fetched two nicely cut glasses, and settled them in front of them. They sat side by side like two passengers on a bus. Kis had tears in his eyes. His cheek had turned a violent shade of red.

"I haven't seen him since the war—" he began.

"Have a drink," said Karel, poured him a glass, and placed it to his lips. Kis gave signs of struggle, then relented at once when Karel turned his eyes on him. Feeding him like a toddler, Karel poured the whole of the glass down his throat. It was followed by a second. Kis's sweat had spread from his face to his whole body, a patch of wet emerging on his fatty chest. There was a smell to it quite out of keeping with its freshness. Casually, as though not to startle him, Karel stretched an arm behind Kis's neck and took hold of his far earlobe between forefinger and thumb.

"He came here, I suppose," Karel said, "sometime in the past two weeks." His fingers pinched a little, relented when Kis spoke.

"Once. He only came once."

"Go on, tell me about it."

But Kis wasn't talking.

"What's the big secret? I already know you are—" Neumann stretched out his free arm, swivelled the hand, and let it droop affectedly from his strong wrist. "Whatever you call it."

He took hold of the decanter, forced another drink on Kis. A second pinch, a little more forceful, prodded him into story. And every time Kis stopped, Karel hurt him a little and fed him booze. After a while he started speaking less guardedly. Perhaps he had begun to enjoy his confession.

"He came maybe a week ago. Just walked up to the door. I didn't recognize him."

"Thin?"

"Yes. And—" He looked for the word. "—dishevelled. I was entertaining guests, and he simply walked in, not saying a word, not even a greeting. Sat in a corner of the room, eyes on the wall. The guests left pretty fast. I expected him to talk then, but he simply sat there, waiting."

"Why did you think he had come?"

"I don't know. To say hello, I suppose."

"Look at you sweat! There was more to it than that."

"We had not parted—That is to say, we parted in perfect equanimity. But later, during the war—"

"You weren't drafted."

"No. Heart trouble. But then, in '43—" He looked up terrified, awaited eagerly his glass of brandy. "—they caught me. A denunciation. I was interrogated. Everyone kept shouting at me. They wanted names."

"And you gave them Beer's."

"Yes. Not right away, you understand. But soon enough."

"And now you thought that Beer had come to have it out."

"I thought he was dead. But there he was, sitting in my living room. Smelly he was, nothing like his old self. Thin as a rail. And the way he looked at me: shifty, always from the corner of one eye. So there I was, babbling, saying nothing really, and all the time I was wondering how much did he know. Then it occurred to me that he was giving me a chance. To make a clean breast of it. That he had said to himself, sitting in the camp, 'If Gustl tells me, of his own free will, I will let it pass. But if he doesn't—well, then.' I swear I almost saw it: him sitting in his prison clothes, a pink triangle on the chest, plotting revenge. So I came out with it, and even while I was talking, I could see he was surprised. I faltered, but I had already said too much; I had to finish my story. He just looked at me, and it struck me that he was still a very handsome man, he just needed a good wash. 'Nineteen forty-three,' he said, the first thing he'd said all night. 'The Russians took me in '43.' He started grinning then, like a madman, one eye staring at the wall. Next thing I knew, he had changed topic and started telling me all about this girl he used to know, some sort of cripple; how he'd sworn to find her, see she was all right. He got very agitated, as a matter of fact. I didn't say a word. It occurred to me that he was lonely. Nobody else around in whom he could confide. That struck me as odd, you know. He is a doctor, after all. He must know any number of people, but he came to me."

Kis smiled, as though cheered by the thought of having been the subject of such privilege. "Next I knew, he got up and walked out, shook my hand on his way out the door. It's the last I've seen of him." He paused, licked his lips, searching them for brandy. "Has he really disappeared?"

Neumann did not answer, sat pondering Kis's words. His right hand was still thrown around the fat man's shoulders, holding on to his ear. The left was pouring out the last of the liquor, a sip for them each.

"It's a good story," he said at length, as though he were evaluating a manuscript. "The problem is, one couldn't really print it. Only darkly hint, perhaps. 'Fruit-love. Sundered by the swastika.' Scandalous, but it won't do." He shrugged, swallowed the contents of his glass. "You know what sells these days? Espionage. 'The Cold War.' That's what people want to read. Especially abroad." He patted Kis's knee, grateful to him that he had helped him establish the point. "How about you, then? Did you go to a camp?"

Kis shook his head. "I underwent re-education," he said vaguely.

"Really?"

"There was an operation . . ."

Karel stared at him, then burst into a good-natured laugh. "They chopped off your balls? Christ almighty, the things they came up with! But listen to this. I had a comrade in the army, had one of his testicles shot off. From behind, mind. Bullet came in from under his arse, shot his testicle clean off. Not a scratch on the rest of him—not the arse, not the thigh, not his peter. There was a physics student there with us, tried to work it out. The trajectory. Said it was impossible. Against the laws of nature. A real joker he was, too. The guy with the shot-off bollock, I mean. One day, on leave, we go to this brothel. We are hardly through the door when he throws down his gloves and pulls down his pants. 'I demand satisfaction,' he shouts. The girls laughed and laughed." He stopped, again patted Kis's knee. "But I suppose it's different when they take away both."

He yawned, rose from the couch. "One last thing, Kis," he said. "Did Beer mention which camp he was in? In Russia. Did he mention a number, or a name?"

Kis shook his head, looked at him in confusion. "No."

"Fine, forget about it. If Beer's wife comes back—" He paused, considered. "She won't, you know, but if she does, just stick to your story. You haven't seen him since '39. To avoid complications. Don't you agree? Gustl?"

"Yes."

"Well then! *Na shledanou*, my sweaty friend."

And walked out without another word.

4.

She asked him what he had learned.

He told her. "Nothing."

"Nothing? You were up there a long time."

"I wanted to make sure."

"He hasn't seen Anton?"

"Not since the war."

"Good."

She did not hide that she was pleased. Why shouldn't she be? Some part of her had feared that they would find him there, cuddled into the warmth of Kis's bedding; that he would stare at her with limp, embarrassed eyes; stretch and sink back into pillows.

"I'm thirsty," she said. "Let's find a café."

They walked some minutes and chose a hotel café whose painted sign insisted on hard currency. A third of the tables were already taken: officers, journalists, NCOs in civilian dress. Most of them spoke English; in the foyer, a slender youth in a dinner jacket stood barking French obscenities into the phone. They chose a table by the window. She was amused when Karel pulled back the chair for her; helped her out of her light summer coat. The big Czech was in an expansive mood and bantered with the waiter, who turned out to be Moravian, from Zlín. On the Moravian's recommendation he ordered pot roast with dumplings and bread, two different types of cake; a glass of beer and a coffee. Anna stuck to water. She watched Karel eat, hurriedly, crudely stabbing the spoon into his open mouth. She wanted to ask, Do you think Anton loved him? But it was impossible to ask this simple question.

"So that's that," she said instead, and he nodded, coughed up gravy, held the rest down with a swig of beer.

"Mind if I have another?"

"Go ahead."

It was understood that she would pay.

He waved over the waiter, asked for a beer along with the bill. The man bowed, smiled, shuffled, at once obsequious and fiercely independent, a Viennese waiter born in Zlín. They used to write feuilleton articles about figures such as him. Outside, across the street, there was a neat gap where there had once stood a building. In the muddy yard crouched a child, sinking pebbles in a puddle, his buttocks outlined by a double print of dirt. Anna Beer lit a cigarette.

The bill came and was presented to Karel, who glanced at it then handed it to her. She pulled out her purse, counted the money, the big Czech counting along with her, gauging her wealth. She caught his look, over-turned her purse, pushed the money across the table. He stared at the little pile of coins, dark eyes puzzled under the overhang of brow.

"Can you find him for me?" she asked. "There'll be more if you do."

His face shifted in surprise. "So you really want to find him?"

She nodded, thought. "Yes."

"You think he's changed?"

"You tell me."

Neumann spread his fingers on the tablecloth, a noncommittal gesture. He had yet to touch the money. "And all the years before," he asked, ignoring her question, "when you were married?" He paused, grinned at her, his meaty tongue hunting for crumbs along the corners of his lips.

"Did I know? Was it love, or was I just happy to have a husband pay my bills?" She sat unflinching before his brazen smile, chin up, shoulders squared, hid her doubt behind her beauty. "You wouldn't understand, Herr Neumann."

"True, true, I wouldn't." He leaned back and carried on, giving prominence to his accent. "It reminds me, though, of little adventure I had. This was before war. This girl and I, we were in love. Her parents did not like me, so we ran away, to Vienna, and found a room with landlord who did not care we weren't married. Yarmilla, she was called, a redhead, legs all the way up to her arse. Anyway, one day I come home and she's in bed with the landlord. I turn around, go to a tavern, get good and drunk. When I come home, she's still in bed, looking at me same way you are looking at me now. Proud, you see, daring me to tell her off. So I don't tell her off. I simply ask her, 'Why did you do it? Are you worried about the rent?' She looks at me, considers. 'No,' she says. 'For love.' So I go away again and chew on it, this 'for love.' I have another round of beers, then coffee, then more beers, until money is gone. 'Very well,' I say, when I come back second time. 'For love. But we might as well save on rent too.'" He laughed, unrestrained, the whole café turning to watch.

Anna stubbed out her cigarette. "You are a show-off," she said, irritated, amused. "The sort of man that will brag about anything. His poverty, his baseness, the holes in his socks. Just for a laugh." She paused, touched his hand with her fingertips as though to assure herself that he was real. "How is it that someone like Anton is your friend?"

He shrugged, a heave of mighty shoulders; swept the coins into his pocket. "I'll find him for you," he said, reached forward, swallowing her hand in his. "Or Sophička will. She's already making calls."

He sat petting her hand until she pulled it away from him. "Let's go home," she said.

The tip she left was rather meagre. The Moravian waiter scooped it up and sadly shook his head in their wake.

5.

She had expected him to part ways with her on the first-floor landing, but Neumann dogged her steps all the way to her apartment door.

"I thought I'd take a nap," he answered her questioning glance. "Downstairs—the bed is too small." He held his hands out mere inches apart. "It's like curling up in shoebox.

"Please," he added, not without a brazen charm. "For mercy of God, and Comrade Beer."

She thought of denying him, but it seemed pointless. Karel Neumann was working for her now, looking for her missing husband. Either he would find him—or she would return to Paris. There was something else to it too: his outsized buffoonery might help fill the flat. The previous night she had walked listlessly through its empty rooms, her heart suspended between foreboding and boredom. Her heart, she thought, *suspended*; pictured it, too, a purplish lump of sodden muscle hanging from a nylon thread, a scrap of butcher's paper sticking to its side.

"Don't make a habit of it," she said, and unlocked the door.

He grunted his thanks and disappeared into the study. She closed the door behind him then went to change into her dressing gown. Cigarettes and a bottle of wine whiled away the evening, the Czech quiet now, catching up on uncramped sleep.

Four

1.

Robert arrived at the stroke of eight. The bell rang, hesitantly, singly, and there he was, the boy from the train, still wearing his dark suit. His face was flushed red, the broken eye drooping in its socket.

The rest of him was beaming at her. "Remember me, Frau Beer? Robert Seidel—we met on the train." He wiped his feet, smiled, whispered conspiratorially, "I copied your address from your luggage tag."

She took his coat and led him to the kitchen.

He sat down without taking in the details of the room, started talking without invitation, words spilling out of him, carried away by an enthusiasm that proved hard to resist.

"It's already the third time I came by today. I tried at three, and then again at five. But you were always out. So I headed back into the city, walked around. The funny thing is, it didn't hit me until today—and even then not all at once. That this is my home. But then, this afternoon, between your door and the Ringstrasse, with every step it suddenly grew on me, precisely this feeling that this is *home*, the city I grew up in, and all of a sudden I have tears in my eyes and I am staring at some building, and quite an ordinary one at that, just another building among many, and I want to hug and kiss it or something like that, I'm really moved." He shook his head, flushed and merry, filled to the brim with his own foolishness. "And then this worker started yelling at me not to stand in the way like a blasted oaf (his words were coarser than that,

134

but that was the gist of it) and I—well I just wanted to go over and hug and kiss him too. Isn't that funny?" Robert laughed. "Just picture it—if I had kissed him! He'd have broken the other eye! It's like something you read in a book."

He looked around himself, suddenly conscious of his surroundings, accepted the glass of water she put down in front of him. Really she should have been serving him milk. Her wineglass was on the windowsill, and she fetched it over, sat down across from him, registered his eyes swooping down the curve of her close-fitting dressing gown. His train of thought was so transparent, she very nearly laughed out loud.

"So where is your husband?" he asked.

"Out," she said, unwilling at that moment to go over the details of her predicament. "And how are things at home, Robert Seidel?"

"Home?" he grinned. "You just wouldn't believe—"

And he told her, in great detail, everything that had happened to him since he parted with her outside the train station. He did so not in the order the events occurred, but the way a drunk tells a story, rushing first to whatever was most exciting, then realizing that what he was describing made no sense if he did not explain something else altogether, and thus continuously chasing back upon himself and getting into a tangle. He seemed to know himself that this mode of telling a story was both inefficient and confusing, but rather than changing it and starting over, he simply laughed and redoubled his efforts, speaking fervently with that same hot, urgent flush on his cheeks.

"In a word," he finished, at long last (he must have been talking for the better part of an hour, dwelling on details, his feelings, the shade of a hat), "Wolfgang's in jail eating Hungarian goulash. And I—I haven't had a square meal in days."

He tucked in cheerfully when she cut him some slices of bread and cold sausage. Anna watched him eat as she had done with Karel Neumann. It was one of the female roles that men enjoyed and she did not resent. There was something heartening about an appetite.

"So," she summarized, picking through his story and wondering distractedly if she should tell him hers, "your brother is a war criminal, your mother an addict, and there is a man watching the house. It's like something by Dumas."

"Yes," he said, unable to hide his excitement. "Isn't it marvellous?"

"It'll be quite a trial. The sins of Austria coming down on your brother's head. If they choose to revisit them, that is. They may not. Let sleeping dogs lie. It's the national pastime." She lit a cigarette, blew smoke at the boy. "What about the other thing? Did he do it? Attack his father?"

Robert hesitated. "I don't know," he said at length. "Eva does." He smiled somehow nervously, grew bashful. "From what you've heard," he asked, "do you think she likes me?"

She laughed, watched the warmth that spread across his skin. "I should think she loves you a little already. You're very easy to love." She suppressed the urge to pet his cheek. "And you?" she asked instead. "Do you like this Eva?"

Robert nodded, stopped. "She has a hunchback. Though not really a hunchback." He swivelled around in his chair, placed his hands on the base of his neck. "Something about the spine." He turned back to face her, looked shyly at her face. "She's not as pretty as you."

She smiled, flattered despite herself, ran a hand through her hair. "Next you'll tell me you're in love with me. That I've been haunting your dreams."

"Frau Beer!" he said, embarrassed.

"Call me Anna."

"Anna? I thought it was Gudrun."

"I prefer Anna. Though my husband calls me Gudrun. Anton and Anna, he says. Too silly. I dare say he's right."

At the mention of her husband Robert flinched, looked about himself. "Is he really out?" he asked furtively. "I thought I heard something."

She shook her head, charmed by this boy. "Is this why you kept coming here today? To declare yourself?"

He rose, almost knocking over his chair. "No," he protested. "You're married. And besides—" He gestured wildly, ran out of words and reasons, jumped a little when she got up too.

"Well, it's late," she said vaguely, adjusted the belt that shaped her dressing gown. She made no motion for the door.

He rounded the table to shake her hand goodbye, stepped too close, and nearly trod on her toe, then stood distracted, holding on to her palm as though he had lost his bearings and was at a loss to say what might come next. His pale face had grown paler yet, no trace now of its earlier flush.

"What now?" she asked. "You want to kiss me?"

Robert frowned and nodded, lifted his head (he was a good inch shorter than her) and searched with his mouth for a patch of proffered cheek.

She smiled, evaded him. "Not like that," she chided. "Like this."

She took him by the scruff of his neck, swooped down on him, taking his lips in hers, slipped a tongue into his open mouth, and ran it between lips and gums. Anna felt the boy's excitement grow against her hip and his immediate attempt to shift his weight away from her; followed the motion, backing him into the wall. From habit—a long history of kisses— she dropped one hand and put it on the tender portion of his inner thigh; the other hand still pressed to his neck and hair, her lips exploring his, the scent of his skin sweet in her nose.

And just like that he came, not ten heartbeats into their kiss. She felt the jerk under her fingertips, heard him moan into her mouth. It surprised her, happened without warning, went on for longer than she was accustomed (she had never had a lover quite so young). The moisture seeped through the thin wool of his trousers onto the tips of her long fingers; she raised her hand and stared at it, then wiped it dry against the downy curve of his pale cheek. All this she did firmly yet tenderly, not from play or calculation, nor yet from love, simply to give him pleasure, something maternal rising in her and mixing uneasily with the heat of her blood. Her caress was too old for him—she understood this. It had had many lessons and came burdened with technique: the echo of other couplings, other lovers written into every touch. And yet she smiled quite tenderly and held on to him a moment longer. He allowed himself to be held.

When they stepped away from one another, Karel Neumann was in the room.

2.

He walked in without hurry, his shirt unbuttoned over his cotton vest, stinky despite his morning bath; turned to the larder and fetched a beer.

"Neumann, Karel," he nodded calmly to young Robert, pushed out the stopper with a flick of his thumb.

Anna looked at him. "You've been listening," she said. She did not say watching. But then, what did it matter to her what Karel Neumann might have heard or seen? "It's time for you to leave."

"Yes," he agreed. "Sophička will be waiting. She gets frisky after dinner." He smiled, stayed where he was, drinking his beer.

Robert, flushed and panting, kept staring at him and adjusting his clothes, the trousers sticking to his thigh. "It's time to leave," he repeated mechanically. His eyes fell on the kitchen clock, which showed the time as ten past nine (it was a little fast). A great haste overcame Robert; he ran out into the hallway, paced up and down searching for his coat. He had avoided looking at Anna since their kiss; kept muttering to himself in great excitement.

It was impossible to make out his words.

He headed for the door. His fingers were shaking and proved unable to work the lock. It was left to Karel to open it for him. He too had fetched his coat, and he slipped into his unlaced boots. The two men stepped out onto the landing and started on the stairs together. Halfway down the first flight the boy detached himself, made a racket tearing down the stairs.

Anna closed and locked the door behind them.

He's running to his crooked maid, it flashed in her. The next moment the thought was greeted by another. It sent her to her husband's study and the torn letter sitting on the desk. It was addressed to an orphanage and described the undulations of a twisted spine.

She read and reread the letter, then upended all his drawers, determined to make a thorough search of her husband's correspondence.

3.

Karel followed the boy. He did so openly and without haste, taking not the least precaution, simply dogged him with his steady step. The boy made it easy for him. He ran some thirty, forty yards then slowed down and continued instead at a slow, distracted, shambling pace, heading to Hernals, the working-class district to the west. After some three or four blocks he stopped beneath a street lamp (dusk was falling and the lamp had only just been turned on), staring at a smudge of blood that ran from the bottom of a shuttered door across the width of the pavement to the grate of the gutter. One look at the sign above the door would have informed him it was a butcher's shop, but he never raised his head; stood still instead, his brow furrowed, as though puzzling over the shape of the stain. And in general the boy seemed to get stuck on details—first the stain, then a broken bottle standing in a windowsill, where it contrived to catch the failing light of the sun; a bare-chested man standing in his open window high above, breathing smoke into the night. Each of these observations would stop him dead in his tracks and root him to the ground; a moment later he would catch himself, start, and carry on down the street. It did not take long for Neumann to tire of the chase and cut into a bar.

It was a workers' tavern, quite empty at this hour; commanded an intersection, dirty windows blind to the boy's retreat. Karel sat, ordered a brandy; invited the barkeep to stay and talk.

"Ever seen a spider eat a fly, friend?"

The man shrugged and said nothing, wiped the table with a sodden rag.

"Well, it ain't pretty. Like eating an olive. You suck it dry and spit out the pit." He pursed his lips, spat into his hand. "And all the while he is in love. With a girl called Anneliese."

"The husband, then. Comrade Beer. Say the Russians took him. Hypothetically, I mean. For rooting around in some general's soul. It's not impossible, after all."

"What I need, my friend, is an informant. Someone who sells secrets, on the quiet, from out the back room of some dive." (Here Neumann looked up and scrutinized the little barroom.)

"Do you know what a double agent is, friend? No? A man on the make. Empty pockets and a story to tell."

The barman finally broke his silence. "Sounds like half the city."

"You know, friend, I like you. Why don't you get me another."

And he finished his glass and pushed it over to the barkeep, dug in his pockets for Anna Beer's change.

4.

Robert walked. He soon found himself in unfamiliar surroundings. There weren't many people in the streets, though some of the windows stood open, the sound of voices carrying into the night. There were arguments and laughter; an old man shouting, yelping, behind a curtain, cursing his rotten teeth. Robert listened without hearing, circled rubble, horse dung, piles of refuse, as so often lost in thought.

What he was thinking about was sex: "physical love" as he liked to call it, somewhat pedantically, using a phrase he had picked from a book. About this physical love Robert had formed two rather contradictory opinions to which he subscribed in quick rotation, and at times quite simultaneously. The first of these opinions was that sex—physical love—was a tender, joyful, healthy, even holy thing; that it befitted a young man to be in love "fully, passionately and above all with his body" (to talk about the soul in this connection would have been retrograde and gauche); the other that sex, on the contrary, was a vile and somehow sinful thing, degrading to the man but above all to the woman; that it did not and could not do otherwise than estrange two people from one another who were bound to regard each other henceforth with shame; and that, anyway, he wanted to become a priest. All this—with the exception of his planned priesthood, which was secret—he had expounded many times to his boarding school friends, who had alternately teased him for his prudishness and shrugged at his fiery vision of passion (most of them were absorbed by no more abstract a question than whether they'd dare approach the village whore).

For all his many speeches Robert had, until that night, never held a girl or kissed one in earnest, and had been in love only once, from afar, with a baker's daughter whose stockings had a fetching habit of sliding down towards her ankles. The attachment had withered when a schoolmate reported he had paid her chocolate to reach down his pants.

Despite his attempts to keep his mind focused on this more general and, as it were, philosophical plane, Robert's thoughts kept leaping quite naturally and inadvertently to Gudrun—Anna!—Beer and the moment of intimacy they had shared. But here the "problem of sex" that he had settled so clearly (if inconsistently) in the abstract seemed infinitely more confused. Every time he went over the scene in his head, a strange sort of tremor took hold of him and he marched on as though breathless, waiting for it to subside. The thing was, he could decidedly make no sense of the scene. Had he really gone to visit Anna in order to secure some token of her affection? But how did things get to the point they had?

Anna's behaviour, too, struck him as extraordinary, and it was not long before he found himself looking for excuses for her shamelessness. Robert found them in her long estrangement from her husband. *It's changed her somehow*, he mused. *She must have been chaste before. But ever since, she's been in turmoil.*

But no matter how often he repeated the phrases, clinging most especially to those two words, *chaste* and *turmoil*, which seemed to him singularly fitting and endowed with a strange poetic power that attested to their truth, Anna Beer seemed less beautiful to him now than she had on the

141

train. He knew he would never think of her again without the memory of her hand upon his lap.

Just as he came to this somewhat mournful conclusion, a new thought fell on him with sudden force. "And who was the man who walked into the kitchen? He wasn't her husband, that's for sure. How he winked at me! Like a proper cad. Only he was charming, too, and part of me wanted to wink right back."

This last bit, incidentally, he muttered quite audibly, even loudly, so that a passerby, a worker in a greasy waistcoat, who was carrying beer, or perhaps milk, in an opaque flask, stopped and looked after him in consternation. Robert did not notice him. His outburst had nudged his thoughts right back to where they had started, and as he finally entered the familiar surroundings of his stepfather's neighbourhood, he found himself reliving once again not only his meeting with Anna Beer but also his conversation with Eva, who had taunted him precisely by saying that he'd failed to kiss her when he'd had the opportunity.

"It's Anna who should have the crooked back," it suddenly came to him. "But what nonsense, stupid nonsense!

"All the same," he carried on, "I wonder if she's still awake."

Again he had spoken out loud, and again he frightened a lone pedestrian, who started and quickly moved out of his way. It was a vagrant draped in a scarf and heavy coat. There was little chance Robert would have recognized him as the watcher had the man not started running no sooner had they passed.

Robert heard it and gave chase at once.

5.

He caught him, not on the street that rose to the hillside park, nor on the wall separating the one from the other, but, having scrambled over, in the cabbage leaf–scented darkness of the far side, amongst vegetable patches and tree stumps whittled to their roots by a population starved for firewood: two bodies colliding shoulder to hip and tumbling to the ground. One, the older, came to rest in the dirt, mud-smeared, winded, clawing at the earth and the weight that sat astride him. A dirty fist rose into the moon, rained down upon the vagrant. Robert was not so much hitting the man as knocking on his rib cage, one time, two times, three, heat in his mouth along with a question—"Who are you? Who are you?"—sown carelessly, with no hope of an answer. Indeed there was none. After some minutes the stranger ceased in his struggle and lay still in the calf-high weeds, his scarf dislodged and trailing past him like a noose. His breath came heavy, in irregular shivers; he coughed and seemed to breathe no more.

Quickly, afraid that he was smothering him, Robert shifted his weight; kept a hand on the man's shirt and slipped to one side of him, crouching low beside his chest.

"Who are you?" he asked again, calmer now. "Why are you watching the house?"

He never saw the fist that hit him, heavy, weighted with a large flat stone. It crashed into his chest with that peculiar thump of rock displacing meat and bone. For a minute or so Robert felt he was drowning; his right hand hooked into some part of the vagrant's clothing while the man flapped and struggled against his grip. The sound of ripping cloth freed him; Robert watched helpless as the man leapt up and ran away. After ten paces the stranger stopped, looked back with frightened eyes, the soldier's greatcoat drooping from his skinny frame. Then he turned, clambered over a chest-high section of the wall, and was soon lost from sight; a patter of footsteps as he raced along the pavement on the other side.

Clouds ate the moon; disgorged some slivers; mopped them up. Robert gasped his first breath in the darkness; lay retching, massaging his chest. In his hand he held a square of cloth that at first glance he believed to be a fistful of lining from the stranger's coat. On closer inspection it proved to be the whole of his inner pocket, ripped out at the seams. Clutching it, Robert rose, still winded, then ran heedless, stumbling after his lost prey.

But it was useless, the trail gone cold, no sound or movement in the street. Disappointed, breathless, doubled over, he slipped a finger past the torn cotton lip of the pocket he was holding, pricked his finger on some sort of metal pin. A second probing, more careful now, produced a passport photo double-stapled to the ripped corner of a sheet of paper. He held it, smoothed it, turned his back on the moon. Its light, cloud-bitten, uncertain, found a face, one staple buried in her forehead. Robert stared and could not stop his hands from shaking; whistled, swore, and hobbled back towards the house.

6.

The Seidel villa was brightly lit, and silent. Robert did not stop to kick off his shoes; spread muck racing up the stairs. His one thought was to find Eva. Her room was at the far end of the second floor. He had been to its door on two previous occasions and both times found it locked, unresponsive to his knocks. Today it stood open, the room behind it narrow and long and crowded with furniture. At the far end, underneath the window, stood a bed. He ran in, impatient, realized too late that Eva was not hiding in the clutter; turned on his heel and collided with her at the door. She was wearing nothing apart from a towel knotted halfway down the freckled plain between her narrow throat and girlish breasts; was in a hurry, too, to cross the distance from the nearby bathroom, her crooked back laid bare for prying eyes to see. The collision threatened the knot that held her towel; he found himself reaching out with both his hands to stop its slide, grabbed her at one armpit and the stretch of flank that grew directly from her hip. The dirt-stained hands left marks on skin and towel. He forgot to close his eyes before a momentary flash of breast.

She would not raise her face; ducked away from him, shouting, then remembered her spine; walked backwards, wet hair streaming down her shoulders; threw a book at him, a shoe, some knickers, the rusty tin that held her pencils.

"Look," he said, taking cover from this indiscriminate hail; placed the photo on the chair beside him, turned around, and walked out. He didn't close the door; crouched next to it, his back against the frame, his bruised chest swelling, hurting, making it difficult to breathe.

He did not hear her move. He expected the door to slam behind him; that she would curse him, chase him, call him names. After some minutes he became aware of the scent of flowers stealing through the corridor, threading a path from the bathtub to her room. It took him a while to understand it was her soap, the smell of hair so freshly washed. Breathless, reckless, he followed the smell, stuck his head around the corner of her door.

She had taken the photo from the chair to her pillow: sat on her bed, naked legs tucked under, wet hair dripping on her sheets. He drew close to her, bent over the picture, still stapled to a corner of typing paper, its torn edge discoloured by old blood. The blue ring of a rubber stamp cut through the photo, smudged letters curving through the cheek. It was a girl, no older than eleven or twelve. Though the photo cut off at the collarbones, there was no mistaking the kink that governed shoulders and neck. Her hair had been lighter then, a stringy sort of blond that had been braided into pigtails at both sides. One strand had come loose and hung down across her eye, her nose, her lips.

"I saw him," he said, standing bowed as though in prayer. "Just now. He hit me in the chest, but I ripped out his pocket." Shyly he placed the dirty rag onto her sheet. It too was blackened by old blood.

Eva looked up at him. It was only now he saw she had been crying. The face beneath the tears bore an expression he had not seen her wear before, of meekness and hope, a shy kind of longing. She noticed his wonder and grew angry at once, rancour spreading through her features. But when she lowered her eyes again, back to the photo, something of the earlier expression crept back into her lips and eyes.

Robert sat down on the floor by the bed. The window was closed, its pane holding her reflection, two girls kneeling on the bedding, proud and tender all at once. With a sudden movement she turned her back on her twin, leaned hard against the window; picked up the hat that lay upturned near the footboard of her bed. An adjustment of its brim served as cover for wiping her eyes. She reached for the photo then thought better of it, left it where it was on the curve of her pillow, the linen clean and without crease.

"He was here today," she said.

"The watcher? He was in the house?"

"I thought I heard him. In the basement somewhere." She attempted a smile. "Unless it was rats."

Robert tried to fathom the implications of what she was saying. He stared at her in her towel and hat, long shins mottled with light bruises.

"He must know you. He has your picture. Why does he not just ring the door—"

She interrupted him. "You saw him. Up close. What does he look like?"

He thought, recalled the face, lean cheeks bleached by moonlight. "Thin. Scared. I only saw him for a second."

"Scared?"

"Or maybe crazy." He told her of their fight. "We wrestled. Like Jacob and the angel."

Her spite was like a dog guarding against her own weakness. "An angel?" she said. "You're a poet. Full of shit."

It was his cue to leave, but he didn't; stayed where he was instead, spread out on the floor beside her bed. Above him he heard her shift, lie down flat upon one side. After some minutes, as though by chance, one hand began to dangle past the mattress's edge: slim, calloused fingers, the nails chewed down to stubs.

"Piss off," she mumbled, and he reached to take hold of her hand. He held it palm to palm at first, then interlaced the fingers, his shoulder growing stiff from being locked in an awkward angle.

"Turn off the light," she said, and he did; stood up, closed the door, and flicked the switch, then retraced his steps to that patch of floor beneath her bed and strummed his fingers gently through the bones, the tendons, of her drooping hand.

7.

While Robert lay, tracing metacarpal bones beneath the white of Eva's skin, too shy even to press them to his lips, elsewhere in the city a man and a woman, long married and as such familiar with each other's hands and mouths (and much else besides), sat up in bed discussing a letter, hand-delivered that afternoon, which pertained to their youngest son. Encrypted as it was in a densely bureaucratic German, and as such illegible to both husband and wife, the letter's only assailable point came in the form of an underlined heading that read *Ladung,* a word that, depending on context, might be translated as "ammunition," "load," or "summons," and seemed to absorb the more sinister aspects of each meaning with each successive reading.

A crow watched their argument (for an argument it quickly became, split along lines of gender, in which the woman's role is to protect her child, and the man's to toughen him up) with considerable interest, then jerked, pecked at its feathers, converting parasites to food. A moment later it dropped from the windowsill, fell groundward then skyward, with an ease that might have startled Newton. High up it fell in with some brethren. They flew into the failing moon.

8.

And what about these crows? A branch of the family *Corvidae,* there are, according to the usual authorities, some forty species of crow. With the exception of New Zealand, Antarctica, and some oceanic islands, they inhabit every known land mass and are, as a genus, some twelve million years old. Crows have long been regarded as the most intelligent of birds, capable of counting to at least four, associating abstract symbols with real-life objects or actions, and adept at mimicking the voices of other birds and mammals, including those of humans, cats, and dogs. The social and behavioural patterns of each species are adapted to its habitat. In the wide plains in North America the common crow can form flocks of up to two hundred thousand individuals and travel, for food, up to fifty miles a day. The European carrion crow prefers smaller associations, though it too will band together, often at dusk, to form large clouds of feather and caw. In the immediate aftermath of the Second World War, the reduced agricultural output drew many thousands of crows to the city, the site of refuse, and of high-density death.

To believe, then, that of all these birds we should find the very one we last saw swooping from a windowsill in grubby Hernals alight two miles to the west (as the crow flies), in a narrow courtyard once dominated by a chestnut tree and lying open to view to the back windows of Anna Beer's apartment, is to believe in coincidence as the prime mover of all story. And yet there is something familiar about this bird, the jerky swivel of its head, the solemn strides it takes across the roof's wet tiling. There it stalks; stops, convulses, retches; performs, with the disturbing lack of self-consciousness peculiar to animals and children—and with the complete stoicism in the face of habitual humiliation, found, amongst humankind, only in the very old—a ritual known to naturalists as "pelleting," in which the indigestible portions of the recent (gustatory) past are dredged up and spat out, pressed into a tight wad of matter from which a patient man may pick a wealth of components, including teeth, fur, feathers, bones, and the exoskeletons of insects. Why it is that birds must purge in this peculiar way, and why men—not all men, of course, and some women too, though in small proportion—feel compelled to tackle this question, armed with tweezers and a scientific bent, does not concern us here. The bird, in any case, spat a pellet; and Anna, some thirty feet up, oblivious, slept, her lips pursed around the memory of a kiss more robbed than stolen.

Part Three

Most made it back. Including those taken at Stalingrad, some three million Wehrmacht soldiers were incarcerated in Soviet prisoner-of-war camps. A little under two million returned. There were camps in which the ration supply soon normalized. In Camp 50, in Frolovo, north of Stalingrad, a Latvian major by the name of Pichelgast encouraged prisoners to read the classic works of German literature. He founded a chess club, an orchestra, and a dramatic troupe. In Camp 286, in Tallinn, Estonia, the prisoners rebuilt the city theatre and concert hall and were invited to its inaugural concert. In Camp 27, in Krasnogorsk, prisoners had vegetable patches and held sporting competitions. In a small sub-unit of this camp the Soviet Military Secret Service trained an elite of German Communists who would later run the GDR.

The prisoners were paid for their work, assuming they fulfilled the daily norm. It was a matter of luck: being paired with strong and knowledgeable workers, nobody weak or sick. For those less fortunate in their work companions there were other modes of self-advancement. The skilled could trade their expertise: in building scales, or knives, or lighters; speaking Russian; advising on escapes. Then there were those who grew friendly with the camp authorities. No jail can operate without informants. It is said that the pen-pushers— the teachers and clerks, engineers and journalists, those unused to physical privations—took to spying more readily than their less educated comrades. Conversion, too, was popular: to Marxism, the faith of the victors. Like all

151

converts, some were in earnest, while others were lured by the opportunity for social advancement. Privileged inmates were given passes to leave the camps. Some had friends amongst the civilian population of the neighbouring village or town. A few had lovers. A number were shot when trying to escape.

Of those who returned, some brought friends back from the camps, dear as brothers. Some brought God, the Revolution, or a wooden leg. Some brought enemies: born of politics, of inequality and loaded dice, of information bought and sold between prisoners and guards.

One

1.

The man with the torn pocket stood hunched forward in the cellar's dark. He was wearing a pair of work gloves and had tied the scarf over his mouth to shield himself from the smells of putrefaction. First he cleared the newspapers away from the body. Some of them were moist, stuck to the man's face and hands, leaving smudges on his livid skin. He fished for a sack, reached in with one arm, and retrieved a fistful of a fine crystalline powder, more pink than white. Like a man who salts his garden path against the winter ice, the man threw fistfuls of the powder over the corpse. A sharp antiseptic smell spread through the cellar room and cut through the fumes of decay. The man waited for the dust to settle, turning away and closing his eyes lest they become irritated. Only then did he bend down and, breathing still through the fabric of his lambswool scarf, begin to arrange the man's shirt collar and retie his necktie, smooth out his waistcoat over the maggot-studded mess that was his shirt. Throughout these various actions his lips were moving as though he were rehearsing benedictions for the dead. In his head the words were quite audible.

"I saw her again, brother. Once at the window, and then, when she went out, I followed, keeping well behind. How changed she looks! Three times she turned, or maybe it was three times three. But I hid and stayed out of sight."

He paused, blew his nose through a gap in the coils of scarf.

"I went to see him too. Herr Seidel. From curiosity, I suppose, idle, idle.

153

I snuck into his room and held my hat in hand, but in its crown I formed a fist. I swear his eyes moved when he saw me.

"The young man is the son. Robert, they call him. I met him today, nearly ran him over in the street. He saw me and we fought."

The man grinned, bent forward, tapped the corpse upon its open eye. The sound was surprising, a bird pecking on glass, having mistaken its reflection.

"A handsome lad," he said. "Has a broken eye like you.

"We wrestled," he went on, "amongst cabbage leaves. Our teacher used to tell it, how the angel tried to get away. Strong as an ox he was, the teacher said. The angel hit him on the thigh and it popped out of its socket, going plop." (He shook off a glove, slipped a dirty thumb between his lips, hooked it into the soft part of his cheek, then flicked the thumb away from him, produced a sound as of a stone that has been hurled into a village well, the wet, low drumbeat of its impact.)

"I hit him on the chest, brother, a nice flat stone, and he lay there gaping, gasping, a fish pulled fast from out the river. *Jakob*, I should have said to him, *Israel*, the angel gave him a new name just for holding on with all his strength.

"Suppose then, brother, I'm an angel, and the angel, really, he was God, wrestling madly in the mud."

The man grinned a wild grin through his slipping scarf, looked about himself, made sure there was no witness to his blasphemy.

"Suppose then, brother, I am God, and everything obeys if only I go say it. Go on, then, get up, you lazy swine! Go on, Lazarus, get up, get up, let's warm some soup and play a hand of cards."

And he laughed and cackled to himself, and in his head it sounded loud and merry.

2.

A noise cut short his laughter. It came from outside the room, the scrape of metal across stone. The man recognized the sound. Someone was trying to force open the bent metal door at the top of the stairs that led into the cellar. Quickly, picking his way through the littered floor, he crossed the room and peeked out into the corridor.

Daylight filtered down from up above, was joined by the cone of a flashlight that roamed the bottom step. The man watched it with great concentration, fear spreading through his hollow eyes. He had been nervous ever since his encounter with the boys and at once looked for a hiding place. Across from him, on the other side of the corridor that formed a T with the short stairwell, the door stood open on a warren of wooden storage booths, each roughly built from planks of wood, and half of them still packed with wartime junk. If he could but make his way across, it would be an easy thing to disappear; it'd take a dozen men with dogs—and patience—to sift each cubicle for stowaways. But to run across meant to expose himself to the beam of the flashlight and the eyes of its owner. He had no idea who it was that was standing there, watching, breathing, shuffling at the top. Thus transfixed by indecision to a spot halfway between the room at his back and the stairwell ahead—shoulders slumped, chin raised, a quiet heave to his quick breathing—the man with the torn pocket stood bargaining with God. He pledged prayers, fasting, "to return on home"; repented in earnest that he had laid claim to God's immortal name; ran his hands beseechingly through the stubble of his close-cropped head.

Then, from one moment to the next, whatever sacrifice he offered was accepted. The cone of light twitched, wavered, then withdrew. He moved like a man released from doubt; ran past the stairwell with three silent springs. A glance upwards showed him a stranger in a light summer suit. He had squeezed through the gap and now stood on the landing with his back to the stairs, applying his weight to the bent door, trying to force it open another foot: one shoulder dug into the metal, the face as though buried in the crook of his raised arm; his buttocks quivering with the exertion. The watcher passed the stairs unnoticed, ran into the darkness ahead; he rounded a corner, dropped to his haunches, and listened for the sound of the man's pursuit.

It did not come at once. The door moaned, gave an inch or two, then wedged its corner into the ground. Footsteps followed, none too fast, stopped at the bottom of the stairs. The beam of the flashlight turned right first, towards the part of the cellar the watcher had picked for a hiding place. It advanced to the door frame, shone its way past the slatted doors of a score of wooden cages, then turned around upon itself and guided the stranger's feet the other way. All sound stopped once he stepped into the room that held the body; the watcher strained his ears but could not hear.

It was curiosity that made him follow. He did not move for several minutes, wrestled with himself as he had wrestled with the boy; prayed, too, a dozen fleeting benedictions poured into the ear of God; crept forward, step by step, until he stood once again near the bottom of the stairs and looked ahead. The light of the stranger's torch was no longer moving. He had placed it on the floor some two yards from the body, the beam pointing inward, projecting his shadow onto the wall. The man had sunk to one knee: the hands thrown forward, each movement elongated, flitting darkly across naked brick. There was something held between his fingers that might well have been a knife.

It would have been easy now and prudent for the man with the torn pocket to make good his escape: walk to the top of the stairs and squeeze his way through the half-open door, into the yard and the anonymity of the city. He inched forward instead, eager to see, and exchange the shadow play for the sight of its source, a portly man neither short nor tall, stooping with one knee of his light summer suit pegged down into the cellar's dirt. His head was turned away from the watcher; his hand armed not with a knife but with a pen, whose capped tip he used to poke at parts of the dead man's body. The other hand was clapped over his mouth. He turned his profile to the light, and for a moment one could see his eyes, great watery orbs blinking under fleshy lids that looked as though they had been painted onto the fronts of his big spectacles. He pulled them off, produced a handkerchief, crouched squinting, rubbing at their lenses, his eyes, diminished, looking tender, newborn, in their tight pink pockets. An intuition pricked him, whipped his chin round to the door.

"Who's there?" he said, squinting square into the flashlight's beam. He rushed to place the glasses back on his nose, their lenses turning into pools of hard, flat light; then bent to pick the flashlight off the ground, the handkerchief still wrapped around his fingers. Halfway up, the metal tube escaped his cotton-slickened grasp. It fell, ejected cap and batteries, which spun and rolled along the floor, following the subtle tilt of the foundations. By the time the stranger's eyes had adjusted to the murky dark and he had taken his query—"Who's there? Who's there?"—into the corridor, the watcher had long scaled the steps and pushed his skinny body through the gap into the sunlight.

Beneath him, underground, the stranger returned to the corpse and completed his search of its few pockets. He found nothing apart from a box of matches stuck together by a viscous mass of old black blood.

3.

This was how they found the body: Nepomuk Frisch, the detective to whom Anna Beer had made her report regarding her missing husband, had a ten-year-old daughter by the name of Gertrud, who was universally known as Trudi. Trudi Frisch had been sick these past few weeks from a respiratory disease to which the doctors had been hesitant to attach a name. She had been feeling better of late, and because she was bored, and because her condition was no longer judged contagious, she had, despite the prescription that she must not leave her bed, been allowed a small number of visitors, as long as these came singly, behaved, and did not stay longer than an hour at a time. It came as no surprise to her father, who was perceptive and involved in his daughter's emotional life to a degree few fathers were, that the principal visitor was a boy called Karlchen, the youngest son of an artisan family, a shy and somewhat weepy lad with whom she went to school. Karlchen and Trudi were lovers of sorts: some weeks ago they had exchanged a careful, snotty kiss and agreed to marry one another when they came of age. All that remained was to fix the desired number of offspring.

Frisch had had a firm talk with Trudi prior to admitting Karlchen to her bedside. He extracted the promise that there would be no further kissing until she was better, explaining to his daughter that despite the doctor's assessment he was concerned that she might pass on her disease. Trudi agreed willingly and informed Karlchen at once that he was in mortal danger from her lips, but might, if he so wished, take the risk of holding her hand. Frisch left the two children with Karlchen sitting on a stool by Trudi's bedside, tilting his body away from her face and clutching her hand across the maximum distance their two arms would afford.

When the boy left an hour later and displayed some signs of agitation, Frisch was inclined to blame it on the boy's fear of contagion. But Trudi too looked flushed and agitated when he looked in on her, as though she were fretting over some momentous thought. There had been no time to question her that day (Frisch was attending his regular *Skat* round and left Trudi in the care of a neighbour), and besides, he preferred to have Trudi sort through her thoughts by herself.

The next evening he noticed that she remained in a state of nervous tension and was obviously working her way towards some kind of confession. Frisch made a point of sitting with her, telling her about his day at the station, the new litter of puppies the city had acquired for police training, and the odd phone call he had received from the Soviet authority regarding one of Vienna's many missing men. He was in the habit of sharing his work concerns with his daughter, much as he had done with his late wife. That evening he took his time over his report, hoping that his show of candour would inspire her own.

She lay there listening to his words with childish solemnity, asked some questions about the phone call (Were they speaking Russian? If they weren't, how did he know who was calling? And why were they so interested in some "sigh-key-olly-gist" anyway—was it because Stalin was sick?), then waved him closer, grabbed the fleshy part of her cheek between index finger and thumb, gave it a thoughtful little yank, and told him that Karlchen had a secret that she mustn't tell.

"What sort of secret?"

She hesitated, pulled once again at her cheek, a characteristic gesture that she shared with her dead mother. A cough rose in her, light at first then turning into the wet spasm of her disease. He wiped her mouth with a handkerchief, noted the colour of the phlegm, a light yellow, less violent a shade than it had been only a week before.

"You must promise," she said, "that you won't tell."

He thought before he answered. "Is it the sort of secret one tells the police?"

She nodded.

"I can promise to keep Karlchen out of it."

He saw she did not like his answer.

"He won't even know that you told."

She wrinkled her brow. "I'll tell him," she said after some thought. "It isn't fair otherwise."

"You like Karlchen a great deal, don't you?"

"His sister died," she said. "He told me about it, and I said about Mother."

"Yes," said Frisch, running his fingers through her knotty hair. "You like him a great deal."

They smiled and hugged (though he noticed she took care not to kiss him lest he catch her disease). And then Trudi told him the story of how Karlchen, his brother Franzl, and their friend, "fat" Adalbert Steinbeisser, had found a dead man in a basement with his fingers spread "like a trod-on spider, only white." Frisch listened, nodded, and wished Trudi a good night.

Since he had promised Trudi to keep Karlchen out of it, he tracked down Steinbeisser instead, who in any case was three years older and would serve as a more reliable witness. He waited for him outside his apartment building the following afternoon, having found his parents' address in the central registry office, then stepped up to the moon-faced boy as he came running out the courtyard gate and, flashing his police badge, requested a word.

In a few quick words (Frisch had invited the boy to sit on the step, then stood towering over him), and without making any direct reference to Karlchen or the body, the inspector informed Steinbeisser that the police "had long had their eye on him" and "knew what he was up to." The boy burst into tears almost at once and confessed a whole series of small crimes, including his ongoing surveillance of the girls' changing room at the nearby gymnasium. It took some prodding, however, to wrest from him the secret of the dead body, and indeed he seemed puzzled that the police would be interested in something that had, upon investigation, turned out to be an embarrassing mistake. While it was true, he said, wiping furiously at his tears, that his dog Rüdiger had broken his leash while they were out amongst the ruins looking for bullet casings and had led him to a cellar where Rüdiger had circled and barked at something that looked like the arm of a human corpse sticking out from a pile of old newspapers, it had turned out that the arm belonged to nobody more exciting than a live vagrant. With the help of a map Steinbeisser was able to identify the house in whose cellar the incident had taken place; he also gave up his accomplices without the slightest compunction, correcting Frisch's spelling of their last name when the inspector produced a notepad to scribble down the information with an officious air.

There was work to be done in the office that afternoon, and so Frisch postponed his visit to the cellar to the following morning. Unwilling to make it an official matter before he'd had a look for himself, but at the same time strangely confident that the story Karlchen had told Trudi was accurate in all its details, he took the Number Two tram early the next day; disembarked, it became clear, a stop too early, and walked some fifteen minutes until he found the house he was looking for. The door to the basement was stuck; he fought with it for a considerable length of time and was annoyed to lose a coat button as he squeezed his girth through the too-narrow gap.

Down in the cellar, kneeling next to the corpse and trying in vain to establish the cause of death, he had felt for a moment as though he was being observed. On consideration he'd dismissed the notion, retraced his steps up the staircase, and returned to the street to look for a telephone. He found one at last some five blocks away, in a corner pharmacy whose owner grudgingly admitted to owning a line. Twenty minutes later he was back at the cellar door, lighting a cigarette, and waiting for the forensic technician to arrive.

4.

It was a shoddy sort of operation. The duty sergeant from the local police station and the forensic technician Frisch requested from headquarters arrived within a half-hour of one another but hadn't thought to bring along the police photographer, who had to be roused with a separate phone call. Some French NCOs showed up at the scene, ostensibly sent there to observe proceedings, and immediately started on a game of cards. Frisch's own deputy drove up in the station's motor car, was sent away in search of coffee, came back some twenty minutes later with two cups of a cold, foul brew that they resorted to pouring down the gutter. The photographer arrived at last but had forgotten his flash; some hard words were exchanged before one of the uniformed policemen was dispatched to fetch it. A crowd gathered in the courtyard, ignored the orders to disperse: ragged, hungry-looking men and women who kept their distance from the police and awaited patiently the sight of the corpse. Frisch tried to approach some of these watchers and canvass them for information but was met by shaking heads and grunted assertions that they knew "nothing whatsoever" about "it." Already the certainty seemed to have taken hold amongst the crowd that what had taken place was a murder. A bum with a new red scarf tied high over his face scuttled away when the inspector approached him, then stood rubbing his hands as though he were warming them above a fire in one corner of the yard, staring at Frisch across the distance.

At long last the crime scene had been documented and a hearse ordered to transport the body to the morgue. In anticipation of its arrival they carried the body up from the cellar on a stretcher that one of the sergeants had been thoughtful enough to bring along. Soon enough they had laid the dead man out on the pavement, but the hearse was slow to show. The crowd gathered, pressing in on the policemen and the corpse. Frisch suggested they cover its face, but there was no sheet or towel to be found and nobody wanted to stain their coat. So they stood around the corpse with its livid face, trying to shield it with their bodies, while the afternoon sun burned down on them. The spectators stood in a ring, murmuring, sniffing the air for the whiff of decay. There were about twenty of them now, men, women, children, craning their necks for a look. From the back row Frisch heard a voice declaim distinctly, if quietly, "He looks like a Jew." And though he could find no one who would admit to starting the rumour, it soon got around that a Jew had been found killed, or rather "butchered" with a knife or an axe. The rumour spread not only among the crowd (and where did they come from, these crowds, in the middle of the working day?), but also—once the hearse had finally arrived and they had heaved the body onto the rubber sheet inside—at the police station and morgue, so that the pathologist later greeted Frisch with a wink and a sly whisper that "he's looking mighty ripe, your Jew."

It was late afternoon by then, and Frisch was sitting slumped forward on a stool in the morgue's examination room, fighting the smell with a series of cigarettes. There was one other body in the room, already examined and tagged, and covered with a fresh white linen sheet. Frisch watched the pathologist, a Dr. Kranz, perform the external examination, then excused himself when he started on the more invasive procedures. An hour later, having stretched his legs and eaten some food, he returned to the morgue and waited for Kranz outside his office, pacing the corridor with short, even steps. The doctor approached at last, still drying his hands on the hem of his lab coat, and curtly invited him inside. They sat down across from each other and waited for the secretary to come and pour out their coffee. The pathologist bridged the wait by filling out some paperwork, rushing his pen across a pre-typed form and setting down his signature with considerable satisfaction.

This Dr. Kranz was an interesting fellow. Tall, handsome, and sporting a perpetual tan, he was also a notorious sloven whose office was filled with stacks of papers, slides, and all manners of junk, to the point that there was very little empty floor space. His lab coat and suit showed signs of a habitual and almost affected neglect, and it was not uncommon to find stains on his shirt or a tear in his cuff. When somebody commented on his rather disreputable appearance, Kranz would answer him only with a knowing wink. Indeed there was a terrible slyness to everything he said or did, as though he were hinting at some secret level of irony pertaining to all his actions and expecting his interlocutor to share in the joke. At the same time he spoke very formally and precisely, if with a broad Carinthian inflection, which itself had the effect of undermining his words, or rather of lending to them an air of mockery: it sounded as though a country bumpkin had somehow stumbled on a medical paper and was now reading it with great seriousness and gravity. His political past, Frisch knew, was similarly ambiguous. Though a member of the SS medical corps from '42, Kranz had nonetheless been denazified and reinstated in his job with a minimum of fuss—a matter, however, to which he never made reference. Even though he was known to be married, Josef Kranz wore no ring and never so much as mentioned his wife.

The coffee came, was made from real beans. Frisch took a sip, held it in his mouth until it was cool enough to swallow.

"It was a homicide then?" he asked. "The man in the cellar?"

"Yes. He was dragged down the stairs and beaten. Widespread internal hemorrhaging; rupture of the liver, kidney, and spleen. Five fractured ribs, one of which penetrated the right pleural cavity and lung. And any number of facial fractures, all of which were caused by the impact of a blunt object, most likely a boot."

"Somebody really had it in for him."

The pathologist nodded, then raised a wry, ironic finger. "Naturally, it is merely conjecture."

"How long had he been there? In the cellar."

Kranz leaned forward, his voice growing animated with professional excitement—though this too was accompanied by a sly little wink that lent a false note to his answer. "That's very difficult to say with exactitude. Someone did their best to slow down putrefaction. His intestines were removed, and some kind of saline solution injected, to displace the blood. The interesting thing is that, whoever it was, they sewed him up afterwards. Quite competently, actually."

"A surgeon?"

A smile. "More likely an internist. Or a gifted seamstress."

"What else?"

"He was stripped and washed. The skin was rubbed in something, an arsenic compound by the smell of it. When that didn't keep the flies off, they resorted to carbolic."

"The reddish powder."

"Precisely. A common-enough antiseptic, though applied in quantity it has a tendency to corrode the skin. Between that and the bruising, identification will be very difficult." He gestured to his face, indicating the places where the victim's skin was burned. "Though the glass eye should prove helpful, I suppose. I imagine you examined the clothes, Inspector. Was there a monogram, or a label?"

"Yes. At the back of the trousers. The cut is somewhat old-fashioned. From the thirties, I should say, though in good-enough nick."

"And is the tailor still in business?"

Frisch shook his head. "A Sigmund Rosenstern. First district. Deceased."

"Ah. Too bad. Well, I suppose it's not your case, anyway. Not your district."

Frisch nodded at that, sipped his coffee. "Who is the other corpse?" he asked.

"He was pulled out of the canal early this morning. The papers are full with it already. Some journalist took a nice photo."

"Suicide?"

The pathologist smiled his noncommittal smile. "I should think so. Lungs full of water, blood full of alcohol, and a fracture in the lower third of his tibia from something he hit in the water." He picked the report from a mound upon his table. "Eberhart Puck, thirty-four, unemployed. A veteran, naturally; it accounts for the frozen-off toes. POW till '47. No permanent address. Last known employment: November 1937. Night watchman, Rothmann & Seidel, Electrical Works. Two arrests for vagrancy, pre-war, and an Iron Cross for blowing up a tank. No wonder he tended to despair." Kranz dropped the report carelessly, rose, and stretched. "You think the war broke some little part of him and it finally caught up? Or did he just grow sick of begging?" He waited for an answer, shrugged, and walked Frisch to the door. "I better get back to work."

They shook hands in the doorway.

"I would be obliged, Dr. Kranz, if you would call me if you notice anything else. About the one-eyed man."

"As you wish. *Au revoir.*"

"Goodbye," answered Frisch, thinking back to a time when they would have taken leave by raising their right arms, a gesture Kranz had performed with a peculiar flourish. Frisch had never been sure whether it was designed to signal his zest or his ironic distance. "My regards to the wife."

He left the morgue and hurried home to sit with Trudi. It was too late, he decided, to go trouble Anna Beer.

Two

Sunshine woke her, pressed its heat into her neck. Eva turned and knew at once that she had overslept. Light streamed through her bedroom window, found patterns on the dusty pane, along with the great net of a spider, already clear of morning dew. Her shadow fell on the insect as she freed herself from the thin blanket; and when her hand brushed the pane, it danced its eight legs clockwise round the spiral pattern of its web, its belly light, the waist as though strangled by a corset. Eva yawned, and smiled; combed her fingers through her hair. A soft, bright moan startled her, recalled her to a sense of haste.

It was not she who had moaned.

She had planned to get up early and leave the house before Robert knew that she was gone. There he was, lying on the floor next to her bed, his face buried deep in the bulk of a down pillow. He was wearing shirt and trousers. His stockinged feet peeked out from the bottom of the tangled blanket he held hugged against his chest. Dream drew sounds from him, too slurred to register as speech. His breath was regular and heavy. He would not wake for a good time yet.

Two nights ago, when he had barged into her room and shown her the photo, Eva had fallen asleep holding his hand; had woken in the middle of the night and been surprised to find him there, curled up sleeping on the naked floor. Annoyed, but at the same time careful not to wake him, she had fetched him a spare pillow and a wool blanket from the hallway cupboard; had slipped the one under his head, the other over his slight shoulders, and had watched in moonlight the rapid movement of his dreaming eye, the other dreamless, still, beneath its vein-embroidered lid. Above them, in the attic, the crows had been restless, cawed and scuffled through the hours of the night.

The next day Eva had run around the house with petulant impatience, watching, waiting for the man with the red scarf. The boy had followed her wherever she went, earnest and chatty, intent on burdening her with confessions big and small (his plans for entering the priesthood, now abandoned; his dead father, good or bad?; the schoolyard scuffle that had cracked his eye). From time to time he paused to press her with questions about the photo and her past. She told him nothing, mocked and abused him, had him scrub the dishes, mop the floor; fed her anger on his unfazed equanimity, the gentle, trusting upslope of his smile. Night came and he padded after her with puppyish resolve, lingered when she disappeared into the bathroom, still probing with his questions, the heel of one hand rubbing the great bruise on his chest.

When he said good night to her outside her room, she surprised herself by taking his hand and pulling him once again towards the patch of floor next to her bed. He crouched, then curled up like a pet; looked up at her in trusting wonder as she slipped between her covers and took possession of his upstretched hand. The weather was warm, the window ajar; Yussuf strutting on the windowsill before swooping down to search the moonlit ground for prey.

On this, their second night, sleep did not come easily to Eva. She tossed beneath her blanket, flipped the pillow, searched for rest. The curtain was open over the window by her bed, moonlight etching sharply all the contours of the room.

After some hours of uneasy dozing she pushed her head past the edge of the bed until it hung directly over his. Robert was lying on his back, his face gentle, trusting even in sleep, his shirt front buttoned to the throat. *He is like I used to be*, it rose in her, dredged up a yearning for her childhood, while spit collected in her down-turned cheeks. She waited until it had filled the hollow of her rolled-up tongue, then let it slide past the firm purse of her lips: a stringy drop of spit that descended on its own thread like a spider and hung from a mouth prepared to whistle or to kiss.

The first such missive hit the pillow by the side of Robert's ear; it formed a foaming bubble that slowly seeped into the cover. On the second attempt she hit the socket of his eye. He woke at once, spit streaming past his open lid and down his temple; saw a third fat droplet thread its way towards his forehead; jumped up, laughing, to his feet and into bed; raised his pillow high above his head and brought it down into her giggling face. They fought like children, then lay wrestling like adults. It took a moment before she understood that he was kissing her: a wetness on her collar and her neck.

She stiffened when he touched her spine.

"You're beautiful," he whispered, fingers sliding down the ridges of her vertebrae.

She slipped out of his arms and pushed him from the bed with hands and feet. He landed with a thump, looked back at her upon the mattress, kindness, pity, shining in his moonlit eye.

"Don't," she said, and he reached again to hold her hand.

They fell asleep without exchanging another word.

Now, awake, the morning sun colouring her dirty pane, she dismissed these nightly fumblings; rose, stepped over Robert, and got dressed as quickly as she could. Her hat was the last garment she donned, and the one over which she took the most care, adjusting its brim in front of the mirror. Then she chose a book from the pile she had pilfered from his suitcase, put it in the linen sack that served her as a handbag, turned, contented, and left the room.

2.

She made a mistake then. Rather than leaving the house at once, Eva—sleep-creased, thirsty—went into the kitchen first. She ran rather than walked, and had already passed the doorway when she noticed Robert's mother sitting at the table, intent on the task of transferring spoonfuls of white powder from a large tin to a row of saucers she had lined up in front of her. Her presence took Eva by surprise. Frau Seidel was not known to be an early riser.

A second mistake: Eva spoke. Found a glass, filled it, drained it, cast an eye on the tin's label. And spoke.

"So we have rats," she said.

She could have left it there, but didn't. She had learned the expression at the orphanage, where it served to underwrite a complex system of coercion: *The devil rides her. The devil must be driven out.*

Well, the devil rode her now.

"Be careful not to mix it up, Frau Seidel. With all your other powders, I mean."

Frau Seidel did not react until Eva turned to place the glass in the sink. "You can't have him," she said; transferred a scoop of poison from tin to saucer. "Don't think I haven't noticed. And don't you get pregnant. It won't help. My son is not for you."

Stung and angry, Eva rushed out; returned again, the devil firmly in his saddle, stooped in the kitchen doorway, lacing up her shoes. "This man Robert has seen. The one who's watching the house. You think it's *him*, don't you? Believe me, I'm rather hoping it is not. But perhaps, who knows, it might be *him* after all. It's curious he doesn't come forward, isn't it? It's eating you up, this waiting; asking yourself, What does he want? Oh, I can see it, the way you poke your head out, trembling, every time some ragamuffin rings the door for a penny or a bite to eat. And when the postman comes, God, you nearly snatch the letters from his hand. But so far: nothing, not a word. You know, I think he's waiting for the trial. He wants to hear what Wolfgang has to say for himself."

Eva might have said more but ran out of breath and lace to knot. They locked eyes for a moment, too fleetingly to take each other's measure or to tally up the score. Then Eva turned without another word and slammed the door on the way out.

3.

The inspector rang while Anna was still in bed. It was eight in the morning; her unconscious strained to incorporate the ringing into dream. She woke at last, pulled on a dressing gown, supposed it must be Neumann come to take another bath. When she opened the door, it took her a moment to place the man's face: the plump figure with its placid gestures; the thick glasses and the neatly parted hair. It was only when he wished her a "Good morning" with the even drone of his voice that she recalled the scene at the police station. His name, he said, was Frisch. There was no weight in his arm as he shook her hand.

"Have you found him?" she asked, feeling naked without her makeup. "My husband."

The man frowned, folded one hand into the other. "So he hasn't come home."

Gently, in quiet, soothing phrases, he explained to her that the police had found the body of a man whom they had not been able to identify. Would she be so kind as to accompany him to the morgue?

The word startled her. "He is dead then."

He shook his head, flashed her a helpless smile. "I'm afraid it's up to you to tell us."

She excused herself and ran into the bedroom to get dressed.

When she emerged some minutes later, the inspector had let himself into the living room and stood with his head tilted to one side, reading off the titles on their bookshelf. He noticed her presence and straightened.

"It's a lovely flat you have here, Frau Doktor. Nice and big."

"Yes," she said, uncertain whether he was expressing admiration or resentment. His voice was as gentle and even as when he had invited her to identify her husband in the city morgue.

"I brought a car," he said, walked ahead, and opened the front door. "After you."

Halfway down the stairwell they ran into the crooked girl. Some part of Anna recognized her at once, or rather her hat, its bright red draining her complexion. The boy's description had dwelled upon its colour. The girl too looked up in recognition; slowed her step, cast an eye at Anna's companion, then suddenly whipped past them, almost running up the stairs. From behind, her spine looked painfully twisted; her cotton dress too flimsy to mask its line.

The detective noticed Anna's interest. "Who was that?"

"Nobody."

Above them the steps grew fainter, stopped. Anna had no doubt that the girl was headed for their flat. She remained standing with her back to the detective, her chin raised into the stairwell, listening for the ring of her own doorbell.

"Is there something you forgot upstairs?"

"No," said Anna, turned around. "Let's go."

Perhaps she should have confided in the policeman and told him about her husband's letters, his dogged search for a crippled orphan. But then— none of it mattered, if Anton was dead.

4.

Frisch's car was parked right outside the building. Anna paid no attention to the route and looked up in surprise when they pulled up in front of a nondescript building at the back of the city hospital, not ten minutes down the road. Somehow she had expected a longer journey. She hastened to get out, then noticed that the detective had not stirred in his seat. He appeared deep in thought. The car door open, the heel of one shoe already placed upon the curb, she looked back at him over one shoulder. His eyes blinked, encased in glass, the lids and lashes amplified in their quick motion. He glanced at her without moving his head: a tender, watery gaze, red-rimmed and kind. The face beneath the spectacles did not hold the same emotion. When he spoke, it was in the same calm, fluid drone. It was as though he were giving her dictation.

"The man's body has been severely beaten," he said. "There are swellings and chemical burns. He has been dead for close to a week. The marks of decay are—unpleasant." He paused, nodded to her. "Shall we?"

Frisch led her into the building. In the gateway stood a porter's booth. While Frisch signed them in, Anna found her reflection in its glass; the light-green blouse and auburn hair, her lipstick glowing brightly in her pale and powdered face. She had dressed as though she were on her way to collect her husband at the train station; then on to a picnic in the gardens of Schönbrunn. Behind the glass, the old, pockmarked porter concluded she must be staring at him. He flashed her a grin of yellowed teeth. A half-eaten sausage lay on an open newspaper, looked grey and waxen in the booth's dim light.

Frisch led her into a corridor on their left, then on down the stairs. There was parquet flooring even in the basement, its wood dirty and grooved from the passing of gurneys. A man in a crumpled lab coat greeted them and introduced himself as the chief pathologist; bowed from the waist to plant a kiss on her hand; then ushered her into a room with a delicate push upon her waist. He was tall, handsome, his accent pronounced and musical; the hands and face tanned despite a life spent in the cellars of a morgue. They marched her to a high metal table with a solemnity that reminded her of walking down the aisle towards the altar: each of them holding on to one elbow, lest she run away.

"In your own time, Frau Beer."

The pathologist flashed her a wry little smile then withdrew half a step. As she peeled back the well-starched sheet (and how many times had it been washed?), the two men behind her launched into a quiet conversation. She listened to them, distractedly, as she uncovered the corpse's face.

"Have there been any developments?"

"We had a close look at the dental work. A steel bridge across the upper right molars. Soviet workmanship."

"So he was a POW in Russia."

"Unless he is Russian. Was, rather. Inspector Höfel called this morning. He thinks he was killed upstairs then dragged into the basement. A butcher's shop, though really just an empty shell; they were doing renovations. The workmen remember a bloodstain."

"When?"

"Six, seven days, maybe more. There's three of them and they don't agree. Like all witnesses."

"How about the eye?"

"Ah, the eye. Quite a mystery, actually. Exquisite workmanship. We haven't been able to determine its provenance. I checked with the standard suppliers of prosthetics, but their eyes are nothing like this. I put it back in, thinking it might help with identification."

The eye was the only human thing about the face that Anna had uncovered. In many ways there was no face at all. There was a mouth, of course, but the teeth behind the lips were broken, the jawbone cracked; they'd had to tie it with a ribbon to the skull. What remained of the face was displaced and swollen. Forehead and cheeks were naked flesh. Something had burned away the skin. The left brow and left cheekbone had risen like dough and fused over a swollen hole. On the other side, under an eyebrow split at the centre by a small vertical scar, sat the prosthetic eye. It looked outsized in its shrunk socket, the only thing of definite dimension in the pulpy mess of lesioned flesh.

Anna held her breath and kept staring at the eye. It was very intricately worked, the iris structured into layers, clear amber grains embedded in three shades of blue, each a snowflake pattern radiating from the pupil's central well. In the bright light of the morgue the eye's milky glass had turned transparent, become infused with something like an inner glow. A root system of capillaries spread from the depths of it: tender, light-pink tendrils fanning out towards the surface and the light. The lid that clung to its outer edges gave it a frame of amber lashes, each gently curving outwards, away from the glass. It was a lovely, human eye, alive with an intelligence intrinsic to its design. The dead man watched her coldly, without judgment.

She forced herself to ignore his scrutiny and concentrate instead on the line and shade of the man's hair. It emerged from out the swollen skull as though each hair had been planted there by hand. Was it possible that Anton had greyed, his hair receded, quite this much? The scalp looked mottled between the thinning tufts, as though covered by some rash. She inspected the ears, found one to be blackened, the other waxen, fragile, incomplete, its rim chewed away into an undulating line. A coarse black hair stuck out of the moulded cartilage ridge near its centre (Anton would have known its anatomical name). It was ugly even in the context of the corpse, a slander on her husband's sense of dignity, so much of which resided in his being perfectly turned out.

If this was, in fact, her husband.

She tried to picture him, compare him to the thing spread out before her on the table, but found she remembered only Anton's photo, his features sharply drawn in black-and-white. The pathologist, as though sensing her indecision, stepped closer and quietly began to pull down the sheet, inch by inch. Like the face, the body was a mess: white, chalky planes rising into blackened peaks at those points where the body must have rested on the ground; the sewn-up flaps of surgical incision; sparse body hair looking stuck into the waxy skin. Anton's chest had been broader, she found herself thinking, but perhaps the memory had become adulterated by some other lover's frame. They passed the belly button, the lower abdomen. The whole area beneath the rib cage looked sunk, scooped out, criss-crossed with stitches.

Through the chemicals and her fear she finally grew aware of the smell. Still the pathologist continued peeling back the sheet until it had passed the halfway point of the corpse's thighs. She found him looking at her, his light-boned features a tidy mask of curiosity. Disturbed, she realized that he wanted her to make an identification based on the shape of the man's sex. Even this part of his body had been mistreated, the left side of the scrotum a blackened, swollen clump. She looked at the curve of the man's penis and turned away; pushed a hand over her open mouth, spreading lipstick across her palm.

"The trouble is," the pathologist whispered in his musical Carinthian, "he lived quite a few hours after he was beaten. The swelling is unusually advanced."

Anna ran out into the hallway. The air was fresher there. For a moment she stood, leaning heavily against a wall, her diaphragm going through spasms as she heaved up stomach juices into throat and mouth. She found a handkerchief in her pocket and pressed it to her lips until the spasm passed. Despite her discomfort she was acutely aware of her physical surroundings, the scarred parquet floor and dirty yellow walls, scuffed in places where a gurney had been rammed into the plaster. All her upset resided in her body. Her head was remarkably clear.

When she looked back to the door, she saw that Frisch had followed her out into the hallway. There was a kindly look in his outsized eyes. He pointed to a bench some five steps down the corridor and insisted she sit down. After a moment's hesitation, standing in front of her so that she was forced to face the buttons of his fly, he sat down next to her and folded his hands together over his chest.

"Did you recognize him?" he asked, the voice even and gentle.

She shook her head. "I cannot tell."

"I see."

She looked over at him, caught off guard by his tone. "What happens now?"

"The detective who is in charge of the investigation will want to close the case. They will bury the body." He leaned forward, placed his palms on his knees. "There is a Soviet functionary who keeps calling my office. Never quite gives his full credentials. He says he is taking an interest in your husband's disappearance." He smiled somehow sadly, as though trying to reconcile himself to life's many mysteries. "Is there anybody else who might be able to attempt identification?"

She stared at him blankly.

"How about this Neumann that you mentioned at the station? I tried to locate him, but he does not seem to be registered in Vienna. Surely he would know about the eye."

"Neumann," she exclaimed. "But of course! He will be able to—I need a telephone."

She jumped to her feet, cast around for a phone with sudden impatience. Frisch rose beside her without matching her hurry. He thought it over for a moment then led her to an office down the hall marked *Dr. Kranz*. The door was unlocked, the office a mess of papers and equipment. She dug around in her handbag until she found the scrap of paper on which she had noted down the number for Sophie Coburn's flat, then picked up the receiver and dialed. The voice that answered was unknown to her.

"Who do you want?"

She forced herself to be polite. "This is Anna Beer speaking. I am looking for Karel Neumann. Frau Coburn's—relative." When the voice did not respond, she added, "The big man, a Czech."

"Wait."

She heard footsteps lead away from the phone, then the sound of someone knocking on a door. Some seconds later the footsteps returned.

"Nobody there."

The man hung up before she had time to leave a message. She rushed out of the office, looked back at Frisch. "Don't bury him. I'll fetch Neumann."

Without waiting for an answer, afraid somehow that he would stop her, sabotage her sudden sense of purpose, she ran out of the building. Outside, in the glaring sunshine, it took her a moment to orient herself and locate the nearest tram stop. She walked over and joined the throng of people standing there, waiting for their tram.

5.

When Anna Beer arrived home some twenty minutes later, she found the crooked girl sitting on the steps beside her door, passing the time with a book. Anna had quite forgotten their earlier meeting, and had run up to her flat with the sole intention of washing her face and taking some Aspirin before setting off in search of Neumann. The girl rose as Anna approached her; frowned, took a step forward, then sideways as though to circumvent her, pass her, and go flying down the stairs. Every movement she made was pulled off kilter by the twist that locked her spine. For all that, she was not without the gift of grace: long skittish legs, a little bony at the knee. The book she had been reading hung lightly from her twirling wrist and followed its gyrations. Two of her fingers were shoved into its pages. On her head there perched the hat that did not suit.

Anna brushed past her, unlocked her door, swung it open, and gestured her inside. "I'm Anna Beer," she said, once the girl had cleared the threshold. "How do you do?"

The girl ignored the greeting, looked around. Her feet carried her down the central corridor. At every doorway she paused, looked inside, in her eyes a look of solemn reverie. When she approached the bedroom, Anna thought of stopping her, then watched impassively as the girl entered the room and came to a halt before the unmade bed. There reigned in Anna a quiet anger already mixed with resignation. The anger, she realized, was directed at Anton. When she spoke, it lent to her voice a clipped formality.

"You have been here before," she said to the girl. "You lived across from here, in the building's rear wing. Anneliese Grotter. At first I did not remember, but then it came to me. A little girl with a sailor's collar buttoned to her dress. Your father dropped you when you were a toddler, broke your back."

The girl looked over to her, proud and impassive, then turned back towards the bed.

"I asked around about you," said Anna. "A lady upstairs told me you two were friends: *'the doctor and his little girl.'* And then your father died and you disappeared. Social services must have picked you up.

"Tell me something," Anna continued, stepped up behind her, reached an arm past the girl's shoulder, and pointed to the photo of the young woman that hung above the bed. "Who the hell is that?"

This time the girl did react: rounded the bed as though to escape Anna's proximity, then turned, her voice bellicose and small. "You'll never understand it all. You weren't here." But she herself looked spooked by the haziness of the past.

"If you are not here to help, get out."

The girl held her ground. "Where's Anton?"

"Anton's dead," said Anna, and felt a single tear spring from her eye. She blinked and made sure no others followed. "Damn you, you brat. Anton's dead."

The girl watched the tear run down her face, from cheekbone to nose and on, to the painted curve of Anna's upper lip. In her own features insolence gave way to consternation. She started shaking her head long before she spoke.

"That's impossible."

And just like that, a trace of hope joined the anger in Anna's voice. "Impossible? Why?"

"Robert has seen him. He's been at the house." She paused, riffled the pages of her book as though looking for a passage, then pressed it shut with an odd defiance and—as though wishing to rid herself of its temptation—threw it quickly on the bed. "A man in a red scarf. He has been hanging about all week."

Anna frowned, recalled Robert's account of his homecoming. A mysterious stranger holding vigil outside the house. It wasn't much to build one's hopes on.

"Did you speak to him?"

The girl shook her head. "No. I waited. All day yesterday. He didn't come." She paused, sucked in her lower lip. "Can it really be that he's dead?"

"The police showed me a body. It's disfigured. I could not tell . . ." Anna trailed off, watched in wonder as relief transformed the hunchback's features. Moved, trying to transfer some of this faith into her own heart, Anna reached out and touched the girl's hair with the back of one hand. "He was looking for you, you know. Writing to orphanages, all across the country. He was inquiring about an Anneliese Grotter. But you had given them a false name."

The girl dodged the caress, crossing her arms across her chest and retreating almost to the window. "They found out in the end," she said. "Someone double-checked my papers. But by then I was fifteen and had gone into service."

"With the Seidels."

"How do you know that?"

"Robert," Anna said. "Robert was here and told me."

The girl flinched at her use of Robert's name, then pulled herself up to her full height. "He kissed you," she whispered. "He confessed."

Peeved, their connection ruptured, the girl who called herself Eva marched out of the room and down the corridor, heading for the apartment door. It was only when she had opened it that it occurred to her that there might be more to say.

"What now?" she asked.

"You go on home and talk to this watcher. If you can find him. I will return to the morgue. There is somebody who may be able to help with identification. One way or the other."

The girl nodded, ran down the stairs without another word. Anna called after her as she took the first bend. "He abandoned me too, you know."

The girl did not appear to hear. Perhaps her voice had not carried.

Back in the bedroom Anna discovered that Eva had forgotten her book. She picked it up, thumbed through its pages, and was intrigued to find amongst *Young Werther's Sorrows* a passport photo of a younger Eva, aged twelve or thirteen, with long fair hair and a stalk of neck very thin and brittle. It was an institutional picture, loveless and sterile, and yet there was a warmth to the young face that the girl had since mislaid.

Three

1.

Sophie and Karel had yet to leave her room. They had been woken, entangled on her tiny bed, by the ringing of the hallway phone. One of their neighbours had answered it, had knocked on their door, Sophie sleepy, trying to formulate an answer through her yawn. Before she'd had time to find her voice, Karel had gently pressed her back into the pillow and covered her mouth with his. When making love, he liked to lift her out from under his great frame and settle her astride himself, her small, mobile face alive with thoughts and sounds and pleasure, until all expression yielded to an aimless dance of tics and twitches, the mouth a thin-lipped oval breathing oh-oh-oh.

Afterwards she covered herself quickly: slipped into her underwear, then pulled a dressing gown round her shoulders. This discomfort at her nudity never failed to amuse him, and he watched her efforts while sprawling on the too-small bed, rubbing dry his sticky thighs with the heel of his great hand. The other hand cast around for smokes and matches. He smoked without stirring: the cigarette wedged into a gap between his lower teeth and jutting upwards from his heavy jaw. Every four or five drags a wag of his chin would rid its tip of ashes. They landed on the bedding or the floor, or sometimes scattered in the hair upon his chest. Once in a while he burned himself; sat up and chased the ember with a spit-wet finger. The sheet beneath him was riddled with a dozen tiny, black-rimmed holes.

At nine or thereabouts Sophie left the room to make breakfast, returned from the communal kitchen with coffee and two buttered rolls. As she turned her back and settled the mugs on her small, much-cluttered table, he grabbed her round the waist and through the silk of her fine dressing gown buried his face inside her butt. She fell on top of him, laughed then struggled, grew angry when he pinned her wrists above her head; then drifted from reproach to pleasure, the muscles of her face now frantically aflutter, a swarm of moths trapped under glass. The moths dispersed and he released her; watched her scramble back into her knickers; picked up the coffee, complained that it was cold. She smiled and buttoned up her blouse.

"Who do you think it was who called this morning?" she asked when she was dressed, running a brush through her bobbed hair. "It might have been important."

The big man shrugged. "They call again."

They spoke in English. He understood one word out of every three.

"Yes, I suppose they will."

She sat down on the chair, bit into a roll, and washed it down with lukewarm coffee, then read through the half-written page that stuck out of her newly acquired typewriter. The paragraph seemed to displease her: her lips tightened, and two parallel lines formed on the bridge of her nose. Karel had become adept at reading her face and quickly began to dress.

"I'm stuck," she complained, watched him tuck his manhood into his trousers. Karel Neumann did not hold with underwear. "There's too much information missing."

"Information," he said. "Yes, yes."

"I can't write the story if I don't learn more. I have a nice piece here on camp life, but it's all been done before. Beer is an inmate; he catches the eye of the major running the camp; they strike up a friendship of sorts. That's a nice angle. He becomes the major's psychiatrist. That's also good—a prison guard with problems. But what exactly was he suffering from, this major?"

"Suffer?"

"Yes. The nature of his illness. Major Sherapov." She tapped a finger against the side of her head.

Karel nodded. "Right, right. He crazy."

"Yes, but what was it? Some form of shell shock? Neurosis, anxiety? Anxiety would be good—the pressures of running a camp. See, the way I look at it, there are two sides to this story. Two protagonists. On the one side there is the doctor who walks over to his commander's barracks every morning and tends to his enemy's mind. A righteous man, acting from a sense of duty to the Hippocratic oath. And then, on the other side there is his jailor, who is breaking down. A modern man: trapped in the rat race, alienated from his labour. There's not a reader who won't identify with that."

Karel nodded, picked through her words, latched onto one of the few he understood. "Rat," he said. "Yes, yes. Much rat. In the beginning we sometimes hunt. Like in Remarque. You read Remarque?" He thought about it, translated the title. "*In West Nothing New*."

"*All Quiet on the Western Front*. But what I am saying, Karel, is I need the medical file. Sherapov's medical file."

"Medical file?"

"Yes. A record of his illness. Can your contact provide it? Your contact, Karel: the spy. Can he get it?"

Karel considered this. "Maybe. Expensive."

"How much?"

He shrugged, and she found her purse, picked through it, gave him three hundred shillings in cash.

"It's all I can spare. If he wants more—" She paused, grabbed Karel by the wrist. "Tell him I want to meet him. Speak to him in person. Otherwise . . ." She trailed off.

He looked down at her tiny hand, then picked it up and kissed it. "Okay," he said. "I go, make arrangement. Back tonight, tomorrow. You wait."

"I will call my friends at the embassy. See whether they have made progress with the Russians. You are positive Beer is still in Vienna?"

Karel shrugged. "Contact say yes."

He put on his coat, bent down one more time to kiss Sophie goodbye. "You wait. Write story. Win Pulzer."

"Pulitzer," she corrected; hugged him and smiled. "There's another story I'm after. A court drama. Fascist son attempts to murder his father. I am meeting his lawyer today."

"Goot, goot," said Karel, finished the coffee, bolted the roll, and left.

2.

Out on the landing Karel Neumann paused for a moment, trying to make up his mind which way to turn. Perhaps he should visit Anna. He could use a hot bath and it would afford him time to think. On the other hand there was a chance Sophie would look up Anna Beer sometime that morning, and while he trusted himself to be able to account for his presence, it struck him as an unnecessary complication. Sophie might be upset. He liked the little journalist, her earnest energy, the way she stooped over her typewriter, peering through her reading glasses, laboriously shaping every word.

While he was still standing on the landing making his deliberations, a young woman of maybe eighteen years came running down the stairs. He noticed first her skinny legs and knobbly knees, then the extravagant hat that sat perched upon her brow. The hump became obvious only when she passed him and rattled down the next flight of stairs. All at once the memory of their nocturnal encounter came back to him, along with the long, rambling story Robert had told Anna Beer. Without hesitation he followed her, his long strides matching the pace of her run, down the stairs and out into the street. She headed for the tram stop, joined the throng of people standing there, but grew sick of waiting almost at once; turned west and started walking. Karel kept a good ten paces behind her until they reached a quiet stretch on the far side of the Gürtel, then caught up to her and started walking by her side. Within five strides she stopped, turned around to him, recognition then annoyance passing through her features.

"The drunk," she said, chin raised, spoiling for a fight. "Piss off."

"Now, now, Anneliese. No need to get gruff."

The mention of her name slowed her down a bit, but she fought through it, carried on down the road. They passed a greengrocer's, a bakery: a queue of women blocking the pavement, ration cards in hand. She rounded them then stopped abruptly, raised a little fist to his nose.

"Who the hell are you?"

"Neumann, Karel, Flag-Junker-Exempted, lately prisoner of war. Beer and I were comrades. His wife has asked me to find him." He switched into English, adapted a phrase he had heard at the movies. "I'm Bohemian gumshoe," he said. "Private Czech Dick." He winked, but she did not react. Perhaps she did not go to the pictures.

Unperturbed, he carried on. "You talked to her just now, didn't you? Frau Anna Beer? I saw you come down the stairs."

The girl nodded, squared her shoulders, her anger shifting away from Karel, back to the woman she'd just left.

"Some wife, eh?" Karel commiserated, then added, "Beer never cared for her. But he loved you."

The words cheered her despite her misgivings: green eyes curious, her features frozen halfway to a smile. It invited him to continue.

"Beer told me about you. Like a lost daughter, he always said, the child he never had. Talked about finding you, helping you out. Can't count on it, though, now that he's disappeared. Looks like the Russkies have rounded him up again. Could be years before he gets out." He lowered his voice, bent forward so that their faces were level. "Not an easy life, if you don't mind me saying. First the orphanage, then maid to some rich asshole. The son a killer, the wife a bitch, and you in the middle, just trying to get by. Oh, you're a tough one. Took your knocks and grew smart on them. Underneath, though"—he thumped his chest as though he were speaking about himself, not her—"tender like a soldier's ass in winter."

She stared back at him, startled, confused.

"Piles," he explained. "Every second soldier on the front. It's what Anton used to say: a good age for proctologists. Pardon if I'm being free."

Again she did not laugh, but rather listened to him with a peculiar intensity, her whole being poured into that stare. Had she owned a knife, she might have put it to his throat. It meant that much to her.

"How do you know all this?" she asked. "About me; things at my house?"

"I've run into Robert. You spend time around that boy, he'll tell you the colour of his mother's knickers. There were some like that at the front. Always busy telling you their lives. It ran out of them like snot."

He grinned, glad the girl was talking to him and no longer thinking of running away. A pretty lass, actually, never mind the little hump. "Looks like he's taken a shine to you in any case. But you know that already."

Some colour rose to her cheeks, confirmed his guesswork.

"I see, I see, things have progressed from the shine. Well, good for you, kid."

She shoved him, hard, in the chest, her arms looking brittle as she over-extended the elbows. Karel stood unmoved, then followed after her when she turned away from him and again started walking by her side. It wasn't hard to match her stride. They had taught him in the army.

"Not a bad find, you know. Honourable and so forth. Stands to inherit. I doubt she'll let him, though. Marry a cripple. And boys like that, they take care not to break their mamas' hearts. Chink them, maybe, from time to time. But never break."

She ignored him, walked on as though she had not heard. He gave it some twenty yards before he spoke again. "All I am saying is, ask yourself where you want to be in six months' time."

From his pocket he took the money Sophie had given him, peeled off a hundred-shilling bill, then snatched her hand from the air beside him and forced the money into it. "Anybody else ever done this for you? Given you something for nothing?"

She opened her hand, stared at the money. He could see that she very much wanted to throw it away, on the ground or at his face. All the same he felt certain she wouldn't. Thrift would not let her: the memory of a hundred hungry nights turned into habit. Hard to shake what's grown into your bones.

"What's this?" she asked, still holding the bill, at once suspicious and intrigued.

"A gift. For daughter of lost comrade." He wagged his chin, offered her a cigarette. "Maybe you'll pay me back one day."

She recoiled two steps, then reached across the gap and snatched the cigarette. It took her some effort to muster her sneer. "You think you're the devil or something? Fishing for souls."

He laughed, lit up, passed the match to her. "A soldier home from war. That's all."

She took a quick puff, swallowed it, held it down. Jailbirds smoked like that, making each cigarette count. As did orphans; or so it seemed.

"Anna Beer says he's dead," the girl told him. "She saw him in the morgue. Only she isn't sure." Her anger shook her hand, two fingers clamped around the cigarette in an inverted Victory sign. It's what the British did, when they told you to fuck off. "She's his wife and she isn't sure."

"Beer? In the morgue?" said Karel. "Shit." He looked around himself, as though wishing to appeal to the few passersby for their thoughts on the matter; smoke curling from his open lips past cheek and nose.

"It's not true," Eva continued. "I've seen him."

"You have?"

"Almost." She hesitated, and might have said more, then decided against it, slipped the money into the pocket of her dress.

When she turned away from him, Karel Neumann did not follow. Instead he turned around himself and headed back to the apartment. It was only when he reached their street that he changed his mind once more; ducked into a side street and walked back towards the Gürtel. There was a tavern there that he liked, and he had money in his pocket. Before long he was sitting in front of a mug of beer, a line of schnapps glasses keeping it company.

"You celebrating?" the waitress asked him in her surly manner.

"Mourning," he said, produced a handkerchief, and blew his nose.

Behind them a man slipped into the public house and sat alone, smoking, wrapped in a dark coat. If there indeed were spies infiltrating every corner of the city, Karel mused, they would look just like that man.

3.

A sound woke him, the tap of beak on glass. Robert raised his head and saw a crow sit in the window, in its jaws the carcass of some insect. It shook its head, tore the remnants of a spider's web; swallowed, cawed, then took offence at its reflection and once again pecked smartly at the glass.

It took some moments before Robert realized that he wasn't in his room. Girls' stockings settled the question, dangled limply from the backboard. Robert smiled and stretched, felt a great pain rising in his chest. The bruise was coming out in green and purple across the sternum and the curve of his left ribs; he had felt feverish for much of the past day. Now, as he hopped out of bed and struggled into trousers, he once again felt a clammy light-headedness take hold of him. He shook his head to clear it and gently buttoned up the shirt, wincing every time his muscles moved within the bruise.

It was tempting to linger in Eva's room. He had never been in there alone and found himself looking over the things that lay out in the open, on her table and commode. There was a brush there, its bristles half clogged with hairs; some pens, some books, a blouse that she was mending with a needle stuck into its sleeve. A second blouse hung airing from a hanger. He approached and sniffed it for a trace of Eva, found it smelled of bleach and lilac soap. Against one wall she had stacked some tins of food of English manufacture. There were no pictures hanging on the walls, no scrap of decoration; no childhood toys tucked in a box along with postcards, presents, letters received from long-forgotten friends; no pretty pages cut from fashion magazines. He opened the wardrobe, found little there apart from a dun, much-mended shift; three empty hangers, a scarf on a fourth, loosely knotted to its hook. Discouraged, closing the wardrobe door, he realized he had been searching for Eva's past. There was none; just the sombre absence of all luxury, relieved only by the pages of some seven novels, Kästner, Kleist, Zweig, and Mann, all in cheap editions, spilling pages from their broken spines.

Robert left the room. He went to the toilet first, then on to his own room, changed his shirt for a fresh one, combed out his tangled hair. A quick survey of kitchen and living room convinced him that Eva was either in her hideout or had gone out. Nor did he see his mother; there was a quiet to the house that suggested he might be altogether alone. He headed back up, intent on climbing to the attic, when he heard the distinct noise of someone retching. It came from Poldi's room, stopped him in his tracks: a noise so violent he concluded it was caused by real distress. Slowly, unsure what to expect, he approached the door and knocked. To his surprise the voice that answered was quite cheery.

"Come in, come in. Ah, it's you, Robert. Well, don't be shy."

Poldi was lying belly down in bed, with her shoulders, neck, and head thrown over the mattress's edge. Beneath her stood a fancy metal bucket intended for the icing of champagne. Its bottom was filled with watery sick. The smell that rose from it was intense; above all sour. While Poldi rolled over and propped herself up against some pillows, Robert quickly rounded the bed and opened the window. He returned to her side, watched her wipe her mouth with a dirty handkerchief, and tried to ignore the fact that one of her breasts was showing through her threadbare nightie.

"You're sick."

She shrugged, watched him stoop to remove the bucket. He'd have to hose it down outside. But when he touched it, she put a hand on his arm and shook her head.

"Leave it. I might need it again." She rubbed her stomach. For a confused moment he concluded she was telling him that she was hungry. She saw the look and laughed.

"I'm, you know," she said, and kept on rubbing. "Bun in the ol' oven. Muzzle toff, eh?"

He stared at her, then found himself won over to her mood. "Pregnant!" he said. "Well, congratulations. That's wonderful. Does Wolfgang know?"

"Not yet." She did not seem unduly concerned by this fact, gestured for Robert to sit. "I thought you could tell him. Gentle, like."

Her drawn young face lit up when Robert followed her invitation and sat down on the edge of the bed. When sober there was an open, trusting quality to Poldi that he had not encountered in anyone else since returning to Vienna. Perhaps it was because she wasn't very bright. In a gesture of spontaneous affection she placed a hand on the side of his cheek, then started wagging a finger in front of his face.

"So what's this with you and Eva?"

He blushed, beamed, slapped away her finger's admonition. "Who told you?"

"Yer mother did. I heard her arguing with Eva. You've been sleeping with her!" She cackled, then coughed. "You rogue, you!"

Robert did his best to defend himself. "All I did was take her hand. Two nights ago. I wasn't planning on it or anything. She was upset."

"And then you jumped her bones! Did you—" She formed a circle with the thumb and finger of her left hand, then punctured the hole with the index finger of the right. It was not a gesture Robert had ever seen a woman make.

He shook his head in vigorous denial. "Of course not. I just, you know. Held her."

Poldi laughed and clapped her hands. "Held the maid!" she repeated, happy for him.

"Listen, Poldi. There's something I've been meaning to ask." He paused, gathered his courage. "Did Herr Seidel ever—You see, I heard a nurse say it. At the hospital. That he and Eva—And Wolfgang too." He blushed, found himself repeating her gesture.

Poldi watched it with a giggle. "Nothin' like that. Wolfgang wouldn't; he's faithful, he is. And Herr Seidel, he was, you know. Being kind, like."

Robert was far from reassured. "He was in love with her, wasn't he?"

Poldi thought, shook her head. "You know what he said to me once? I passed him in the corridor, a little sloshed, like, going to the loo. There I sit, peein,' and when I get out, he's there, waiting for me. 'I object to you on principle,' he says. 'On what?' I says. 'On principle.' Standing there with his hands on his trouser seams, like he is about to sing the feckin' anthem. And that's how it is with Eva too."

"He loves her on principle?"

She shrugged, embarrassed to be taken so seriously. "Summat like that."

They laughed and the phone started ringing in the house below. Both Poldi and he quieted down at once to listen for some further sound, but nothing carried up the two flights of stairs.

"I better look—" he said, and Poldi nodded.

"Thanks for stopping in. You're sweet, Robert Seidel."

She lifted her arms up over her head, a dancer's gesture, forearms crossing at the wrists; her lean breasts rising with the movement. He could not tell whether she was stretching or seducing him, a pot of vomit rancid by her side. Outside in the corridor the air was sweet and fresh. He hurried to the stairwell, heard his name being called from down below.

"Robert, Robert!"

It was his mother's voice.

"That was the clinic. They say he's awake."

Robert ran down the stairs, too startled yet to take stock of his emotions. Outside, climbing into the taxi they had summoned, they saw Eva walk towards them up the street. Quickly, ignoring his mother's protestations, Robert opened the car door and explained the situation; ushered her inside.

For once, Eva did as she was bidden, sat beside him, her hand a fist inside the pocket of her dress.

4.

They came and crowded his bedside. Paul Hermann Seidel was awake, yet felt as though enclosed by a glass cage. He had in fact been awake for two whole days without anyone's noticing, until he had committed the imprudence of moving his eyes while a physician was present. The doctor and nurse had questioned him without success. Seidel felt quite capable of speech now and was no longer afraid that every word might bring on a renewed seizure; but at the same time he had not only no desire to speak but felt something akin to nausea when he contemplated interacting with those who had assembled—to watch him die, why else?—and observed them with detached hostility, wishing only they would leave.

But they did not leave, and at length, almost against his will, his thoughts disengaged themselves from his own vital processes and fastened one last time on the people surrounding his bed. There was his second wife, Klara, sitting on a chair, her plump hands folded in her lap, and he remembered with sudden clarity a certain night when she had served him dinner and he—quite naturally, as though the thought had only just occurred to him—asked her to remove her apron and join him at the table. She had eaten her dinner with her eyes on her plate, never raising them to meet his, a blush on her cheek that seemed impossible to connect to the flaccid, calculating creature sitting across from him and yearning only for his death.

Seidel's gaze fell next on her son, who paced nervously from one corner to the other, his soles squeaking at every turn; then on the cripple, their maid, who stood head bowed, a fist thrust into her pocket. Of all the details he observed, this alone roused his curiosity, the question of what she was holding there, and holding so desperately, the row of knuckles visible through the fabric of her skirt. Then he blinked and the thought vanished. And a great blankness came over him that was not sleep nor quite yet death, but simply the discontinuation of all thought. It would spit him back to wakefulness an hour hence, leaving him with no recognition of the passage of time.

He had woken first precisely in this manner—alert and wary, as though yanked from a dark cupboard—to find a man standing, hat in hand, half-way into the room. He had stood there long enough for them to fall into the rhythm of each other's breathing: his stubbly throat corralled by a red scarf. The man had fled when a nurse approached and left Seidel to wonder whether he knew him. It was then that he'd felt the change in himself: the question had held for him no interest. His mind had discarded it, turned inward; had listened to his pulse, the rush of blood, the pressure slowly mounting in his skull.

Time and again he dreamt: not in those intervals of abrupt oblivion, but in between, awake, his eyes wide open, gazing calmly into the room. It was always the same dream. He was a boy, still young enough to wear short trousers and dressed to go to church, and was holding a ledger book up to his mother. The dream was rich in detail: his dark blue Sunday suit with the three-quarter-length trousers; the satin bow that hung limply from his throat; the ledger's leather binding and the column marked Charity in his own spiky script; his mother's breath scented with lemons, and the dark, rich folds of her dress. And yet for all these details there was no affect to the dream—no fear, no love, no sense of loss—just a dull sense of inevitability as he dreamt it over and over.

He remembered also, intermittently, abstractly, scenes from his life: how he had spat in the schoolhouse paper bin one day and been punished by the teacher; the painting of a yellow horse that had hung above the bed in his grandfather's house; the look of a worker, a woman, whom he had dismissed for stealing copper wire, accusatory and weepy, a thick brown mole jutting from her eyelid.

And he remembered too the fall he had endured, the onrush of air, the sudden feeling of weightlessness coupled with disbelief that he (a man, a factory owner!) should be falling through the air. But to this too his mind proved incapable of clinging, just as the thought of his son, Wolfgang, passed through him without emotion, crowded out by the all-consuming awareness of his own dying.

At dusk they sent for a priest, to administer last rites. Seidel felt soothed by the strange, solemn, abstract words, then forgot about them and the fat-cheeked priest no sooner had he left, and returned his attention to his body, gently flexing his puffy wrists and hands, waterlogged with liquid he could no longer pass. His wife left within half an hour of the priest, nervous, sweaty, in need of the tonic her unscrupulous doctor prescribed. Eva followed shortly after: stooped low to look him in the face, reached out with a palm that curled into itself before it reached him; turned on her heel and went.

It was the boy who stayed longest; stayed from duty rather than love, the stubborn determination to do what was right. He had long quit his pacing and sat now on the chair his mother had abandoned, his head folded in his hands. For a moment Seidel wanted to reach out and warn him: tell him how he'd wasted all his life trying to do things from duty, against his inclinations, his vanity, his greed (and how pressing had been this greed, how omnipresent and how joyless; and how hard had he worked to reconcile it with his "conscience," until his conscience itself had been absorbed into a system of accounting in which he assigned values to every passing act of decency and took out loans at interest like some petty Jew). He wanted to tell him all this and simultaneously confess, explain himself (for how had it started, this joyless, nagging love of money?; had he been born with it or had it been given to him, and if so by whom?; and the weight of duty, how had it come to him, and whatever for?). But the moment when he might have moved and interacted with the world had passed. The hand no longer obeyed. Soon the wish too faded away and returned him again to that sense of perfect isolation, focused only on the breath that filled, then left, his lungs.

Paul Hermann Seidel died in the early hours of the morning, the boy still sitting by his side, sleeping, his chin rolled tight into his body.

Four

It was Sophie who located Karel in the end, drunk in one of the bars near the Gürtel, having walked for hours from one establishment to another and endured the stares of their male clientele. She brought him back as a mother might return a child in disgrace, pulling him by the elbow, her mobile face showing all the marks of vexation, but careful all the same to guide him across potholes and curbs without his falling.

They took a cab to the morgue. Sophie insisted on coming along and sat in the front while Anna shared the back seat with the hulking shape of Karel, who slumped against the window, red-faced and reeking of spirits. It was unclear to Anna whether he had understood the purpose of their journey or the nature of their destination. It would have taken only a moment to ask him whether her husband had had a glass eye, but she found in herself a strange reluctance to be prematurely robbed of all illusion. Instead she sat and observed the drunk with a hostility she herself could not explain.

Frisch met them outside the building as he had promised he would. Anna had called ahead and got hold of him at the police station. The large eyes swimming in his glasses seemed to reflect some of her own suppressed excitement. For all that, his voice was as monotonous as ever as he shook hands with both Sophie and Karel then guided them past the porter into the morgue. It was a quarter past four and many of the staff had already gone home. They were met outside the examination room by the same tanned doctor in his creased lab coat. He was smoking a cigarette, dropping ashes onto his trousers and the floor.

Inside the examination room the smells of the morning seemed to have intensified. They filed in, Frisch in the lead, then huddled by the door, far from the gurney that held the dead man. When the pathologist crossed the room in order to remove the sheet, she looked away and fastened her eyes on Karel's face instead. The big man approached the corpse with a slow, unsteady stride. Disgust, unease, spoke from his features, were quickly chased by incredulity. He bent low, threw a questioning glance first at her then at Frisch, confused, suspicious, as though they were having him on somehow; returned his attention to the body, peeled a knotty finger from one massive fist and slowly lowered it to the corpse's face. Even the pathologist winced when he pressed down on the glass eye. It gave, and produced a wet little squeak. Again Karel turned his face towards them, the cheeks flushed from either drink or anger. He released the eye; stood up; walked quickly over to the door.

"It's not him."

She did not believe him. "How do you know?"

"He had his appendix out. In camp. This one—" He tapped his own pubic bone through his trousers. "Stitches across the belly. But no scar!"

"And the eye?"

He bent down to her, anger, vodka, in his breath. "The eye is his all right. Bastards stuck it in another face."

When they left the morgue some ten minutes later, not Anna, nor Frisch, nor Karel, nor yet Sophie noticed the pair of men standing in a nearby doorway, smoking, watching them go their separate ways.

2.

Trudi heard her father come in quietly that evening. She heard him sneak into the bathroom and wash his hands, and knew by the length of time he took over the task that he had handled a dead person that day. It was not clear to her whether his hands were actually covered in blood or whether it was the smell that he was scrubbing off so arduously; did not know for sure how dead people smelled, though she had once seen a hedgehog broken in a gutter, had sniffed at it and watched the flies alight from its small body. When her father finally came out of the bathroom, he found her in the corridor, nose curled, breathing in his scent.

"You shouldn't be barefoot," he said.

"I'm not cold."

"All the same. Your slippers are right here."

He took her by the hand and led her to the kitchen. They had dinner together, rye bread and *Speck*, some slices of tomato, a mug of tea for the girl and a beer for the detective.

"Who died?" she asked, picking her teeth with one finger for residue of sticky bread.

He did not bother to deny it. "You see," he said, surly with disappointment, "I really don't know."

She laid a hand on his arm as she had seen her mother do in moments of crisis or grief, and together, bound by the gesture, they finished the food one-handed, then sat in silence until it was time to go to bed.

3.

Once darkness had settled on the city, two men broke into the city morgue in ——gasse.

There was a night attendant who manned the little booth near the entrance, but he had stepped out for a moment to answer the call of nature, and the pair used his absence to break into the premises. There was no finesse to their entry. They simply broke down the door. It took them longer than they expected to orient themselves within the building and locate the corpse with the glass eye. They found it at last in a room reserved for refrigeration; wrapped it in the oilcloth they had brought for the purpose. As luck would have it, the night attendant returned to his post just as they were crossing back through the gateway. He was still adjusting his braces. A scuffle ensued during which the attendant was thrown to the ground and repeatedly kicked. When questioned the next morning, he asserted that the men had been speaking some foreign tongue that might have been Russian, or Yiddish, or perhaps even French. A report was drawn up and filed with all four of the occupational authorities. They each denied knowledge and promised to investigate. The identity of the corpse, meanwhile, remained unresolved.

4.

The same night the corpse was stolen, Karel Neumann also disappeared. He had, Sophie Coburn later told Anna, not returned home with her after their visit to the morgue, but had gone out instead to "wash the stink of death out of his mouth." When he had not turned up by the evening of the next day, Sophie made the rounds of the public houses he frequented and soon caught his trace in a bar called Erdmann's, whose painted female clientele implied that its owner had diversified his business interests. The barman remembered Karel, a habitual customer. He had arrived after midnight, drunk steadily for an hour or two, then been joined at the table by two men in long dark overcoats. They had talked, neither aggressively nor in a particularly friendly manner, and had left together, the big man supported by a stranger on either side. The barman had not been close enough to overhear their discussion, though he indicated that they had spoken with an accent, or "at any rate did not belong." Sophie thanked him and interviewed some of the Erdmann's habitués, none of whom was able to add anything of substance. She spent another day waiting for Karel, then notified Frisch of his disappearance, though she did not file an official report. There seemed to be little point.

It was understood that Karel Neumann was once again in Russian custody.

BOOK TWO

Part One

There was a story that made the rounds amongst the inmates of the Russian camps. It was about a man, a soldier, returning home from the Great War. He must have been young, of course, but they imagined him old, the way they felt themselves. Some liked to give a date to his return. December 1918: the day before Christmas. The sixth of January, 1919: the feast of the Epiphany. Wintertime, in any case; snow on the ground. He is late coming home; an injury, in most versions of the story, has detained him since the armistice. His arm is in a sling. He is a farmer, a joiner, a postal clerk. In no version of the story is he rich.

Here is how it goes: The man arrives at the local train station late one evening, then walks the five miles to his village. He walks slowly, head bowed, hobbling. It's gone midnight when he arrives; not a light burning in his house. He is about to rouse his wife by knocking, then remembers; bends down, retrieves the key from under a loose brick. The front hallway opens straight into the kitchen; floorboards creaking with his every step. There is no fire in the oven, no coals to make one; a painted cupboard stacked with dishes; a kitchen table and some chairs. The man is about to go on, find his wife and his bed, but something stops him. A man's coat is thrown over the back of a chair. He walks over, runs a hand over the wool. The coat isn't his. His eyes find his wife's slippers, not two feet from the coat. Again and again he looks at the slippers, then at the coat; strokes it, all the while listening into the quiet of the house.

203

It does not come to him at once, the sound, but once he is conscious of it, there can be no doubt of its origin. Two people breathing, one louder than the other, a throaty exhalation that isn't yet a snore. He sits down on the chair, careful not to disturb the coat over its back; sits in the draft between window and door, and listens to this breathing that isn't yet a snore. By morning he is frozen solid. It's the man who finds him, the wife's brother, who has come to wait with her for her husband's return.

The first of the German POWs were released from American incarceration as early as May 1945. The last returned from Russia in 1955. Those first ones, they were soldiers, not inmates, the camp no more than an episode at the close of the war. Back home they found their cities in ruins, their wives half starved, their children running the black markets; the streets alive with occupying soldiers; refugees; DPs; KZ survivors; profiteers; journalists and film crews; the fear of a winter without coal.

Those who came last, in '55, found their cities rebuilt, the Economic Miracle in full swing, Marshall monies paying dividends; found their wives aged, their places in their beds usurped, their daughters copying fashions from American magazines. These men were different; some had been soldiers for one year and prisoners for thirteen. They returned as anachronisms, shaped by the struggle of the camps; spoke Russian, read Marx—and found a democratic world devoted to consumption.

Both groups might have told the story, during the hours of transport, going home. Not one of them froze in the draft "between window and door." But then again: who knows?

One

1.

It was the twenty-second of October. A cold spell had taken hold of the city and seemed to suggest an early winter. In Karlchen and Franzl's room in ——gasse, Karlchen's mother was helping him dress. The boy kept shivering under her hands as she smoothed out his dress shirt and coat and bent down to give his shabby shoes another polish. He seemed unable to stop fidgeting, shifted his weight from one foot to the other, and had to be reminded to hold still. His face had taken on an unhealthy reddish sheen; only the centre of his cheeks refused to fill with blood and stood out in pale blotches. She pinched them once or twice, hard enough to draw a wince, but it was useless. Perhaps he had simply caught a cold.

It had not been easy to procure formal clothing for the boy. There had been several discussions on the subject between herself and her husband. There was, of course, no money for a new suit, nor indeed for a used one that was in decent nick. For a while they had considered sacrificing her husband's good coat and having it altered, but in the end she had been able to convince a cousin from St. Pölten to send them their elder son's Communion suit, provided they paid for the postage and promised not to shorten either sleeves or legs. As a consequence both jacket and breeches looked large on the boy. The trousers had to be belted nearer the chest than the waist, and the child's hands kept disappearing in the sleeves.

Karlchen, for his part, endured his mother's touches and adjustments without complaint and watched his brother watch him from across the room with an expression that was half jealous, half angry, and not without a note of sympathetic fear. During breakfast Karlchen had to wrap a handkerchief around his chest and shoulders and place another in his lap so that there was no danger of staining the suit—and this despite the fact that they were eating nothing apart from bread with a little butter and some slices of boiled egg.

There was, to the boy, something odd in the way his parents treated him that morning, an air of reverence that cut across all pretence of treating him normally, even gruffly, as his mother poured out a quarter mug of milk for him and his father scolded him for chewing his bread so messily and leaving crumbs on the table. And in this reverence there sounded something different yet, a kind of distaste, as though he had contracted a disease to which they now felt obliged to tend. For the first time in his life Karlchen had the feeling of standing apart from his family. He might have cried but was gripped by an unconscious fear that he would not be comforted.

"Time to get going," his father said at last, and hurried into his coat. They walked hand in hand, the father leading, the boy trailing, taking two steps for his father's one, watching dust attach itself to the remnants of polish on his shoes. When the courthouse came into sight, grey and forbidding, the father momentarily paused in his stride, causing his son to collide with his thigh.

"I didn't," the boy said quietly, squirming at the end of the parental wrist. "I swear. I didn't do anything wrong."

His father reached down, straightened his collar, and did not respond.

2.

They entered the building. A porter listened to his father's request, nodded somehow gravely, and called over an usher. They were led down a series of long, barren corridors, surprisingly shabby in appearance; not narrow, but vaulted so high as to appear narrow, their footsteps ringing in the frigid air. A row of dirty windows was set high above their heads and admitted no glimpse of the outside world, the shadow of bars falling on the endless stretch of tiling. It seemed they had walked a long time before they arrived at their destination, a narrow, airless waiting room furnished solely with a wooden bench on which they presently sat down. A clock hung on the wall across, very large, like a station clock. The usher cautioned Karlchen's father to wait until he returned for the boy, then disappeared through a set of double doors that belched a roar of noise as he hastily squeezed through the gap. A silence fell that, far from being dispelled by the low murmur which soaked through the doors, found in it an accomplice, as it did in the sudden, audible movements of the clock. They were alone.

They waited the better part of an hour. From the first the boy was drawn to the doors. He slid down the bench in order to sit as close to them as possible, his father sliding down alongside, wordless, hostile, reaching across to tighten Karlchen's tie. After some minutes the boy began to distinguish variations in the whisper of the doors. There was, for one, the hubbub of voices, subdued and yet excited, and pierced at times by a laugh, a cough, the sudden bark of censure. From time to time a hush would fall, not a silence exactly, but a noise in its own right, the low, shivering hum of restrained anticipation. Steps fell into the silence, long, careful strides, and once a man shouted, "I object!" The more the boy listed to the noise, the more he yearned to pass beyond those doors—and feared it too, with the same dumb, wrenching fear he knew only from dreams. His collar chafed and his hands were sweaty, and he flinched when his father turned to run broad-pronged fingers through his hair (they had forgotten to bring a comb).

"Here," his father said, dug a paper bag from the pocket of his starch-stiff suit. He picked a sweet and passed it swiftly, almost with a kind of anger, then watched as Karlchen pushed it past his lips. It sat on his tongue like a stone, then suddenly grew soft and attached itself to one of his molars; sugared woodruff colouring his spit. Karlchen dug for it with one finger, pried loose the sweet, his father's eyes still on him, watching him as he folded his spit-slick finger back into his palm and hid it quickly in the pocket of his too-large coat.

The minute hand on the clock face moved then quivered, time marching on in reluctant, fettered steps.

At long last the doors opened, spilling voices, laughter, and the usher, who gestured without words then turned at once and slipped back into the room.

Karlchen's father did not stir. The boy walked in alone, into the roar of noise beyond the heavy double doors.

3.

To his surprise Karlchen entered the great hall of Vienna's criminal court not from the front—that is to say, from the side where members of the public sat in densely packed rows—but from the back, behind the rostrum of judges. For a moment he froze, feeling as though he had by accident taken the wrong door at the cinema and found himself trapped in front of the luminescence of its giant screen. He did not stop in the doorway for more than a second, however; then ducked his head and ran after the usher. In six, seven steps he had arrived at the chair pointed out to him. He thus gained only a fleeting impression of the auditorium. What he saw, above all, was a sea of ladies' hats behind which cowered a crowd of people. He did not, in this first glance, see any face that he recognized.

He was asked to sit. He could not have said whether it was the usher who asked him or one of the judges, or someone else altogether; in the noise of the hall the words came to him diffusely, like the hum of traffic, or a thought formed in his own head.

Karlchen sat. To his confusion he found that the chair did not face the auditorium as he had expected (he had for a week now imagined how it would be, lying awake at night to his brother's even breathing), but the row of judges in black, who sat somehow elevated behind their giant desk and were framed by a vast expanse of ornate wall and ceiling. His own chair, too, struck Karlchen as unnecessarily big and uncomfortable, and as he slid around in it, one arm tangling in the too-high armrest, his skin came alive with the sensation of everyone's watching.

Shyly, compulsively, and only dimly aware that someone was talking to him, he craned his neck to once again scan the audience. He saw fingers pointing, was distracted for a moment by the row of sketch artists who sat to one side with large pads of papers hoisted on their knees, then found himself drawn to a young man with feverish eyes who sat in the first row and who was missing not only a leg and an arm, but one entire side of his body, including his shoulder, half his chest, and some of his abdomen. Karlchen heard someone call his name but could not wrest his eyes from this half man, occupied by the question of how his body looked under the shirt (the man kept it from gaping with the help of some clothespins).

He looks like a fish ate him, it ran through him. *Or a whole swarm of fish.* And he kept on staring at the horrible eroded edge of his torso, and the place where his rib cage should have flared.

"Young man," the voice spoke again, and he turned at last, reluctant, looked up, and saw that one of the judges, the one in the middle, was speaking to him. "Did you hear what I said?"

Karlchen nodded, blushed.

"You will tell the truth, then?"

Again the boy nodded.

"You must speak up. So the stenographer can record your answer."

"Yes," he said, and then again, afraid he had not been loud enough. But each time, what emerged from his lips was little more than a yelp. Behind him, in the sea of sounds that was the audience, he could hear the rising tide of discontent.

4.

The boy was questioned in the late morning of the third day of the trial. The first day had almost entirely been taken up by formalities, including the swearing-in of the jurors, the reading of the arraignment, the opening statements, and the defendant's plea. It was only towards the late afternoon that the first witness had been called. But despite the fact that there was nothing in the arraignment, the speeches, or indeed the statement of this first witness that could be of surprise to anyone who had read a newspaper in the week or so coming up to the trial, the rows of the criminal court were packed to the last seat. Indeed there were reports about a lively and somewhat shameless trade in admission tickets being conducted not ten steps from the great hall's front doors. All this frenzy was owing to the fact that the first day was widely regarded as the earliest opportunity to meet all of the trial's major "actors," about whom there had already been so much talk.

Apart from the defendant himself, interest on this first day had centred on the figure of the prosecutor on the one hand and Wolfgang's defence lawyer on the other. They were, it was decided, a study in contrast, a contrast that extended to the physical, political, even spiritual dimensions. Representing the State was one Julius Fejn. Dr. Fejn was widely believed to be either one-quarter or one-half Jewish, which is to say (by the system of classification only so recently lifted) a mongrel, who had however survived the war years with minimal inconvenience thanks to the intervention of his wife, who was the daughter of a well-respected opera critic and consequently well connected. In any case (it was said, in tones ranging from surprise to a sulky sort of anger) Fejn did not *look* Jewish, was blond, tall, with a burgher's girth and heavy jowls, and the cutest little button of a nose in his fleshy, ruddy, but otherwise remarkably patrician face. When he spoke, it was with a sonorous, clear, if somewhat lazy delivery that in times of great excitement embraced the ghost of a lisp. It was in this lisp that the connoisseurs of such matters (there was amongst the audience more than one) located something affected, overdone, in bad taste, and consequently Jewish, even though the voice held, of course, no hint of a Yiddish intonation and Dr. Fejn spoke in the purest of German, conscientiously inflected with a touch of Viennese.

Dr. Fejn was facing off against quite a different sort of man, a short and tidy figure who looked as though he had been starched and pressed along with his clothes: a sort of Robespierre of defence lawyers, unyielding in his thought and habits, who had a manner of speaking to witnesses in a dry, flat, quiet voice that invariably succeeded in suggesting that they had not only insulted him, personally, but the moral order of the universe as such (and, really, that these were one and the same). His name was Ratenkolb. He too was rumoured to have been a "victim of recent events," and indeed it was said that his father, a Socialist, had been jailed immediately after the annexation, had caught a chill in prison, and had died as a consequence (albeit a year later and once again a free man). Dr. Ratenkolb had not maintained his practice during the war years, though whether from choice or because he had been blacklisted was a matter of dispute.

As for the presiding judge, the case had originally gone to one Klemens Meutziller, a fearsome tyrant of a man who had a habit of clearing the courtroom at the slightest provocation and who was known to bully prosecutors, defence lawyers, and witnesses alike, all in the name of common sense. And generally the Right Honourable Dr. Meutziller was said to hate any kind of verbiage and florid speech, as well as any kind of posturing. But just a few days before the court date the judge had suddenly taken ill, and quite seriously at that. Consequently the case went to one of the assistant judges on the case, a certain Bratschul, Alois by Christian name: a timid, indecisive soul who had earned his appointment more through societal connection than any show of legal brilliance, and suffered from some kind of gastric condition that often saw him squirm in his judge's chair with a mild-mannered impatience. It was therefore expected that rather than embracing the strong, some might say inquisitorial, role accorded to him by the Austrian legal system, he would sit back and allow prosecution and defence to dictate proceedings to a considerable degree.

All this, and much more besides, Anna Beer had learned from Sophie Coburn, who, despite her fragmentary German, seemed to have an impressive array of sources at her command, as well as a willingness to fill in the blanks with bold intuitive steps. Some other details Anna had learned by herself. She had not at first wanted to come to the trial at all, but the boredom of her situation, as well as the fact that it would have been impolite not to make use of the much-coveted entrance ticket Sophie had procured for her, convinced her otherwise. After her initial visit, midway through the opening afternoon, she found herself returning to the trial day after day, until her fellow spectators became as familiar to her as the judges and jurors, and she was able to pick out new faces and mark conspicuous absences almost as well as Sophie herself.

Anna had come to distinguish three distinct groups in this audience, though they did not, of course, identify themselves as such and sat scattered throughout the hall. The first—perhaps the largest, if also the quietest—was made up of men and women who all shared in a somewhat unhealthy and, as it were, downtrodden appearance. Quite a few of them appeared to be crippled, while others had the air, if not always the scars, of having endured violence of some form or another; were pale, thin, badly dressed, and sat on the benches with quiet, unmoved faces, their hands in their laps. There were many older people amongst this group. Though they tended to betray little emotion throughout the trial, it was understood that they were, to a man, hostile to the accused and had come to witness his condemnation.

The second group, on the other hand, were uniformly young men, many of them well turned out, with hale and pleasant faces. They were, as a group, broadly sympathetic to Wolfgang and in sympathy with one another; indeed many of them seemed to know one other and exchanged looks, sometimes handshakes, albeit in a strangely guarded, even furtive manner that ran counter to their general mood, which was confident and cheerful. It did not take much imagination to picture them dressed in uniforms; in the right sort of setting they would have made quite a dashing impression.

In addition to these two there was a third, more varied group, less committed in their sympathies, that treated the trial quite openly as a form of entertainment. These more casual spectators often took great care over their toilette and came dressed as though going to church or even the opera. The majority were women. They tended to come early and secure the first few rows. A number wore jewellery and a handful brought their lorgnettes so as to better study the scene before them. There was, amongst this group, a lot of whispering and coughing, and the occasional request, not always voiced politely, to remove a wide-brimmed hat that was blocking the view.

Chiefly these young and well-to-do women seemed interested in the accused and often focused their attention solely on him, though he sat with his back to the audience and could, at best, only be studied in quarter profile. Anna could well understand their interest. Wolfgang had surprised her on his first appearance: was handsome, tall, and long-limbed, given to moods, and at times appeared bored; was hostile and scowling during one witness statement then boyish and distracted during the next, digging around in his pockets or nervously playing with a deck of cards under the little desk behind which he had been placed.

This last detail—the card playing—was, Anna observed, noticed by more than one juror. Their reaction was hard to read: some seemed to judge him a frivolous young man, and hence guilty; others looked on with greater charity and rather seemed to wish they had a deck of cards to play with too. As far as the general disposition of the jurors was concerned, the older and less educated amongst them, along with the stout banker's widow who was the sole representative of her sex, seemed to incline towards Wolfgang and to take an almost paternal interest in him; while two or three of the younger men, who looked, at times, as if they would not mind doing away with their own fathers given half the chance, were consequently amongst the most judgmental of those in attendance and seemed to already have consigned Wolfgang to the gallows. It was, Anna would reflect in the evenings, a mystery how any sort of verdict was to be distilled from all these disparate elements and impressions.

5.

At the point the boy was called in, a new and unprecedented sense of suspense hung over the room. The cause for this excitement was as follows: Earlier that morning a string of policemen had been questioned about the defendant's confession. This confession had already been the subject of several newspaper reports and was generally regarded as unassailable proof of the defendant's guilt, especially since the defendant had not withdrawn it but simply insisted "that it did not count for a thing."

But strange to say, that was precisely how things turned out. According to the arresting officers the accused had made an oral confession no sooner had he been picked up by the authorities for shuffling around the city with bare, bloody feet and behaving like a drunk. He had, they said, "spilled the beans at once," which is to say even before they arrived at the station; had insisted on his guilt with particular vehemence and in "colourful language"; beaten his breast, cried, threatened to kill himself, and generally made quite a spectacle of himself. The confession had then been typed up "straight away" and allegedly been signed. But precisely this document now appeared to have been "misplaced." No trace of it could be found either in the investigative file or at the station house itself. A carbon copy existed and was produced but proved to be unsigned. The overall impression was that the original had also never been signed, and that, assuming a confession had been made at all, it had only been made orally, and that by the time the document had been presented to the defendant (the carbon was dated two days after the incident) he had refused to sign. It was at this point that the prosecution called Karlchen as their next witness.

The initial impression made by the boy was a negative one. He looked small, distracted, even neurasthenic; was fidgeting in his seat and craning his neck around its backrest; kept scanning the audience as though he were expecting one of the spectators to come forward and help him out of his predicament, and staring at a young crippled man whom he seemed to regard with enmity and fear. While many in the audience felt a certain sympathy for the boy, few were inclined to consider him a reliable witness. The thought must have occurred to the prosecutor, who, after all the judge's questions had been met with what now seemed like an obstinate silence, rose, smoothed down his robes, and begged the judge's permission to "have a go" himself.

"So," he said, in a kindly, self-assured voice, "it's not how you'd expected, eh?"

The boy did not answer.

"More people than you bargained for, I suppose. And those lorgnettes! You must feel like an exhibit."

Again he received no answer. The prosecutor followed Karlchen's gaze, adjudged its subject.

"Does that man frighten you?" he asked. "I am sure he does not mean to. All it is, he's lost an arm and a leg. Well, and a bit of the trunk too, I suppose." (Laughter in the audience.)

"There now, I believe we have made him blush. Let's give him a rest, why don't we? Why don't you look at me instead? I am not all that frightening, am I? Yes, that's right, turn your head forward. Can you see those gentlemen to the right? On the rostrum? No, not the judges. Over there, I mean, to your right. Those are the jurors, the men—and the woman—who will be asked to hand down a verdict in this case. You see them? All they want is for you to tell them what you saw on the twenty-fifth of June of this year. Nothing more, nothing less. You will manage that much, won't you? Of course you will.

"But I see it's not a good place to start. Well, then. 'Karl Theodor Heinrich.' Isn't that what the judge just called you? That's a very grown-up name. In fact it's three very grown-up names. Quite a mouthful, really. I don't suppose they call you that at home? They don't, do they? I see you are shaking your head.

"Come, now, won't you tell the jurors what they call you at home?"

The boy listened to all these explanations and questions with the air of someone gagging on his own breath. His mouth was wide open, his ears were burning red. In his desperation he once again turned to the audience, shook loose the vision of the crippled man, and at last found what he was looking for. A young girl, witnessing his predicament, had convinced her father to let her clamber onto his lap so as to be more visible and now stood up to attract the boy's attention. Her face was a pale mask of the most intense concentration; her hands bunched into fists and raised up before her—not as a threat, but rather in entreaty, their knuckles buried deep into her cheeks. It was as though she were willing her little friend to speak. And strange to say, the boy, upon finding her and exchanging that first gaze, calmed down almost at once, turned back to the prosecutor, and answered his question.

"Karlchen," he said. "They call me Karlchen."

A sigh went through the audience, of almost physical relief. The prosecutor straightened, took a second to flash a smile of good-natured triumph at the jurors, then bent forward towards the boy.

"Of course they do. They used to call me Julchen, you know. From Julius. I never much cared for it." He laughed and invited the audience to laugh along. Some spell of tension had been broken. "Well, now, Karlchen. We want to talk about the events of the twenty-fifth of June. But I see you are still a little nervous. Let us start somewhere a little easier, then. To talk ourselves warm, so to speak. It's what my mother used to say, that the tongue's a muscle like any other. For instance, can you tell us what you had for breakfast this morning?"

The boy considered it, a little taken aback by the inquiry. "A slice of bread with butter. But I didn't finish it. Half a boiled egg; I shared mine with Franzl. And some milk."

"Franzl? That's your brother, I take it. Did he also eat just one slice of bread?"

"No. He had two. And the rest of mine."

"How about the way here, then? Did you take the tram?"

But no, the boy had not taken the tram, he had walked with his father. What route had they taken? And how long until they'd arrived? And in the courthouse itself, what had Karlchen noticed? For instance, at the doorway, did they turn right or did they turn left; and how many stair-cases did they pass?

The prosecutor kept up this ream of questions for some minutes, while the boy gave increasingly precise, and at times very detailed, answers. The point of the exercise, naturally, was to impress upon the jurors that, far from being the nervous, shifty, dim-witted child they might at first have taken him for, Karlchen was in fact a sharp observer with a good memory, and as such made an excellent witness. The defence lawyer, Dr. Ratenkolb, was consequently none too happy about this line of questioning, and at several points seemed about to object that it was irrelevant, but Anna could see that he feared to alienate both audience and jurors, who were enjoying the interlude. So he sat, frowning at the boy with some severity, and held his peace. At long last, though, Ratenkolb could no longer hide his irritation. He jumped up from his seat and shouted that "this game has gone on long enough" (though he did not, of course, actually shout, but rather spoke in a precise, irritated voice that was as good as shouting, only quieter). Sighing on his chair, the presiding judge agreed and instructed Dr. Fejn to "please move to the matter at hand."

The prosecutor, at any rate, was almost done with the preliminary part of his interrogation. He had arrived by now at a summary of Karlchen's last birthday, or rather at a detailed list of the various and, it must be said, rather shabby presents he had received.

"You are twelve, then," Fejn finished, not at all ruffled by Dr. Ratenkolb's complaint, and knowing full well that the number was wrong.

"Ten," the boy corrected, looking pleased.

"Why, of course. It's just that you remember everything so well. Do you know who Hans Gross is? No? Well, I suppose he is dead now. He was Europe's premier authority on crime. Still is—ask any policeman! A good Austrian, incidentally, from Graz. You know what he said about witnesses? He said—" (At this point he took up a book he had lying on his little desk face down to mark the passage in question.) "Here it is: 'Experience shows that in many situations the most reliable witness of all is a healthy boy between seven to ten years of age who knows nothing as yet of love and hate, ambition and hypocrisy, nor of the considerations of religion, rank, et cetera.'"

Fejn closed the book with a thump and smiled a smile that left no doubt that he had just scored a point in the contest that was afoot, and that each little point brought him closer to victory.

The next moment the smile had vanished and, with the air of a man turning up his shirt sleeves to get started at long last on the task at hand, he once again turned to the boy.

6.

Prosecutor (gravely, signalling to boy and jurors alike the seriousness of his intentions): "To business, then. Where were you, Karl Theodor Heinrich Landauer, on the afternoon of June 25 of this year?"

Boy: "I was playing in the little park on ——gasse."

Prosecutor: "The park on ——gasse. That's across from the shirt factory, isn't it?"

Boy: "Yes. But it's bombed out."

Prosecutor: "So it is. Were you alone?"

Boy: "Yes, alone. Franzl was there at first, or rather we were across the road, looking for bullet casings in the rubble. But he kept teasing me, so in the end I ran off and played by myself."

Prosecutor: "And what game were you playing, all by yourself?"

Boy: "Marbles."

Prosecutor: "Marbles, hm. Were you throwing them or what?"

Boy (shaking his head): "No, I was just playing. Separating the colours. Making piles."

Prosecutor: "And then?"

Boy: "A man came and sat down on the bench."

Prosecutor: "What time was that? When the man came?"

Boy: "Two."

Prosecutor (thoughtfully, with an exaggerated sternness): "Two o'clock? How do you know? You don't own a watch, do you? No, I should imagine not, you are a little too young."

Boy (unfazed now, convinced he can account for himself): "The bell had just rung."

Prosecutor: "What bell?"

Boy: "Maria Treu. It rings on the hour."

Prosecutor: "You are sure?"

Boy: "Yes."

Prosecutor: "How can you be so sure? It could have been some other church. Announcing a funeral perhaps. Or a wedding."

Boy: "There's no other church nearby. Apart from St. Francis. But St. Francis got bombed. Besides, they don't sound alike."

Prosecutor (nodding, as though grudgingly convinced by overwhelming evidence): "Very well, then, two o'clock. So a man comes, sits down. What is his aspect?"

Boy: "His what?"

Prosecutor: "What does he look like? Is he a clerk who has nipped out to read the paper? A drunk? A cavalier in a top hat?"

Boy (thinking about it): "He was tired. He sort of plonked down." (Titters in the audience.) "And he wasn't wearing any shoes."

Prosecutor: "How far away were you when he, as you put it, plonked down? Ten steps? Fifteen?" (He steps out from behind the prosecutor's bench and walks away from the boy, moving ten steps down the aisle.)

Boy: "Not that far."

Prosecutor: "How far, then? Tell me when to stop." (Approaches again, in a slow, formal manner, almost a march. The boy does not stop him until he is three steps from his chair.)

Prosecutor (miming a whistle, without making any actual sound): "This close, then. How about you? Did you walk up to him?"

Boy (nodding, biting his lip): "Yes."

Prosecutor: "Why? You didn't know him from Adam. Why approach him?"

Boy (looking up at him, suspicious, as though sensing a breach of trust): "He wasn't wearing any shoes."

Prosecutor: "Come, now. Surely you have seen men without shoes before."

Boy (after a pause): "There used to be many." (A wave of his hand serves to indicate the past.) "Not so many now." (Another pause.) "The thing was, his feet were bleeding."

Prosecutor (quietly, so as not to interrupt the boy's rhythm or the spell his shy little voice has begun to weave in the courtroom): "So what did you say?"

Boy: "I asked him, 'Does it hurt?'"

Prosecutor: "And?"

Boy: "He didn't answer. So I left him alone. But then he's beckoning to me, asking me to sit down beside him."

Prosecutor: "And you did? That was brave."

Boy (flushing): "I was curious."

Prosecutor: "What did he do then?"

Boy: "He started whispering, only quite loudly, right in my ear. 'You better remember this,' he says. 'They will want to hear about it. The police.' And then he smiled." (He demonstrates the smile, thin-lipped, lopsided, fleeting. Perhaps he is, at precisely this moment, just as afraid as the man he describes.)

Prosecutor: "And then what did he say?"

Boy: "'I've done my old man.' Just that. He said it twice. And then he raised his eyebrow."

Prosecutor: "What did you think he meant by that phrase?"

Boy (without hesitation): "That he killed his pa."

A murmur goes through the courtroom. Somebody coughs, and a woman's voice is heard, quiet yet piercing: "Of course he did."

7.

Dr. Fejn turned away from the boy, head bowed, as though deep in thought. There was to the moment an enormous theatrical tension. The drama had to be played out. There was not a soul in the audience who wished to hurry it along.

"Is he here?" he asked quietly, but received no immediate answer. "Stand up, look around. Do you see the man who talked to you on the park bench on the twenty-fifth of June and told you that he murdered his own father?"

Shyly, hesitantly, the boy stood up from his chair and turned around. Indeed it seemed that Karlchen had not noticed the defendant until this moment, though he was sitting not four steps from the boy, albeit to one side and at a right angle, facing the prosecutor rather than the witness. Wolfgang sat with his head bowed, too tall for his chair with its little desk, and as though folded up underneath. He did not look at the boy right away. Only after some moments, feeling his gaze on him, and without moving his head, did he raise his eyes and acknowledge him, in a way that was not in the least unfriendly but, on the contrary, almost light-hearted, as if with a wink. The boy had enough of a sense of the drama of the occasion to stretch out a hand and point.

"It's him," he said quietly.

"You are certain."

"Yes."

"How many marbles did you have? The day in the park? You said you were making piles. You must have counted them."

"Forty-three. Twenty-one red, eighteen blue, and four green."

"And how many do you have now?"

"Forty-one."

"You lost two?"

"I got three new ones, and gave five to a friend."

"That must be someone very special."

The boy raised his chin, his eyes found the little girl who had willed him to speech. Dr. Fejn followed his gaze and made sure the jurors did too.

"I see. The prosecution rests its case."

8.

The defence lawyer was given the word. He stood up, took a moment to smooth out his clothing, and then did an odd little movement in which he rolled from heels to toes, as though stretching out his feet and calves. It was hard to say whether the movement was calculated or habitual, but it did have the effect of shifting attention away from the events that had just transpired and onto this prim little man. With the permission of the presiding judge Dr. Ratenkolb too stepped out from behind his desk and took half a step towards the boy. For a full minute or more he stood, taking the boy's measure, somewhat sneeringly, it must be said, and with evident distaste, as though studying a stain on the wall.

"'I've done my old man,'" he echoed at last, in a flat, pedantic voice that served to bring out the theatrical absurdity of the phrase. "I suppose you go to see a lot of pictures."

The boy did not react, sat there, wide-eyed, staring up at the lawyer. It must have occurred to him that he was facing an adversary and was now under direct attack. But there was nothing in his young arsenal that could have informed his defence.

"What was the weather like?" Dr. Ratenkolb asked, moving away from his witness and speaking as though to the jury.

The boy was struck dumb. His earlier fear seemed to have rushed back on him.

"Come, now. Was it sunny, perhaps? A warm day?"

The boy nodded, then realized the man could not see him. He tried to answer, whispered a spit-wet "Yes," looked over to Trudi for help.

"Yes? Then how is it that the meteorological institute recorded showers for that afternoon and precisely at two o'clock? You said it was two, did you not? You heard the ringing of Maria Treu?"

He sneered, turned, transfixed the boy. Karlchen's voice was very small.

"The rain came later. It was sunny. And then later it rained."

"Later? Is that when you met the other man? The one who told you he'd killed his wife, and ten blooming Americans besides?"

He went on in this manner for some more minutes, discrediting one by one all the points to which the boy had testified. The lawyer's sneering manner was disliked by the audience and the jurors, yet all the same his words sowed doubt where before there had been certainty, and the boy's assertions appeared in a new light, uncertain, tentative, adulterated by fantasy. No sooner had the boy been dismissed than the court was adjourned.

Two

1.

Anna left the courthouse by a side entrance and immediately crossed the road to escape the huddle of spectators who had gathered on the pavement, where they stood smoking, exchanging impressions. The trial would not resume for two full hours. Sophie had declined Anna's invitation to lunch: she had, the journalist said, some notes to type up. There was time to go home, but Anna felt herself drawn to one of the cafés just a short way up the road, in the immediate vicinity of the city hospital. She chose a table by the window and had not yet ordered when she saw the plump, myopic figure of Detective Frisch walk past outside, his daughter in tow. Anna had noticed them at the trial, and now found herself rapping a knuckle against the window and waving them in. Frisch looked up, pale eyes startled in their thick-lensed frames. His daughter spoke to him, obviously displeased by the invitation, and was pulling him along. A second rap encouraged Frisch's resistance to the girl's hurry. He entered the café. In an inversion of gender roles Anna stood to shake his hand.

"How do you do, Detective? Please, you must join me." She pointed at the chairs across the table.

The detective demurred, forgot to return her hand, his fingers moist in her palm. "We only came in to say good day. This is Gertrud. Trudi, Frau Anna Beer."

It was reassuring to hear his voice, that slow, pedantic drone, unruffled despite his clammy hand.

"I did not know you had remained in town. Has your husband—"

She shook her head, smiled from coquettish habit, then nipped her lip as though to punish it. "There has been no news. Nor of Neumann—the Czech, you remember, the drunk. I have petitioned the Soviet authorities for information. Frau Coburn has a friend in diplomatic circles. It's all very hopeless. There was another lead, some vagrant this girl told me about, who she thought—But he too seems to have quite disappeared. If I don't hear within the next month or so, I'll be off . . ."

She shrugged, rescued her hand from his grasp, gestured God knew where; to Paris, she supposed, which she seemed to locate just behind the entrance to the hospital. In his pedantic manner Frisch followed the gesture, looked over at the row of squat old buildings with their yellow, flaking paint.

"He used to work right there, you know. My husband. We would meet here, in this café, for lunch. He liked the pickled herring. Imagine living with a man who smelled of raw onion half the time."

She paused, detected the falsehood in her story, remembered Anton's habit of brushing his teeth when he came home from work. He had been nothing if not fastidious.

"But this is silly, our standing around like this. Please, Herr Frisch, sit. I beg you."

While the detective was still making up his mind, looking at his daughter as though to solicit her permission, Robert Seidel passed the café. He was walking without looking, hands buried in his trouser pockets, chewing on a cheek. Anna had spent many hours watching him at the trial; only rarely had he met her eye. He sat every day near the front of the courtroom like an island unto himself: the only representative of the defendant's family. Up close, she noticed he'd grown his hair and had filled in a little in the face. It rather suited him.

As though alerted by a sixth sense Robert looked up, saw them clustered around the table; recognized her, flushed, and hurried on. There was a curious rhythm to his walk, shoulders moving in counterpoint to his legs. Frisch watched after him, a hint of curiosity in his outsized eyes, and finally resolved to sit, pulling his daughter onto the chair next to him.

"You know the defendant's brother, Frau Beer? I noticed you in court and wondered what interest you—"

"We met on the train," she smiled. "And it appears your daughter is friends with today's star witness." She turned to the child. "He seems a little sweet on you, my dear."

The girl did not acknowledge her smile; pulled a face instead. It was hard to pinpoint the cause of her hostility. Anna turned her attention back to the father.

"In any case, it helps pass the time. The trial, I mean."

The waiter came to take their order. At Anna's insistence the detective agreed to a coffee. His daughter rebuffed her repeated offer of "an ice." For herself Anna ordered the herring she had just mythologized; did not eat it, but spent a quarter hour stabbing a fork in its cold flesh and combing all the onion to one side. Frisch finished his coffee in two slow, decorous sips, then sat studying her, ignoring his daughter's glare. After a moment's hesitation he sent the girl to play outside.

"You'll be right out," Trudi said, more command than question.

"In two minutes."

She nodded and ran out.

Anna grew tired of poking at capers. She pushed the plate to one side, lit a cigarette. "There is something you wish to say?" she asked.

He nodded but did not speak at once, had placed his hands side by side on the table. "We never followed up on the blood. In your apartment, I mean. You said there was a patch of blood. You washed it off, you said."

"So?"

Again it took him several moments to speak. She wondered whether he was composing his thoughts or if this was an interrogation method that had long hardened into habit. The waiter approached then immediately withdrew, sensing their change of mood.

"I investigated a case some months ago. A man was found dead in his apartment. Poisoned, as it turned out. A prisoner of war; he hadn't been back for much more than six weeks. His wife was very pretty. An interesting woman, proud and lively, with a beautiful smile. She's never admitted to the crime."

She laughed, smoke flying out of mouth and nostrils. "You suspect me, then?"

He dismissed the notion with a wave of his hand. "Of course not."

It was as though she had missed the point of his little story.

"Are you going to," he asked her gently. "Be all right on your own? Until your husband returns, I mean."

She looked at him and wondered when she had last been propositioned with such kindness. He saw her glance and at once understood; took off his glasses, revealing a pale face and pale, naked eyes.

"I've always been ugly," he said.

Spontaneously, touched by his tone—calm, punctilious, devoid of self-pity—she lent forward, plucked his hand off the table, and planted a kiss on its back.

"You're a good man." She did not know what she meant by the phrase. He smelled surprisingly pleasant, of aftershave and dried-in sweat.

When she leaned back in her chair, the girl was there, storming to the table.

"We must go," she said. "Karlchen will be waiting."

"Yes, of course." Frisch rose.

"You are not going back to the trial, Detective? From what I hear, this afternoon might turn out to be rather interesting. At least Frau Coburn thinks so."

He shook his head, offered his hand in parting. "You will let me know," he said, "when you have news from your husband?"

Anna thought it good of him that he did not say "if."

2.

When the trial resumed early that afternoon, the court spent the first hour or so on the examination of a string of witnesses who had all seen Wolfgang on the day of his father's fall. They could do little more than corroborate that the defendant had been in such and such a place at such and such a time; had been disorientated, swaying and ranting; and had not been wearing shoes. On the whole these witnesses lent credibility to Karlchen's statement, though the defence lawyer, Ratenkolb, managed to draw from one witness, a paperhanger's apprentice, the stubborn avowal that he had seen Wolfgang "precisely at two" at a spot a good mile from the little park Karlchen had indicated. Moreover, all the witnesses readily admitted that the physical and mental state of the defendant had been consistent with his being drunk. Indeed they had been fully convinced at the time that there was nothing at all the matter with Wolfgang—other than being "lit like a howitzer," as the paperhanger's apprentice put it—and had only changed their minds after they'd read the newspaper coverage of the murder. By a quarter to three, therefore, it was felt that the entire case hinged on the statement made by a nervous little boy who might have heard nothing more implicating than a drunk's sodden grumble about an oppressive and, truth be told, rather niggardly father.

At this point the trial arrived at a critical juncture. The question everyone was asking themselves was whether the judge would allow witnesses unrelated to the incident itself who would, in the prosecutor's words, establish "not only a pattern of violence" in the defendant's actions, "but positively identify the murder as his handiwork." The defence lawyer had argued that since the defendant had, after all, "only one father," no past act, violent or not, could help shed light on what was, last he had checked, an accusation of parricide. He'd spoken vehemently against a "trial by character," which he intimated was unworthy of a civilized state that had, dare he allude to it, only so recently shed the "mantle of tyranny" (the phrase caused some debate: did it imply, for instance, that tyranny had never been more than a superficial aspect of Austria's political landscape?).

In any case it had become known amongst the public (though the devil knows how: in judicial terms, Anna later heard, it was utter nonsense) that this question had been debated not only in the courtroom itself—where it occupied some few minutes—but more hotly and exhaustively "behind closed doors"; and that the panel of judges had decided to withhold its final judgment on the matter until the first of these witnesses was called.

This moment had now arrived. If the presiding judge refused to call the next witness, then the prosecution's case was as good as complete. If, on the other hand, the witness was heard, the prosecution's case was not only not complete, but the whole trial would very quickly transform into a different trial altogether, for it was understood that the witnesses the prosecution wished to call were men and women the accused had met, and indeed interrogated, during his time as an SS officer in the Secret State Police and were, for want of a better word, his "victims," that is to say a string of Jews, Gypsies, Socialists, and anti-socials whom he had maltreated as an officer of the then law. The significance of the moment was felt all the more strongly because, to everyone's surprise, no charges had been filed against Wolfgang for his conduct during the war years, neither by the criminal prosecutor nor by the representative of the People's Courts that had been set up for precisely this purpose. There was to be no other trial.

Consequently a hush went through the courtroom when the prosecutor announced that he wished to call the next witness. All eyes turned to the presiding judge. Dr. Ratenkolb once again objected to the proposal in the strictest terms, but his comments were brief and *pro forma*; it was not, at this point, a question of arguing a point. The judge sat, looked over the courtroom, and hesitated. He looked like a man who had made up his mind but now suddenly found himself wavering. He opened his mouth, closed it again; looked over at the representatives of the press, domestic and foreign, who had been given a row to themselves, then at the audience as a whole; at the florid, patrician face of the prosecutor, who precisely at this moment very softly injected into the silence that most Jewish of statements: "Be a mensch." A murmur went through the room, half of outrage (for was it not bad taste for the prosecutor to remind one and all, at precisely this time, of his own Jewishness, and of the, as it were, "Jewish dimension" that hung—albeit obliquely—over the whole trial and could be summed up with those twin letters, SS), half of expectation, as those amongst the audience who had themselves run afoul of truncheons, fists, and bullets placed all their hopes on this "Be a mensch."

For another ten or twenty seconds the judge held his peace, then swallowed, looked down at his papers, and grumpily instructed the prosecutor to "get on with it." Whether he "was quietly resentful of this well-fed Jew who was seeking to parade Austria's shame so shamelessly," as Sophie Coburn later put it in an article she sold to the Toronto *Globe and Mail*, and only did it because he felt that "the eyes of the world were upon him," Anna had no means of judging. It must be nice, she felt, to find oneself with such unmediated access to another human being's soul. On the whole she was inclined to think it a sort of fraud.

All at once a great feeling of haste seemed to take hold of the court. It was clear from the judge's behaviour that he wanted this phase of the trial to be over and done with as quickly as possible. He called no further recess, made only the most cursory pretence of examining the witnesses himself, and hurried the prosecution along wherever possible.

What could have been a strung-out process lasting a day or more thus became a highly condensed spectacle that ran into the early hours of the evening. Witness after witness was called, then rushed through a description of his or her arrest, the conditions at the Gestapo prison, the beatings and humiliations. A number added accounts of violence they had experienced on the streets or in their own apartments. Those amongst the audience who had expected tales of bestial torture—fuelled by the rich rumours that had long attached themselves to that fearful acronym, Gestapo, and its leather-coated goons—were disappointed. The men and women who testified had been slapped, kicked, and beaten; they had been called "pigs" and "sluts" and "bastards" and left to freeze in barren cells. Wolfgang, it must be added, seemed to have been far from the worst of their jailers. Other figures surfaced in the witness statements and were named with peculiar emphasis ("Rosenheim"; "Langfuhr"; "that monster, Hein"). Nonetheless the portrait drawn of the defendant was far from flattering: he emerged as a young man of temper, physically overpowering, and habituated to acts of considerable cruelty.

The demeanour of the witnesses, incidentally, was by no means uniform. Some were tearful, some proud. Some stared at the defendant in solemn hatred, while others smiled at him with timid nervousness even as they described how he'd taken them "by the ear" and repeatedly slammed their heads into the tabletop "as though bouncing a ball." Most witnesses seemed to experience discomfort, even shame, at making public the abuse they had endured or witnessed, though one or two seemed to enjoy their sudden stardom. A cleaning lady for the Gestapo headquarters, for instance, who testified to the cries of pain emitting from the cells and especially from the basement of the facility, sat on the witness chair in an elaborate coiffure and recounted her impressions with such zest that even the prosecutor judged it best to dismiss her as quickly as possible lest her air of self-satisfaction influence the jurors against her.

The defendant, it should be added, listened with remarkable equanimity to the string of witnesses who had queued up to testify to his brutality. Only once did he lose his outward calm, when the fifth or sixth such witness (the order had been carefully arranged by the prosecutor, who was aware of the repetitive nature of the statements and feared nothing so much as boring the court) recounted his interrogation. It had taken place on February 2, 1942, "a year to the day prior to the capitulation at Stalingrad," as the man explained with odd insistence. His name was Klein; a fine-boned figure with a full head of white hair and a pair of tortoiseshell glasses. Klein was dressed very primly, but not only had his jacket been patched in a number of places, but his glasses too showed a fine hairline crack over his small, lively, somewhat watery eyes. He was, in short, the model of a decent man who had fallen on hard times. It did not hurt that, as the prosecutor pointed out in passing, he was the same age as the defendant's supposed victim. In a brisk, quiet voice Klein recounted his arrest, his imprisonment in a holding cell, "as small as a coffin," and the humiliation of a strip search.

"I was interrogated the next morning at half past eight," he finished, then looked to the prosecutor for permission to carry on.

"Can you tell the court who was present at the interrogation?"

"Kriminalassistent Seidel. The accused." He turned and pointed at Wolfgang. "And an older officer by the name of Pfalhuhn."

"They introduced themselves by name?"

"Why wouldn't they?" the witness asked quietly. "They were our masters."

"What was the point of the interrogation?"

"They wanted me to sign a confession. I had been denounced for 'sabotage of the war effort.' I had made some comments indicating that we would lose the war."

"This was when? Your comments, I mean."

"November 1941. They showed me the statement. The name of my accuser was blacked out."

"November 1941. That was perceptive of you. Did you sign the confession?"

"I refused."

"Even though the accusation was accurate?"

"I had predicted we would lose the war. I did not sabotage the war effort."

"Indeed. What happened then? Were you bullied?"

The witness here gave a little shrug, indicating the silliness of the question. "They called me a traitor. I was repeatedly slapped."

"By the accused?"

"No, by Pfalhuhn. He had large puffy hands and some very sharp rings."

"You were insulted and beaten. Was that all?"

"No. When I continued in my refusal, the two men exchanged some whispers. The older officer then left the room. As soon as he was gone, Kriminalassistent Seidel asked me to get up from the chair and walk over to the window."

"He dragged you over?"

"Not at all. He stood, went ahead, opened it, and then asked me to join him there."

"What did you do?"

Again that minuscule shrug. "I had no choice. I walked over to him."

"Frightened, no doubt."

"I did not know what he was up to. I imagined he wanted to show me something. I was afraid they had arrested my wife and imagined her standing in the courtyard."

"And was she?"

"No. There was no courtyard. Just an air shaft. You could barely see the sky above."

"What happened then?"

"The accused bid me lean out. He said, 'Go on, take a look, right to the bottom.'"

"You did, naturally."

"I hesitated. Next I knew, he had grabbed me by my jacket and hurled me onto the windowsill. It knocked the wind out of me. My legs were scrambling, hitting the radiator underneath the window. I cut open both knees."

"And the accused?"

"He held me by the collar of my jacket." Klein took a hold of it himself, sat on the witness chair, dragging his jacket halfway over his ears. "I could feel the buttons straining at my chest. Thirty feet to the bottom of the air shaft. There was a frozen puddle there, and rubbish. He kept yelling at me, right in my ear. 'Filth,' he said, again and again, just the one word, and I still could not breathe."

"And then?"

"He hauled me back in. Walked me back over to the chair. He had thrown his arm over my shoulder and watched me as I signed, ruffling my hair. Of all the things he did—" He paused, breathless, made as if to ruffle his own hair, then smoothed it instead, suddenly embarrassed. "That false camaraderie," he went on, tears gathering behind his cracked glasses. "I dream of it sometimes, and I—" He choked and broke off.

At this point, even before Klein had a chance to finish his statement, Wolfgang leapt out of his chair, almost falling over the little desk in front of him, and took two steps towards the witness. His face was bloodless, and his right hand was crushing the deck of cards he'd been holding. It was unclear whether he was about to hit the man or apologize. The witness, at any rate, had risen from his own chair and stood, chin raised, as though inviting a blow. But before either of them could so much as utter a word, Ratenkolb let out a sharp, whip-like hiss that was immediately followed by the much milder order to "Please sit down, Herr Seidel. It is customary to let your counsel handle the cross-examination." The words caused some ripples in the audience, something akin to laughter. It stopped Wolfgang in his tracks.

Even then it was not apparent what he would do: for three, four heartbeats Wolfgang remained where he was, halfway between his own chair and the witness's. There were those who swore afterwards they saw him shake with tension. Then he turned abruptly and returned to his place. During the short moment when he walked back to his chair, there stole across his face a peculiar and somewhat haughty smile that, it must be said, made a rather poor impression, most especially on the well-to-do ladies who had otherwise rooted for this young "hussar."

"One last question, Herr Klein," the prosecutor shouted into the growing din of the courtroom. "When you read that Herr Seidel's father had fallen out of his window, did you have any doubt that he had been thrown out by his son?"

The witness's answer was lost in Ratenkolb's yell of "Objection." It was, in truth, not needed.

Wolfgang's case was as good as lost.

3.

Robert rushed out of the courtroom no sooner had the last witness of the day been dismissed, pushing past the people sitting next to him, making liberal use of his elbows. He was one of the first to leave the great hall, whose marbled grandiosity extended no further than an arched doorway. It spilled him into a shabby little corridor marked by dirt and broken tiles.

Poldi was not waiting outside the door as they had agreed but some ten steps to his left, up a short flight of stairs and pressed into the shadows of the wall. She was wearing a new dress, which is to say one of his mother's dresses, which Robert had sneaked out of her wardrobe and Poldi had altered, clumsily it must be said, and which now clung unbecomingly to her abdomen and chest. Her eyes were on the floor, as though she were counting tiles. Robert ran up to her and reached for her arm.

"There you are! For a moment I thought you had left. The session overran. But come, we better hurry. I don't know if they'll wait for us."

Poldi did not come along at once; kept staring at the floor, a stubborn note to her voice. "They'll wait. They haven't got a choice, have they? I mean, *he* en't back yet either. And besides, you're chummy with the guard."

"It's the judge's assistant I'm worried about. He has to be present—otherwise they won't let us see him. He's already making an exception, you know. It's long past visiting hours."

"Well, go on, then. Only don't run. I'm in a certain condition, I am."

They set off. Robert seemed unable to impress on her their need for haste, had to pull her along by the crook of her arm like a reluctant child. They didn't have far to go: the remand prison was in the same building that housed the criminal court. They sped down corridors the length of a city block. As they approached the prison entrance Poldi came to a sudden halt and dislodged herself from Robert's grip.

"I en't ready," she complained, touching her temples in an oddly affected gesture, Bette Davis coming down with *le petit mal*. "I have to look my best. Otherwise, what good is it to visit, eh, pet?"

She smiled at her hand mirror, licked a smear of lipstick off her teeth.

It was Poldi's first visit to the prison. Ever since Wolfgang's arrest she had refused all contact, claiming at first she was too sick to leave the house (she did in fact suffer from almost constant nausea and could be heard throwing up not only in the mornings but practically any time of the day and night), then insisting she'd make "a bad impression on them guards" and would "conspire 'em against him" (she proved resilient to Robert's argument that the guards had nothing whatsoever to do with the outcome of the trial). Wolfgang, for his part, had seemed undecided whether or not he wanted to see his wife. At times he had asked about her, badgering Robert for all the details of her pregnancy and asking questions of such physical intimacy that they flustered his stepbrother. Then entire days would pass when he displayed no interest in his wife and dismissed any suggestion of a future visit, often in terms crudely insulting to Poldi.

Robert had come to see his stepbrother three or four times a week since their first meeting three months ago and, in the course of time, had grown familiar with his bewildering range of moods. Quite often, during the first few minutes of these visits, Wolfgang appeared to Robert a changed man, which is to say thoughtful, chastened, engaged in the scrupulous examination of his past. But inevitably a sneering, mocking mood would take possession of him before the visit was over, and more often than not the interview ended on a caustic, even sour note.

Part of the frustration of these exchanges derived from their setting: visiting rules demanded that they not discuss the trial, nor Wolfgang's supposed crime. Often they found themselves reduced to the rehearsal of childhood anecdotes. It was, Robert had explained to Eva, not a situation "conducive to the baring of souls." She had laughed and warned him he should beware his didn't curdle on exposure. Robert, undaunted, had redoubled his efforts to talk Poldi into making a visit. Three days ago she had finally agreed and at once launched into frantic preparations. It was only now that she'd suddenly grown tardy.

As it turned out, there was no need for any hurry. The young man who

represented the judge during these meetings had himself attended the trial
and had arrived, Robert was told, "not a minute ago," as had the prisoner,
who was even now being conducted into the visiting room. They signed
the guard's ledger and listened to his recital of the rules.

"So you finally got her to come, Robert," the man added familiarly, tracing with his eyes the clumsy, looping letters with which Poldi had spelled
out her name. He started relating some prison gossip, then thought better
of it when he noticed Poldi's mood. "Nervous, are we? Come in, then, it's
right over here."

Indeed it was hardly more than ten steps. As though by silent agreement they stopped one more time outside the door.

"You go on ahead, Frau Seidel," the guard encouraged her gently.

Poldi faced her little mirror before opening the door.

4.

Wolfgang was smoking. He sat slouching on a chair, both elbows on the
table, the cigarette wedged between fingers that were threaded through his
hair. When he heard the door, he looked up with no special show of interest. His eyes found Poldi, arrested her step; examined her from head to toe
with great deliberation and a certain virile cruelty. She in turn submitted
to his gaze, a little shamelessly, it felt to Robert, pushing her chest forward
(she had filled out in the course of the pregnancy) and allowing herself to
be appraised.

"What's that, then?" Wolfgang said, his eyes on the abundant fabric of
her sleeves. "A curtain?"

She coloured but did not reply.

"I should leave you two alone," said Robert, already retreating.

"No, no, stay," Wolfgang instructed him, his eyes still gathering in his
wife. "I insist. My whole life is played out before an audience these days."
He gestured to the judge's assistant and the guard, who were standing by
the far wall and whispering to one another in low voices. "You might as

well join the crowd." He shifted his gaze to Robert. "But I forgot. You *want* to leave. You are terribly disappointed with me. After all you've heard, I mean." He pointed at Poldi, a stabbing motion, sharp and accusing. "Was she there?"

Robert shook his head. "She didn't want to come in. Besides, there were no tickets. She waited outside the door."

"Look at her blushing, though. She *knows*. She eavesdropped."

Robert did not reply. All at once he remembered where she'd waited for him, pressed into the shadows of the wall, like a child pretending she'd been good.

"Well, screw it. So everybody knows."

Neither Robert nor Poldi made any movement to sit down. Robert looked very pale in his dark suit.

"Go on, little brother. You have something to say?"

"How could you?" Robert asked meekly. "Beat a little man like that?"

"What, the one with the cracked glasses?" Wolfgang gave a crooked grin. "And what do you bet he has another pair at home? Without any crack. You can picture him at his sink in the morning, trying out both pairs. Or maybe he dropped the glasses on the way over—by accident of course. But look, the Herr Assistant-Court-Official is getting nervous. We mustn't discuss the trial."

He shook his head in mock exasperation that nonetheless seemed to bleed the anger out of him; flicked away a curling inch of ash and ground the cigarette into the tabletop.

"You remember, Robert, when we were children, Dad would take us fishing sometimes. He insisted we clean our own fish. First you slit them open with a narrow knife. From asshole to gills, so to speak. And then—" Wolfgang hooked two fingers, mimed the process of wrenching out the guts, then wiped his hand upon his tie. "I remember you didn't like it at first. You may even have cried. But after a while—" He shrugged, sour, amused. "You got to be pretty good at it, little brother. The blood didn't bother you at all."

Wolfgang turned his attention back to Poldi. He rose from his chair and walked over to her until they were no more than a foot apart. "You're sure it's mine, eh?"

She nodded, dry-eyed, hands folded over her stomach.

"Ah, give us a kiss, then." He pulled her towards him, kissed her lips in a greedy, forceful manner, then immediately pushed her away again; swore, rounded the table, dropped back onto his chair. "Time you went, kid. You need your beauty sleep.

"That's my wife," he added, much too loudly, as though yelling at the guard. "Tits out, preggers, half her teeth missing. Wasn't me, in case you wondered." He flushed in renewed anger, bared his own teeth, raised one fist in a mock punch. "And they say I called them filth. What if I did, though?"

He lit a new cigarette, turned once again to Poldi, looked pained. "You're still here? Stop staring at me with those cow eyes. You heard it: I throw old men out the window. Me, the father of your child. Sleep on it, I tell you, see how it sits with you in the morning."

Calmly, not rushing, Poldi turned and walked to the door. Robert made to follow her, but Wolfgang stopped him.

"How is *Mother*?" he barked at his back.

"She is well. She sends her regards."

"Does she now? Any special message perhaps?"

Robert shook his head. "She says you are sure to be acquitted. She is praying for you."

Wolfgang grinned. "Praying? That means she's nervous. Tell her I'm thinking of testifying. Making a clean breast of it, once and for all. And Robert, tell her I'm parched in here. Can she send me some bottles? She's rich now, isn't she? She can afford to splurge. One can't take it with you: make sure to tell her that. She's the type who thinks you can."

Robert ran out then, caught up with Poldi, crushed by the feeling he did not know his brother at all.

Three

1.

He told Eva about it later. They were sitting on the floor of his bedroom, her legs splayed, her back against the bed frame, Robert sprawling with his bottom between her hips, leaning lightly on her chest. These days they often sat like that. She could not see his face this way but, then again, he could not see her back. He had a lovely, narrow, upright neck. She liked to breathe him in: stick her nose in the space where the collar gaped at the nape and inhale. It was the smell of being cared for, sweet, a little sweaty, suggestive of bedtime as a child. To believe in it was like believing in God, or Father Christmas. She reached around with both her hands and laced her fingers across his chest; held him tight against her doubt.

In the course of the past two months, Eva and Robert had established a pattern for their relationship. They spent the day apart, hardly talking, he busy playing messenger between Wolfgang and the world; she procuring necessities on the markets, running the household, avoiding his mother. At night they met, shyly, in the corridor outside her room. On the whole there was little talk, or rather little conversation. He liked to speak, upend his mind. She would listen and ration her responses, from caution, habit; because she distrusted the contents of her head. Lately she'd found a better foil for the darkness of her thoughts.

"So it looks like he's found some joy in it," she said, when Robert had finished his account of Poldi's prison visit. "Being a villain. At least she didn't cry. Almost dignified. Or did she start howling once you were outside?"

Robert shook his head; a twist of bone and tendon in his neck. She stuck her tongue out, touched a mole straddling his hairline; withdrew it again to listen to his answer.

"I found her outside the courthouse. She was tearing the sleeves off her dress, tearing at the seams, but she had sewn them on so hard, the fabric tore instead; a crowd of people around looking at her like a madwoman. When she noticed me, she set off for the tram stop. I tried to console her, but she wasn't listening. All of a sudden she turned and said, 'He needs me.' She said it so tenderly, it nearly broke my heart. 'He was horrible to you,' I said, but she shushed me, fingers to my cheek. 'Don't you see?' she said. 'He's ashamed.' I thought she meant the dress, she's not much of a seamstress, after all, and it did look a bit of a mess. 'We can buy you a new one,' I started, but she just laughed. 'Oh, no, not like that,' she said. 'He's ashamed. Because of what he did. Before you. But also before me.' The tram came; we sat across from one another, and now her eyes were filling up. 'The way he looked at me,' she kept on saying. 'He still wants me.'"

Robert paused, obviously moved. It distracted from his smell, fanned a spark of cruelty in Eva.

"He *wants* her. Wolfgang leers at her across a room and she thinks it is love."

"Well, perhaps it is." He turned so he could see her face, his cheek now level with her mouth. "She stands by him in any case. She wants me to take her back tomorrow, 'so he can shout at me some more.' When we got back to the house, she climbed the stairs like a queen."

Eva snorted: warm breath into the windings of his ear. "You will, of course. Escort her back and watch him insult her some more. Because in your heart you'd already forgiven him the moment you left his cell. It didn't take ten steps." She paused, her mood suspended between tenderness and anger. "The thing is, you think he repents. It comes out all wrong, of course, but he repents. And you know what, he probably thinks so himself. That he's—what's the word you like so much?—'resurrected'; ready to acknowledge the 'blot on his soul.' But it didn't bother him, that blot, not when it was just him who knew, him and his victims, and the people who paid his wages. Even last week he didn't care one ounce about that blot; he might even have prided himself on it, that he had the strength where others were weak. But now it's in the papers—and he, he is shaking in his boots."

Robert did not contradict her. She felt like punishing him but kissed him instead: slipped to his side, turned him by the chin, and crushed his lips with hers. For a moment it won out against everything else, and a soft-ness crept up in her that she longed for and feared.

"You love me, then?" Robert asked, his voice shy, light, boyish. They had played this game before. She had long rehearsed her line.

"Why not?" she smiled. "Any day now you'll be rich."

"Say that you love me."

"Love?" she said, no longer quite so playful. "I'm an orphan. They cut out our hearts at the gates. Didn't you know?"

A crow cawed, flew in through the half-open window, the curtain catching on its wing. It was Yussuf; she had raised him from a chick. He landed on the headboard of her bed; hopped onto her shoulder, then settled on his.

"You've stolen his heart," she complained, then realized it was true.

"I think it's my jacket. Black. I remind him of his mother."

She did not show her hurt at once. It was another lesson of the orphanage: that one is a fool to divulge one's tender spots. They kissed again, her eyes wide open, Yussuf cawing in her ear. She chased the bird, jumped up, made for the door. Mechanically, Robert stood up to follow.

"Where are you going?" he asked.

"To piss. You want to walk me to the bowl?"

Her irritation spent itself in the slamming of the door. By the time she'd reached the stairs, her anger had already flown.

2.

Eva did not go to the toilet, but rather downstairs, to the kitchen, wishing to eat and to collect a bundle of food. It was past nine o'clock at night. She walked along without turning on a light, the hallway carpet crusty under her naked feet, opened the kitchen door, found a shadow pressed against the window. Frau Seidel turned momentarily, just long enough to ascertain who had come. Then her attention wandered back into the moonlit night.

Unperturbed, Eva went through the cupboards. There was a drawer to which only she had the key. She took out the bundle she had come for, put it ready by the door; reached back into the drawer for a tin, spooned corned beef onto salt crackers. In the quiet of the kitchen her chewing sounded very loud. She wondered sometimes what Frau Seidel ate; most of the cupboards were empty of food. Not that she cared if the woman lived or starved.

"What is it?" she asked at last, curious despite herself. "Still looking for ghosts?"

"I saw him," the older woman replied after a pause. "I saw him clear as day. He's out there somewhere."

Eva failed to mask her interest. "You saw him tonight?"

She received a grunt in reply.

"I'm surprised you haven't got a shotgun there. Ready to pick him off."

The shadow shifted, pressed something to her bosom. For a glum moment Eva considered whether she had accidentally hit the mark. Surely the woman was not as crazy as that.

"The moon's too bright," Frau Seidel said presently, though she remained standing at the window. "He won't come back."

She turned around at last, saw the half-eaten plate of crackers, reached for it then stopped her hand.

"Go ahead," muttered Eva. "Have it. I'm done."

She walked away, stopped, watched Frau Seidel stuff her face.

"The trial took an interesting turn today. Robert told me. Wolfgang's sure to be convicted."

Frau Seidel grunted, chewed.

"You know," Eva carried on, "I didn't understand at first. For the longest time I thought that all you wanted was for Wolfgang to get off and come home. But that's nonsense. He's not your blood, after all. Better if Robert gets it all. The factory, I mean."

Frau Seidel moved a hand. At first Eva thought she was shaking her fist at her, or making an obscene gesture. But she was just chasing a cracker that had got stuck to her teeth.

"He says he'll testify, Wolfgang does. He told Robert to tell you. That he wants to 'make a clean breast of things.'" Eva paused. "Of course, it mightn't get to that. They called me as a witness, you see. Tomorrow afternoon."

"What will you say?" It came out muffled, soggy, between fingers, shards of cracker flying through the dark. Then: "There's money."

Eva snorted. "Yes, I suppose there is. And a berth to Ecuador. Or the Argentines. I imagine you've already packed my suitcase. How much will you pay me? No, tell me, I want to know what I'm worth." She waited, received no response, Frau Seidel hiding behind mastication. "You know what I want," Eva added at last.

"You can't have him."

"We've had this conversation. And look whose bed I'll be sleeping in tonight."

Eva picked up the bundle, left the kitchen, and the house, without another word. Outside, in the pale light of the waning moon, a ghost made water in the thorny shelter of the hedge.

3.

It was a cold night, cloudy, each inhalation thick with rotting leaves. Still buttoning her coat, Eva hurried down the hill. She had timed it well: the tram arrived as she approached the stop. She found a seat, watched the people around her. There was a fat-faced boy who was holding his dog by its collar; his knees bright red where he'd scraped them and had them daubed with iodine. A drunk hung in the leather handles that were fastened at regular intervals to the ceiling; he had threaded his wrists through their hoops, lost his footing in every bend, then pulled himself upright in the straights. A GI in uniform climbed on two stops down the road; he found her face, smiled, then caught sight of her hump; grimaced and passed her a cigarette in consolation. She found some matches in her pocket and lit it at once; spat smoke at her reflection in the glass. For the whole of the journey she never once glanced back at the tram compartment behind.

She changed trams when she reached the Gürtel, then got off and walked the last few hundred yards. It was one of the city's least salubrious areas, home to hookers, pimps, drunks, and vagrants. Outside a public house there stood a crowd of men watching two adolescents fight. They might have been sixteen years old: knives out, one arm cut and blood-slick from bicep to the bone-grip in his palm. She pushed straight through the crowd, ignored the stares of the men. Her back offered her protection: if her face drew them to her, her hump chased them off.

There was something else that gave her confidence. For the past three months, ever since Robert had brought her the photo of her younger self, she had nurtured the fantasy that the stranger had been watching her. Not the house, not Robert, nor yet his mother, but precisely her. So precious was this hope, and yet so fragile, that she took care never to ascribe to the man his proper name. He was as elusive to her as a dream. No one but Robert had ever seen him, and even Robert had not clapped eyes on the watcher since the night they had wrestled in the mud. There were times, to be sure, when, out running errands, she thought she'd caught a glimpse of him from the corner of her eye. He looked just like Robert had said: a shabby figure in a long red scarf. Initially she had turned at every street corner and tried to catch him out, but had since decided that he had reasons to be shy. In some childish recess of her heart she had long supplied him with a role. He was her guardian angel. Nothing could happen to her. He foresaw the future. He could walk through walls. One touch and he'd uncoil her spine.

Another twenty steps brought her to her destination. She climbed the steps, cleared the threshold without hesitation. It was an establishment somewhere between hotel and flophouse: a half-lit lobby, the air bitter with cold smoke. The concierge raised a greeting hand. He recognized her from previous visits; she did not know whether he took her for a whore. She climbed the naked stairs to the fifth floor, walked the narrow corridor nearly to the end: peeling wallpaper, dark halos scorched by bulbs screwed high into the wall. Seven rooms, some reverberating with the squeak of beds behind their flimsy doors; metronomes of coin-timed love.

The room at whose door Eva stopped was quiet. She knocked and turned the handle with one motion, found the door resistant to her push. She tried again, pushed harder; earned a yelp, the dance of agitated paws, the door flying open on a narrow, dirty room. Two beds stood side by side. One sheltered a sick man covered up with blankets; the other a giant who sat, dwarfing its frame, cradling a yelping three-legged mutt.

"*Grüss Gott,* Anneliese, *ahoj*, and welcome!" said Karel Neumann. "Come in, but be gentle. You almost hacked off tail of my new friend."

Eva nodded a greeting, and took two steps into the dirty room.

4.

He started talking at once, not even waiting until she had closed the door, dropping articles in his familiar manner, and all the while stroking the little dog, first its back, then, once it had rolled over in his giant hands, its pink and almost furless belly.

"How do you like him? I named him Franz Josef, after emperor. Something about whiskers. He came in this morning, when I was eating breakfast, cold sausage on dry roll. Put his snout right in my crotch, like a right little strumpet. Manager wants to throw him out, give him a good hiding. But why, I ask you, he's just looking for scraps, just like the rest of us. Got into a fight, see?" He grabbed the dog's hindquarters and showed her the stump. "A proper Austrian: three paws and an appetite. Until a year ago he was German, and had a pedigree certificate to prove it. Now he's a patriot. Applying for damages, for the thrashing he received in war. For all that, he's good boy, frisky. Gets around just fine. It's only when he pees he's in trouble. He has to squat, see, like a girl. If he tries to lift a leg, he lands on his ass."

Neumann smiled, tossed the dog onto the floor, where it immediately set to licking its tail, then picked up a newspaper that lay crumpled by the side of his bed.

"Have you seen this?" he carried on without transition. "The evening paper. Got it hot off the press. The ink was still wet. The whole thing is about the trial: blow by blow, who said what, and what did the ladies wear. Only, the spelling's pretty crummy. Look here, they wrote 'sensationel.' And every other time, 'Herr Klein' becomes 'Herr Kleun.' They do better with the pictures. I open the paper not an hour ago, and look who I find, third row from the front? Frau Anna Beer." He stabbed with one finger at a half-page illustration depicting the courtroom audience. The scene was rendered with draftsman-like precision. "Does her justice, no? A hand-some woman. Pretty hat. You think she got it in Paris?"

"How would I know?" Eva replied, irritated, and fingered her own hat as though it had been criticized by comparison.

"Ah, don't grow angry, Lieschen. Sit, sit." He pointed to the foot of his dirty bed. "Sit and talk. You brought me food? You're an angel, you are."

He unpacked the bundle she had brought and immediately set to demolishing its contents.

They had met two weeks previously. She had been out making pur-chases. Specifically, she had been looking for silk stockings, motivated by an incoherent but vivid desire to show off her legs "when the time came" (she was very careful never once to shape the word "engagement," let alone "wedding," even to herself). The search had brought her to a rubble-strewn courtyard in the fifth district. A number of people, not all of them shabbily dressed, stood nonchalantly next to bundles of goods, not all of them illegal; some boys on the lookout near the gate. Neumann was there, haggling with a man who was leaning on his bicycle with a rucksack worth of produce. She recognized him at once—who else had his frame? As she followed him from vendor to vendor (he seemed to be trying to trade his coat, to no great success), her hand fingered the money she had received from him. It had remained, all those weeks, intact in her pocket, folded in half and made fast to the fabric with a safety pin. She'd had no occasion to break so large a bill.

At length he too noticed her: whirled around, tried to place her, scanned her hump, and started grinning. "Anneliese!" he called, as though greeting an old friend. "Fancy meeting you here."

Her answer was curt. "Karel Neumann. You're broke."

A shrug of the shoulders. "Always. And last time I was handing out the dough like I was growing it."

They did not appear to bother him, these vagaries of property and loss. Nonetheless the remark placed on her the weight of obligation.

She nearly gave it back. The bill was right there in her fist, she even slipped it out of her pocket. But then she stuck it back onto the pin her fingers had so dexterously undone; dug around the much-washed cotton and produced a number of coins, spread them out along her upstretched palm. He watched all this with peculiar focus, as though aware of the lightning struggle precipitated by his casual remark. For a moment there settled between them a kind of perfect understanding. A quiver ran through her, of shame then anger, but—with a grace she had not suspected in him—he diffused it at once, allowing her to pretend he had not noticed her act of aborted generosity; took the coins, shook them jangling in the cup of his great fist, and spoke.

"I need a drink. Want one?"

She said no; he bought her one anyway, at the shabby public house right on the corner of the dirty yard, the patrons little more than beggars, nursing dirty mugs of homemade schnapps. She had never before sat with a man to drink. No one around her seemed to see anything unusual in the act.

"I haven't seen you since that day," she said, uneasy with the situation. "I expected to find you loafing around."

"So you haven't heard?" he answered, surprised. "I *disappeared*. The Russians picked me up." He sounded hesitant, as though he could hardly credit it himself. "Two months of questions, day and night. Then they let me go again. Funny, eh?"

"Did you see Anton?"

The note of hope caught his attention. He shook his head. "They must still have him," he said curtly, all his usual humour gone out of his voice.

He went on drinking until he had run through all her coins. She sat there watching him, still on her first glass, each sip a caustic burn on tongue and gums. When the money was gone, Karel staggered to his feet with drunken sadness and reached over to shake her hand.

"So long, Lieschen."

"What are you going to do?"

"Emmy-grate," he said, drawling out the word as though it were some private joke. "Yah-merika. Or maybe Canada. Wherever they'll have me. I already have a passport. That is to say, I almost do. I know a man who knows a man . . ." He gestured vaguely over one shoulder. "I just need the money."

"You could ask Anna Beer. Does she know you are back?"

He frowned. "I thought about going to her. To her, or to my Sophie. No good, though. There'll be a thousand questions. And in the end, they'll go to the police. And once the police get involved . . ." He shook his head as though to clear some inner fog, turned away from her then swung right back, grabbed for her arm but missed it, his left foot losing its grip on the slick tiling. "Whatever else you may hear," he whispered to her as he picked himself up, "he loves you, your Anton. He went looking for you. He told me so himself."

She gave him ten yards' head start then followed after him, wishing to find out where he lived.

5.

Since that day, she had gone to see him five or six times. From her second visit she'd been bringing him food. Her reason, she told herself, was this: Karel Neumann was her only connection to Anton Beer. He had seen him, talked to him, as recently as four months ago; had told him about Eva. Her own memory of Beer was disconcertingly vague. He had taken her in after her father had died (her mother had left them in her infancy). There had been some others who had helped, but it was the doctor who remained with her. One scene in particular: Beer at the kitchen table, buttering bread. There had been strawberry preserves that morning: an earthenware jar. Eva would have been most distraught had anyone suggested it had been glass. Her childhood had ended a day or two later; there had been a teddy, a hedgehog, and a box of coloured pencils.

But it wasn't just Beer that brought her back to Neumann. Truth be told, they hardly spoke of him. She had no interest in soldiers' anecdotes, did not want to see the man cheapened by accounts of his trudging through the Russian mud. The big Czech himself offered her something she had never had. Naturally, she did not trust him; the orphanage had proofed her against trust. Nonetheless she found that she could talk to him. There was to him a crude sort of honesty that was refreshing, new to her: not the heartfelt earnestness of Robert, with its poetic yearning for a final truth, but something coarser, simpler, more aligned with her experience of the world. Then too, one could never feel ashamed before him, for he was entirely shameless. All that was sour in her nature—all that rankled—could be let out of the box, show itself; preen. Not that she took to talk easily; she weighed every word, guarded it, whistled some back. Even so, more escaped than she would have expected: he summoned them forth, proved astonishingly adept at guessing her thoughts and feelings; it was as though they neighboured on his own. And thus a friendship sprang up between the giant and the crooked girl—a friendship threaded with caution, barbs, and scornful disavowal— but a friendship nonetheless. It only added to its flavour that they conducted it in secret. She held on to it as insurance against the frailties of love.

Up in his room he now stood, stretching and feeding the last of the food to his dog, while she loafed on his bed and thumbed through the paper. Other than her handouts it was not clear what he lived on. True, he hardly paid any rent. Nobody else had wanted to share the room with the sick man. They did not even know his name. He was a young lad, blond, the eyes an eerie shade of grey that turned transparent in the lamplight. A woman had brought him, unloaded him on the manager, and paid a month in advance. Twice a day she stopped by, fed him, changed him, combed his hair. It was a mystery that he was still alive. Much of the time he lay in a sort of delirium, muttering to himself in Polish: a tumour the size of a wasp's nest grown into the soft parts of his throat. He should have been in hospital, but it was clear he had no papers. A DP camp might have taken him, but it appeared he preferred the flophouse. Eva did not blame him. She thought of camps as another type of orphanage.

Karel, at any rate, did not seem in any way put out by the sick man. From time to time he walked up to him, squeezed a sponge of water against his lips or moistened his eyes; slipped off his diapers when he had fouled himself. Mostly, though, he just ignored him. For all they knew, he had not a word of German.

"So," Karel said, lighting a cigarette and leaning his bulk against the frame of the open window. "Talk to me. How is the lover boy?"

She picked up his bantering tone, mirrored it. "Absurd. You know what he tells me yesterday? He looks at me, real serious. I am combing my hair, sitting on my bed, and he sidles up, actually sidles, eyes wet with his thought, falls to his knees, and asks me to tell him my life story. 'You can tell me everything, everything,' he says, and that he's 'infinitely beneath me.' It's because I have 'suffered' while he was being 'pampered' in Switzerland, or something of the sort." She smiled in attempted mockery. "I swear he has it from a novel. He reads such trash."

Karel laughed and wagged his finger. "Liese, Liese, Liese. What a silly girl you are. You love this boy, he's the first who's been nice to you, you even stay up at night, thinking of his kisses. Don't say you don't—you admitted it the other day, not directly, of course, but all the same. And yet you come here to sneer at him."

She flushed at his reprimand, grew more reflective. "I told him today that his brother has a blot on his soul."

"Let me guess. You know because you yourself—" He screwed a thumb into his temple as though squashing a bug, and at the same time wrinkled his nose, to mark a bad smell. "It's why we get on, eh? My own soul—a *Scheißhaufen*. Pile of feckin' turds. But singing voice is a nice baritone. It balances out." He grinned, produced a flask from his pocket, took a swig. "And how is Mama? Picked out a wedding dress for you yet?"

"She'll see me buried first."

"Screw her, then. What do you care about her blessing? Run away with him. Or won't he go?" He studied her, seemed to catch something in her expression. "No, that's not it. You want him, but you also want the inheritance. Greedy, eh? No, no, don't get mad, Liese. What's to admitting it?"

She sat there, angry, then thoughtful. There was something tentative to her justification, as though it were the first time she was trying it out.

"It'll make me straight," she explained. "The money." When he looked at her, baffled, she reached around herself, patted her back.

"Surgery?" he asked, confused.

"Not like that. But if I wore furs—do you think anyone would notice I'm bent?"

He thought about this, brow furrowed. "Does the boy mind?" he asked at last.

She blanched. "I suppose," she whispered. "Surely. He must."

"Then why would he marry you?" The question was brutal, but the big face was kind.

"Pity."

"That's awful, Liese, just awful. But there, you don't quite mean it. You say it with a quiver. Like you're hoping it's a lie. It might be, at that. It's you who won't believe it."

She started, surprised by this assessment, coloured at the thought that she had given away so much. All the same it was hard to stop. She had so rarely spoken her mind.

"In any case, she *will* give her consent. I'm going to testify. I was meant to go on three days ago, right at the start of things, but I cried off sick. Earned myself a reprimand! They put me at the end instead. For the finale!" Her eyes flashed. "She's already tried to bribe me. She'll soon meet my price."

"She really thinks you can save Wolfgang? What does she care about her stepson, anyway?"

"It isn't that. She's worried about losing the factory. And the house." She smiled, pleased by her sense of power. "You should see how she skulks around. Not a wink of sleep. Stands by the window all night, on the lookout for the watcher. I swear she has a gun."

Karel leaned forward, interested, one hand stroking his big chin. "I don't get it," he said. "Who is this watcher?"

Eva hesitated before she answered, unsure what she might lose by sharing the truth. But what good was it, her secret, if she never once got to show it off? "He is a Jew."

"Go on."

"Arnim Rothmann. Has a ring, doesn't it: 'Rothmann & Seidel.'" She sketched the ampersand.

Karel whistled. "Seidel's partner."

"Senior partner. The factory used to be his. The house, too. Till '38."

"I see. Seidel stole them from him. Why fret, though? That was the fashion, wasn't it? Aryanization. Half of Vienna changed hands."

She shook her head. "Not like this. There was a contract. Some sort of buyback clause. I found Frau Seidel rummaging for it not half an hour after they had scraped her husband off the front lawn."

"So ever since the war ended, they have been waiting for Rothmann to come back and ask for the keys!" The big man laughed, pushed off the wall, and started pacing the room, the mutt, Franz Josef, tangling in his feet. "No wonder she is snorting powders. How about him, though, the right honourable Paul Seidel, RIP? Was he willing to pay up?" He stopped abruptly as a new thought dawned on his face. "Or was it Rothmann who pushed Seidel? He came back, half crazy from the camps, asked for his share. They had a fight!" He returned to his pacing, took a few more turns, digesting the idea. "Is that how it was? But then, how does Wolfgang fit into it all?"

But Eva had no intention of parting with all her secrets. "Who's to say," she said blandly. "Perhaps the stranger isn't Rothmann at all. Rothmann was fat: Frau Seidel has a photo. Though of course—"

"Why yes. The Auschwitz diet."

She shook her head, thoughtful, defiant. "It could be a mix-up. Perhaps he is simply some madman. Or—"

"Beer? You're still holding out hope, eh?" He made a face. "Forget about Beer. The Russians have him. He is in Siberia, mining for ore."

She flinched but did not answer.

"What is he to you, anyway? He was nice to you when you were a child. It isn't much."

She stared back at him, defiant. "He didn't forget about me."

"No," he admitted. "He talked about you all the time." And he told her again how Anton Beer had told him that she was the sweetest girl in all the world.

She listened in silence, slipped out some minutes later, feeling happy; walked the dark streets of the Gürtel, picturing Anton Beer walking like an angel at her back, wings spread and holding a slim white umbrella lest a drop of rain disturb her peace.

6.

Robert was asleep when she returned to the house. He lay, still dressed, underneath the open window, a book open on his chest; a cold draft whistling through the room as she opened the door.

Eva crept inside on tiptoe. She took off her clothes and crawled naked into bed with him; lay on her flank and did not touch him with more than one breast pressed gently into the fold of his black jacket.

"I love you," she tried, hesitantly, shyly, not quite in earnest, the way a child might try it out on the playground, playing "family" with the six-year-old son of a butcher who has snot dangling from his nose. "Will you run away with me? To Yah-merika?"

He sighed in his sleep and did not wake.

Four

1.

Halfway between the State Opera House and the Burgtheater, on the western side of Vienna's most sumptuous street, the Ringstrasse, which encircles the inner city like a wedding band—or a vise—there lies, boxed in by those architectural twins the Natural History Museum and the Art History Museum, a small but beautifully manicured park whose geometric bushes and ornate benches had to contend, at the time, with a mound of rubble that had been swept there from adjacent streets and formed a sizable pile. In this park, on one of the benches not far from the rubble, there sat, on a damp day in late October, a policeman's daughter in a mud-streaked dress and a runty little boy who had recently served as witness in a murder trial. The two children were deep in discussion. They had stuck their heads together and were not so much speaking as transferring confidences from mouth to ear. The subject of their pow-wow was the weighty question of whether the girl's father harboured feelings for Frau Anna Beer. The girl—Trudi—rather inclined to the opinion that he did.

"I saw her kiss his hand. Like this." She acted out the scene she had witnessed in the café, using Karlchen's hand for a prop. "She isn't even very pretty. She's got a mean face. But father is feeling lonely. Ever since Mammy died."

Karlchen sat there, rubbing the back of his hand. They were eating candies that his brother, Franz, had procured. Her kiss had been sticky.

"Maybe it's her bum," he said at length. "Steinbeisser says that it's the bum that matters. It has to be round. From underneath."

Trudi bit down on her lip, intrigued by this theory, which was quite new to her. "Mine's flat," she said, getting up from the bench, drawing the dress tight around her body, and looking down over one shoulder.

"That's because you're a girl. It only grows once you turn into a woman." He paused, followed her gaze, the two of them studying her rump with close attention. "When it does, it'll be just right. You'll see."

The topic closed, he pulled a torn and wrinkled comic book from his pocket and offered it to his friend. It showed a muscular woman in a short, star-spangled skirt and boots. She was lifting a car and throwing it at some men. Her bum was very round indeed. The words, Karlchen explained to his friend, were in English: speech was in bubbles and thought was in clouds; fat words meant someone was shouting. *Woman* was English for Frau. Karlchen had traded an American boy for the comic: seventeen marbles, the negotiations handled with gestures and nods.

They slid closer together, sat thigh to thigh, and tried to make sense of the story. There was no problem identifying Wonderfrau's enemies: they wore big-shouldered suits and brandished guns; they did not shave. The simple fact of their conspicuousness impressed itself upon the girl.

Without introduction, she started talking about the trial.

"Father says that if the man is convicted, they will hang him. They pull out the floor from under you and then you die."

The boy understood her at once. The thought was not new to him. "It's because of what I said," he whispered. Then added, "Do you think he's a bad man?"

Trudi mulled it over. "I thought he looked nice," she said at last. She might have said "handsome," but felt it was too old for her; their neighbour had said it when she'd seen his picture in the paper: "That poor, handsome lad."

"Then they'll hang a nice man," the boy said glumly, and cursed himself for having spoken the truth.

2.

On the fourth day of the trial of Wolfgang Seidel, suspected parricide, the court was as crowded as ever. If anything, more people were jostling for space in the corridors outside the great hall, trying to push their way in and arguing with the ushers. The ushers had their hands full, for there were some in the crowd who seemed hell-bent on pressing their point. At long last they closed the doors and took position just inside the court-room, from where they followed the trial with the same rapt attention as the audience. There was a rumour, fanned by a report in the papers, that the defendant had recanted his earlier refusal to testify and would be called up that very day. The jurors too seemed to have heard of it; one could discern a new level of interest amongst their ranks.

First, though, the chief prosecutor, Dr. Fejn, was to continue with his interrogation of those witnesses who could testify to Wolfgang's propensity to violence. Just as Fejn was about to start, however, the presiding judge, Bratschul, interrupted him, leaned forward, and in a somewhat malicious phrase requested that he "spare" the court all witnesses other than those "who have been thrown out of windows, or nearly so." This phrase, unusu-ally bellicose for this otherwise rather mild-mannered man, people at once ascribed to a "hemorrhoidal attack," whose effects, it was said, could also be traced in his complexion, which, truth be told, was a little sallow that day.

Not wishing to make an enemy of Bratschul, Fejn bowed to his pressure, hemorrhoidally induced or otherwise, and immediately produced a fat lit-tle seamstress who had been threatened in a manner very similar to the pre-vious night's witness, Klein. She too had been asked to walk to the window to look into the yard beneath, then been "thrown onto the windowsill" and "dangled by the neck." But where Klein had moved the court with his cracked tortoiseshell glasses and quiet certainty, the seamstress lacked charisma, and her statement, while corroborating the defendant's modus operandi, failed to draw much of a reaction from either jury or audience. Seeing this, Dr. Fejn dismissed her at once and quietly declared that "he did not wish to belabour a point already made abundantly clear, or repeat facts already present in the minds of our most perceptive jury" (here he gave a little bow). The little speech was greeted by generous applause on the side of the audience. There could be little doubt that Fejn had carried his point. After the briefest of adjournments the defence was given the floor.

3.

Dr. Ratenkolb went to work very methodically. The first witness he interviewed was a self-satisfied doctor by the name of Schiefental. Schiefental was a familiar face. On the first day of the trial he had testified regarding the wounds found on Herr Seidel's body and had drawn a careful distinction between lesions and breaks he had acquired during a fight that preceded his fall, and those caused by the impact with the ground itself. The former included a bruise at the back of his head caused by a blow from the victim's office telephone (the object in question, one corner soiled by a smear of dried blood, had been passed around amongst the jury). In a memorable moment, designed to drive home the sheer brutality of the attack, Schiefental had himself swung the telephone with all his might, explaining that a right-handed man of such-and-such a height had struck the blow from such-and-such an angle, all the while looking at the defendant in blunt accusation. At the time Ratenkolb, aware of the effect made by these words, had asked no questions but had reserved the right to do so "at a later point." This "later point" had now arrived.

No sooner had the doctor taken his seat and made the customary promise to tell the truth (there was no formal oath) than Ratenkolb begged him to clarify if the wounds inflicted by the fight, including that infamous "collision" with the telephone, had been life-threatening. Schiefental answered in the negative.

"The blow did not fracture the skull."

"And was there anything about the wounds caused by the fall," Ratenkolb went on to ask, "that suggests that the man had been thrown rather than fallen?"

"Not with any certainty."

"In other words, no."

"Correct."

"Which is to say that the deceased may not have been pushed at all. He could have had a fight and then, say, leapt from the window of his own volition." (A murmur went through the court at this suggestion, half of anger, half of curiosity.)

"It's possible, I suppose."

"How much time might have passed between the wounds suffered during his fight and the wounds suffered from the fall?"

"Impossible to say. Not much, at any rate."

"No more than a day?"

"No more than a few hours. The swelling—"

But Ratenkolb interrupted him. "Note," he said dryly to the jury, looking over at them and speaking in particular to an elderly schoolteacher who sat in the first row, "that the deceased might have been alive for several hours after he was involved in a fight with an unknown assailant."

He dismissed Schiefental with a wave of his hand.

The next person called was a Professor Dr. Ferdinand Bündl, a bent, elderly psychiatrist who operated a well-regarded private practice in the first district. His arrival was not unexpected. Many of the real and self-proclaimed experts who followed the trial had long expected that Ratenkolb's defence would arrive at a point where Wolfgang's criminal responsibility was put into question, and at least one paper had openly speculated about the "psychiatric defence," using the thoroughly antiquated term "temporary insanity" to sketch what it had in mind. But when the judge had concluded his initial examination of Professor Bündl, which included the question of whether the defendant was to be considered sane ("Quite," the old man answered curtly), the defence lawyer displayed not the slightest interest in the topic. He focused instead on the defendant's father. What he wanted to know was whether Herr Seidel, "that is to say the deceased," had ever come to consult Bündl in a professional capacity. The answer was a quiet, musical "In-deed."

"He came to you," Ratenkolb said into the sudden quiet of the court-room, "not because he wanted to speak about his son, or his wife, but because of himself."

"Ye-hes."

"Why did he come? I beg you to remember that your patient's death absolves you from your oath of confidentiality. What was his condition?"

The old man cleared his throat then opened his arms in an expressive gesture until his palms were stretched out on either side of him. "It was far from clear. He did not have any obvious symptoms. He was anxious and asked whether I could help him."

"Anxious?"

"In-deed."

"What about?"

"He would not say. It was all rather vague."

"What did you advise him to do?"

"He came twice, each time looking at me with a certain—um—expectation. An expectation, yes. As though he were waiting for me to say some magic word. I was a little put out. The second time, I said, 'Perhaps you should talk to a priest.' He gave me a queer little smile and said, 'I have. But nothing would come out there either. Funny, eh?'"

"What was his general frame of mind?"

"He was thoughtful."

"Melancholy."

"Per-haps. It is not a clinical term."

Ratenkolb nodded, lowered his voice, his brow furrowed like that of a man who, despite his inclinations, forced himself to consider all the possi-bilities. "Do you think it possible," he asked, "that Herr Seidel committed suicide?"

The old man took his time considering his answer. When it came, there was a touch of flippancy to it. "Possible?" he said. "Why not? A great many people do."

Fejn questioned him after that, but was unable to dispel the feeling that the defence was gaining ground.

4.

Throughout the day Ratenkolb pursued a patient, two-pronged attack on the presumption of his client's guilt. The first and primary part of his strategy was to lend an air of plausibility to the theory that Seidel had taken his own life. He did so by interviewing a string of witnesses—from Seidel's factory manager to a triumvirate of business magnates with whom the deceased had been in the habit of consuming a carafe of wine on Wednesday evenings—and eliciting their impressions regarding Seidel's mental state in the weeks leading up to his death. While none of these witnesses could be tempted by the word "suicide," which Ratenkolb would, as it were, dangle before their noses like some forbidden fruit, they all agreed that Seidel had been "preoccupied" and "nervous." More than one hinted at domestic unhappiness precipitated not by Wolfgang (of whose presence in Vienna not one of the witnesses had been aware) but by "the widow Seidel." Ratenkolb seized upon this opening at once. The deceased would not be the first man, he insinuated to the jury, to grow despondent over sharing his life with a loveless wife.

The second prong of the defence lawyer's strategy was quite different in nature. It aimed at dispersing the bad impression made by the witnesses who had testified to Wolfgang's brutality and sought to establish the defendant as a man both chastened and reformed. This attempt centred on a single witness, a coarse young woman wearing traditional peasant costume, as though she were going to a country church on Sunday. The prosecutor, Fejn, watched her take the witness seat with suspicion and surprise: she had been on the prosecution's witness list until the judge had ordered Fejn to cut short his interrogation. Ratenkolb pounced on her at once.

"Do you know this man, Fräulein Hofer?" he asked, pointing to the defendant.

Her answer had the nature of a sneer. "Sure do."

"Can you describe the circumstances under which you met the accused?"

"He beat me."

"Where?"

"At the cop shop, that's where."

Ratenkolb directed her to be more specific. In a short few minutes they established the reason and time frame for her incarceration by the Gestapo. She had cut up a neighbour's SA uniform with a pair of scissors. As it turned out, the action had had personal rather than political motives. After some further questions Ratenkolb returned to the subject of her beating.

"Did the accused threaten to throw you out of any windows, Fräulein Hofer?"

"Windows? No. He slapped me. And pinched my ear. And my, you know . . ." (She pointed vaguely at her rump, rising slightly from her chair as she did so.) "A real pig, he was."

Ratenkolb nodded and turned briefly to the jury, as though to say, "Look, I have no desire to hide anything. My client acted like a cad; alas, it cannot be helped." Then he fastened his eyes back on his witness.

"Did you ever meet him again? After your interrogation, I mean?"

"Yes."

"Could you please describe the circumstances of this other meeting? When and where did it take place?"

She shrugged. "It was some time ago. I think it was June. Summer in any case. I was on the Number Five tram, late in the evening. The next stop, at the train station, he comes on with a woman. I look at him and think to myself, 'I'll be damned if it isn't that nasty young copper, well, he don't look so high and mighty now.' Dirty, he was, carrying a ragged little suitcase. And his woman! You wouldn't believe it. Almost in rags. I swear there wasn't a button left on her blouse. She was, you know: gapin'. The girl sitting next to her even stood up. I think she was afraid of catching lice."

"And what happened then, Fräulein Hofer?"

"So, here we are, me sitting on one side, and them on the other. He looks at me somehow strange, like he recognizes me but also doesn't. I just sit there glaring, thinking how he pinched me, the pig. We go a few stops, and then he suddenly gets up to leave, tugging his woman along."

"Was he in a haste?"

"Sure."

"Why?"

"I was making him, you know. Uncomfortable."

"And then?"

"He bumps me with his suitcase. On the way out. The tram sort of shakes, crossing rails, I guess, and he almost shoves his suitcase on my lap. He catches himself, looks me in the face, not like you normally look at someone, but somehow different, like he's concentrating real hard. I sit there thinking, here we go again, he's going to slap me. But he doesn't slap me. 'I apologize,' he says, real quiet, right in my ear."

"Was he referring to the suitcase, Fräulein Hofer?"

She shrugged. "Nah."

"To what, then?"

Another shrug, then a funny little snort. "You know. All that."

"You mean the interrogation. The slaps and the pinching."

She nodded.

"You think he was sincere?"

She hesitated, but only for a second. "Sure, why not."

"And? Did you forgive him?"

It took her three breaths. "I guess there're worse," she said at last.

For a moment there belonged to this coarse young woman in her country dress an air of dignity that quite electrified the courtroom. Wolfgang looked up to stare at her, and something like a sigh ran through the rows of the jury.

With the judge's permission Ratenkolb dismissed her at once. Before he had a chance to call the next witness, Bratschul interrupted proceedings and ordered an hour-long recess.

5.

Ratenkolb accompanied Wolfgang to his cell. As soon as the guard had removed Wolfgang's handcuffs and locked them in, the lawyer produced his cigarette case and offered it to his client, all the while searching Wolfgang's face with an expression halfway between amusement and anger.

"You shouldn't have looked up," he said. "You were doing just fine, sitting there with that hangdog air. Your chin was nearly on your chest. And then you looked up, just as she was saying you'd apologized to her. For 'all that.' What a naked look you gave her! It was all right there: that you did not recognize her at all and had no memory of the incident whatsoever. You simply bumped her with your suitcase; drunk, I should think, coming back to Vienna with a hole in your pocket and a useless wife. 'Sorry,' that's what you said to her, only on my suggestion she changed it to 'I apologize.' It's just as well she didn't see your face: she might have retracted it. Neither did the jury—one of the old men nearly wept. It's the public in the first two rows you've robbed of their illusions, those who were looking, anyway. Your brother, for one, I could see him grow all pale. Christ, my friend, you are on trial for murder. The least you can do is look contrite."

Wolfgang listened to all this calmly, picking two cigarettes from the case, waiting for Ratenkolb to offer him a light. He did at last, and the young man inhaled a lungful of smoke.

"What does it matter," he decided, smoke in his mouth, "if the jury didn't see?"

Ratenkolb flashed a sour smile. "Never let your lawyer know you're a rotter. It weighs us down."

"It's all rubbish anyway. So I apologized, or I didn't. But the trial, it's about father, isn't it? No apology's going to change that."

"No, no, you've got it all wrong. The trial is about whether or not you are a swine. If you are a swine, then you killed your father and to hell with you. But if you are a good lad, really, deep down that is, well then, let's forget and forgive. Who's to say you shouldn't get off?"

Wolfgang seemed to consider this, smoked the cigarette in deep, efficient drags, lit the second off its end. "What's next, then? Are you going to call in my schoolteachers? They will tell the jury that they never quite figured it out: was I lazy or just plain stupid? Then there is a little widow where I used to go, a seamstress, who specialized in schoolboys. A lovely lady, actually. She can testify that I was a most punctual boy. Never missed an appointment, and didn't overstay my welcome. I was generous, too: I stole money from my father's pocket and didn't like to skimp. Not sure it would do me much good though, as character references go."

"I have something else in mind. When Fejn dug up all those jailbirds, I asked the judge for permission to call some of your former colleagues. Ross-länder, Bienenkopf, Schramm. And half a dozen others. I've put together quite a list."

Wolfgang spat smoke. "You're calling the Gestapo crowd? It'll bury me! The jury already thinks I'm a brute. No point reminding them."

"On the contrary. It will show them what well-brought-up young men served in this most necessary branch of the state machinery. They've all come fresh from the barber. I called them all personally yesterday to remind them to polish their shoes. And they will all say the same thing: that you were responsible, diligent, calm. And that you loved your father."

"You paid them off?"

Ratenkolb frowned. "No, of course not. It's how they remember you."

"Shite." Wolfgang shook his head in genuine wonder, started pacing the cell. Of the many emotions that marked his countenance, impatience ran topmost. "So when am I coming on?"

"Not until the end, if I can help it. We want to take our time with this part of the proceedings; put some distance between the prosecution's case and the jury." Ratenkolb smiled that humourless smile of his, his eyes on his client's movements. "That's assuming, of course, you put on a good performance. We haven't rehearsed it. What exactly will you say?"

Wolfgang smiled, drew a figure in the air with the burning tip of his cigarette. "Depends how the mood takes me."

"You're thinking of jumping off a cliff, aren't you? Some dramatic confession; in your head you've already phrased it, trying to find the most shocking words. It'll feel good—for a second. Then the ground will hit you. Or rather it won't. The noose will break your fall."

"It's my neck."

"I hate losing."

Wolfgang almost laughed. "So tell them your client screwed your strategy. People will understand."

They smoked another cigarette.

"In any case," Ratenkolb said, "we'll see what the little hunchback can produce for us. I am leaving her for tomorrow too."

"She hates me."

The lawyer shook his head. "Not hate, no. Indifference. But there are other interests involved."

6.

When the trial resumed, at a quarter past three, the first thing Anna Beer noticed was that Robert had left. It was the first time he had absented himself from the proceedings; she wondered what it was about the last witness's testimony that had turned him away.

The afternoon proved wearisome, young men smiling with good teeth and musing on the weight of duty. Not even Fejn's remonstrations could draw from them a bead of sweat. The long procession of witnesses was enlivened only by the rumour, spreading like wildfire through the courtroom, that a lone woman was stalking the hallways outside the courtroom and that this woman—confused in her bearing and muttering angrily to herself— was none other than the accused's mother. A man in the audience, a shabby little postal clerk who had taken his holidays to attend the proceedings, from "civic interest" as he put it, even claimed that she had spoken to him during the recess and had pressed him to tell her whether "the hunchback has spoken yet." Several members of the public in attendance, Sophie Coburn among them, took it upon themselves to locate this mysterious woman and ascertain whether she was indeed the defendant's mother. They found her not far from the doors of the courtroom, conversing with an usher; she was holding him by the sleeve of his uniform and making him swear an oath to something or other. The woman left soon after, shaking a fist at this huddle of spectators, her plump face shaking with indignation. It was quickly decided that she was merely some madwoman who had stumbled into the courthouse: the defendant's mother was rich, it was said, and would not be seen dead in that shabby dress from which a dirty negligee protruded at the back. Anna listened to Sophie's whispered description without comment, calling to mind Robert's account of his reunion with his mother. She saw no reason in fuelling the little journalist's hunger for sensation.

Ratenkolb's list of witnesses was not yet exhausted when the weary judge rose from his chair and called for an end to the day's proceedings. It was gone six by then. Anna and Sophie walked out together, the latter with a distracted sense of urgency that had clung to her the whole day. Anna was about to ask if she would join her for dinner when a man who had been standing in the shadow of the building stepped close to them and, with a wave of his hand, requested a private conversation. His hat and overcoat, and the failing light, made it difficult to study his face and figure, but there was something about his gesture—a studied elegance not quite feminine—that made recognition immediate.

"Herr Kis," Anna greeted her husband's lover.

"Frau Beer." His bow held something repulsive for her, insinuated a familiarity, even a tenderness, entirely foreign to their relationship. "I saw your picture in the papers. In the trial coverage. The sketch artist admires your beauty." He smiled weakly, obviously nervous, both cheeks dappled with light acne.

"What do you want?" she asked.

He shook his head, flustered by her tone, raised a gloved hand to run it along the line of his moustache. "I have been thinking about Anton," he said after a pause. "I simply cannot comprehend—" His eyes grew soft;

not weepy, mind, but simply soft, filled with remembrance of sweet hours past. It took an effort to remain civil to this man.

"Have you seen him, Herr Kis?"

"No, no."

"Do you know where he is?"

He shook his head, wearily, sadly, the brim of his soft hat lending drama to the movement.

"Then I have no wish to speak to you."

She turned and he tried to stop her, put his hand to her arm. Her fist came up unexpectedly. It did not hit him but hovered an inch from his face. She uncoiled one finger, defusing the fist but not the gesture; stabbed it into his upturned collar, a dozen epithets for his kind rising to her tongue, barnyard phrases she had not known were hers to command. Kis flushed as she began listing them, ran off in hasty little steps that her wounded heart called mincing. Some twenty yards from her he slipped upon the cobbles, dipped his arse into a dirty puddle, then quickly hobbled out of sight.

When Anna Beer turned to search for Sophie, the little journalist was nowhere to be found.

7.

Sophie was glad she had been able to give Anna Beer the slip without the need for explanation. She had what she thought of as a private matter to attend to. Despite the many hours they had spent together, no real friendship had sprung up between the journalist and the doctor's wife. There was something cold, unyielding, to Anna that was alien to Sophie; it went beyond reserve and seemed too relentless to be simply a matter of temperament. It was as though Anna Beer had taught herself to stand apart. Sophie had a good understanding of the reasons for this—Karel Neumann had explained it all quite graphically—but nonetheless found it hard not to place the blame on Anna, the spurned wife.

Herself, she could have used a friend. She was sick of Vienna, of the soldiers and checkpoints, the broken buildings and dirty urchins, the greedy begging for her castoffs; was sick, too, of the shared apartment, the scheming tenants, the filthy hallway, the squalor of her tiny room; was sick even of this trial that she covered so diligently and that was beginning to make her name, somewhere, on the other side of the ocean, where there stood an empty house full of photos of a man who had burned to death for raining bombs upon this city. The longer she stayed, the more she found herself isolated. Even her friends at the embassy returned fewer and fewer of her phone calls. She was a crackpot, a paranoid, had ruffled feathers in her search for Anton Beer.

Sophie had come, half a year ago, to mourn her husband and to earn a reputation for her pen. Back then these goals had seemed to her harmonious. Now, sitting at home stooped over typed-up notes, she caught a mocking note in the face reflected by the wardrobe mirror, before it was lost in the rehearsal of a hundred neurasthenic ticks.

She arrived at her destination. She had been there before and found it much as she had left it: a side-street tavern hosting shabby clerks and careworn workers; a group of British soldiers doting on some local girls. Sophie's arrival called forth the type of scrutiny familiar to unaccompanied women. Her tailored wealth attracted notice, if not the scrawny body that it dressed; her face too foreign to invite the risk of an approach. She sat down at a table, asked for the waiter who had called her on the telephone the previous night, and slipped him a coin as soon as he appeared.

"You must order a drink," he said, pocketing the coin. "If you're going to sit.

"What?" he added, in answer to her inquiring glance. "I've told you all I know. If you want more, you've got to ask her." He pointed to a waitress who was sitting, knees pushed wide, astride a soldier's thigh and laughing at his joke. "It's her that saw him. Only she's busy now. I'll let her know you're here."

She nodded, ordered wine and water in her broken German, sat and watched, but looked away whenever someone gave her a searching glance.

The waitress took her time, or rather the soldier did, sat drinking with his comrades, one arm wrapped about the woman's waist. She was neither young nor yet middle-aged; a bluff face and a bluff body, not without a fleshy sort of charm. What she did command was a brazen sort of wit: they traded jokes, she and the soldier, drank down shots of apple brandy to giggling, broken-Englished toasts; the soldier's hand on her stomach, holding on to those maternal rolls of fat. He rose at last, walked her over to the entrance. She came to a halt when Sophie waved at her; stood for a moment, one arm hooked into the soldier's, torn between two different sources of income; then turned to her suitor, whispered something in his ear, and waddled off, hips swinging, to the back door and the stairwell beyond that housed the toilet. Sophie followed her at once.

They spoke on the minuscule landing, the toilet door leaning open between them, its painted wood scarred with a hundred invitations and rebuttals, heart-framed commemorations of young love. The floor was littered with strips of newspaper that had been dropped while similar strips were put to sanitary use. Sophie felt her eyes pick through the headlines even as she phrased her question.

"The waiter—Herr Frobel—he called me last night to say he saw the man I'm looking for. Now he tells me it's you who saw him. Is that true?"

The woman shrugged and turned one hand to show a calloused palm. A coin got her started. Her English was surprisingly good.

"I heard that some weeks ago you came here to ask for the giant," she said. "I had not the telephone number. Frobel has. So he makes the call. He wanted to earn some shillings too."

"He got his coin. But it's you who saw him. Karel Neumann. That's who I've been looking for."

The waitress shook her head. "His name I do not know. But it's the one that was here, three, four months ago. Drinks much. A big man. Very ugly. Thin, no meat on the bones, but his shoulders like a bull." She spread her arms. "A giant."

"Tell me all you know. Here, I'll give you five more shillings. That's all you're getting."

The waitress took the money and made an odd movement with her body. On reflection Sophie identified it as a curtsy.

"It was like this. He comes in two days ago. Before midday. Nobody was here, only I, cleaning. He buys beer to take home. I need somewhere to put it. He has no glass, but has old—" She hesitated, pointed to the light hanging off a cord inside the toilet. "A *Scheinwerfer*."

"A bulb? A lamp of some kind?"

"A lamp, yes. From the front of a motorcycle. Like this." She formed her hands into a globe some six inches across. "He says, pour beer in here. I want to see money first. He pays, I pour. Four litres go in and the lamp is not half full. He drinks a little from top. Then he goes."

"Did you follow him?"

"No. I was cleaning, I must stay. But I asked around. People have seen him. They say he lives on Gürtel somewhere. And that he has a girlfriend."

"A girlfriend?"

The waitress laughed, threw her shoulders up and forward, retracted her neck. "Girl with lump. On her back. Young, I hear." She laughed again, then noticed the effect her words were having on the journalist. "You like him?" she asked, surprised. "I see. He belongs to you. I'm sorry. He'll come back."

But Sophie had already come to a decision; stood chin raised in defiance of her emotions and the implications of the waitress's news. "It wasn't him," she said. "Not Karel. He'd contact me if he'd escaped. To ask for money if nothing else." She smiled a half smile, too unformed to call bitter, then dismissed the waitress with a movement of her head. "Go. Your soldier is waiting. I have given you all I'm going to."

To Sophie's surprise the woman did not argue, but rather left her with a comradely clap upon one shoulder, her hand as strong as any man's.

No sooner had she gone than Sophie Coburn locked herself in the toilet and sat in the dark upon the wooden lid, not crying, not thinking, her square heels planted amongst the scraps of soggy newspaper strewn upon the ground.

8.

The night was growing late. Eva was restless, contrived reasons to walk into the kitchen, sat at the table chewing crackers, chocolate, tinned sardines. Frau Seidel never turned to look. She seemed immobile, rooted to the spot; stood by the window, eyes fixed on the glass. Yesterday's newspaper announcing that Eva would testify lay where she had left it the previous night, thrown upon the kitchen sideboard, the section circled in red ink.

The day had not gone as planned. All morning, dressing, brushing her hair, Eva had waited for Frau Seidel to notice the paper and intervene: to approach her, beg her, sell her son. Eva had waited so long that she arrived at the courthouse long after the appointed hour. Robert had been there, greeted her outside the courthouse, led her inside. He was friendly with the ushers, was allowed to sit with her in the waiting room reserved for witnesses, an unspoken question in his eyes. Around nightfall a clerk had relieved them: her testimony had been postponed. When they arrived back home, Frau Seidel had already taken up her station, mute, unyielding, absorbed in the study of the yard.

Frustrated, too worn out to challenge her directly, Eva left the kitchen, went upstairs. She got ready for bed, shooed Yussuf off her pillow, dirty claw prints on the linen. Robert was there, looking at her but avoiding her eyes.

"You are afraid to ask," she accused him. "'*What will you say? When you walk through that door tomorrow? Will you bury my brother or rescue him?'* It's been written all over your mug the entire day."

He blanched, fidgeted, sat on the bed, and lay down on his side. "Just tell the truth," he said.

"You don't mean it. You might not like the truth. But then, it'd be immoral to ask me to lie."

He did not answer, and she climbed behind him so her hump was to the wall. He was wearing his nightshirt and a pair of underpants. She knew both intimately. In the past few months Eva had returned to doing the washing.

"Turn off the light," she said. "And close the window. It's cold."

"Did you talk to Mother?"

"Turn off the light," she repeated, and after some minutes he got up and did.

9.

The girl had finally gone upstairs. Frau Seidel stood immobile for some further minutes, then sighed and took a vial out of the pocket of her cardigan, mixed some drops into a glass of water, drank it down. Each of her movements was reflected in the window's dirty pane. Her handbag lay on the windowsill, a bundle wrapped in a dishcloth at the top. The garden outside was totally dark. As the drug took its effect, a detached calm rose up in her like the waterline of a hot bath. She sat down at the kitchen table, her legs very heavy, stretched them out across a second chair.

When she woke, she was disorientated at first; was cold too, her feet wooden and dead to the touch. It took some minutes to stamp new circulation into her heels and toes, a painful tingling that cut through the drug. It might have been midnight by now: a waxing moon clinging to the window frame. Its light caught the newspaper, the red circle around paragraph five. *Herr Seidel's charwoman*, it read, *one Anneliese Gruber. Further sensations are expected.* They seemed unable to get a single fact straight.

Her feet revived, her body heavy, Frau Seidel rose and started on the stairs. She bypassed the first floor, carrying on up; walked the long corridor that led to the maid's quarters. Outside she stopped, dug in her handbag, her shoulders hunched. She opened the door, peered inside, waited for her eyes to adjust. They lay on their sides, her front pressed into his back, both heads on the pillow, one behind the other. Emotion came to her, came dimly, through the wall of opiates; not all of it was laced with spite. Her son looked peaceful, happy, his hair very dark. She could count his breaths by the rise and fall of his narrow chest; a snort of cold in his nose when he exhaled. The room was icy, they had failed to close the window properly, had kicked the too-thin duvet down to the level of their waists.

The open door added a draft to the cold, and it was this draft that woke them, first him, then her: two pale faces, stirring, robbed of features by the dark. She spoke to the girl, not to him.

"You can have him," she declared, her hand in her handbag, amongst vials, tissues, a dead weight wrapped in threadbare cotton.

The girl sat up enough to signal confrontation. "How do I know?" she whispered. "That you'll honour the bargain?"

"He heard it, didn't he?" Frau Seidel said. "You have it, I say. My consent."

She waited for some further humiliation: chest squared, chin drawn into the soft skin of her throat.

"Thank you," said the girl on the bed, said it almost softly.

Frau Seidel closed the door before her son could add his thanks.

Five

1.

Anna was in bed when the doorbell rang. She woke, disorientated, within the sweat-damp tangle of her hair. For some strange reason she decided that it must be Frisch bringing news of Anton. She rose quickly, slipped into her dressing gown, hurried over icy floorboards without taking the time to locate her slippers. A hand run through her hair and a quick adjustment of the belt had to suffice as her toilette. She opened the door with a touch of drama: head cocked, brow raised, one fist pressed into a pushed-out hip. Her excitement was misplaced.

It was Sophie.

"What time is it?" asked Anna.

"Ten past six."

"You're early."

"I couldn't sleep. I was hoping you'd be up."

Anna let her in. It was tempting to send her away and crawl back into the warmth of her bed, but there was on Sophie's face a restless urgency that appealed to Anna's sense of decency if not to her compassion.

"Come in, then. Let's have some coffee."

They sat in the kitchen, or rather Anna sat, one naked leg crossed over the other. Sophie busied herself with setting the table for breakfast as though she were the host and Anna her guest. Anna let her do it; took a cigarette from the pack lying open on the table and asked Sophie for a light. The journalist hurried to the stove and found the matches.

"Would you like one?" Anna offered, then leaned towards the struck match with a habitual movement, her lips pursed around the cigarette end, her eyelids lowered, showing off long lashes.

"Coffee first. Here, I'll put on the pot.

"The trial starts at eight," Sophie added when she had finally sat down and wrapped her hands around a steaming cup.

Some day-old rolls lay in a basket between them; a china saucer with an ounce or two of butter; a glass of synthetic honey; the grey wedge of liverwurst that had not been wrapped properly and had dried out. Neither of them showed any interest in the food.

"You will come, won't you, Anna? It's the last day. We might even get a verdict. Depending on the jury, of course."

Anna did not answer at once; sipped her coffee, remarked on the absence of lipstick, whose flavour she associated with the drink.

"What is it you came to tell me?" she asked at last. It came out more gently than she expected, as though the words themselves carried enough weight to dissolve her petty irritation. Sophie noticed it too, the formality of her phrase; sat up in her chair, a flutter of emotions on her brow and cheeks.

"Have you," she asked very cautiously, her eyes on the table, "in the course of your life, I mean—Have you slept with many men?"

Again the answer was gentle. "Is that what you woke me for?"

"Yes. In a way."

"Five or six," Anna said. "Six. For comfort, mostly." She smiled: the sort of smile that effaces emotion. "I chose rich men." She could have softened her answer; explained that there was more to it than that. That she had been lonely, in need of evidence that men liked her; that it was only her husband she had failed to seduce. But Sophie wasn't listening; and at any rate, Anna hated excuses.

"I only ever slept with my husband. And, you know—with Neumann." Sophie paused, kept her eyes on the saucers, the honey, and the liverwurst. "He's a better lover than my husband was. It's not that he does anything very different. I mean, the . . . mechanics, they are the same, give or take. But—" Here she looked up with a reckless sort of courage. "I liked it better. He made me feel things, I hadn't—And the things that would come out of my mouth . . . I probably kept half the courtyard entertained."

Anna wanted to laugh at her, ask her what it was about this morning that had triggered the thought of her past ecstasies; wondered too whether Sophie would be sitting there, suspended between shame and self-discovery, had Karel still occupied her bed and conjured obscenities from the mouth of his lover. *What beasts we are,* she mused, *that it requires loneliness to trigger our sense of guilt.*

What she said was: "We do not choose what we desire." The moment she said it, it sounded wrong to her, bookish, like something Anton would have said, a phrase from a treatise on the stockyard of one's soul. Sophie heard it too, and correctly identified the phrase's likely origin.

"Like your husband," she said. "Forgive me, Anna. Karel told me. That Herr Beer . . . " She paused, lost confidence in her word of choice, found a stand-in. "About his inclinations, I mean. It must be difficult for the wife. After all, you still love—And yet . . . "

Anna rose, disentangled her hands from her coffee cup, walked quickly to the door. "I think we have exchanged quite enough confidences for one morning. If you will excuse me now, Sophie, I must dress."

When they walked to the courthouse an hour later, neither one of them made any reference to their earlier conversation.

2.

Dark caws, the scrape of claws upon unvarnished wood, then the muffled clap of wings on air and a dance of four-toed, hopping acclamation. The birds were preaching again, a rhythm of call and multi-voiced response. It sank into her sleep and commandeered her childhood memories: rode them raw against their inclinations. The pastor of her native village throwing dirt into an open grave, his frock coat torn under one arm, yellowed linen underneath; behind him, on a table laden with her sister's wedding feast, her uncle's wireless was making static-punctured speech; and a speckled Great Dane known as Liebling dragged through the dirt the puzzle of his tractor-broken hip.

She woke sweating, her belly heavy with retained water and the growing child, the need to piss pressing urgent on her bladder. Poldi climbed out of bed, squatted low over the chamber pot, relieved herself, then sat down bare-assed on the floor, her back aching, her memory still clinging to poor Liebling, that painful slither, paw over paw. From the attic there travelled a renewed chorus of caws; crows circling the house, more every day, as though to mark its carcass for their peers. She grabbed a slipper that peeked from a pile of dirty clothing; lobbed it hard against the ceiling, earned a burst of renewed agitation, a dozen birds hopping, screeching, trading perches. It had been impossible, these past few weeks, to play any music. Every time she put on a record, the birds responded, drowned whole symphonies within their screams. She'd been falling asleep with her hands clapped around her ears.

She left the room. Downstairs, Frau Seidel's door stood ajar, the bed untouched, one window open to the October cold. On the ground floor a half-drunk cup of herbal tea upon the kitchen sideboard; everything much cleaner now that the boy lived in the house. Hungry, Poldi tried a handful of drawers, found most of them locked. They had left some bread out for her, a thimbleful of margarine; some dried-out cheese, a packet of malt coffee. The charity of relatives. She ate some bread and cheese, hungered after something sweet.

There was a larder at the back of the kitchen, three steps deep and vivid with the smells of former bounty. Now it stood bereft of food, save for a sack of flour, a basket of spuds, and a mound of onions covered with rough canvas sacking. At the back the row of shelves hung somehow crooked, as though one side had been pushed into the wall. It was only after stepping close that Poldi realized the entire section swung on hinges, like a door. Behind it a flight of stairs led downwards, to an unknown part of the cellar.

She descended slowly, less from any sense of trepidation than mindful of her own clumsiness, the slowly shifting centre of her body's gravity. The room at the bottom held a bed and chair, a cot, and some more shelving; a bare concrete floor, cracked in parts, glazed with a patina of mould. The room was lit by a tall floor lamp with a flower-patterned, tasselled shade. It stood by the dirty cot like a dandy at the bedside of a pauper; spread a soft, red-tinted glow. The light gave weight and volume to the figure sitting at the table, spooning jam into her mouth. The tabletop was cluttered with tins and jars.

"Frau Seidel! You gave me a right fright. I had no idea there was a room down here." Poldi spoke quickly, unsure what would be her reception. "I suppose you en't goin' to the trial, then?"

Frau Seidel shook her head without looking up.

"Me neither. He asked that I don't go, Wolfgang did. I went to see him last night. He was pale, and in a bit of a temper. I suppose he must be nervous and all. Said he had in-di-gest-shien. I could tell. He smelled a little from the mouth." Poldi smiled, conjured the memory of their sour kiss. "He'll get off, won't he, Frau Seidel?"

The emotion behind the question was so raw that even Frau Seidel seemed startled. She paused, looked over, a spoonful of jam still in her mouth. Then she swallowed, raised a plump wrist to her eyes, read the time on her gold watch.

"Ten o'clock. The little cripple will have testified by now. It's all up to her." Anger flooded her features, changed the direction of her thought. "The conceited little bitch. Thinks I'm an idiot or something. She kept the food locked away all these months and never once realized I had this."

She pointed at the rows of shelves laden with jars. Poldi followed the gesture, first with her eyes then with her feet, and quickly realized that the entire supply consisted of store-bought jam and tinned fruit. There had to be a hundred jars lining the shelves.

"Apricot!" she called out in childish excitement, reached for a jar. "If it's all right with you." She turned to solicit permission, a hint of curtsy to her movement. "Got a sweet tooth, I have. It's been months since I had jam."

Frau Seidel did not object, and Poldi brought the jar to the table. She ate with her fingers, fishing out the sticky chunks of fruit and licking them off with obvious relish.

"And what's this here?" she asked halfway through the jar, reached for one of the larger tins that sat on the table, then recoiled when she saw the tar-black skull printed on the label.

Frau Seidel watched her, grinned, stuck her jam-smeared spoon into the open tin. She scooped out a quantity of fine white powder, stirred it into the dregs of the jam jar in front of her. Carefully, moving with surprising dexterity, she laid the jar on the ground then rolled it across the room in the direction of the shelves. The jar disappeared in the shadows at their base: a grating sound as glass rolled over concrete. Poldi made to say something, but was cut off by a warning finger. They sat and waited, heard nothing. Then a subtle movement of the jar, a quarter turn, the scritch-scratch of a careful paw.

"Rats?" Poldi asked. The notion failed to disgust her. She had been fighting vermin all her life.

Frau Seidel nodded, her face a mask of dried-in makeup. "They know it smells funny, but they eat it anyway." She spat on the spoon, wiped it on the hem of her dress, then opened a fresh jar of jam and resumed eating. "I kill a dozen every week. They breed like   " She broke off, stuck for a comparison, then looked over at Poldi and fixed her eyes on her stomach and lap. "You're feeling well?" she asked abruptly, the voice slipping instantly from triumph to sympathy.

Poldi shrugged, one hand to her abdomen. "All right, I suppose. Peein' a lot. And chucking up my lunch." She got up from her chair, walked over to the unmade cot, struck anew by the oddity of her surroundings. "But what about this room? You come here to sleep, do you?"

Frau Seidel shook her head, all sympathy extinguished. "*He* stayed here. In '42. You can still smell him in the sheets." Her nose wrinkled. "Have you read the numbers? One million, five million, ten!" Frau Seidel swallowed, stuck a tongue into the pocket of one cheek, found sufficient spit to wet her venom. "You'd have thought they could have got this one. He came here the morning they rounded them all up: his wife and daughter, his father, his mother-in-law. He'd run away. Sat in our basement, sweating, saying, 'I've got to go.' Only he didn't. Four days he stayed; the house full of servants, all those curious eyes! Seidel refused to kick him out. Not that he didn't want to, mind. But it wasn't *right*. Running to church every three minutes, and to the crapper. Stomach ulcer. Because we owed him, you see. Well, he left in the end, gave himself up to the police and asked to be brought to his wife. And what a disgusting face he had, such cheeks, always greasy, hanging down over his bones." She touched her own face as though fearing she'd taken on the man's features; took hold of the fatty tissue of her throat and stuffed it under the high collar of her blouse. "It's been almost six years, and the room still smells of Jew."

Poldi looked at her, rose, and slowly climbed the stairs. At the top she spoke, sadly, quietly, though loud enough to make herself heard.

"You're mad, you are," she said.

Back in her room the ceiling sang with mating crows. Poldi lay down, stuffed fingers in her ears, and prayed for Wolfgang.

3.

"Would you describe your duties to the court, Fräulein Grotter?"

"My duties? I'm a servant. I do what I am told."

"Quite, quite. There is no need to grow angry. I suppose you must be nervous."

"Must I?"

"Well, at any rate, it's only natural, with all these people watching. But really there is nothing to it. Just tell the truth."

"Well, get on with it, Herr Prosecutor. I have chores to see to."

From the first, then, Prosecutor Fejn seemed a little put out by the final witness of the trial. The person he had met to prepare her testimony some weeks earlier had been quite a different entity: taciturn, for one; dull to the point of stupidity. He recalled a working girl dressed in her Sunday best, her virgin bosom sheltered in much-mended lace. Her statement had been as colourless as her clothes.

Today she was different. Anneliese Grotter—Eva—had appeared in court in a getup that was nothing short of provocative. She wore a scarlet hat cocked at a precarious angle and an old dress that seemed too tight, too short for her: it accentuated her breasts, her hump, and invited a view of her naked calves stretched out before her in the witness chair. There were other details of her costume that drew the eye. She had painted her lips, the colour clashing with the hat, but had left her eyes naked; had brought no jacket or cardigan and sat with exaggerated stiffness in her chair, turning only her head on occasion to stare flatly at the members of the jury. When her eyes fell on the defendant, she made no effort to hide a sneering indifference to his fate.

"We won't detain you for long," Fejn continued, dissolving his consternation in a smile. "Far be it from the court to interpose itself between you and the household linen." He paused just long enough for the first wave of audience titters to arrive, then waved off the joviality as though it were his regretful duty. "To business, though. I really only have a single little question. Where were you at midday on June 25, Fräulein Grotter?"

"That's your 'single little question,' Herr Dr. Fejn? I was in the Seidel residence." She made as though to rise, had to be shooed back into her chair; her expression haughty, spiteful, each movement hampered by her hump.

"And what were you doing?"

"At noon? Cleaning the toilet, I expect. Or the mirrors, perhaps. Some annoying little task."

"You were in the bathroom, then."

"In one of the bathrooms. Top floor. Where the young Herr Seidel has his room."

"And while you were there, going about the cleaning, did you see the accused?"

Fejn pointed, and her eyes duly followed, studied Wolfgang coldly head to foot.

"I did."

"Doing what?"

"He was getting dressed. And talking to his wife."

"What state was he in?"

"He was drunk."

"Please, Fräulein Grotter. You seem rather eloquent when you put your mind to it. Describe the scene for us."

She snorted, adjusted her hat, scratched—actually scratched—the place where her upper arm disappeared into her sleeve. "It was like this," she said. "The accused was in his pyjamas and had just stormed up the stairs. He was pulling on his clothes, yelling at his wife. His face was flushed and he was reeling. I believe he slumped against the wall once or twice while attempting to step into his trousers. A matter of balance. He'd left the door wide open, so I could see it all quite clearly."

"Where did the accused come from?"

"His father's study."

Fejn hid his surprise behind the shuffle of notes. They made no mention of this detail. "From his father's study! You know this for a fact?"

"Yes, of course. I could hear them shout at each other. I couldn't make out the words, but they were shouting. Then he banged the door, ran up the stairs, and yelled at his wife instead."

"And what is it he was yelling at his wife? Surely you could hear the words this time around?"

"He was cursing his father."

"What exactly did he say?"

"Oh, just incoherent words. 'Bastard,' 'asshole,' 'hypocrite.' He may have called him a cunt."

The word froze Fejn for a moment, and he looked around him like a man wishing to ascertain that he had not misheard. But the jurors and spectators mirrored his shock. From the ranks of the jurors came a single cackle, suppressed to be sure, but quite audible in the sudden silence of the room. Eva searched out its origin, pinpointed the youngest of the jurors, a department store clerk not much older than herself, and bestowed on him a look of frank amusement.

"I am merely quoting the accused."

Fejn recovered, smoothed down his hair. His robes billowed with the motion. "And what, er, was the defendant's tone as he made these remarks?"

"His tone?" She smiled up at Fejn, pursed her painted lips, deliberated. "Murderous."

"Murderous?" Fejn repeated, gratified, appeased, his voice still ranging through the octaves. "What happened then?"

"He left. Stormed out, you would say. He banged all the doors."

"Did he put on his shoes, Fräulein Grotter?"

"No. I saw him holding them in one hand, but then he threw one as he was yelling and dropped the other. He left sweaty marks on the stairs. The socks, I mean. They were far from clean."

"And when was the next time you saw the elder Herr Seidel?"

"Never. Not conscious, that is. A little later there was shouting in the street. They'd found his body."

"Thank you, Fräulein Grotter, that will be all. The prosecution is done with this witness."

Fejn bowed to the judge, took out his handkerchief, and wiped sweat off his brow.

4.

Ratenkolb took over. He did not speak at once but rather sat at his desk, shuffling through papers, the eyes of the court upon him.

"Fräulein Grotter," he said at last. "I notice that there are significant discrepancies between your police statement and the report of the investigative judge."

She did not answer but merely looked at him: naked, hostile eyes.

"What I mean to say, Fräulein Grotter, is that initially you refused to make any statement at all."

"So?"

"You have no comment to make?"

"You have asked no question."

Ratenkolb nodded slowly to himself as though he appreciated her precision. "Let me put it like this, then, Fräulein Grotter. What changed your mind?"

"At first, I did not want to get involved. A maid must know her place."

"Come, come, you do not strike the court as such a wallflower."

"Well, then, I thought the police could do their job without my help."

"The investigative judge convinced you otherwise?"

"Evidently."

A pause commenced, during which Ratenkolb once again leafed through his papers. "Tell me," he asked thoughtfully. "Do you like the accused?"

"Not especially. He beat up people for a living."

"You were afraid of him? You seem like a bold young woman."

"My station in life necessitates caution."

"So you are not put out that the defendant has not been in the house these past months?"

"Put out? No. For all I care, he can go to hell."

"Well," said Ratenkolb, "it's beginning to look like he may." He bowed his head, took a moment, then spoke as though to his desk. "One last question, though. A matter of a minor discrepancy. Or perhaps an oversight. In the report, I mean. The time you saw the defendant leave the house without his shoes on—the day he called his father names—when exactly was that?"

"Around noon."

"You are certain?"

"There are several clocks in the house. I heard the chime."

"And when was Herr Seidel's body found?"

"At half past one."

"Yes," said Ratenkolb. "That agrees with the other witness statements. A whole hour and a half after his son threw him out the window. How do you explain the lag?"

"How do I explain it?" Eva sneered. "I suppose nobody passed the house. Or they did pass but had their noses in the air. One would have to look over the little fence."

"Quite." Ratenkolb waited, smoothed his jacket and waistcoat, consulted his papers. "Do you remember what you did after you had cleaned the upstairs bathroom?"

"I swept the stairs."

"And then?"

"Windows. Front parlour, then dining room, then kitchen."

"You are certain?"

"I follow a routine, Herr Ratenkolb. The twenty-fifth was a Friday. I swept the stairs then cleaned the downstairs windows."

"Bathroom, stairs, windows. An odd routine, if you'll excuse my saying so."

"You want to tell me how to clean house? Come over sometime. You can give me lessons."

Ratenkolb smiled thinly at her joke. "Please, Fräulein Grotter. This is a murder trial after all. Can you tell us at what time you cleaned the windows in the parlour?"

"At twelve-thirty."

"You sound very certain."

"I am."

"Well, in that case you have lied to us, Fräulein Grotter. You told the court that you did not see Herr Seidel's body until some passersby drew your attention to it by the noise they made out on the street."

"That is correct."

"But surely the windows of the front parlour look out onto the front lawn."

"They do."

"Is it possible that you could have cleaned the windows in the front parlour at half past twelve in the afternoon and not seen the body of your employer lying broken and bleeding right in front of you?"

A whisper went through the audience, a sort of collective bracing.

"Is it possible?" she repeated lightly, lazy with the words. "No, of course not. He fell not five steps from the window. I assure you, the front lawn was quite empty at the time."

Pandemonium broke out, was stoked rather than soothed by the drumming of Judge Bratschul's gavel. Fejn had leapt out of his chair and was gesticulating wildly. The word "perjury" was heard from a variety of corners; for once, all sides of the audience seemed equally outraged. Eva sat through it all with exceptional calm; was a little flushed, it is true, and held her hands knotted against her stomach, but made no other movement, her chin held high, poking from the shadow of her hat.

Eventually the judge's entreaties brought some semblance of order to the room. Cautioning Fejn to return to his seat, he addressed the witness directly.

"Fräulein Grotter. You will have noticed that your statement has thrown the court into quite a state—yes, yes, quite a state. You see, the sequence of events on June 25 is a matter of great importance. We have a witness, one of the neighbours, who discovered Herr Seidel's body at around half past one. And other witnesses who saw the defendant—barefoot—at around two. It was assumed—that is, the prosecution has assumed—that he left the house in the wake of—*after*, you understand, *after*—Herr Seidel was thrown—or let's say fell, one mustn't influence the jury!—out the window of his study. Now you tell us the defendant left the house while his father was still inside. May I point out that there are, um, grave penalties for lying in court, very grave penalties, and that, if you are mistaken, this, perhaps, is the last point at which you can correct, that is take it back, and, in short, enlighten the court . . ." He trailed off, exhausted, sat kneading his gavel between nervous, blue-veined hands.

Eva looked at him with an air of total unconcern. "Herr Judge," she answered quietly. "On the day of Herr Seidel's accident, a policeman came to the house to ask me questions. He was rude and I was upset, so I did not answer his questions. He did not try very hard. I heard him tell his colleague that I was an imbecile and a cripple. Six weeks later an investigative judge requested my presence in the courthouse. He made me wait in a shabby little corridor. There was a long line of people and only one chair. When it was my turn, I went in and closed the door. He was sitting behind his desk, nose buried in some papers. I wondered would he say "Good day" at least, but he never even looked at me, just sat there thumbing through his papers for the whole duration of the interview. He asked me a whole ream of questions, some of them quite personal. I answered them, though he talked too much and did not listen. Whenever he liked what I said, he nodded to the typist to fire away. You have the report in front of you. He read it back to me at the end. It sounded accurate, so I signed it. Then, last month, the prosecutor came by the house, to 'inspect the crime scene' and to read my statement out to me again. He came in, drank three cups of tea, and ate all our biscuits. 'Just stick to the truth,' he said in between bites, and waved the paper at me. And so I have. I think you will find that nothing in the report contradicts anything I've said in court. I assumed the goal of the questions was to ascertain that the defendant was angry with his father. He was. He called him names. I have related some of his language for you. I cannot be held responsible for questions that the investigator omitted to ask."

She came to an end. More colour had entered her cheeks. Perhaps, at long last, the gravity of the occasion had become present to her.

"But surely you had read the papers!" the judge exclaimed. "You knew what was at stake."

She reeled off a phrase too tidy not to have been rehearsed. "I refuse to be responsible for your assumptions."

There was more shouting after that, and more work for the gavel, but after a few more minutes the witness was dismissed.

5.

The moment Eva had finished, while the court was still in uproar and the judge's gavel was once again swinging in his bony fist as though he were hammering flat a schnitzel, Robert pushed his way to the end of the bench and quickly ran out of the courthouse looking very pale under his mop of black hair. She came out a few minutes later, a coat pulled around her shoulders hiding the thin dress.

"Well," she said, looking hard into his face. "You're not staying for the end? Wolfgang has declined to testify, so they have moved straight to the summations. Fejn goes first. He asked for a recess, but the judge wants to be done with it all."

Robert spoke softly, shuffled his feet. "It's a fraud, isn't it? It was all pre-arranged. You told Ratenkolb what to ask."

"I sent him a note this morning. So what?"

"You did not have to do it like that. There was no need to make them hate you. You could have been nice."

She grimaced, wiped at her lipstick with the back of her hand. "I thought about it. Playing the sweet little idiot. In a sailor's collar, no less. I'd have taken you as a model: the bumbling, happy fool. But you know what: it would have been hard to keep a straight face." She forced a smile, searched his face again with a look that belied her nonchalance. "Anyway," she said now in quite a different voice, "it's best if they hate me. They needed a villain. Now they can let Wolfgang off the hook." She bit her lip. "It's what you want, isn't it?"

"Yes, Eva. Thank you."

He could not help it; his eyes welled up with tears, the left one droop-ing, its lid sliding down. She reached over to tuck it back, her hand clumsy, the gesture new to their courtship. He let her do it, patient, trust-ing, took hold of her hand before she could withdraw.

"Whatever happens," he said, "whatever the verdict, let's have dinner tonight. I mean all of us. A family dinner."

"With napkins, and Mama doling out soup?"

"Yes."

She frowned; made herself free of his hand; turned to leave.

"Where are you going, Eva?"

"We'll need food, won't we? And I need stockings."

"Stockings? Whatever for?"

He watched her cheeks colour, with pleasure rather than embarrassment. "You'll ask me tonight, won't you? At dinner."

He trembled just a little, or maybe his voice did; a chill wind cutting through his clothing. "Yes."

"I want to wear stockings when you ask me. Silk stockings. Like a lady."

He nodded eagerly, mirrored her smile. Then a worry took hold of his pale face. "I have to stay here. The jury might—that's to say, you never know how quickly they will—"

"Stay," she said, kissed him quickly on the cheek, then skipped off. Halfway down the street, he noticed, she took off her hat despite the cold and crumpled it under one arm.

6.

It would have been nice if there had been some paint. Blue would have been good, to suggest a metallic sheen; a dollop of black to conjure the darkness of the cockpit. The boys were alone in their room; dusk in the window, and the clatter of a passing tram. Franzl was building the airplane out of some planks of wood. He had already cut the wings, using a broken-off saw that he had found somewhere, and glued them to the body. Karlchen would have liked to help him—he had an idea how to shape the plane's rudder—but had yet to be invited. To hide his sense of expectation he lay spread out on the bed, leafing through his comic book. Truth be told, he was bored with his acquisition. In retrospect seventeen marbles seemed rather steep for a dozen pages full of little pictures. It was not impossible that he'd been had.

Their father came home, heavy boots out in the corridor. The boys did not acknowledge his arrival, and yet they noticed it, each in his own way, and measured his mood by the length of his stride and the time it took him to hang his coat. And though neither of them said anything, the saw ceased working for some moments, and the comic book's pages remained unturned. Straining his ears, Karlchen could hear Father talk to Mother in the kitchen. She made a sound, something like a squeal, that might have communicated any number of emotions. Almost at once an argument ensued. Only their father's voice carried, its tenor, not the words. It was more chiding than angry. He fell silent, walked down the corridor, slammed the apartment door to lock himself in the toilet off the stairwell outside—each of his movements so familiar that Karlchen could picture it down to the details. The boy seized the opportunity to jump up off the bed, slip out of the room and into the kitchen. Franz looked after him then rammed shut the door of their bedroom with a shove of his foot.

Karlchen half expected to find his mother crying. But she was dry-eyed, stirring soup, humming a ditty to herself. When she noticed her son, she first threw an eye at the apartment door then waved him over; crouched down to him and wrapped her apron skirt around his shoulders as though swaddling him in a blanket. He allowed himself to be crushed against her bosom; smelled her; offered the back of his head to her kiss.

"He's innocent," she whispered, nuzzling him. "The man at the trial. It's just been announced. They let him go."

He did not answer, held on to her until she rose again and shook him out of the crumpled apron. They had dinner, talking of other things, his father drinking beer, reading the paper. Only later, sitting on the hallway toilet in the dark, the only room whose door he could lock, did Karlchen allow his tears of relief to flow.

7.

The verdict was handed down a little after five. At three, Robert, sick to the stomach with waiting, and anxious to make arrangements for that night's dinner, had run home. He'd roused his mother, who was sleeping in the drawing room, and discovered that Eva had already dropped off several parcels of food in the kitchen then left again, presumably still hunting for stockings. For an hour he fussed and gave instructions; convinced first his mother, then a nervous, sickly Poldi that Wolfgang would be "acquitted without fail" and that they must prepare a worthy welcome for him. When he left, the two women were standing shoulder to shoulder rinsing and drying the good Meissen and arguing about the preparations for the roast.

When Robert returned to the courthouse, the judge had just recalled the jury to deliver its verdict. So overwhelmed was Robert by the occasion that he could not later recall any actual words. The judge spoke, then the foreman of the jury; a sigh went through the crowd. It was only when his brother stood up and turned to the public benches with a broad and somewhat stupid smile that Robert understood. Robert hastily shook his brother's hand across the railing, told him to hurry (there were some formalities to take care of that would detain Wolfgang for no more than an hour), then ran home as fast as he could.

Back at the house the preparations had faltered. Poldi had left after some argument or other and his mother sat blankly at the kitchen table, picking apart a crust of bread. Eva had yet to return.

Robert refused to be daunted. He shouted out his news, rallied the troops; sent Poldi into a dance of joy, then into a frenzy of preparation as she searched her wardrobe for something to wear. Robert had no time to serve as critic. He tore down the stairs, ran to the kitchen; tied an apron to his tidy frame. Pleading, cajoling, Robert got his mother to explain how to prepare the meat; browned the pork loin in a casserole then surrounded it with chunks of onion and stuffed it in the oven. Rushing, a manic joy taking hold of him, he began to set the table; stopped to sweep the dirty floor and beat the dust out of the chair cushions, then begged his mother to iron the good tablecloth that he found neatly folded at the bottom of a cupboard. As he arranged the soup bowls, he realized they had no soup and immediately ran back to the kitchen to boil up the bones Eva had brought. While he stood at the counter, cutting vegetables into the thin broth, his mother entered the kitchen with a pile of embroidered napkins and began folding them. He looked over at her, grateful, and she beckoned him close with the curl of one finger.

"I had a dream last night," she whispered. "A dog was nuzzling me, right in the stomach. But also he was feeding. The muzzle was wet."

"That's terrible, Mother."

She waved away his concern, folded a napkin. "Only a dream."

Some minutes later, standing by his shoulder as he was peeling the last of the carrots, she bent over to him, kissed his cheek. "Are you happy, Robert?"

"Very happy, Mama. You will see, everything will be all right."

She seemed embarrassed but also pleased, excused herself, and returned a half-hour later glassy-eyed, edgy, out of sorts.

"It's a hard life," she muttered to his inquiring look. But the good mood held, despite her fix of drugs.

At length the house was as though transformed. Robert had found candles and lit a row of candelabra; the table silver, a little tarnished, reflected their light. Each place setting was flanked by two glasses of fine Bohemian crystal, a tumbler and a wineglass, chosen for their beauty rather than their function (he had yet to locate the wine). The plates and bowls were pure white porcelain and seemed to glow on the dark blue tablecloth, a painted symbol on their backs vouchsafing their provenance. Outside it had started to rain, and the grim weather made a pleasing contrast to the cozy scene inside. The smell of pork roast filled the house. Robert had changed into a fresh shirt and tie and done his best to polish his shoes. The kitchen was cleaned, and at the last minute he had even remembered to put on the potatoes: the nervous titter of the lid over boiling water.

Now all there was left to do was wait and make sure the meat did not get overcooked. Both Wolfgang and Eva were long overdue.

At half past seven Poldi came down, sat in a corner with a cheerful grin, rubbing her tummy and darning some old socks. She was dressed plainly, but her blouse was clean and she had washed and brushed her hair. They sat across from one another and waited.

Eva returned. She came in wet, sodden hat in hand. "How long do I have?" she called as Robert ran to meet her in the hallway. "I want to take a bath."

"Hurry. The meat is getting tough. Wolfgang will be back any minute."

She nodded, kicked off her dirty shoes, headed for the stairs. Before she had taken two steps, he caught up with her, pulled her quickly through the door into the front parlour, kissed her as he had not done before, which is to say firmly, on the lips, holding her cheeks between his palms and taking time to taste her breath. She did not struggle, but when he paused, her look was suspicious. "Why?" she asked.

"You are my—That is, we will marry, won't we?"

"Yes."

"So there." He kissed her again, holding her firmly, leaning into her, feeling her body pressing into his.

When they were done, she blushed and smiled. "You do this rather well," she whispered, seeming younger, stripped of her defences. She ran off before he had a chance for a third embrace; skipped up the stairs like a child.

Robert looked after her, leaning on the door frame, hands shoved into pockets: the only blemish on his happiness the sombre recognition that it was Anna Beer who had taught him how to kiss.

8.

Wolfgang did not return, and Eva would not come down. He called to her after ten minutes, and again after fifteen, received a hollered answer that she was on her way. Then, nothing. Robert called again, his young voice rising up the stairwell. His mother and Poldi were sitting on armchairs in the drawing room; sat stiffly, hands folded in their laps, the younger woman nervous, determined not to crease her blouse, his mother glassy-eyed and frowning. He called a fourth time, was answered by silence.

"We must eat," his mother urged behind him. "The meat is drying out."

"Wait. Just one little minute. I'll run up and fetch her."

He went reluctantly, calling Eva's name, afraid to anger her by their impatience. The door to her room stood wide open: clothes on the floor, a wet towel thrown over the footboard of the bed; her smell in the air, clean skin and soap. He approached the bathroom, knocked with awkward delicacy. Eva was neither combing her hair nor doing her ablutions. He called once again, much quieter now, more a mumbling than a shout; stood motionless, his hand still on the bathroom door, and listened into the house. He heard nothing; too little: the creaking of windows battered by the rain.

It was the quiet that drew him to the attic.

He did not run but rather walked in a hurried yet compacted step. For a fraction of a second he found himself transported to Herr Seidel's funeral where he had walked with a similar gait behind the pallbearers, impatient, nipping at their heels, yet hampered in each step by the solemn rhythm of the occasion; had walked distracted, by the hail of acorns thumping on the casket, and the shift of public mood that overnight had transformed him from a schoolboy to "the young Herr Seidel," the prospective heir to a great fortune; a crowd of mourners at his back walking with a similarly tethered slowness, straining against their wish to be done with the funeral and move on to the repast that would follow. So strong was this momentary vision that he stopped, wheeled around, stared down the corridor behind: five yards of carpet, the soft, wallpapered walls, and a hint of scent that attested Eva must have passed.

He reached the ladder leading up to the attic, the trap door open, silence up above. "Eva," he tried again, "Eva, Eva!" frightened now, with no hope of an answer, mounted the rungs with careful, halting steps. As his head cleared the attic floor, he saw first of all Eva's rump, outlined sharply in a new, tight-fitting dress; a dark seam running, heel to hem, up each shapely calf. Eva had found some stockings. She stood bent forward at the waist. When she came up, both hands were burdened by black, heavy rags. It was only when one slipped her grasp and disgorged a spray of feathers that he recognized them as crows.

9.

Just like Robert, it had been the silence that had drawn her. She'd been dressed and ready, a drop of new perfume dabbed onto the bone between her breasts. No lipstick, if only to invoke no memory of the morning: a clean, scrubbed, *virgin* face, the lashes curled with Italian mascara: petroleum jelly and coal. She had heard him call for her, and had answered—"On my way"—cherishing the domesticity of the phrase, a moment snatched from the pictures. One last straightening of the stockings (they were slightly too big for her) and a quick clamber onto the top of a stool so she could admire her legs in the bathroom mirror, the mirror too low now to reflect her hump. There she stood, smiling, and became conscious of it: the silence of the attic.

No matter, she needed to hurry, he was waiting for her. She made it to the top of the stairs, looked down, heard him pacing at the bottom. The sound of it, leather soles on parquet floor; it reinforced the absence of any sound above. And yet she made to run down; wanted to tell him how cleverly she had bargained for the food and stockings, and how she was certain, today, that the angel had shadowed her on the ride back on the tram. But she'd forgotten her earrings. They were mere trinkets to be sure, silver, if that, each shaped into a simple hoop. Still, she had bought them, they were part of her costume, would draw the candles, look fetching in their living light. She hurried back, found them, put them on, then went left, not right, when she exited her room, for what harm could it do, just to take a peek? Climbing the ladder in pumps had not been easy; she'd giggled when she'd slipped.

There were seventeen of them. That's the first thing she did, stand there and count. Who would have thought that they liked jam? It had been spooned onto small squares of bread and placed at intervals upon the floor; each dollop flecked with fine white powder. There'd been enough to kill off the whole roost.

She did not remove the little traps; climbed up and started piling birds into a heap. There was no delicacy to her movements. She picked them up by twos and threes—by the neck, the wing, the scrawny feet—and dumped them in a pile. Only once did she hesitate, when she found Yussuf in the corner, his dark eyes just as blank as they'd been in life. She closed a fist over his head, felt the beak dig into the base of her palm; picked him up and carried him around, kicking at the others now, building them into a messy mound. Somewhere along the line she noticed Robert. Half a bridegroom, the body cut off by the trap door at the waist, his left eye lolling lazy in its socket. He looked pale, but then again, he always did.

She did not trust herself to speak, but the next moment it slipped out, drily, as though she had scripted the line.

"Your mother made me an engagement present. A sort of promise of what's to come."

He started shaking his head even before she had finished. "Perhaps it wasn't her, Eva. We need to—"

She hit him. It was not meant to dislodge him from the ladder; was a push more than a punch, born of frustration, the need to silence his excuses; one hand planted on his face, the other, bird-burdened, slamming hard into his chest. His soles squeaked. Then he fell.

Perhaps his head hit the rungs. At any rate he landed awkwardly, lay crumpled at the base. She came down after him, feet forward, butt to the ladder, thinking, *He can see right up my skirt.* Her pumps caught in the rungs, but she held on; the crow stashed in her armpit, one wing loose, flapping outwards, attempting to soar. She reached the floor, bent down to him; a deadly stillness to his frame. She should have nursed him, but kicked him instead, a look of anguish on her face; one, two, three vicious little kicks that hit him in the chest, the throat, the face; then ran, the bird back in her fist, riding the air behind like a broken kite.

10.

Afterwards, one of the things that revealed her to herself was the fact that she did not leave the house at once. Rather she went to her room, knelt down by her bed, and found the slit within her mattress in which she had deposited her savings. She took them, put on her coat, struggled with the sleeve until she realized she had to let go of the crow to fit her arm through the hole. She picked the bird up again before she ran down the stairs. There was no thought in her head to punish the mother; at any rate not yet. All she wanted was to leave.

Outside, the rain fell heavier than ever. She had left behind the hat. A three-minute sprint down to the tram stop. The tram's headlight startled her, caught the blackness spreading from her wrist. She dropped it in a puddle, as simply and mechanically as she had picked it up, the carcass of a *Speck*-tamed pet; climbed on the tram and sat on the wooden bench with her hands on her gut, breathing hard through her open mouth. The doors closed, a drunk jumped out at the last second, the tram moved off.

By the time she looked back, it was too late to see the man step out of the shadows of the building, bend down to the crow, and gently pick it out of its puddle. He wrapped it in a red woollen scarf, then followed the tracks into the city.

The only person who noticed him at all was the drunk who had left the tram at the last moment and immediately started charging up the hill, drawn by the promise of a meal and a pregnant wife who would laugh at his jokes and not begrudge him the bottle he'd drunk to celebrate his innocence.

11.

He didn't expect her, not on the day of the verdict. The evening paper was full of her, a half-page sketch, sitting proud and crooked on the witness chair. *Good for you*, he thought, the mutt happy, curled up on his lap.

The church clock had stuck nine when she came in. She was soaked to the bone. She peeled out of her overcoat then stood there almost naked, her blouse and dress clinging to her skin. She had the most lovely breasts.

"Here," Karel said, handing her a rag that served him as a towel; then, realizing its uselessness, he threw her the blanket that covered his bed. "Dry off, you'll catch your death." There was, at this moment, no trace of accent in his German.

She wasn't crying. It had looked like it, her face dripping with water, mascara streaks heavy on her cheeks. But when she dried off, her complexion was clear. Franz Josef, the mutt, ran up to her, licked her ankles through stockings that looked wet and new. She shook him off gently enough, dug into her coat pocket, threw her purse at Karel where he was sitting on his bed. He opened it, counted the money.

"I want to go with you," she said before he could ask. "To Canada. Or wherever it is you are going."

Karel nodded, counted the money once more, looked up. "It won't be enough," he said. "Passports are expensive."

She stared at him, wrapped in his blanket, damp hair standing on end from how she'd towelled it off.

He found in his heart the wish to make her happy.

"Perhaps it is time we locate that Jew of yours," he said, and the Pole in the bed next to them sat up and shouted, "*Świnio, świnio,*" before collapsing back into his pillow, the tumour at his throat soft and lumpy like a sponge.

Part Two

The Germans too took prisoners. About five and a half million Russian soldiers were taken into custody. Some 3.3 million died: 60 percent. One hundred and forty thousand were murdered outright: picked out by the "Security Police" for their race or their politics and shot. The vast majority, however, were killed through labour. Amongst this population, starvation was not simply a matter of faulty supply lines and food shortages. It was the continuation of racial war by other means. By central order, many such prisoners' calorie intake was made a function of their productivity. The weaker they got, the less they produced, the more they starved, and in their skeletal lethargy confirmed the indolence of Slavs.

The number of POWs was dwarfed by that of forced workers. Some twelve million people were pressed into service both in the occupied territories and in the Reich itself. Close to three million Soviet citizens found themselves abducted and pressed into factory and farm work, many of them young women and teenage girls. In the late stages of the war these forced labourers represented a quarter of the Reich's workforce. The permutations of their employment were rich and varied. Some built military installations—bunkers, tank defences, U-boat ports, V-1 launch pads, clad in the green uniforms of Operation Todt, an organization whose name, by a stroke of orthographic irony, is only a silent consonant removed from the German word for "death." Some assembled guns, grenades, mortars; built Fords and Volkswagens; mined for coal, iron, copper.

From Berlin factories to the Ruhr Valley mines, from the northern ports to Austrian oil refineries, few were the companies yoked to the Reich's war effort that did not make use of slaves. Irregularities were common; children fathered; prisoners murdered; workers used for private gain.

On occasion subtler, more human irregularities arose. An Oberhausen machinist recalls how a pair of Soviet workers lent to him by his employer repaired his private, bomb-strafed roof. For three days and nights they lived amongst his family, sharing their food; sat on stools, perhaps, around a kitchen table made festive in their honour by the Sunday tablecloth, a pair of daughters gawking at these men with hollow eyes who rebuilt their attic beams and roof bricks and tiles, and left thankful for their three days' holiday from hell.

One

At three o'clock in the morning Aleksei Semyonovich Kozlov, resident of the fourth floor of apartment building thirteen in —— Street in Alma-Ata, the capital and industrial heart of the Soviet Empire's second-largest constituent republic, was pacing the floor beside the bed of his five-year-old daughter, Yulia. It was, incidentally, quite a new apartment building, with central heating and good electrical wiring, and, what is more, twenty-four-hour hot water. He and his family had moved there quite recently, after years of waiting on a list, and had only been able to secure it due to Aleksei's "spotless" and "heroic" war record.

But none of that mattered now. Yulia was sick, her cheeks burning red and her blond hair clinging to her forehead. What had started as a light temperature early in the afternoon had turned into a raging fever. Her stomach was swollen, and she answered all their attempts to minister to her with the same piercing animal shrieks that were quite simply unbearable. Aleksei's wife stood by the telephone in the corridor. They had already called the hospital a half-dozen times, each time receiving the promise that an ambulance, and a doctor, would be dispatched "at once." She had just asked the operator to once again connect her to the hospital when the doorbell rang.

"I'll go," he said, hurried past her, his feet clumsy in their well-worn slippers that were not made for haste.

There were two of them, dressed in overcoats, their hats still on their heads. This confused him for a moment—that they should have shown up as a pair—until he chanced on the happy idea that the life of his daughter was so important that two men had been dispatched. Without listening to their announcement—this was no time for introductions, they must hurry, hurry!—and impatiently shaking himself free when one of them grabbed his sleeve, he ran ahead into the flat and led them to his daughter's bedside.

But now something strange began to happen. Rather than examining the girl, or even approaching her bedside, one of the men started talking, and talked not at all like a human being at the bedside of a sick child, but in those crisp, precise, practised phrases that did not belong to the human but to quite another sphere of life. At the same time they stared at him with a certain expectation and even frowned in consternation when he did not react to their words at all, but rather stood there, both hands stretched towards his daughter, inviting them to step up to her bed. As for what precisely they were saying, he could make neither head nor tail of it. The words reached him, but he was unable to attach any meaning to them; brushed them away, turned to his daughter, and reached for her little hand, an action she answered once more with a high, yelping shriek. He looked over to his wife and was surprised to find her crying. She turned away, left the nursery, and went across the corridor into their own bedroom. Through the open door he watched her pull out a suitcase and pack clothes into it, above all his socks and felt booties, and underwear of the warmest kind.

"Here," she suddenly shouted, running back across the corridor, "you must put this on," and handed him his dress uniform, the row of military honours neatly pinned to its chest. "You have been arrested, you fool."

Down in the car, nobody would speak to him. He sat on the back seat in his uniform and the thick winter coat his wife had pressed on him. One of the men was next to him, the other was driving. Aleksei sat there, overheated, placid, still trying to make sense of that word, "arrest." He put a hand to his chest, ran a finger up and down his honours as though along the keys of a piano.

"I am a war hero," he said, distractedly and without force.

"Quiet, friend," the man next to him advised. "Best to save your strength."

They gave him a cigarette and drove him to the squat grey building that served as the local headquarters of the secret police.

He was processed, stripped, searched, put into a holding cell. He tried to sleep, but the light was kept on in the room and his hands had to show above the blanket at all times. When he finally managed, a man came to shout at him that there was "no sleeping in daytime." He protested he was innocent.

"My daughter is sick," he explained to the guard. "I must send a message home."

The guard reassured him. "You can explain it all to the investigator."

"When?" he asked.

"When it is your turn."

"I insist on seeing him right now."

"You insist?" the guard repeated, his peasant face turning mean. "I'll smash in your head, you shit, you prostitute."

His first interrogation came some forty-eight hours into his arrest. He had barely slept, but the moment the guard stepped into his room and barked at him to follow, he felt wide awake, and confident. Finally he'd have a chance to explain himself and clear up this misunderstanding. At the very least he would have word from his wife, or be able to send her a message. What he must do, he decided, was to explain to the investigators that Yulia was sick. These were no peasant imbeciles after all, but educated men. He had heard somewhere perhaps at his office—that the new head of the secret police hailed from Moscow; he had been seen at the opera (or maybe it was the symphony), and it was said he had cried after a particularly beautiful passage, shouting "Bravo! Bravo!" with such enthusiasm that the entire audience had fallen in with him. Kovalyov, that was his name, Vladimir Petrovich. Though, of course, perhaps it was not he but someone else who would head the investigation, and there was no telling what sort of person that might be.

As Aleksei entered the office in which he was to be questioned—no different from any other government office, really, a cramped little space with a table and a lamp and a black telephone standing at one end—he was still trying to resolve the question of whether he should insist at once on Kovalyov being summoned to take charge of proceedings, or whether he should wait and see, take the measure of the man behind the desk. This man, in any case, sat up, looked at Aleksei across the metal frame of his round little glasses, waited for him to sit down on the bare wooden chair, and then returned his gaze to the file spread out in front of him. A secretary took a seat right behind Aleksei's chair, crossed her legs in front of her (she had a charming figure; it was odd that he should notice it, but he did, stared for a moment at the exposed skin of her plump, pretty forearms and wrists), and readied a piece of paper as though for dictation.

"Name?" the investigator asked, not looking up.

"My name? What's this? You had me arrested, but you don't know who I am?"

The man frowned. "It's for the record. Surely you understand. I did not expect to meet in you a habitual saboteur."

Flushing, feeling the sting of the rebuke, Aleksei hastily gave his name.

"Birthplace?"

He named the village in which he'd been born.

"Occupation?"

It went on like this for a little while: simply, smoothly, without fuss.

"You served in the war?"

"Yes."

"With the final rank of?"

He named the rank.

"And your final command?"

"Camp commander for Prisoner-of-War Camp 97."

"Number of prisoners?"

For the next few hours the questions kept on coming, and little by little, in imperceptible steps, Aleksei's confidence and comfort slowly began to fade and transform into quite a different feeling. The chair beneath his rump seemed to become harder and harder, and the light shining from the room's single lamp appeared to him brighter and brighter and more and more painful to the eyes. Slowly, too, an irritation began to rise in him, and the more the interrogator made him dwell on this or that detail during his time as camp commander, the more Aleksei called to mind his years of service to the Fatherland and the gratitude expressed to him by the State. The young man across from him, by contrast, looked as though he had left school not more than a year ago; it was even possible, it struck Aleksei, that he had not served at all. As his irritation grew, the questions increasingly began to repeat themselves, as though his interrogator expected him to get entangled in the most elementary of falsehoods and was intending to accuse him of having fabricated the most basic facts of his life. In time Aleksei's irritation transformed into a cold, towering rage.

"But you know all this," he spat at last, having been asked for the third time to describe his duties and responsibilities at the camp, and to name the number of prisoners at different stages of the war. "There, I can see it from here. You have my record in front of you."

His interrogator did not respond, in fact did not even look up, but simply repeated his question with a mildness that seemed calculated to fan the flames of Aleksei's fury.

"Look here," he suddenly shouted. "My daughter is sick. It is clear that you are wholly incompetent. I demand to see—"

He did not get much further. Even as he started raging, the investigator sat up, opened a little drawer in his desk, reached in, and coolly withdrew a small object and placed it on the table. It was a prosthetic eye, made of glass and fashioned in beautiful and astonishing detail. Without alluding to it, the investigator began to roll the eye—shaped like the head of an ice-cream scoop, at once semi-spherical and hollow—back and forth under one finger.

"Comrade Kozlov," he said, still in the same mild tone. "You insist on your innocence and yet you won't lend assistance to our inquiry. Surely you can see yourself that this makes us suspicious. Incidentally, I have yet to accuse you of anything. Let us return then to the question. In October 1943, how many prisoners were transferred from—"

And with one blow all confidence and bluster had been taken from Aleksei. He curled his head into his chest, forgot all about the little secretary behind him with the pretty, fleshy forearms, and answered every question quickly, ingratiatingly, all the while filling his clothes with rank, cold sweat.

Two

1.

Three days after the trial of Wolfgang Seidel had come to a close, in occupied Vienna, a tall, broad-shouldered man, whose German was selectively marked by Czech intonation, was making the rounds of the city's backyards and cellars, talking to workers, vagrants, ragpickers, and schoolchildren. He was not wearing an overcoat and was evidently freezing in his dirty shirt and waistcoat; walked with a certain furtiveness, his hands stuffed into the relative warmth of his armpits, a tatty rag tied around his face and head as though he were suffering from toothache. His inquiries led him to a former factory yard. The front building had been patched up and now housed a butcher's shop; the inner courtyard looked out over a mound of rubble that marked the spot where the building's back wing had once stood.

He entered it hesitantly, scanning the yard with suspicion; approached the cellar door that, warped and broken, stood open no wider than a crack. He stopped at the door for some minutes, staring into the dark of a cellar stairwell, soft calls of inquiry issuing from his lips; then shrugged his massive shoulders and quickly left the yard.

The man warmed up at a public house some blocks down the road, drank two shots of rowanberry schnapps with systematic small sips, asked the proprietor about a "bum with a red woollen scarf," then continued his search out in the bitingly cold wind. By the time he returned to the section of town where Vienna's shabbiest hotels had chosen to congregate, he was frozen to the bone.

He walked quickly, hurrying home, and it was only by chance that, passing the establishment two doors down from his destination, he noticed a woman standing at the reception desk, talking in loud, broken German at the bored youth who was on duty. It struck him as curious that he would recognize her from the back: there was nothing very remarkable about her silhouette. She wore an expensive coat and had a certain way of tossing her head.

He hurried on past, ducked into the doorway of his own hotel, walked up the stairs. The door was not locked. Eva was sitting on the narrow bed, a newspaper open on her lap. They had taken turns sleeping on the floor. She looked up as he entered, pushed the paper away from her.

He read the page's rubric, then attempted to read her face. "Obituaries? Still worried, are you? There's no need." He unwrapped the rag from around his head, his hands clumsy with cold. "If he were dead, it'd be all over the papers. His brother's a celebrity after all. As are you." He bent down to her, tried to catch her eye. "He's probably sitting at home, pining for you. Go home and he'll eat out of your hand."

She refused to look up, ignored his words. "Did you find him?" she asked.

He shook his head. "Not yet."

"What if you don't? Or if he refuses to help? All this time, and he hasn't asked them for a dime." She looked hard at him, her eyes full of pent-up anger. She had been looking at him like that ever since she came. "We don't even know it's him."

"We need the money," he said phlegmatically. "No money, no papers."

"We could steal it."

"Steal it? Stealing is hard work." He gestured her up, his eyes taking inventory of their meagre belongings. "In any case, we have to move."

"Again?"

"I saw Sophie just now. Snooping around, asking after me." He smiled. "One thing about me, I'm hard to miss." He collected their few things.

"What does she want from you?" Eva asked.

He considered it, a hint of buffoonery creeping into his voice. "I don't know. Must be she misses me. Because of charming personality."

"Just go down and tell her to leave you alone."

"I thought about it. Too dangerous." He took her by the arm, hurried her along the corridor and down the back stairs. "She's jilted lover. No telling what she'll do."

Eva refused to share in his joke.

2.

Robert came to her mid-morning in November, the trial ten days past. Anna received him in the kitchen, as she did with all her callers. When they sat down, it occurred to her that the last time they had been in the room together, they had parted with a kiss. She could see he was thinking about it too, his eyes on the spot where she'd cornered him. Anna smiled but did not comment. It would have been cruel to make him squirm.

"What can I do for you?" she asked blandly, studied his face. The right eye was marked by the late stages of a shiner. Other than that he looked dapper and well fed.

"Eva has disappeared. You know—the maid." He blushed over the word, hurried on. "You saw her at the trial. We were about to get engaged, but then—" He recounted to her the story of his woes. "I asked Mother, why did she kill the crows? She point-blank denied it. I'm no longer speaking to her."

"You should save your anger for the girl. It's a wonder you didn't break your neck."

He shook his head, unwilling to hear any criticism directed at Eva. "That's just it," he said. "She might think I'm angry with her. I can't find her anywhere. Then today it struck me that maybe she came here. She knows your husband, you know."

"She met him when she was ten years old. And now she's decided he's a saint. Her father died and Anton put her up for a week—but I don't know the details. In any case, she hasn't been here."

He nodded glumly, looked around himself, noticed for the first time the trunk that sat open in one corner, half packed with household things. "He hasn't come back?" he asked her gently.

She feigned unconcern. These days it was awfully easy to feign. "The police tell me he's in Russia. Back in a camp."

"Do you believe them?"

"Sometimes I think he's right here, in the street, looking up at this window; a shabby figure in a shabbier coat. Lost in the world. Have you noticed how many men like that are walking around the city these days? I turn a corner and that's all there seems to be: shabby, lost men, looking at me with vacant eyes. Oh, there must be women like that too. But I don't seem to notice them. Perhaps they are hiding indoors."

He listened, looked again at the half-packed trunk. "Don't go," he said, entreatingly. "Not yet. Give him more time."

"How long do you want me to wait?"

He frowned, stood up, started pacing. "I started praying again," he said abruptly, not pausing in his step. "I used to pray a lot, you see. Before I came here; I even wanted to become a priest. Sometimes I think everything went wrong because I stopped."

She laughed, lightly she hoped, and rose from her chair. "Go," she said, leading him out into the hallway. "Find your girl. If she wants to be found. And leave God out of it."

He followed, took heart. "I will find her," he said. "After all, my father was a detective. It must run in the family."

"Ah, yes. The famed Inspector Teuben. You never told me how he died."

"Mother says it was a stroke. While he was out and about. In the line of duty." Anna could tell he liked the phrase. "That's all she ever said."

"You should ask her. But no, I forgot: you're not speaking to her."

He almost shared her smile. "She got a letter the other day," he said. "She was very upset."

"What was it?"

He shook his head. "She didn't show it to me, and I didn't ask."

"And you didn't sneak into her bedroom to read it on the sly? No, I suppose you wouldn't. It'd be *dishonest*." She smiled again. "You really are a very funny little man."

The phone started ringing. It was there in the hallway, not two feet from where they were standing, unaccountably shrill. She let it ring until it fell silent.

"Someone had it fixed," she explained while Robert slipped into his coat. "A policeman. He showers me with attention." She wrote her number on a used envelope. "Call any time."

He flinched when she gave him the envelope and let her hand linger for a moment on his.

"God," she said. "It was just one little kiss."

He nodded and ran out the door as though stung.

3.

The silence burdened her. Not a squawk came through the ceiling. She had tried dispelling it with records but had found that she had lost her joy in opera. Besides, Wolfgang had complained. She had spent hours at the window, hoping for the sight of some survivors. But it was the season of flight, not of return.

"We should move into a bigger room, Wolfie."

She said it quietly, more to herself than to her husband, who lay stretched out on the bed in his underclothes. The pillow framed his unshaven face. His upper body was wrapped in crumpled blanket, his legs sticking out, dirt stamped into the heels of his old military socks. She stood on the far side of the bed, both hands pressed into the small of her back, rubbing warmth into sore muscles.

315

"There's no space for a cot in here. There's the big bedroom down-stairs." She paused. "Frau Seidel won't say nothing. You're in charge now, en't you? The master of the house."

She used the phrase awkwardly, pinning an odd hope to it. The thought had been on her mind of late, that she was now *mistress*. She'd played with it shyly, in her pocket as it were, not daring to bring it to the light.

"Shut your hole." He never so much as raised his head from the pillow.

"At least get out of bed, Wolfie. I've got to change the sheets. They smell. It's been two weeks."

Wolfgang neither moved nor answered. After two days of drunken cel-ebration he had fallen into a black funk, not leaving the bed for more than a moment, let alone the house. He had even stopped drinking; ate little, stared at the wall.

She stepped closer, lowered herself onto the far side of the bed. "It's all right to go out, you know. They let you off." She paused, considered reaching for his hand, but did not dare touch him. "So what if people talk. People always talk. Let them."

He rolled onto his side, turned his back on her; a wedge of dark hair poking from the elastic of his underpants, marking the cleft of his but-tocks. Poldi stretched out next to him, cast around for a topic that might capture his interest.

"Frau Seidel got a letter today. Second one this week."

She studied the nape of Wolfgang's neck but could discern no reaction.

"I had a look at it. While she was washin'." She paused for effect. "It's from that Jew. The one that used to live here, in the basement. He wants money."

"There were no Jews living in no basement." There was, in Wolfgang's irritation, just a hint of curiosity.

"Were too. I saw the bed and all. But I bet they didn't tell you. Afraid that you'd blab. Bein' still in school and all." Pleased at having got Wolf-gang's attention, Poldi stroked her belly and carried on. "I've been think-ing about it since she told. How come he left his wife and child." She closed her eyes as though she were literally trying to picture it. "Maybe they got sep'rated in all the mess, while they was being rounded up. People yelling at them, everybody scared. Or maybe they had a fight the evenin' before, a bad one, and he spent the night away, hooked on a bottle." She shook her head, saddened by her inability to step into their lives. "He must have come here feeling so ashamed. And every minute he stayed—"

Wolfgang turned around at her, looked at her with something more than condescension. Wonder, perhaps. "My wife's a romantic," he said. "Who would've guessed?"

It was her turn to ignore him. "I know how it was," she went on. "My father was a union man. Red as they come. They locked him up too, you know."

"Next you'll tell me you're a Communist yourself. Spent the war in the resistance. That titty-bar was just a front."

Poldi bit her lip. "She wants to see you, Frau Seidel does. In the drawing room at three. She said to tell you it's important."

This drew a chuckle from her husband. "In the drawing room at three? It appears I've been summoned. Did she say I should wear a tux?"

He rose from the bed very suddenly, stepped into his trousers, and, still in undershirt and socks, left the room.

4.

There were two sets of curtains, one behind the other. The inner was a sheer curtain made from cotton lace; the outer, a heavy velvet drape in a vivid shade of bronze. It proved impossible to shut the window with both curtains hanging out: the velvet was too thick. She tried several times, putting her weight against the glass. In the end she used a piece of string to tie the handle to its neighbour. It would prevent the window from blowing open but left it gaping a good few inches. Outside, the curtains billowed in the wind until the weight of the rain settled them, the velvet's bronze turning a flat brown. Her hands felt raw from the cold and the exertion; arthritic pain deep in the joints. Without looking back, Klara Seidel left her late husband's study and hurried back into her bedroom.

She settled down to lighter work; sat at her vanity and saw to her hair. There was a brush she liked that Seidel had given her for their first anniversary: solid silver, its handle and back inlaid with ivory, the horsehair bristles a light, speckled grey. Her eyes avoided the mirror. She worked by touch alone, each movement the echo of some childhood original, her entire life measured out in five-inch strokes. On occasion she caught a glimpse of the woman sitting across from her, frightened eyes and bloated jowls. It would have been good to reapply her makeup, but to do so required a longer meeting face to face. Powder served as a stopgap; hid her face, obscured the mirror in fine mist.

Soothed, her face a blank, a trail of particles shadowing her every movement, she reached into the vanity's drawer and withdrew a leather-bound album of photos. In recent weeks she had often had recourse to its comforts. Setting it down required the rearranging of bottles in front of her; a clink of glass on glass. She lined them up along the mirror's base, arranged them by size; arthritic fingers making order with exaggerated care. She paused over a particular bottle, removed the stopper, took a pinch, and dropped it quickly on her tongue. Eyes closed, she opened the album to a random page.

There was no chronology to the progression of pictures. She had arranged them quite recently, by size, mood, and association; had cut herself loose from the tyranny of sequence. Nonetheless it was all there: her childhood, both weddings, Robert's christening, the time Herr Baron von Schirach had shaken her hand. A reception of the National Socialist Women's League; the mayor's birthday; a commemorative postcard of the Führer's visit in 1938. Mum, Dad, three brothers; an albumen print of Grandpa, looking young and dapper in his Sunday suit.

There were pictures she lingered over. A picture of Robert, taken at school, dressed formally in jacket and tie; he had sent it one Christmas, a declaration of love neatly written on its back. A Sunday outing with her first husband, Franz Teuben, holding a gingerbread heart against his breast. The picture had been taken at the Prater amusement park; from his hat there grew the spokes of the great Ferris wheel. It might have been 1934 or '35; they were, neither of them, yet wearing their Party pins. She studied his face quite without emotion. Her love for him resided on the level of pure fact. True, things had been imperfect. Franz had drunk and gambled; had beaten her; had strayed, other women's smells clinging to the inside of his underwear, a half snatch of memory of her sniffing, crying, scrubbing at stains with a brick of soap. Nor had Franz had any real commitment to the Party; it merely suited his career.

As for herself she hardly ever read the papers; listened to the radio with no investment in the words. It was only in 1941, the year of victory, and of her second wedding, that she had become more involved. At first it was the social aspect that had drawn her: she, a policeman's widow, was suddenly courted to join the Women's League; helped organize the celebrations for the Day of Youth; raised funds for winter clothing for the soldiers at the front. Gradually, though, through the weeks and months of mouthing phrases, something else had taken hold. She had learned Nazism the way one learns any language: through constant repetition. It had felt good, for once, to be certain, on the side of the winners: a lifetime of anxiety taken off her shoulders. Of course, by then she'd become rich.

Of Paul Seidel there were only two photos in the album: the first, a staged wedding picture in which they gazed into one another's eyes; the second, part of a news clipping that praised his charity work. In both of them he looked very handsome, if slightly pinched. He had buried his old wife and married the new; had watched with trepidation her gradual transformation from maid to socialite to ideologue. For him the Party had been a business partner, to be negotiated with friendly distrust. His son had felt this lack of commitment and thrown himself into a frenzy of sloganeering. They learned from one another: in no time at all both Wolfgang and Klara spoke fluent Goebbels all day long.

She paused in her perusal, looked up, avoided once again the eyes of the powdered woman in the mirror. Anxiety took hold of her, came from nowhere, like the touch of a draft. Her moods were restless, like a trapped fly, now calm and quiet, now hurling its weight against the glass wall of its prison. Without hesitation she reached for one of the bottles, withdrew the glass pipette, placed two drops on the back of one hand, and licked them off; her eyes watering with its bitterness. The drug worked quickly, offered distance from herself. All at once it was as though she and the woman in the mirror had traded places. Gratified, she returned the bottle to its place.

Klara could no longer recall with any certainty when she'd first had recourse to her medicine. Certainly it had started before the bomb raids, the food shortages, the radio speeches instructing them to hang on. It had been so easy to procure. She'd simply asked the pharmacist for something to steady her nerves; a week later she'd requested a pick-me-up. The names entranced her: Luminal, Veronal, Pervitin, Benzedrine, codeine, pethidine, mixed at various concentrations. Powders, liquids, pills. She remembered a woman at a party, young and graceful, a gold chain slung around the long stalk of her neck, dipping its pendant deep into her cleavage.

"Try this," the young woman had said at the cloakroom mirror. "Our soldiers take it at the front." She kept it in a silver compact inscribed with a fashionable rune.

"I have my own," Klara had giggled, and they had traded tastes; the sudden rise of the girl's nipples, laughter as she danced back out into the crowded room.

"Try this," she mouthed now to the woman in the mirror, trying to recapture the moment's careless gaiety, "try this," the woman sour, swollen, unimpressed.

She closed the photo album in front of her, planted her fists on its leather, and pressed her head into her aching knuckles.

When next she looked up, Wolfgang was in the room. It could not have been much after noon.

5.

"You're early," she said, finding his eyes in the mirror. He stood, half dressed, at the centre of the room; a wedge of cigarette curling from the corner of his mouth.

"Does it matter?"

"I gave instructions."

"So you did."

She seemed more awake today, more present than he had seen her in some time. He thought of saying as much. He said, "You're losing your hair. There, at the back."

Her hand came up before she could stop it, searched her head for thinning hair. Then it was banished to her lap.

"I want to be friends." She said it carefully, a pleading note to her voice. For a moment he almost believed it.

"You know," he answered, "you never congratulated me. On getting off. True, true, I've not been social. Still, you could've found a way. A card would have been nice, maybe some flowers." He grinned, sucked smoke, let it stream from nose and mouth. "Or is it that you are disgruntled after all? For a while there, Robert looked to be the sole heir. Other than you, I mean."

He took a step closer, watched her shift her eyes in the mirror. "You know, you don't even love him very much. Was it his picture you were looking at just now?" He pointed to the album. "No, I didn't think so. You want him to be happy, of course—that is to say, you want him to be rich. But love? You don't have the knack." He shrugged. "Then again, who am I to talk? You sent for me, *Mother*. Here I am. What is it you want?"

She took her time with the answer; swallowed her spite and raised herself up in her chair. "We're being blackmailed."

Her hand slipped into the album in front of her, withdrew two pieces of paper, handed them to him. They were letters, typewritten and unsigned.

"Do you remember him well?" she asked while he was reading.

"Of course. He ate dinner here, two, three times a week. It's his house."

"Well, he finally came out of the woodwork. He found us all the same, even after you shut up your father."

Wolfgang ignored the insinuation. "It says here," he said, "you are to hang a curtain out the study window. As a sign you agree to the conditions. Will you—"

"I already have."

He handed back the letters. "So you'll pay."

"Let's go downstairs," she said, "and sit down in the drawing room. Talk it over."

He noticed, amused, that she took her handbag along for their interview, and a quart bottle of powders.

6.

Robert returned. He no longer entered the house with any hope of finding Eva there. Every day he walked for hours: asked in hotels, marketplaces, hospitals. All he had to help him was her hump: he owned no photo of her, was unsure which name she was using. The problem wasn't that he got blank stares; the city, it seemed, was full of hunchbacks, a score of false leads. Towards the end of the second week he gave up on asking; walked the streets, staring at passersby, then lost himself in thought and worry, allowing his feet to carry him wherever they wished. Once he was held up at knifepoint and stripped of his good coat; another time he walked headlong into a fight. Detective work, it appeared, did not run in his blood.

He entered the house, kicked off his shoes, carried his umbrella into the kitchen to drip onto the tiles. Hunger gnawed at him. He had brought bread home, unpacked it, cut a slice. He'd just put on the kettle when he heard his brother's voice.

"Robert?" it called. "Over here, in the larder. And now on down the stairs—you have to push at the back shelf. Yes, that's right, come on down. God, what a racket you made just now. And you probably thought you were as quiet as a mouse. But everything carries through the floor. It's like moving around on a drum."

Robert descended into the cellar. Wolfgang was sprawling on an unmade cot, a bottle of liquor wedged between his thighs. There were open jam jars on the floor.

"Ah, the look on your mug just now. Priceless! I didn't know about it either. All the exploring we did as kids, and we never dreamt there was a secret cellar. But sit, sit, join my little party. Only close the door. We want to be alone. Good, good. And now slide the chair closer. That's it. Ah, brother, here we meet again!"

He giggled, took a swig, passed the bottle over to Robert. He demurred.

"Not to your taste, eh? How about this?" He reached under the pillow behind his back, produced a small brown apothecary bottle with a handkerchief stuffed down the neck in lieu of a stopper. "Mama's little pick-me-up. Have you ever tried it?"

Robert shook his head. "Did you steal it?"

"Steal? No, no, she gave it to me. Like giving a child a treat. Perhaps she thinks it'll give me courage. It might at that." He pulled out the hanky with a little flourish, poured a small mound of powder into the palm of his hand. "Go on, little brother. Let me corrupt you just a bit."

Robert hesitated. "What do you do with it?"

"Take a pinch, rub it into your gums. That's it. Like eating powdered sugar. Only bitter. It works right away, doesn't it? Sends a buzzing down your pecker." He laughed. "Ah, yes, Mama and I had a nice little chat today. Real cozy it was."

Robert, energized, his senses crawling, took another pinch of powder. "What did you talk about?"

"Rothmann, Arnim Rothmann. The fat man. You don't remember him? Hm. And here I thought you would." Wolfgang sat up, took a pull on the liquor bottle, waved Robert closer yet. "A story, then. A family yarn. Best story there is."

He burped happily, closed his eyes to collect himself, held on to Robert's

323

shoulder. "Once upon a time there was a businessman, an Austrian by the name of Seidel, who invested all his money in a factory run by a fat Jew. God knows what they were making exactly, radio parts, transistors, who cares. The factory did well, in any case. The Jew wanted to expand. But for this he needed money: capital. He was a convert, our Jew, went to church every Sunday. Which is where he knew Seidel from. They got talking one afternoon, in the back pew. You can picture them sitting there, haggling. Conducting their business, with the blessing of the Lord.

"Things proceeded quickly. The Austrian, Seidel, well, he wasn't daft. He knew a good thing when he saw it. He put in all his money, everything save for some bonds, and before the month was out, he'd become the Jew's junior partner. This was in 1931 or '32: early days. They worked side by side and made one another rich.

"Now the thing to remember is that up to this point the Seidels had been small fry. Upstarts, that's the word; their money so new it put a blush on their cheeks. Grandpa, you see, was a shopkeeper. Came from the country and started selling hosiery. A crude man, but clever all the same. He made a small fortune somehow before the Great War and then held on to it when everyone else lost theirs. Mean as they come: he saved up every penny he ever made. Might be there was a little Jew in him too.

"In any case, the factory flourished, and Dad grew rich. Buried the old shopkeeper, started going to a better church. We moved into a flat in the first district; he bought himself a nice tweed suit. Then '38 rolled around. The Reich paid us a visit and decided to stay. And here something interesting happened. On that day—the day the army walked in, when all those people lined the streets, clapping, hailing Hitler—well, on that very day, it wasn't even clear what was really happening yet, some hooligan stepped up to fat Jew and knocked his hat off his head. It was nothing worse than that, but it happened in his own factory. One of his engineers. They got into an argument, right on the shop floor, and the man knocked his hat off.

"Rothmann took it as a sign of the times.

"Now the Jew proved to have vision. Prescient, that's what he was, like a Gypsy woman with her cards. That very day, he came to Father and made him another business proposition. He'd sell the factory to him, all of it, for a very modest price. There was a condition, of course. Any time he wanted to, Rothmann could buy it right back. Oh, it was more complicated than that, they drew up a whole contract, but that was the gist of it. They signed the papers and that was that. Seidel was the sole owner.

"It didn't stop there, either. Two weeks later, the Jew came back and sold father his house. Same conditions, same outcome, he even sold the furniture. Rothmann and family moved into more modest lodgings. We moved in here and everyone sent flowers. Only my mother did not join the celebrations. She was already sick, a hundred pounds going on eighty, thin as a stick.

"Now at the time, all this seemed crazy, or at any rate premature. Then the wave of Aryanizations hit all across Austria and Jewish businesses were being sold off for a pittance, whether they wanted to or not. And all at once Rothmann looked like a genius, let me tell you. He had Aryanized before the season—but on his conditions. We, meanwhile, lived like kings. We buried my mother six months after the move.

"By the time your mother came into the house, we'd got used to it all. You won't remember how pleased she was with herself: one day she was the maid in a nice, perky uniform, the next she was bossing around her own. It's funny, all that energy Father had spent on leaving the shop keeper in him behind. But the moment he'd made it, entered the first circles—cigars, cognac, a private booth at the opera—he went and married a bit of rough. She learned fast, your mother did, transformed herself into a lady. Only, when she wanted something, the fishwife would come peeking out.

"Those were glory times in any case; we never had so many servants. Life would have been grand, if it hadn't been for that Jew. Every other day he'd come for dinner, sometimes with his whole family in tow. Father practically fawned on him. It was, 'Try this cigar, Herr Rothmann, I had it sent from overseas,' and, 'Take the good chair, Herr Rothmann, here, by the fire, it's chilly out,' 'Such a delight to see you, you must come back soon,' on and on—and me already in the police! It was then your mother and I started discussing Party business over dinner. Good God, we had such fun.

"One time, early on—I remember it like it was yesterday—Rothmann leaned over to your mother, very discreetly, mind, speaking under his breath, and instructed her how to hold the fork, 'in a good household.' You should have seen her blanch. I swear, she signed her soul over to the Party and cheered Rothmann's entire race to the gas chambers just for that 'in a good household.' Not that he was wrong, mind. Your mother handled cutlery like she was digging a latrine.

"Then they stopped coming, the Rothmanns. 'To forestall unwanted attention.' Oh, he was a grandiose bastard, Rothmann was. Fat as a bar-rel, always a sweet in his pocket for you and me. I'm surprised you don't remember. But then, there were a lot of people who came and went. We ran a busy house back then.

"But in the end, even a clever Jew like Rothmann made a mistake. He left it too late to leave the country. He wanted to, kept on talking about London and New York, how he had business connections there. But the wife wouldn't go without her parents, and her parents refused.

"Next thing you know, well, history took its course. They got rounded up and shipped out of town." Wolfgang waved, as though seeing off a departing train, then leaned back and took another swig. "After that, nothing. Until now."

"He's come back."

Wolfgang grinned. "He sent us a letter. And how nicely it's written. You'd swear Fontane wrote it, or maybe Kleist. Says he has been watching us all along."

"The man with the red scarf. He wants everything back."

"Actually, he just wants money. A mere trifle, really. Ours is a modest Jew." He ran a hand through his stubble, gave Robert a sideways glance. "Your mother's not too happy about it, though. We had a little meeting, she and I. Down in the drawing room, real cozy. She closed the door after us, turned the key, then started right in. What a beast that man is, a Jew-swine, a usurer, you know the phrases. I listened to it, she worked herself into a right lather, and then I said, poking fun, like, 'I see you don't want to pay.' That stung her, she went red and started to lecture me. 'It's not about the money,' she said. I laughed. 'You're still fighting the war?' I asked. 'Is that it? You want to win?' She got angrier yet and started shouting at me in earnest. The words she came out with! Right out of the gutter. I pretended I'd taken offence (really, it isn't nice to be shouted at), I rose and walked to the door.

"She stopped me, of course, and all of a sudden she was soft like butter. She took hold of my sleeve and tugged me over to the armchair, gentle, though, making sure I didn't bump my legs. She tugged me down into the seat, sat down on the footstool, just by my side, and as she was talking, she stroked my jacket like she was testing the quality of the fabric, only tender, tender. And how she crooned! 'Wolfie,' she crooned (and when is the last time she called me that!), 'Wolfie, remember when you came home that day, wearing your uniform for the first time. Your father pretended not to notice, but I Remember how we drank jenever together, glass after glass, toasting your new position, I got tipsy real quick, but you kept on pouring, one arm around my shoulder . . .'

"And the funny thing, Robert, was that I did remember and felt moved. It rose before my eyes, jenever and all. Of course I knew she was just buttering me up—it was crude after all, very crude—but all the same, my eyes welled up and I was grateful to her. She sensed my change of mood and, still sitting there on the footstool, stroking my jacket sleeve, she started humming the 'Horst Wessel Lied' and telling me how her first husband, your father, had been fond of whistling it, but somehow with feeling—it's absurd, laughable, and yet I got all soft inside. I even let her hold my hand.

"So we spent a pretty little hour. I wish there'd been tea. And then, at the end, without looking up, without even changing the tone of her voice, she said, 'Will you get rid of that Jew?' 'What will you give me?' I said, unruffled, cozy with the moment. 'One hundred thousand,' she said. 'And twenty percent of the factory.' We shook on it, like the thieves we are.

"You know," he finished, patting the basement wall, "she's a little touched, your mama, but the truth is that half the people on this street, they have a Jew walled in their closet. God, how they are hoping the mortar will hold."

He leaned back, exhausted, took a dash of powder for his pains. Robert sat there very quietly, mulling over his story.

"What does she mean," he asked at last, his voice very quiet, "'get rid of him'?"

Wolfgang did not answer at once. "Scare him off, I suppose. She's decided I'm a good one for the rough stuff. Made a career of it, after all. What's one more Jew?" He sneered, patted Robert's leg. "She knows what I want, your mama. Of course, I could wait for my inheritance. There's a lot more in it than a hundred grand. But, hell, I want out, this minute, go someplace where nobody knows my face." He paused, looked Robert in the eye. "I'm going to be a father, Robert. I want to raise my child someplace where they won't point their finger at us every time we climb on the tram. And besides, it's all nonsense anyway. This letter writer, he isn't Rothmann. He can't be. Rothmann's dead. Father made inquiries, wrote a letter to the authorities. Gassed, they told him. They have some sort of list.

"Your mama doesn't know. If she did, she wouldn't give me a penny. Not until the lawyers force her to. But that'll take weeks, maybe months. Even then, I won't be able to leave. I'd have to stay to run the factory. It's one of Father's stipulations: I've seen the will. I'll have to pay you out and stay."

"I don't want the money," Robert said. "You won't owe me a dime. If you want, I will run the factory for you."

"Perhaps you would at that, little brother. But to live all my life in the shadow of your magnanimity—" Wolfgang shook his head. "No, no. First, let me take a look at this crook. See what he has to say."

7.

They sat in the cellar for another hour. They fetched the bread down and loaded it with jam. Robert sampled the brandy, took more of the drug. Whenever he wanted to turn their conversation back to Rothmann, Wolfgang demurred.

"Tomorrow," Wolfgang said, his eyes already glassy. "Nothing's going to happen till then. We're awaiting 'instructions.'"

Towards evening, lying shoulder to foot on the narrow cot, Robert bumped his head on something hard.

"What's that?" he asked, fishing under the blanket.

"Ah," said Wolfgang, smiling, "it's something else your mother gave me. She pulled it out of her handbag, wrapped into a dishrag, just as it is now. The way she was holding it, I thought it was a hammer."

"But what is it?" Robert asked again, undoing the knots.

"That, little brother, is the Viennese Detective Bureau's standard-issue Walther PPK service pistol your mother has been sleeping with since the autumn of 1939."

Perhaps it was the drug, but they both started giggling and, for the longest time, were unable to stop.

8.

The Walther Polizei Pistole Kriminal is a blowback-operated semi-automatic pistol developed by Fritz Walther in 1931. With its 83-millimetre barrel and a weight of less than 600 grams, the PPK's compact size predisposed it for use by plainclothes detectives and undercover agents wishing to carry a concealed weapon. A variety of safety features enhanced its applicability to urban peacekeeping. The double-action/single-action trigger mechanism ensured that the weapon could be confidently handled even if the safety had been disengaged: to fire the initial shot its operator had to overcome a greater trigger pull weight than for the subsequent single-action shots. A fall arrest system prevented any shots from being fired until the trigger was fully depressed, thus securing the weapon against accidental discharge. Due to its small size the weapon handled best in small and medium-sized hands. Large-handed users wishing for a comfortable position of the small or "pinky" finger had to resort to a special magazine with elongated grip. Like many semi-automatic compact pistols the PPK's hammer had a tendency to pinch the webbing between the operator's thumb and trigger finger when the gun was fired, a phenomenon known as "hammer bite." The problem was addressed by later models built under licence by Smith & Wesson in the U.S.A. through the addition of a so-called beaver tail, an elongation of the upper rear end of the grip. Other than becoming the weapon of choice for detective units across much of Europe, the gun also became standard issue for border patrols both before and after World War II. The PPK was popular amongst German Wehrmacht officers, who acquired it privately and used it as their service handgun. It had the reputation of being a reliable execution weapon.

After the war the PPK's popularity was further buoyed by Ian Fleming's decision to equip his fictional secret service agent with the weapon. There have been other famous users. Hitler shot himself through the right temple with his Walther PPK, serial number 803157, at three-thirty on the afternoon of April 30, 1945. Fourteen years previously Hitler's niece, some say his lover, Angela "Geli" Raubal had committed suicide by shooting herself through the chest and lung with another Walther, also belonging to Hitler. It reputedly took her seventeen hours to die.

In June 1967 a West German plainclothes officer by the name of Karl-Heinz Kurras killed Benno Ohnesorg, a student who had participated in a Berlin demonstration against the visiting Shah of Iran, by shooting him in the back of the head with his Walther PPK. During his criminal investigation and trial Kurras insisted he had acted in self-defence and described having been assaulted by a throng of armed demonstrators. Of the eighty-three witnesses heard in court, the only one to confirm this account was a fellow police officer's wife who lived in the building in whose yard the shooting had taken place. She did not come forward until shortly before the trial, claiming that the officer in charge of the investigation had omitted to question her on this point. The statement of a nine-year-old boy who had watched the shooting from his kitchen window and described a deliberate, almost execution-style killing was treated as unreliable on grounds of his age. The criminal trial acquitted Kurras due to lack of evidence of wrongdoing.

It was not until 2009 that Kurras was discovered to have served as an informant for the East German Ministry for Security, MfS, more popularly known as the Stasi. Internal communications within the MfS reveal bafflement with regard to Kurras's motive for the shooting. He was involved in a later, separate investigation, in which he threatened his Czech maid at gunpoint, trying to force a false witness statement regarding the beating of a press photographer. It is not known whether the gun used in this second incident was also a Walther.

Chekhov said that if you introduce a gun in Act One, it has to go off in Act Three.

He does not tell us what happens if you introduce it in Act Three.

Three

Hunched and freezing, the man with the red scarf was sitting down in his cellar in a parallelogram of pale November light, threading black thread through the eye of a needle. The parallelogram kept moving, renegotiating its angles, taking orders from the sun. He followed it doggedly, inch for inch and foot for foot, then swapped it for its twin when the patch of light was beginning to reach the wall. He had neither a work table nor a chair and had placed a flat wooden board across his knees; worked in a soldier's squat, for hours at a time. The man had done his best to clean the little cellar windows, but even so the light was streaky, criss-crossed by smudges of projected grime. The bird in his hands felt as cold and stiff as a frozen glove.

It was perfectly preserved. There was no bullet hole or cut; the carcass bristling with a seamless coat of jet-black feathers. Each time he slipped a hand inside, it bulged and came to life, a lopsided bird with soaring wings he had just finished wiring into shape. When he withdrew the hand, the bird deflated, became an empty sack whose only point of real solidity was the cleaned and reinserted skull. He had been working on the carcass for two weeks. Very soon now he would stuff it, sew it up.

It was not easy working with a bird. One had to take care not to damage the feathers or tear the delicate skin. He stopped intermittently, warmed his fingers and hands. They had been different before the years of forced labour: thinner, more supple, better suited to such delicate work. Even so, each of his movements was gentle, almost regretful, implied an apology for the crudeness of the act. Had he been stroking a kitten, or bandaging a wounded child, he could not have moved with greater circumspection. He was, at present, trying to ease a split marble into the scooped-out socket of an eye.

It had begun with a long incision and the patient peeling of skin from flesh. The skin had to be scraped free of fat then cured with sodium borate; the skull excised and rid of everything but bone. Then came the patient building of the armature. He had found no clay and had decided on a wire structure that he wrapped in layer upon layer of rags and straw until the body of a bird took shape between his hands, supple enough to simulate the soft contours of life.

The problem throughout was materials. The wire had been easiest, cut at some risk from a bit of wall atop an American compound. Rags and thread he had found after long searching amongst the discarded things in the cellar. He stole the straw by the fistful from a horse stable in Ottakring. There were chemicals he needed, including camphor, arsenic, and potassium carbonate. Some he owned from previous forages, some he stole afresh from a pharmacy on the Gürtel whose back-door hinges he unscrewed in the depth of night, having spent the afternoon observing the shop and making sure its owners did not keep a dog. The eyes were a challenge all their own, and for days he could not think of a solution. In the end he bargained—silently, by gestures—with a child for marbles and paid with a toy horse made from sewn-together rags and straw. He took the marbles home, split and shaped them with a chisel, wedged them in the scraped-out sockets, replaced the skull in the skin, then sewed the eyeholes into place around each artificial lens. The results pleased him, each eye a swirl of midnight blue and red.

He stroked the crow's feathers, rose, and stretched his back. The armature lay ready on a pile of papers. He might finish tonight.

He decided to take a break first and go out looking for the girl. He did so every day, walked a circle of streets he associated with her presence. For the first time since finding her, he had lost sight of her. She had dropped the bird for him to find and had not returned to the house. It was impossible, thought the man with the red scarf, not to see the hand of God in this.

He sat alone sometimes, wrapped in his blankets, wondering whether it was time now to go home.

2.

The phone rang six times before she picked up. He gave his name before she had time to finish her greeting. Her response was conventional, the voice free of excitement.

"Hello, Inspector Frisch. What a surprise. How can I be of service?"

Frisch had long learned to hide his awkwardness behind the drone of his voice. "Good evening, Frau Doktor Beer. I just wanted to make sure the line works. I called before and there was no answer. So I thought I'd try you at night."

"That is kind of you. Well, it works. Thank you again for having it reconnected—I should really have sent a card." Her pause was well judged to draw out the fact of his impertinence. "Was there anything else, Inspector?"

"No. That is to say, perhaps. I requested another look at your husband's file. His investigative file, I mean; a record of all our activities. I wanted to see whether we ever followed up on all the dental records. Concerning the body in the morgue."

"And?"

"It seems that we tried. But we failed to track down any records for your husband. The dentist he frequented prior to the war left the country. Address unknown. Still, there may be other avenues—"

"Very good. Do call if you find something concrete. That would be very kind."

"Of course, Frau Doktor Beer. Will you be staying in Vienna, then?"

"Only until I have packed up the apartment. A few weeks, I imagine. I will make sure to pass on my forwarding address. Good night, Inspector."

She hung up. Frisch stayed on the line another moment, listening into the void, then caught himself and followed suit. When he turned, Trudi was standing next to his desk. She was looking at him with something too childish yet to be called contempt. Embarrassed, Frisch took off his spectacles and polished the lenses on his sleeve.

"She does not want to talk to you."

"No, Trudi. She does not."

"But you'll keep on calling her."

He smiled at the pithiness of her summary: the sad smile of a man used to acknowledging the facts. "Perhaps. You are too young to understand."

"I understand," she said. "You miss Mama. I miss her too."

He winced at this assessment, took her by the hand, led her over to the kitchen. They sat down to have dinner.

"This is something different," he told her as he was slicing the bread. "A different sort of missing." He paused again, put the bread into a basket, fetched the cold cuts from the larder. "It's like you grow a second stomach. When you turn into an adult. You try to forget about it, but when you go to bed at night, it growls."

Trudi processed this. "You want to eat her," she summarized.

He laughed. "Yes, I suppose I do. The way you dream of eating chocolate. You can live without, but . . ."

They had dinner. When they were done and she stood doing the dishes, her feet on a stepping stool so she could reach, he unlocked the hallway cupboard and removed a little bar for her. It was British, still wrapped in tinfoil.

"Here," he said. "This way, at least one of us gets their sweet."

She unwrapped the chocolate, bit off a square, lips and teeth staining brown. "She won't let you, will she?" Trudi asked, chewing.

"Not in a million years," said the detective, sat down at his desk, and read his way once more through Anton Beer's slender file.

3.

To her surprise she got an appointment almost at once. Sophie approached her usual contact at the U.S. embassy, begged them to ring the representative of the Soviet military administration, and within the hour was issued a pass to cross over to the Soviet sector and speak to a secretary of the news and propaganda division. He was bald, bearded, in his thirties; a cordial man with wire-rim glasses. His office, in the second district, was located in a spacious mezzanine apartment that appeared to have been requisitioned from a hunter. Deer heads lined much of the walls, along with more exotic trophies. In the wood-panelled study she sat between the pelts of two spread-eagled bears.

The man's English was excellent, his manner affable. "So we are colleagues," he said, having spent several minutes studying her press credentials with great care. "But what is a pretty little thing like you doing writing articles?"

She blushed and watched him pour tea from a samovar.

"Please," he said, "don't stand on formalities. Just tell me what I can do for you."

"I—I have come for information. It's all a little delicate. I made inquiries before, you see, of the Soviet authorities. And now I am worried that my questions may have led to—But really, I'm at a loss where to begin."

"Just start at the beginning," he encouraged her. "There's no need to rush."

It was not long before the whole story spilled out of her. The man listened attentively, took notes, but rejected her suggestion that her earlier inquiries about Beer's disappearance might have led to the disappearance of a corpse from the city morgue and the arrest of Beer's friend.

"You must not believe everything you hear, my dear," he said. "About Soviet security organs and the like. We are the freest nation in the world. Soon we will have no need for a police force at all." He smiled with considerable warmth. "And besides, when *they* strike"—he let his eyes dart around the room and left it to her to give content to this *they*—"well, it's like a storm cutting through a barley field. It takes what it wants, and afterwards, not a sign: just clean, fresh air."

He rose, escorted her to the door, brushed her hip with his hand as he saw her out. "I wonder whether you would like to have dinner some evening? Or go to the opera, perhaps? I can get hold of tickets. Well, think about it. In any case, it's been a pleasure, Frau Coburn, a real pleasure." He had sent for a car and stood there on the pavement, watching her drive off.

The car took her to the border of the American district, where she transferred to a tram. She was halfway to her apartment building when she got out, changed over to a cab, and headed instead to the hotels and flophouses of the Gürtel, resumed her dogged search for Karel Neumann and the woman with whom he was said to have taken up.

4.

Eva watched him get ready. There wasn't much to do: he owned no clothes other than the ones he was wearing, owned no coat and no scarf, nor even a hat he might have drawn into his brow to mask his features. In fact he made a point of washing his face and shaving. He seemed to believe that blackmail was one of those tasks best performed clean.

It was not clear to her at which point over the past two weeks Karel had given up on finding the man who might be Rothmann and had decided on impersonating him instead. Perhaps he had been planning it all along. When he suggested it to Eva, she had accepted the idea at once. It was much simpler that way. They tracked down a typewriter in a pawnshop. She composed the letters herself, the words shaping themselves into phrases as though she had done this all her life. It seemed frightfully easy, all of a sudden, this getting rich.

At length Karel seemed satisfied with his shave; wiped the soap off his chin, dried off, then tucked the cutthroat in his pocket rather than returning it to the sink. She noticed it and frowned.

"Why are you taking a knife?"

"Just in case."

"You won't need it," she said with peculiar emphasis. "You won't be having any trouble. She'll send Robert. She doesn't trust the other one."

He looked at her for some moments, dug in his pocket, threw the cut-throat onto the bed. "You know," he said, "it's not too late. You can still go back." He reached out a hand as though to touch her, then thought better of it. "Forget about the crows. So the boy didn't stand up to his mother. She won't live forever, you know."

She shook her head. "It's not about the crows."

"Oh, I understand. You're upset. He doesn't love you enough." He shrugged as though to say it was hard to meet her standards. "Or maybe you have this fantasy, buried deep in your heart. That you will go to America with all this money and then ten years down the road you'll return, almost a princess, take a taxi to his house and ring the bell?" He searched her face, found only spite and irritation. "Tell me, Lieschen. Were you always this sour?"

She flashed a smile, bitter, turned, and straightened out before the washstand mirror. It only seemed to emphasize the hump. "Sour? Not at all. I was the sweetest little girl in the whole wide world. People could not wait to pet me. It even worked at the orphanage. The wardens were quite charmed. Then the other girls got jealous."

"They beat it out of you, eh? Ah, the cruelty of children."

His voice was mocking, more from habit than intent. He half expected her to let it drop, but his remark had evidently struck a chord.

"It wasn't just that," she said. "After a few years, I beat them too. The newcomers, the ones that were younger. Weaker." Eva gave him time to process the words then carried on. "I *did* have a fantasy once. When I was living at the orphanage. I'd imagine sneaking down to the kitchen, boiling the kettle, and carrying it back up to the dorm. What I kept picturing was this: standing there in the dark, the kettle tilted in my hands, the water flush with the spout, just inches from the little sleeping face. Not the pouring itself, but the moment just before, when I knew I would pour without fail and nobody could stop me. It's funny that I never imagined scalding the matrons, only the orphans." She shuddered, smiled. "I used to imagine it in great detail. It wasn't revenge, mind. I didn't pick any of the bullies. I chose the quiet girl, the sweetheart, the one they hadn't broken yet. I stood there looking at her locks. I was fourteen then. Timid. Today, I would pour the water." She paused; a long pause, eyes turned inward. At long last her thoughts came to rest on this: "Have you heard about that man, the one who tried to blow up Hitler?"

"Stauffenberg."

"No, the other one. Elsner or something. He sat in his garage and built a bomb. I heard about him on the radio. They called him a hero. Any day now they will make a movie about him, with Jimmy Stewart, you just wait."

Karel grinned. "So that's it, eh? Another fantasy! You're a funny girl, Liese. First you don't speak, not ten words in two weeks, and then it all comes out, what you've been working away at, in some corner of your mind: you want to blow up Hitler. Of course, it's impracticable; you don't know a thing about explosives, and he's dead, the little fucker. Who, then?—No, no, don't be insulted!" She had turned away from him, stood scowling at the mirror. "I'm laughing, but all the same I understand; it's despair, a dark anger of the heart. Mama killed all the crows and no one loves you. So, good, let's rob her a little, it isn't justice, it won't take the orphanage out of your blood, and that nasty steaming kettle, but hell, at least you'll be rich and far away and Robert will be sorry."

"I hate you," she said. And then, in a voice suddenly choked with tears: "What a stupid fool I am."

He tried to reassure her. "What does it matter, all this? The truth is, you never poured the water."

"No, I didn't. I thought that if I did, they would have put me down. Like a dog. Turns out I wanted to live!" She blew her nose, walked over to the bed, picked up the cutthroat. "It is too late. He won't have me, and I'm too ugly." She thumped her chest, not her hump, forced the cutthroat into Karel's hand. "Take it. Make us rich."

They left the hotel together. Out on the street he turned to her one more time before they parted. "You'll send the telegram? At six o'clock. Not before."

"We've been over this."

She watched after him until he was lost in dark and growing mist, then walked to the telegraph office. A clock was hanging on the wall. She waited until the agreed time, filled in the little slip, then went up to the counter.

"Send Urgent," she said, "to be delivered at once."

The man looked at the address. "It'd be quicker to just take a taxi. Cheaper, too. That's what our boy will do."

"Just do as I ask."

When she returned to the hotel, there stood in the corridor outside their door a small woman with foreign features that seemed incapable of settling into any definite expression. She was wrapped into an expensive fur-trimmed coat. As Eva approached, the stranger watched her with a puzzled intensity, but stood aside when Eva drew level.

"Looking for someone?" Eva asked, but received no answer.

When she checked a half-hour later, the shabby hallway stood empty, though there lingered amongst the kitchen smells and dirty walls a hint of French cologne.

5.

Robert and Wolfgang spent the day together waiting. They sat in the kitchen, then the drawing room; drank coffee, ate jam; spoke at intervals with a freedom and intimacy they had not enjoyed even during Wolfgang's time in jail. Later, waiting in the dark of a doorway, counting off the minutes since Wolfgang had left, Robert would revisit these snatches of conversation, sift them for meaning.

"Did she give you the money?" Robert asked.

"She gave me an envelope. It's rather thick."

"You didn't open it?"

"Why bother? We both know what I'd find: a cut-up newspaper. Look"—he held the envelope to the light—"you can make out the print."

"She's determined to cheat, then."

"Don't be too hard on her, Robert. You don't know what it's like to live in a place where you can make a man disappear just with a phone call. And have the radio tell you you did right.

"Besides, we're cheating a cheat."

A half-hour later, rain on the windowpane.

"You know, Wolfie, it's possible he's a relation. A stranger wouldn't know the details. It might be Rothmann's brother. Or his uncle. Or maybe the lists have it wrong. There must be thousands unaccounted for."

A little later he added, "We have to atone."

Wolfgang smiled at the word.

The clock struck one. They heard Robert's mother move deep in the house, walking about. Floorboards creaking, the slither of slippers.

Robert closed the door.

One forty-five.

"Father wanted to give it back, didn't he? That's why he was looking for Rothmann."

"So it's 'Father' all of a sudden?"

"He wanted to give it back. All this time I hated him. But he was a good man, wasn't he?"

"A good man? Ah, Robert, it always comes back to the same thing with you. So what if he was? One thing, though: all the time he was looking for Rothmann, writing letters, talking to past acquaintances, he hoped and prayed the man was dead. The thought of losing it all (well, half, or two-thirds, or whatever it is, but in his mind, let me tell you, he thought of it as all), it gave him an ulcer. All the same, he wrote his letters inquiring, 'Did Rothmann live? What happened to his family?' et cetera, et cetera, always hoping God was watching, taking note."

Wolfgang smiled sourly, took a pinch of drug. "Do you remember the priest at the church? Father Ludwig? God, what a swine he was. Every time some girl got herself pregnant, out of wedlock, I mean, he'd lay into her until she sobbed and was ready to throw herself off a bridge. He'd come here afterwards and brag about it to Father. And then he would join us for dinner and eat and eat and eat. Well, guess what? Father Ludwig was sent to a camp and died a martyr. Devil knows how he got himself arrested, some leaflets of some sort. Father heard it and wrote a letter of complaint. Addressed it to the *Gauleiter* himself. He sealed it up and mulled it over; it sat on his desk till after the war.

"But on the whole, yes, a good man; better than most."

Two twenty-five: time passing erratically, in fits and bursts, Robert watching the clock face, trying to catch it at its tricks.

"Here, Wolfgang, take this and give it to him. I don't care if he's a crook. Just give it to him. What difference does it make?"

"Three thousand? And he whips it out like it's a fiver! Had it flying round his trouser pocket. Where do you have this from?"

"Mother. I know where she keeps it."

"You stole it? Ah, now we've corrupted you in earnest. Very well, I'll take it. If he deserves it—well, we shall see. I half expect him to show with a knife, you know. Or maybe an axe. Split my skull and rob me blind."

Ten to three, the tap of fingers against glass as Wolfgang shakes some powder out of the apothecary jar, its contents moist and sticking to its walls.

"Go on, Robert, have some."

"No. Don't you think you've had enough? It's making you twitchy."

"On the contrary. It's helping me focus. They gave this to our pilots. God, what it must have been like, dropping down on the enemy from the centre of the sun. You know, Robert, there were moments during the war when every little schoolboy felt just like a king."

At half past three Robert's thoughts drifted to Eva.

"I can't find her," he lamented. "I looked everywhere, but she's simply disappeared."

"Be glad," said Wolfgang. "You're better off without.

"It's the sort of love," he added, "that is two-thirds pity. Believe me, Robert. I know."

At four Poldi came to see what they were doing. She sat down, started chatting, was met by cold looks. When she reached for Wolfgang's hand, he brushed her off. She slammed the door on the way out.

Robert looked after her long after she was gone. "How did you meet, you and Poldi?"

"She didn't tell you? She was dancing. In a sort of cabaret. I was ordered to shut it down."

"Did she—Besides dancing, I mean."

"You want to know if she was a whore?" Wolfgang said it calmly. "Who knows? I didn't ask. She did what she needed to survive. It's hard being poor, Robert. Father never understood this." And in a belated flare of anger: "She is the mother of my child."

As the clock inched towards five, Wolfgang's thoughts returned to his father.

"Were you there when he died, Robert? In hospital, I mean."

"Yes, I was."

"Did he say anything?"

"He wasn't conscious."

"He didn't suffer, then."

"I don't know, Wolfie. It was terrible. I watched him die and I didn't care."

Five-fifteen. Dusk had long fallen. It took them a while to notice and turn on the light. Outside, the rain had stopped, the temperature fallen: mist rising off the street like exhalation.

Robert poured himself a glass of water.

Wolfgang rubbed Pervitin into his gums.

"Did you do it, Wolfgang? Because of the money? He kept on writing those letters, looking for Rothmann, giving away your inheritance. You grew angry, and you—"

"Do you really believe that, Robert? That I killed my own father over money?"

Robert hesitated. "Mother believes it. It's not true?"

"I've had my trial. You heard the verdict. That's all I have to say."

"We'll do it together, Wolfie, you and I."

"We have instructions. One person: 'unaccompanied.' If there are two of us, he might not show."

"Then let me go. I'll talk to the man."

Wolfgang smiled. "With a face like that, you could get away with murder. No, Robert. I will—how did Father like to say it?—'carry the cross.'"

At twenty past six a car drove up. They heard the door slam then a ring at the door. The telegram boy passed over a little slip of paper, waited in vain for his tip. Outside, the drizzle had stopped and been replaced by a pale, cloying mist that gave the illusion of light.

Wolfgang read the instructions, passed the slip of paper to Robert.

"Do you know the address?"

"I know the area. Our factory is just around the corner from there." Wolfgang looked at his watch. "I'll call a taxi."

The taxi arrived after fifteen minutes. They were already running late. Two blocks from their destination the brothers got out of the car and watched it speed away. They walked half a city block then stopped in the shelter of a doorway. Wolfgang searched his pockets for a cigarette, but all he found was the gun.

"This will do," he said. "You can see the gateway from here. Over there, next to the butcher's shop." He pointed out into the mist. "We'll do it as agreed. You stand guard here. Whistle if you see something suspicious. If you hear me shout, run and get help."

Robert took hold of Wolfgang's arm. "Don't go, Wolfie. Let the truth come out. It'll be better that way."

For a second it looked as if Wolfgang might be swayed. Then he slowly shook his head. "I might as well take a look," he muttered. "One hundred grand, little brother. I could be in Brazil by Christmas." He turned to leave. "Just watch my back, Robert. Will you do that for me?"

Again Robert held him back. "Promise that you won't—"

"Just as we agreed, Robert. Not a hair on his head. I swear it on my mother's grave."

Without another word Wolfgang started walking down the street.

6.

It was less than fifty yards to the gateway. Wolfgang walked, his hand stuck into his coat pocket, his head thrust forward, peering into the mist. As he went, the feeling stole over him that Poldi was there, walking with him, a half step behind. He turned, cursing himself for his stupidity; walked on, and again felt her there, right past his shoulder, matching him stride for stride. Five yards on, Poldi was replaced by his father, then by Fejn, the prosecutor, shadowing his every step. He caught himself listening for their footfall; changed his pace to catch them out.

Then, as suddenly as it had come on, the feeling lifted. It was as though he had been abandoned. Startled, Wolfgang looked about himself and realized that he was still less than halfway to the gateway. Behind him the darkness had swallowed Robert. The street was empty, devoid of movement other than a ripple in the puddle he had just crossed. Wolfgang squared his shoulders and hurried on.

But the closer he drew to the gateway, the more his haste abandoned him. He got to one knee when he arrived at its entrance, to retie his shoelace; made a hash of it with trembling fingers. Annoyed, he jumped up and stormed on, only to stop again some three steps later, lean against the wall, and stare at the courtyard ahead. In the dark one could make out piles of rubble; moonlight clinging to the mist. Another step, another hesitation. The gun pulled at his wrist; he was not sure when he had drawn it. Disgusted, he shoved the Walther back into his pocket, all the while thinking, *I mustn't use it, Robert will hear*, thinking of him standing there, at his street corner, waiting for his return.

Perhaps it's a sort of trick, it came to him. *Robert's waiting back there so he can wash his hands of things. Afterwards, he will be grateful.*

He pictured Robert's face mouthing the word "atone" and felt his own face freeze into a sneer. And anyway, what if the stranger attacked him first? If he tore open the envelope, saw there was no money inside, then launched himself at Wolfgang? It'd be self-defence. Even Robert would not be able to object.

The main thing is, Wolfgang reminded himself, *I mustn't tell Father*.

He had, at that moment, quite forgotten that his father was dead. An enormous thought seemed to be growing in him, just beyond the threshold of consciousness; he groped for it in irritation, the way a man gropes for the light switch in the dark. Abruptly he began wishing he had brought a knife.

With a knife, I could kill him in silence.

He remembered a friend of his instructing him, a fellow police officer, sitting in their tea kitchen over some sandwiches and making small talk. "Aim for the throat or face," he'd said. "A thick coat will deflect your blade." Stolzfuss—that had been his name; a lad so skinny it was impossible to picture him in a fight. The next moment Stolzfuss was forgotten, and the thought of killing someone seemed nothing short of preposterous.

The war is over after all.

What Wolfgang would do was this: he would smile at the stranger and talk to him quite openly, the way Robert did, holding nothing back.

"You're a crook," Wolfgang would say. "Go on, tell the world all the secrets you like, it won't make any difference. Just do this, friend: wait a week. So I can get my money and leave. Look here, I'll give you ten thousand. A week from Monday. Ten grand for waiting one little week. That's not bad, friend, is it now? So let's shake on it and go have a drink. I know a darling little place nearby. There's a waitress there, oho! And besides, I'll pay, for the booze and for the girls too, if the mood takes you. My little brother's given me some spending money. We can have a right little orgy."

But even as he was thinking this, his hand once again moved back into his pocket and wrapped itself around the butt of his gun. He remembered the interrogations he had performed, their simple brutality, the frightened faces of the prisoners and the calm assurance of his superior sitting next to him, giving orders.

If it's to be done, it's best done quickly, at once, before he even opens his mouth.

He pictured it, the man in the yard, going down after a quick blow (with the butt, the butt, there need be no noise!), then realized that he was picturing Rothmann just as he'd been, a fat, genial man with long, curling eyelashes that gave a special warmth to his eyes. It took an effort to remind himself that the man he would meet was an imposter.

All the better, he thought. *I won't know him. It'll be easier that way.*

But again he stopped in his tracks, shoved the gun back in his pocket. Perhaps, it occurred to him, he had taken too much of his stepmother's drug. He wished he had brought along some brandy, something to wet his throat.

When he finally stepped out into the yard, he was unprepared to find it empty.

7.

Relief flooded Wolfgang, was immediately replaced by anger, then by a feeling of cunning as he realized he might have arrived at the location first. He whirled around, making sure there was nobody behind him; scrutinized the piles of rubble that had been the back building, trying to assess whether a man might be hiding amongst them. At his back he noticed a bent metal door leading to a cellar. Wolfgang approached it, then thought better of it and pretended to lose interest.

On his second circuit of the yard he noticed a piece of brick wall— more than a foot across, the inside still covered with wallpaper—that lay on the ground by itself and had evidently been dragged there from one of the mounds. He crouched down to it, found it marked with chalk glowing strangely in the moon-soaked mist. It said *SEIDEL*, just the one word, large capital letters. Wolfgang pushed the slab aside, and beneath it found a shallow hollow where two courtyard cobbles had been pried loose. A dirty sheet of paper spelled out *HERE*.

Without the slightest hesitation Wolfgang deposited the envelope within this hollow, replaced the slab, and hurried to the gateway. Everything was all abundantly clear to him—almost as though someone had explained it to him. Rothmann *(No, not Rothmann; the stranger, the crook, the man who is trying to rip us off!)* was hiding behind the cellar door. There was no way he would risk someone else coming along and finding the marked slab of wall. No, he was there, right behind the door, eyes fastened on the yard, listening for Wolfgang's footsteps, waiting for him to leave. Wolfgang obliged him and made a point of walking loudly—stamping his feet almost—until he had nearly reached the street. Then he lowered himself to the ground, lay down on the icy cobbles in the gateway, and crawled back seven or eight yards until his face was less than a foot from the threshold to the yard. The gun was out again, his fingers growing stiff around its grip.

He did not have to wait very long. After six or seven minutes there came a scrape as the cellar door dug itself into the courtyard floor. A moment later a figure stepped out into the yard and bent down to the marked slab. The moon-fed half-light distorted his proportions: from Wolfgang's vantage point, peering at him through the sodden mist, the man retrieving the envelope looked as big and rough-hewn as a tree.

Carefully, the gun in his fist, Wolfgang got up off the ground and stepped into the yard. The man did not notice him until Wolfgang was three feet from his broad back.

When Robert entered the yard, not ten minutes later, he found a mauled and bleeding body lying in the dirt.

It took an awful lot of shouting to alert the police.

Four

1.

Sophie did not feel the first drop form, was unaware of it until it hit the water, spread red skirts into the foam. A second followed, hit her drawn-up knee, splattered upon impact. She felt with her hands, came away bloody, then sat calmly, her attention on the droplets' passage. First a quick dash from nostril to upper lip, where they sat, beaded, and swelled, clinging to the thin ledge where two types of skin collide. A moment later, blood-swollen past endurance, the drop would break; would choose a passage left or right, drawing half of a moustache onto her features, then chase on down, past the precipice of jawbone, launch itself into thin air. A quarter heartbeat later—reverting in an instant from trickle back to tear—it would hit her breast, her knee, the white ceramic of the tub. Sophie did nothing to stem the flow; sat, arms hugging bony knees, and watched the cooling water turn from soapy grey to pink.

Somebody—a fellow lodger—knocked on the door, first gently then with increasing force, made speeches in loud German on the code of conduct pertaining to shared bathrooms. She understood not half of it, but the tone was long familiar. It seemed the language was made for this: the judicious venting of rational outrage for the benefit of those whom one knew to be listening out of sight. The water was quite icy now, and Sophie got out, reached for the towel, pulled the plug. She dressed quickly, still without answering the banging on the door, bundled up her dirty underwear and the old stockings, combed her hair. When she stepped out, the fat man outside watched her with embarrassment that only regressed into hostility when she was five steps down the hallway.

"About time!" he shouted after her.

She did not answer, dropped off her dirties in her room, then left the flat and ran up to see Anna. There remained, on the side of her chin, a faint tear-track of blood. The bathtub, too, was ringed by a fine pink waterline that gave her neighbours further reason for gossip and complaint.

2.

She did not wait for Anna to lead her into the kitchen to make her confession. It came out in the corridor, in mid-step, while Anna was still closing the door.

"Karel is back in Vienna," she said. "He's been here for weeks."

She described, too quickly perhaps for Anna to follow all her English, how she had paid people to look for him in bars, and how she had traced him from one shabby hotel to another, always asking for a "giant," always arriving a day or two too late.

"Tonight, I finally caught up with him. Only I was late again. He'd left on some errand, or to go drinking, I don't know."

Anna listened to her and felt a coldness rise in her that it took her a moment to identify as anger. "You should have told me earlier. Frisch needs to question Karel. He escaped the Russians. He will know where Anton is." She pushed past Sophie and fetched her coat.

"There are no Russians. He made them up."

Anna froze, one sleeve dropping from her fingers, flopping empty by her side.

"I knew it months ago. The moment I started asking him questions. It just didn't add up—the names and dates, it all kept changing every time he told the story, and when I pressed him, he just asked for money, to meet a 'contact' he'd picked up in some bar." Sophie paused, awaited a verdict.

Anna did her the favour. Her limited English lent a fitting crudeness to

351

her words. "You kept silent because you enjoyed fucking him? Or because you wanted to write your article?"

"Don't pretend you're surprised, Anna. You must have suspected it too." Sophie looked at her, expectant, but was granted no pardon, no sharing of her guilt. When she carried on, there was genuine wonder in her voice. "All this time I thought you knew. That you held on to the Russians as a sort of insurance against the simplest of explanations. That your husband simply left you."

If Sophie was aware of the hurtful nature of her words, she did not show it. She was absorbed in her own justifications. "I went along with Karel's story because I thought there was a chance there was some truth to it, mixed up with his lies. And then, when I started calling the embassies, it did push some buttons. When that body disappeared, and Karel himself went missing—well, I thought, maybe I had done him an injustice. Maybe he had embellished a little here and there, but the core of it—But he is back and didn't bother to come see me—"

Anna had heard enough. "We must tell the police. Karel knows *something*. He knew about Anton's secret. And he had a key to the flat." She finished putting on her coat, tied a scarf around her neck. "Where do I find him?"

Sophie gave her the address of the hotel. "He's got a new girl," she added hoarsely, her restless features reaching for defiance. "At least I think she is his girl. I was there today and wanted to ask her, whether they—But how do you ask a question like that?" She swallowed, relocated her feelings of betrayal underneath her confusion. "You can't miss her. The one from the trial. She's bent like a miner. How can a man take up with someone like—" She stopped herself, hurried after Anna, who had stepped out onto the landing. "I'll come with you."

Anna shook her head. "Go home," she said in German. "To Toronto, or New York, or wherever it is you belong. Nobody wants you here."

Without locking the door, she ran down the stairs and out onto the street, looking for a cab. By the time she finally found one, three blocks from the house, she had changed her mind about her destination, dug in her purse, and found an address that had been pressed on her weeks ago by a would-be suitor.

"Fifteenth district," she said to the cabbie. "Make it quick."

3.

Anna found the name on the doorbell; she had to ring several times before she was let in. Frisch lived in the back wing of a Union building built in the 1920s, its murals of working men untouched by the war. It was not he but his daughter who opened the door. Anna had no memory of her name.

"Good evening," she said formally, looking down at the child. "I wish to speak to your father."

"He had to go out," the girl said. "To work."

Anna turned to leave.

"You can call him if you like. We have a telephone."

"That would be most kind."

She followed the girl into the small, cramped apartment. It smelled of boiled cauliflower and cigarettes. A coconut runner stretched from entrance to study. A look in the kitchen revealed a heap of dirty dishes; Frisch's socks drying on the radiator, lined up in a messy row.

Frisch's desk, by contrast, was remarkably tidy. Next to the telephone there lay two thin paper files, the first entitled *Anton Beer*. The second was not labelled. The little girl—Gertraut? Gerlinde?—dialed for her, passed her the receiver, then stood by the desk, watching her closely.

Ignoring her stare, wedging the receiver between shoulder and cheek, Anna opened both files. The first contained her "missing persons" statement about Anton, along with a list of witnesses interviewed. It appeared Frisch had done a second round of interviews about a month after his initial investigation that aimed to establish whether her husband "wore a glass eye." His verdict read that "with considerable likelihood" Anton did.

"Several of the witnesses had not been aware of the eye but mention an odd sort of character to his gaze. I attribute their uncertainty to the quality of the prosthetic." The unlabelled file contained police photographs of "unidentified body No. 48 vii 2," along with the pathologist's autopsy notes. She hastily closed it again, unwilling to revisit her trip to the morgue, and uncomfortably aware of the stare of the child by her side. The phone on the other end of the line, meanwhile, kept on ringing. Somewhere at the back of her mind she'd been counting the rings.

The duty sergeant at the local station picked up after the twenty-first, sounding sleepy. He promised to "have a look," and returned after some minutes informing her that Frisch was not at his regular desk; he had been called out to stand in for a colleague at headquarters.

"It's the flu," he apologized. "We are short of hands. Are you a—lady friend?"

Anna left the question unanswered, requested the number of headquarters, called there. This time the call was promptly answered. Yes, Frisch had signed in for duty and in all likelihood "was present in the building." A man was dispatched to track him down. Anna had to wait several minutes for his return, only to be told that Frisch was "not available at the moment." The voice did not offer to take a message. It didn't matter. Anna had none to give. She hung up, picked up the file with the autopsy photos, turned to the girl.

"Tell your father that I will return these tomorrow."

The child nodded gravely, her eyes on Anna, not the file.

"What is it?" Anna said, stopped by this queer stare.

"Father explained it all to me," the girl said, chin raised, proud, as though expecting Anna's anger and determined not to flinch. "How he is hungry, in that other way. You could let him, you know. Just a little. It wouldn't cost you anything."

"Go to bed," said Anna Beer. She only made sense of the words after she'd run out of the house. Perhaps the girl was right, at that. It cost you something, feeding that appetite, but, all things considered, not so very much.

She rode the tram to the city centre, then walked ten minutes to the flat of Gustav Kis.

4.

It started as a routine disturbance. A police patrol was fetched by an elderly man who "just happened to be passing" and had overheard "somebody shouting." On arrival the situation looked to the officers like the aftermath of a run-of-the-mill fight: one man beaten on the ground, another, a youth, sitting next to him, shouting, crying, his hands smeared with blood. It called for an ambulance and an arrest; a night in the drunk tank, most typically, then a glum confession in the morning.

The first complication manifested itself in the fact that the man was dead. Not that it changed anything of substance, but their procedure was expected to be more thorough in cases of homicide, more diligently "by the book." Then there was the matter of the gun. It was lying in the dirt not far from the corpse. It was entirely possible that somewhere in the bloodied face there hid a bullet hole. A shooting might point to premeditated murder. Add to this the boy (for really, he wasn't much more than a boy, eighteen if he was a day, soft down on his lip like there'd been on the lips of those Italian girls one of the officers had occasion to study during the war): amongst his hysterical declarations, his insistence that they search "the cellar, at once," he divulged his name and with it the possibility of scandal. The two officers had a brief conference that resulted in one of them leaving the yard to locate the nearest public telephone. He walked the better part of a mile until he did, dug for some coins and called headquarters. Headquarters, in turn, called Inspector Frisch. Frisch had been sitting at home in his bathtub at the time, doing a crossword and yelling instructions at Trudi to boil another kettle of water. He dressed at once.

When Frisch arrived at the scene, his initial preoccupation was to figure out why he'd been called. While it was true that a good many senior officers were off sick, this wasn't his district and he hadn't been part of the central investigative unit for several years. As soon as he got out of the car and recognized the building, he formed the theory that some clever clerk had noticed he'd filed a report some months ago on another body that had been found on these premises. Or perhaps some of his colleagues had been reluctant to become embroiled in a case that involved a Seidel. There were several amongst them who had reason to be shy of the press.

At the scene everything seemed under control. He tried to make a positive identification himself, but the hard light of his electric torch revealed features too mud- and blood-smeared to interpret. The nose had been broken and hung somehow loose; the teeth caved in and covered in grit. The boy, meanwhile, kept shouting and had to be restrained by one of the officers. He had long been cuffed. Frisch, still crouching near the body, listened to his shrill accusations then ordered his driver to keep a watch on "the suspect" while his two colleagues searched the cellar rooms. They looked at him in confusion until he pointed out to them the bent metal door.

"The cellar," he said. "I've been down there before."

The two officers entered cautiously, truncheons out, then re-emerged after a few minutes holding between them a shabby man dressed in a torn greatcoat and a red woollen scarf. One of the officers also carried out a brown canvas sack.

"You won't believe what's in here!" he called to Frisch, but Frisch gestured for him to be silent.

"Leave it for the station," he said. "And get the police photographer here. We want full documentation."

Unwilling to wait for any of his superiors to have second thoughts and pass the case to his colleagues, Frisch had the two suspects put into his car. The boy kept shouting accusations at the other man and had to be cautioned several times. After some minutes he settled down and sat more quietly, his head turned to the man and scrutinizing his features. It was clear enough that they knew one another; and yet the boy did not seem to know the stranger's name.

At the station, before transferring them to adjacent interrogation rooms, Frisch made a search of their pockets. The Seidel boy had nothing on him other than his wallet and some verses of Rilke copied out on a scrap of paper that he kept in his breast pocket. The man in the red scarf had straw in his trouser pocket and two sewing needles struck through the cuff of his worn shirt. There was a hole at the right side of his coat where the pocket had been torn out. In his left coat pocket they found three items. The first was a torn letter from a Linz orphanage concerning the whereabouts of one Anneliese Grotter. The text made mention of an attached passport photo, now missing. The second item was a crumpled telegram giving details of a train schedule, including its arrival in Vienna. It had been sent by Anna Beer. The third item was a photo of Anna Beer in her mid-twenties, looking radiant in a light, shoulder-free gown. There were neither a wallet nor any personal papers. The man had, as far as Frisch could tell, not a penny to his name.

"Are you Anton Beer?" he asked him, examining the photo.

The man did not respond.

The way his eyes moved, they both had to be real.

5.

They questioned the boy first. He had calmed down since arriving at the station, asked to wash his hands. Frisch considered the request, then calmly refused.

"Later," he said. It seemed to him that it was harder to lie with blood on one's palms. "Tell me what happened."

"I'll try not to make stains," the boy said, sat down on the chair he had been offered, and, leaning forward, folded his hands carefully into the gap between his knees. "Can you tell me—is he really dead?"

"You know he is."

The boy nodded gravely. "We must tell Poldi. His wife."

"All in good time. Please, start at the beginning. What were you doing in that yard?"

The boy told his story. There were obvious omissions. His brother had gone to the yard to "meet somebody." It was "a matter of money." Wolfgang had asked him to wait for his return in a doorway not far from the factory yard. The boy had waited, "five, ten, maybe fifteen minutes," frozen through to the bone. "There was no noise, you see, no sound at all, and he'd made me promise I'd wait," he said, seeking out Frisch's eyes. "I thought, 'If there's a row, there is sure to be some noise.'"

When Wolfgang did not return, Robert decided to walk over to the yard. A body had lain prone in the mist. As he'd bent down to it, he had heard a movement behind him. "I saw a face peeking out from behind a metal door. When I approached, he threw his weight against it. A sign on the door said it was an air-raid shelter. I thought to myself, 'It's a cellar, he can't possibly escape.' Then I returned to the body. The face was so bloody, I kept on hoping it wasn't him."

He paused, raised a hand to rub his cheek or maybe his neck, then remembered the blood. "Wolfgang had a gun, you know. But he never fired a shot."

There was, despite the evasions, a quality of sincerity and honesty about the boy that Frisch found intriguing. He wondered briefly whether such a thing was congenital or acquired, and whether it necessitated habitual truthfulness. But despite these thoughts and the skepticism they implied, he found himself drawn to the boy, whose emotions appeared so simple and unstudied. The image of Anna Beer flashed through his mind: for her the opposite held true. The two, he remembered, had met. Frisch wondered whether Anna had taken to this wonky-eyed boy.

The detective stood up, rounded the table, perched on its far side, closer to Robert. He paused before he spoke, scrutinized the boy. Robert bore it calmly, stole a second to look around the room as though for the first time.

"Is this a holding cell?" he asked.

"An interrogation room."

"It has a telephone," Robert said. "A holding cell would not have a telephone. Nor a desk, I suppose." He blushed, caught himself in the irrelevance of his thought. "It's because my father was a policeman. Inspector Teuben. I was told he worked right here, in this building."

Having finished his inspection, Robert gazed straight into Frisch's eyes. "You will tell me now that I have not been forthright in my statement. That I left bits out."

"Yes."

"What it is, I wasn't sure how to say it. It's funny. Two hours ago I told my brother to let everything come out and to hell with our 'reputation.' But now . . ." He swallowed, thought. "Can you tell me something, Herr Inspektor? The man who did it, the one who hid behind the iron door—Is he a Jew?"

"I have not spoken to him yet."

Robert nodded, distracted, continued the trajectory of his thought. "It makes a difference if he is. In terms of motive, I mean. Whether he had the right—" He sighed, and without further ado launched into a summary of the situation. "We were being blackmailed, you see, that is to say my mother was, by my stepfather's old business partner. But Wolfgang thought it was a fraud and that someone else was sending the letters. He went to that yard tonight to have it out."

It took Frisch another thirty minutes of questions to make sense of this announcement. Robert answered willingly and comprehensively. Only one little detail failed to cohere.

"Why did you not go after him sooner?" he pressed the boy. "You felt uneasy about Wolfgang's plan. Why not sneak after him right away?"

"He made me promise to wait."

"You mean you were scared."

"No," Robert said, "not the way you mean."

"What, then?"

Robert blushed, wrestled with himself. "I didn't want to know. I thought Wolfgang was up to something. Something bad. I didn't want to be there when he did it."

"You loved your brother."

"Yes. And now he is dead."

Frisch sighed, rose from his chair, and informed Robert that he was cleared of all suspicion. "I would like to ask you to wait around for another few hours. There is a waiting room near the entrance."

He did not have the heart to tell the boy that it would fall to him to make a formal identification of the body.

6.

Frisch turned his attention over to his second suspect. When he entered the neighbouring interrogation room, he was annoyed to find it empty. The duty sergeant knew nothing about it, and it took fifteen minutes of walking around the building and knocking on doors to locate the prisoner on the third floor, in a larger interrogation cell equipped with a long table and a good dozen chairs as though it doubled as a meeting room. Two fellow detectives were present, cups of coffee in their hands. They had, they explained, been dragged out of their beds by the chief himself, though both were on the sick, one with a cold, the other with a "gastric complaint." They both seemed chipper enough, however. The investigation, in any case, was no longer Frisch's responsibility, "Sorry to say, old chap." But since Frisch had inspected the crime scene and had already questioned the boy, he was invited to stay and "work this maggot as a team." The stated goal, the older of the detectives announced with a belligerent look at the suspect, was to "get a quick confession and be back in bed before ten." They sat down at the big table with the air of men who had done this a hundred times.

But nothing about the interrogation proved routine. At first it was thought that the man was dumb, or imbecilic. He would not answer a single question. But then, perhaps an hour into the interrogation, with the two detectives alternately yelling or cooing at him, feeding him schnapps and cups of malt coffee, he all at once began to emit a rapid series of words, albeit in a hoarse and barely audible voice. When he was made to speak up (some twenty minutes were spent cajoling him towards this end), it turned out the words were in some foreign tongue that none of them spoke. It was tentatively identified as Russian. A discussion ensued in which the elder detective argued that the man should be turned over to the Soviet authorities immediately, while his colleague wanted an interpreter—"one of ours, an Austrian"—to be fetched, though it was unclear from where. After some inquiries it turned out that the cousin of one of the uniformed policemen on duty had spent three years in a Soviet camp and had had a girl there, "almost a sort of wife," and consequently spoke the language "better than German." They sent a car around to his house and brought back the man, who looked as careworn and emaciated as their prisoner. The two men sat across from each other and exchanged a quiet greeting.

"Get the fuck on with it," the older detective told the interpreter. "We haven't got all night."

But even with the interpreter present, progress was minimal. For the longest time the man refused to give his name. A half-hour of questions finally produced a single, halting, "Israel, formerly Jacob," from which it was inferred he was Jewish, though a quick examination, performed with a crudeness that filled Frisch with shame, informed them he was uncircumcised and bore no concentration camp tattoo. He did not answer the question what he was doing in the basement; nor would he name his nationality, his place of birth, his whereabouts during the war. When asked his age, the prisoner held up a combination of fingers indicating he was either thirty-seven or thirty-eight (his vacillation on the issue was itself frustrating), though he looked twenty years older. He smelled like a badger. It was impossible to sit with him without opening the door.

The only question he answered consistently, albeit with a voice so light it seemed to wither in the air, was whether or not he had this evening killed the man identified as Wolfgang Seidel.

361

"*Nyet.*"

It was beginning to look as if they'd have little use for the interpreter.

They confronted "Israel" with the contents of his pockets. He studied the letter, the telegram, and the photo with a certain tenderness, but declined to give an explanation. The younger detective leaned forward at this point, grabbed their prisoner by the shirt front, and delivered three quick slaps to his left cheek.

"Ask him again," he told the interpreter.

The prisoner bore it calmly, one cheek burning red.

The desk sergeant entered. The detective let go of the prisoner and whipped around, converting frustration into anger. "What is it, you fool?"

The young sergeant apologized profusely and asked Frisch for a word. "Your daughter keeps calling," he explained, still in earshot of the door.

Frisch pulled him along until they had rounded a corner. "Is there something wrong?" he asked in his calm manner.

"She asks when you'll come home."

"I'll be a while."

"She says she is frightened." The young man's eyes pleaded with Frisch on his daughter's behalf. "She is home all alone and cannot sleep. She says she thought about going to the neighbours', but they're off visiting relatives in the country."

Frisch sighed. "Very well. Send a car to pick her up. Here, I'll give you my key. Make sure they lock the door. I don't have an office here, but she can wait with you, can't she? In the waiting room?"

"Of course." The man was so pleased, he seemed ready to run back to his desk. Then he remembered something. "Someone else called. A woman." He searched his pockets as though expecting to turn up a note but didn't. "I believe it was a social call."

"I am not to be disturbed," Frisch told him, hoping against hope that it had been Anna Beer.

7.

Frisch sped back to the interrogation room. The door was half open, the man's body odour noticeable even in the corridor. Frisch stopped and listened to them talk.

"What did he say now?"

"He's a philosopher, I suppose. He says, 'God is a spider, we are stuck in his web.' He says, 'I am the ghost of the past.' He says, 'A crow can fly even if it's dead.' I'm not sure what it means."

"It means he is crazy. We'll shop him to the Soviets and be done with the fucker."

The assistant chief of police appeared in the hallway stifling a yawn. He had stopped by before to inquire about their progress; now he walked past Frisch without acknowledging his salute and leaned his head through the door.

"God, he smells ripe," he said. "Any news?"

"He's a ghost from the past."

"*Of* the past."

"You see what we are up against."

The assistant chief nodded. "Very well, then. Ready his papers and get him out of here. We are charging him with murder but releasing him to the Soviet authorities on grounds of his nationality, et cetera. Have Heinzl help you with the forms, he's good with that sort of thing." Without entering the room, he extended his arm and shook both the detectives' hands. "I congratulate you. Another case solved."

The men grinned and lit cigarettes.

"Are you doing the paperwork now?" Frisch asked, when the assistant chief was gone.

"Nah. It'll keep for the morning. Fancy a nightcap?"

"I'm afraid I can't," Frisch said. "But I can stay and keep an eye on him if you like. I have some paperwork of my own to finish up."

The detectives left. When the interpreter attempted to follow suit, Frisch arrested him by the elbow. "Stay another hour. We aren't quite done here."

The man acquiesced.

They transferred the prisoner to a new interrogation room two floors down. This time Frisch took care to close and lock the door.

Five

1.

The desk sergeant was only a few years older than Robert. He sat behind his desk in an attitude that alternated between a cheerful awareness of his exalted position in life—here he was, barely old enough to shave, a telephone in front of him, manning the front desk at police headquarters during the graveyard shift—and spells of abject boredom, during which he leaned back and went hunting for zits on his cheeks and scrawny neck. Robert's presence in the adjacent waiting room did not seem to incommode him. They had exchanged a greeting when Robert first arrived more than an hour earlier, and since then shared the occasional look of boys too socially inexperienced to decide on an appropriate topic of conversation. Robert wore a distracted and somewhat tragic air that made an approach all the more difficult. Now, though, as the sergeant unwrapped a sandwich he had brought from home and carefully folded the greaseproof paper into an improvised plate, a subject at once innocent and topical presented itself to him.

"Would you like a bite?" he asked, waving the sandwich in the air. "My mother made it. Real salami. And butter, too. And here are some radishes on the side." He ignored Robert's sullen shake of the head, broke the sandwich down the middle, and passed half of it over. "You look like you've been through the wringer," he added. "You are Robert Seidel, aren't you? I've seen your picture in the papers. During the trial. 'Brother of the accused.' The paper said your father was a policeman."

Robert listened to his prattle with a certain amount of annoyance, holding the sandwich at arm's length despite his sudden appetite. Then a new thought dawned in him, indifferent to his grief. He took a first bite and turned around to face the young sergeant.

"I always wanted to come here someday. When I was at school. I used to dream about it. How I'd come here and ask about my father."

The young man smiled, passed over a radish and a salt shaker. "His name was Teuben, right? Before my time, naturally. But I can see if someone can look up the file."

"Could you really?" Robert munched his salted radish.

The desk sergeant gave an enthusiastic nod. "You wait here. I'll ask Lieutenant Mayer. He's got the key to the archives. One of the nice ones, Mayer is. If someone comes while I'm away—well, there is a bell. But anyway, I won't be a minute."

He ran off still chewing on a bite.

Within minutes of his leaving—Robert had just finished the last of his own sandwich—a uniformed police officer entered the station and made his way to the front desk. He was holding by the hand a little girl of maybe ten or eleven years. Robert recognized her from somewhere but could not immediately place her. The policeman craned his neck, trying to locate whoever was on duty. Robert called out to him.

"The desk sergeant will be right back."

The officer nodded, stood undecided. His charge freed herself from his grip and walked into the waiting room.

"It's all right," she said over one shoulder. "Papa said I should wait here." She sat down on the bench next to Robert and seconds later swung her feet up, tucked her heels into her bum, showing off thick stockings. "Really, it'll be all right. I've been here before," she said again.

The officer shrugged. "I'll be going, then."

"Good night," she called after him. Then, without the slightest pause or hesitation, she turned to Robert. "I was afraid at home. Stupid. But it was so dark and the pipes were making noises. I know that it's the pipes.

But still I was afraid. It really is stupid." She seemed wound up, eager to talk. "I'm Trudi."

"Robert."

"I know," she said, without explaining her meaning. "Why are you here?"

"My brother was killed."

She gaped. "The one from the trial?"

"Yes."

"Was it a tram accident? There're a lot of those these days. Papa says it's because people are deh-jected."

Robert closed his eyes. "A man beat him to death. His face—" (he touched his own nose), "it was smashed in. I found him face down in the mud."

Saying it returned the moment to his memory. He stared at the hands he had scrubbed in the station toilet: bloody crescents still under his fingernails, the smell of salt radishes clinging to his skin.

"He just lay there, like a drunk. At first I couldn't even tell it was him. Everything was so dark, and dirty. And then my mind got stuck on the strangest things. I was down in the mud, squatting on my heels, and even as I began to clean him off, my feet started hurting, all my weight was pushed into the toes. And I figured it was the socks, they were too thick for the shoes, or maybe my feet had grown and I laced them up too tight. I pictured how all my toes were jammed into the tips of my shoes, my dark socks dyeing the skin, leaving little bits of fluff on the sweaty bits in between—And all the while I was cradling his head, right here between my knees, and was spitting on him, too, to clean off his face." He swallowed, his throat thick with memory. "And then, just when I realized what a beast I was, holding a dead man and thinking about toes, a shriek came out, right out of my mouth, like someone was reaching in and wringing out my lungs. Next thing I knew, I started shouting in earnest, shouting my head off, forgetting to breathe. But even then, in the midst of all this, I was still thinking, worrying about my socks. It's as though one person was shouting and another was watching, and neither gave a fig about the other."

Robert looked up, startled, realized he was talking to a little girl. "I'm sorry," he said softly. "I'll give you dreams."

Indeed Trudi had grown pale. Nonetheless she shook her head and did her best to reassure him. "The neighbour said he was handsome. She cut his picture from the paper. During the trial. She said he had a noble face." Trudi pursed her lips then added, "Your eye droops. You also had a fight?"

Robert blushed. "A long time ago. At school. It was about my father. This boy kept saying that he was a Nazi—"

But he fell quiet the moment he noticed the sergeant walking back to his desk; leapt up from the bench. The young officer was in the company of an older colleague dressed in civilian clothing. The two men stopped three feet from the desk and entered into a hushed conversation. Robert caught most of it.

"Him?" the older man asked. "But he's tiny. The father was a big old ox. Six foot, fleshy. This one's a shrimp. The same sort of hair, I suppose. Thick, almost like a wig."

Robert quickly bridged the distance that separated him from the two men, making it impossible for them to ignore his presence. "Did you find my father's file?" he asked, and was surprised by his belligerence.

The detective and the young sergeant exchanged a look. When their silence became awkward, the latter took it upon himself to answer.

"He was a well-respected member of the force."

The older man snorted, then quickly forced his head into a nod.

"But the file?" Robert pressed.

"Personnel files are not for public perusal."

"I am his son."

"All the same. The law is the law. Besides: a great many files were displaced after the war."

The detective shrugged and turned away from him. Robert caught him by the elbow.

"You worked with him, didn't you? Please tell me how he died."

The man's face betrayed annoyance, then surprise at Robert's question. His face was ruddy, the skin shot through with a network of veins. Robert stepped closer yet, into the range of the man's sour breath.

"It was an accident. He slipped and bashed in his head. In any case, he was off-duty."

"That's not what I've heard."

"It was a long time ago, boy. Bygones, eh?"

All gentleness left Robert. It fell off him like a burden. He pushed out his chest, crumpled his hands into fists, stood nose to chin with the detective. "I am not a boy, Inspector. I am Robert Seidel, future owner of the Seidel factories. And I just found my brother beaten to death by a thug."

He whipped around, walked away, paused briefly by the girl. "I have to go home now, tell his wife."

"She'll be sad," the girl said. "Everybody will be sad."

"They should be," said Robert. "Wolfgang Seidel was a good man."

2

Anna reasoned like this: Karel had been lying to her; he would do so again. She had no means to compel him to speak the truth. Frisch did, but Frisch was unavailable. There was little point, then, in seeking out Neumann on her own.

The situation was entirely different when it came to Gustav Kis.

She rang his bell. Kis opened at once. He wore a dressing gown and pyjamas, and a look halfway between surprise and gratitude.

"You wanted to tell me something," she said, without reacting to his greeting. "Outside the courthouse. When I called you names." She stepped into the doorway, made it impossible for him to close the door. "Tell me now."

He asked her to wait in the hallway for a moment, then ran into his room. She expected a red-faced lover to emerge, a blanket thrown around his naked loins, then realized from the sounds that escaped the room that Kis was simply tidying up. She followed him without waiting for his summons, caught him fluffing up his pillows with repeated slaps of the hand. The room smelled of food and unwashed linen. Anna stepped over to the window and discreetly opened it a crack before sitting down upon the sofa. She patted the place next to her. Kis hesitated, smoothed out the coverlet on the bed, kept his eyes from meeting hers.

"What was it that you wanted to tell me?" Anna tried again. She was still wearing her hat and coat and gloves. The tension of her smile made her face hurt.

"There was something strange," Kis said, "about that man you took along. That Czech."

"Karel."

"Yes. He seemed to know your husband. At least he acted like he did. But then he asked what camp he had been in, like he didn't know."

She processed this. "Why did he think you would know?" But the answer was obvious. "So you have seen him since the war."

"Once. But he told me not to tell you. The Czech. He beat me. My face swelled up like a melon afterwards."

"Tell me about Anton. When did he come here?"

"About ten days before you did."

"He wanted to—renew your acquaintance."

"He came to talk."

"You slept with him."

"No. I didn't. Not for many years."

"What did you talk about?"

"Nothing. Anton was looking for someone. A crippled girl. He came and he talked and then he went. It was like he'd gone crazy." His eyes pleaded with her not to push the point.

She didn't. Her interest lay elsewhere. "So you told all this to Karel, then figured out he was a crook. And then it took you three whole months until you worked up the courage to waylay me outside the courthouse.

You saw my picture in the paper and had a sudden pang of guilt."

Kis launched into apology, but she cut him short.

"It doesn't matter. What matters is that you know what Anton looks like. Nobody else saw him; only from a distance, in passing, in a stairwell or a crowded street. But you—you were his lover. He came here; you talked to him, studied him, in good light. You'd pick him out amongst a thousand." She patted the sofa again, more forcefully this time. "Sit, Herr Kis. There is something I need you to look at."

She produced the file she had taken from Frisch's desk.

Kis did as he was bidden, preserving a yard of distance between them, accepted the file. He dropped it when he saw the first of the pictures. The photos slipped out and formed a collage upon his carpet. Most of them were close-ups of individual wounds and body parts; with a little effort, Anna mused, one might be able to assemble a life-sized corpse. She stopped Kis when he hastily attempted to stuff the photos back into the file; lowered herself onto her knees next to him and with gloved fingers spread the pictures apart.

"This man was found some months ago," she said very calmly. "He had been murdered in the cellar of an abandoned factory yard. There was a suspicion that it might be Anton." She turned her head to study Kis's face: pale, sweaty, distressed by the gore. "I want your opinion. Is it him?"

He took his time, fixating on the prosthetic eye, which had been photo-graphed both in its socket and separately, lying in a metal bowl, the cam-era's flash shining through it, illuminating the twisting line of the optical nerve, crisp and as though ink-drawn in the fine-grained black and white. Kis stared at it a full minute, seemingly unable to make sense of it.

"It's made from glass," she explained, and felt relief flood her. "You are surprised. So it isn't him. Anton hasn't lost an eye."

Kis did not respond. He shuffled the photos, discarded the face shots: there was little there recalling human features. The rest of the stack he pressed into his chest. It took Anna a while to understand he was crying.

"He kept looking at me funny. One eye screwed into the wall. I thought he'd gone crazy. How was I to know?—It looked so real."

Blood left her head, her hands and feet; she felt sick, unbalanced. "It is him?" she asked, helplessly. "How do you know? There are other one-eyed men. It doesn't mean—"

Kis looked over at her, almost in anger. "Here," he said, throwing down the topmost picture. It was a close-up of the upper left part of the dead man's torso. The bruises stood out in a dark shade of grey.

"His shoulder?" she asked, not comprehending.

"There!" Kis said with renewed vehemence, and pointed. "The three moles. Forming a triangle."

She found the mark he was talking about but did not recognize it. "Are you sure?"

"It's Anton," Kis said. "I used to kiss him there, three kisses, one for each mole."

He burst into tears. She watched him cry. After some minutes she reached out a hand, touched his shoulder, then his face. His skin felt waxen through the leather of her glove.

Kis produced a handkerchief, blew his nose; cast a grateful look in her direction. When he tried to take hold of her hand, she shook him loose. She did so gently, stayed close to him, kneeling on the floor, their heads together like conspirators.

"Did he talk about me?" she asked him quietly. "Before the war."

"Never."

She felt her face freeze into a mask. Kis saw it too.

"All he said was that he felt bad about the lies. He told me again and again. 'I live a life of deception,' he said. He felt guilty before you."

"I loved him," she said, as though Kis had accused her of doing otherwise. It felt natural to use the past tense.

She rose from the floor, sat back down on the couch. Her eyes returned to the autopsy photos. The realization hit her that Anton had been murdered. There had to be a murderer. She remembered the stain on her living room wall; remembered scrubbing it, looking for a bullet hole.

"I must use your telephone."

Kis pointed her to the corridor.

She called the police headquarters and asked for Frisch. She got the same desk sergeant as before.

"He is not to be disturbed."

She hung up.

"What now?" asked Kis.

"I'll go see Neumann," she decided, despite her earlier assessment that it would be futile. "Do you have a gun, Herr Kis?"

"A gun?" Kis asked. "Why would I have a gun?"

He tried to hug her as she left. When she looked back up in the glum light of the stairwell, there was such sorrow in his face that she wished she had let him.

3.

Robert took a taxi home. He paid the driver without tipping, walked up to the door, let himself in. His mother was sitting in the dark of the drawing room. The only reason he noticed her at all was because she was brushing her hair. The brush's silver caught the lamp he had lit in the hallway.

He walked up to her, waited until his eyes had adjusted.

"You are late," she said.

"Wolfie is dead. Beaten to death."

She looked up, surprise on her face, then calculation. He understood at once that she fretted over the blackmailer. There was in her features no hint of sorrow.

"You are a monster," he said. "I told the police everything."

She paled, reached out a hand like a beggar asking for money. "You look just like your father when you're angry."

"I asked about him at the station. I'm beginning to think that he was a monster too." He brushed off her hand and cast around for something else to say. "I must tell Poldi."

The moment he turned, he heard naked feet run away from him. She must have been listening to their conversation from the stairs. He ran after her into the unlighted house. Two floors up Poldi slammed her bedroom door. He heard the key; the sound of her breathing through the wood.

Robert knocked. "Poldi!" he called. "Please."

"Go away!"

"It's about Wolfgang," he said. "I'm so sorry." He fell to his knees, spoke to the gap at the foot of the door. "He told me to wait. He made me promise. And then, I didn't hear a thing. Things would have been different if only I had heard. But there wasn't a sound."

"Poldi," he said, "Wolfie's dead. Please open the door."

She did not answer for the longest time. They sat, each on their side of the door, listening to the other's breathing.

"I killed the crows," she said at last, sorrow, malice in her voice. "So he could sleep. I thought he'd be tired, coming home from jail. They was makin' ever such a ruckus. Nobody told me they was pets.

"You went out together," she added, all in the same breath, "but it's only you that's come back home."

Robert stood up and left before she could say anything else.

<hr />

4.

Before resuming his interrogation of the man with the red scarf, Frisch excused himself and briefly left the room. When he returned, he was carrying the potato sack the officers had found in the cellar. He placed it on the table with exaggerated care and sat down. The interpreter was chain-smoking cigarettes. Frisch looked from one face to the other. Emaciation made the two men look like brothers.

He reached into the sack and pulled out its contents. The interpreter flinched, but the prisoner looked over with a hint of fondness.

"It's very lifelike," Frisch said. "The eyes, the cock of the head, the angle of the wings." He stroked the bird, turned it over in his hands, waited for the interpreter to catch up with his words. "Did you do this? Stuff the crow?"

The man hesitated, then gave a cautious nod.

"It's good work. What's inside? I thought one used sand or perhaps clay. But it feels too light."

The man tried to answer. It took him a while. It appeared that he had become so used to speaking only in his head that actually shaping the words took a conscious effort. He sat there as though trying to vomit the words, his hollow cheeks flushing with embarrassment. At long last he produced two little words that the interpreter rendered as "straw" and "wire."

"You bend the wire into shape? To build an armature?"

A nod.

"I see. You skin the bird, scrape off all the flesh, slip the skin over the armature. And then you sew it up here." Frisch dug amongst the feathers on the bird's underside, exposing the stitching, and earned another nod. "Is that what you do professionally? Taxidermy?"

Again that timid ritual, in which words had to be first mouthed then given volume, as though these two aspects of spoken language were governed by entirely separate faculties. "*Ljubitel.*"

"He says, 'Amateur.' I suppose he means he does it as a hobby."

Frisch blinked. Pale lids fluttered in thick glasses. "We found a dead body. A few months ago. Someone had removed the intestines, then sewed it back shut. I wonder whether the stitching is similar. I can call the pathologist and ask him to take a look." He paused. "You seem to have borrowed the dead man's coat."

The moment the interpreter had rendered Frisch's words, the man grew pale. Twice he started to respond but stopped himself: thin hands flapping in the air in agitation.

Frisch watched him without moving. "Tell me something," he said. "Are you Jewish?"

He received no answer.

"No, I didn't think you were. Nor is Israel your name. A private joke, I suppose. 'Israel formerly Jacob.' From Genesis: the man who wrestled with God. Is that who you are?"

Again he received no reaction. Frisch bent forward until his face was very close to his prisoner. His voice was soft. He did not wish to frighten the man.

"Look here," he said. "There are two dead men. Both were found in the place where you live. Did you kill them?"

A shake of the head, at once forlorn and emphatic, silent lips shaping a "*nyet.*"

"Then help me figure out who did."

The man thought about it. Folded his hands in the attitude of prayer and listened into himself, his lips moving in silent monologue.

When he finally spoke out loud, it sounded like a question.

"He wants to know," the interpreter said, "what will happen to him."

Frisch looked him in the eye. "They want to give you to the Soviets."

The man trembled when he heard it.

"You don't want to go." Frisch leaned back, sat musing, wiped his brow. "Perhaps I can help you," he said. "I will if I can.

"Please," he added, "all I want is the truth."

The man turned his hands to the ceiling: a preacher's gesture. When he spoke, each word seemed smuggled past the threshold of his own temerity.

"*I istina sdelaet vas svobodnymi.*"

"The truth shall set you free."

Frisch took a risk then. "You are at a police station," he said. "The opposite tends to happen here."

It earned him his first smile.

5.

"Please. Give me a name. Something to call you."

"Timofey. Son of Ivan, son of Alexei the spice merchant."

"Timofey. A Russian name. So you are Russian."

"Ukrainian. From Kiev."

"Profession?"

"Chemist."

"Jewish?"

"No."

"Christian, then."

"Orthodox."

"Do you know an Arnim Rothmann?"

"No."

"His wife, his child, any of his relations?"

"No."

"What were you doing in the cellar, Timofey?"

"Hiding."

"From whom?"

"Your people. My people. The wrath of God."

"Is God angry with you?"

"He must be. Look where I am."

Theirs continued to be a three-way conversation, the interpreter's voice sandwiched between Frisch's methodical drone and the prisoner's halting whisper. He had a pleasant voice, the interpreter did, full-bodied even when it was quiet. His diaphragm moved more than his lips. In time Frisch forgot all about his presence, focused solely on his mark. It soon become obvious that he was highly articulate, and just a little mad.

They started with generalities. Timofey had been a German prisoner of war. He had served in the artillery and been taken in the fall of '41 near Orel, then transported westward and used as a slave labourer in a variety of factories. In the confusion of the battle for Vienna he had escaped and hidden from conquered and conqueror alike. It had been easy enough; the city was full of lost souls and there were plenty of corpses from whom to pluck clothes and identification papers. When forced into contact with people, he pretended to be mute. Nobody troubled the walking ghost. He

lived in the sewage canals for a while. Eventually he had found an unoc-
cupied basement. He had lived there ever since.

"By yourself?"

"With my shadow."

"Lonely, I suppose."

"Alone."

"Alone, then. But one day that changed, didn't it? You got company."

"Yes."

"Tell me about that day."

The man nodded, took a sip from the cup of coffee Frisch had fetched
for him, leaned back in his chair, and, with a theatricality borrowed from
some earlier incarnation of his life, gathered his thoughts.

"There was a rainstorm that night," he said at length. "I had gone out
late in the afternoon. The rain surprised me. I decided to sit it out in a
church. A well-attended church: people sleeping on every pew. The rain
did not break until dawn. When I returned to my cellar, he was there. The
body was still warm. He had lived long enough to bruise."

It was the scarf that drew his initial interest, then the warm soldier's
coat. He went through the pockets, found two photos, a telegram, and
a letter, but no money or keys. Then he noticed the eye that stayed alive
long after the other had gone dull.

"It gave me a fright at first," Timofey said, "but then I found beauty in
it. There were such colours to the iris. I took it out and cleaned it off; held
it up into the sun. Patterns on the floor. Whoever made it was an artist."

"'Patterns on the floor,'" Frisch repeated. "You are an educated man,
Timofey. Do you speak English perhaps? French?"

"French."

"So you can read our alphabet. Of course you can. The telegram listed
a date and a time. A train schedule: somebody's time of arrival. You understood it at once."

"Yes."

"And decided to be there to meet the train."

"Yes."

"When did it come in?"

"That very evening. The fifth of July. Nine fifty-five. From Paris."

"Nine fifty-five. So you had all day. Tell me what you did."

"I tried on my new scarf. I'd never in my life felt wool so soft."

Timofey omitted the gutting of the body and had to be prodded; then, in a quiet, timid voice, described a procedure so barbaric Frisch felt sick. "Why?" he asked, but received no answer, was whisked to the train station instead and matters metaphysical.

"The train was late. People waited all night. A close summer night. Some rain at dawn. At last the train arrived. I recognized her from the photo. She looked older but just as fine. A strong woman, a hardness to her chin."

"You followed her home?"

Timofey shook his head. "She took a taxi. I had no means to follow."

"Then what?"

"There was a boy there too. He came with the woman. He set off walking. I followed and he led me to a house. The second photo—the photo I lost—it showed a girl. She lived there. I saw her and came back the next day. The boy chased me off for a while, but I always returned." He made a face, too sly for a madman. "It is good to find a home."

Frisch asked more details about the girl, enough to identify her as Anneliese Grotter. "What was your interest in her?" he pressed Timofey.

The man pondered it. "The dead man had left her to me. An obligation." He crossed himself, studied Frisch's face. "Have you ever felt the hand of God, Herr Commissar? It taps you lightly, on the shoulder. You barely feel it, but all the same it almost shatters your bones."

"My colleagues were right about you, Timofey. You're a philosopher."

"I understand, Herr Commissar. You object. You don't like God. Not here, in your station house. You'd rather have psychology. A motivation. Very well. Let's say this, then: she was just like my sister had been when we were young. An angry girl. Suffering. Alone." Timofey paused, chanced a question. "Was the dead man her father?"

"Beer? Not so far as I know. He received the photo in response to an inquiry. From an orphanage. It appears he was looking for her." He eyed the prisoner. "You never spoke to the girl?"

A smile, only his second. "I don't speak."

"Yes, of course. *You're the ghost of the past.*" Frisch paused, leaned forward. "Tell me why you gutted Beer."

The Russian grew embarrassed. "He was in my cellar. He would soon start to smell. Impossible to bury him there: concrete floors. Too dangerous to carry him out, and too heavy to carry very far. Besides—" He rewrapped his scarf. "I needed someone to talk to."

"So you stuffed him?"

"Not 'stuffed.' I'd have had to skin him, build a skeleton from wire or wood. It'd take weeks. So I tried my hand at embalming. I removed the intestines, thinking they would rot first, then injected him with aluminium salts, trying to push out the blood. I foraged for chemicals and made arsenic soap. In taxidermy, it keeps away the flies." He shook his head, regretful. "He rotted anyway. It was impossible to drain him properly. One would need some sort of pump. Soon the skin was crawling, despite the arsenic. I brushed off dead maggots by the thousands."

"Then what?"

"I thought I'd have to get rid of him. Cut him to pieces perhaps. Bury him, bit by bit. Then you found him. And took him away."

"You saw me?"

A nod.

"I solved your problem."

"But took away my friend."

"So you were alone again. Walking the city. Keeping an eye on the girl." Frisch polished his lenses. "Until tonight. Tell me what happened."

The Russian shrugged, pointy shoulders rising in his threadbare shirt. The cup in front of him was empty.

"I heard noises in the yard. I was working, finishing the stitching." He pointed to the bird. "It did not sound like a fight. There was no screaming. A series of dull blows, like someone was beating their carpet. When I looked out the door, one man was dead in the mud."

"And the other?"

"Walking into the rubble and the mist. Not a man. A shadow. The rubble ten foot high and yet he climbed it, walking straight across the broken side of yard." He sketched the scene with brittle hands. "When he was gone, I ran out to have a look at the body."

"And then?"

"The boy showed up. I heard him coming."

"And hid."

"Yes."

Frisch leaned back in his chair and threaded his thumbs through the armholes of his waistcoat. His fingers rolled themselves into pudgy little fists.

"Two murders, Timofey, and a 'shadow' vanishing in the mist. I can place you at the scene. Starving, frightened, in need of cash." Frisch spoke very softly. The threat was in the words themselves. "I'll never find a better suspect."

The man folded his hands. "God put me there." Ten seconds later: "I dreamt once I was God."

Frisch shook his head, suddenly annoyed. "A tuppenny dream. Every little crook has had it.

"You didn't kill Seidel too, by any chance?" he carried on. "Perhaps you worked in his factory and wanted revenge. Perhaps it wasn't the boy who led you to his house; you had been there before."

Timofey shook his head, more amused than insulted, then paused. "I visited him in hospital. The father. I knew he owned a factory. I figured he must have used prisoners too." His brow furrowed, in wonder, not anger. "I thought I'd find an enemy. Someone to hate."

"So you hate us? Germans, Austrians, whatever it is we are?"

"Only those who held the whip."

"Well," said Frisch, taken aback, "it passed through an awful lot of hands."

The interpreter stood up then, requesting leave to empty his bladder. It occurred to Frisch that the man felt insulted by his assessment. Detective and prisoner sat out his absence in silence.

6.

When the interpreter returned, they backtracked to the subject of the "shadow."

"Describe him for me," Frisch said.

The man's eyes grew shy. "Judas climbing his own gallows."

"Something less poetic."

"He was as tall as a giant and as thin as a wraith. His arms out swinging; the shirt soaked and sticking to his skin."

Frisch pondered this for some moments. "A giant?" he asked. "Two metres, broad shoulders, features as though whittled out of wood?"

"You know him?"

"Yes. Last I heard he was heading to Siberia courtesy of the Soviet state."

It was only when the man winced that Frisch remembered his likely future. Curiosity distracted him from the matter at hand.

"Why don't you want to return?" he asked. "You'll be going home after all. Don't you have a wife?"

"I do." Timofey hesitated, went on. "My family were landowners, Commissar. Class enemies. My grandparents were shot. My father spent ten years in a camp. And now I have collaborated with the enemy. 'Foreign experience.' It's very suspicious. I expect I will get shot."

Frisch glanced at the interpreter, incredulous. "You didn't collaborate. You were a prisoner of war. You had no choice in the matter."

Timofey raised both hands in front of him in a gesture halfway between entreaty and shrug. "Real patriots had the decency to die." His wrists looked so thin it seemed possible to snap off his hands.

"What did you eat all these months?" Frisch asked after a long pause, avoiding his prisoner's eyes.

"Heaven provides."

"You mean you stole," Frisch said softly. "And for a moment there, you had me believing you were innocent."

It earned him a third smile, the weakest of the bunch. There wouldn't be any more.

"Let us return to the day you found Anton Beer."

Frisch proceeded to work his way methodically back over the information, requesting further details about various particulars. Timofey spoke with increasing ease; his answers were frank, witty, consistent. The point came when Frisch realized he was prolonging the interview simply for the sake of speaking: he wished to delay the moment when the man would be taken away, to an unknown fate. At last he ran out of questions. He sent the interpreter away and offered his prisoner a cigarette. But Timofey did not smoke.

"I wonder if they'll really shoot you," Frisch said, aware that he was no longer understood. "If I had known, I wouldn't have arrested you, my friend."

The man sat, quiet and impassive, then raised a bony hand to his face and mimed taking off his glasses. Frisch obeyed. His prisoner sat very still, looking into the detective's myopic eyes. He seemed to find something there that reassured him. When Frisch returned the glasses to his face, Timofey had closed his eyes and was humming a melody, low under his breath.

Frisch stood up, called for the guard, and left the interrogation room.

He went straight to his superiors and requested a warrant for one Karel Neumann, vagrant, suspected at large in Greater Vienna.

Six

1.

Karel came to in a public house on the Gürtel. He had not been unconscious exactly, but neither could he have explained how he'd got there.
His ears rang. It took him a while to understand the cause was physical.
His right ear was blood-clotted and swollen. There was a beer in front of
him, and a schnapps glass in his hand. When he set it down, its sides were
smeared with blood. None of the other patrons seemed to care. When
he rose from the chair, a pain shot through his lung and back. A muddy
puddle had formed around his boots. He dug in his pocket and found a
sodden bill. The landlord changed it for him, and avoided looking at him
for more than a moment.

He left the public house, boarded a tram, pushing his bulk through the
throng of those disembarking. The tram was packed: soldiers, drunks, a
group of university students, all standing shoulder to shoulder.

Feeling dizzy, his tongue swollen too big for his mouth, Karel groped
for the only vacant seat. His hands were shaking, his knuckles hurting; the
shirt sleeves blood- and mud-caked to the elbows. An old woman sat next
to him. She gave him a sour look that mixed fear and anger; clutched her
handbag to her chest. The air oppressed him: sweat, digestive gases, sodden fabrics; the heat of bodies pressed too tight. After two stops he needed
out: swam through the crowd with a sort of breaststroke, leapt out onto
the street. The dizziness stayed with him. He tried to walk but staggered,
scraped his shoulder on a metal grate, roused a nest of rats. Two corners

on, a drunk sat on the pavement, legs spread out before him and holding his head in veiny hands. A bottle was wedged between his thighs.

Slowly, laboriously, Karel slid down next to him. The man did not react. Tiredness overcame him, his back complaining, a hurt deep in his lung.

"Son of a bitch," he murmured. "He must have cracked my ribs."

He sat, nauseated, breathing, a drizzle soaking through his clothes. A realization hit him, raised a giggle soon snuffed out by the ensuing pain.

"I just figured it out. The look that woman gave me. The tram was full, and she didn't want to give up her seat. She knew very well I was an axe murderer —she kept looking at my sleeves—but all the same she wouldn't give it up."

His neighbour was unresponsive, lost in deep stupor or in thought.

"Cold night, eh?" Karel said, but again earned no answer. "And look at me, I'm a real mess. The thing is, friend, I just had a fight. In all my life, I never had a fight like that." He sighed, found himself reliving it. "He came at me from the dark. A gun in his hand, aiming it right at my chest. I thought he was going to shoot and braced for it, balls in my throat, as they say, but he swung it, like it was a club, hit me right in the chest. I slapped it out of his hand, he didn't even bend for it, kept coming at me. I put a fist in his face. He went down, came up kicking. I shattered his nose. Down he went, got up again, leapt at my legs. I kicked him, right on the ear, he was dizzy now, crawling around, not a sound out his mouth. He was looking for his gun. I got there before him, stamped on his fingers. He sank his teeth into my calf, pulled himself up by my belt; kept flailing with his mangled hand. Shit, he nearly broke my jaw. His thumb bent back and flapping against my throat."

He fell silent, pondered it all, his head hurting, teeth loose at the back.

"Like a wind-up doll. Always getting up. Even after I broke his leg."

"How did it end?" the man next to him asked. A high voice: forlorn, wilful, drunk.

Karel shrugged. "I got angry. It's happened before."

The stranger was silent long enough to give the impression he had fallen asleep. Then he gave his verdict. "He wanted to die."

"Bullshit," said Karel. "Nobody wants to die." But he grew thoughtful nonetheless. He turned his head and gave his companion a closer look. He was a big man, fifty or older, dressed in a loden coat, wool jacket, and linen shirt. "I have money," Karel said. "I need a clean shirt."

The man stripped without the slightest hesitation. Karel handed him his soiled shirt, but the drunk made no move to put it on; sat in the rain, his bare chest slick and covered in grey hairs.

"You will catch your death."

"What if I do?" the man asked.

Karel looked at him with anguish, bundled him into his jacket and coat. The man did not fight him, endured his manipulations with perfect equanimity, but like a stubborn child refused to thread his arms through the sleeves.

"I tried to jump in the river," he said, "but I got scared. The water was so dark."

"Sleep on it," Karel said. "Tomorrow's another day."

He dragged him into the shelter of a doorway, lost the clothes en route, gathered them, and once again swaddled the man as best he could.

"You want to know how it ended?" Karel asked, mournful now. "I broke his face and drowned him in a puddle. Then I went through his pockets and took all his money." He displayed the bloodied wad.

The man shook his head in parting, heaved a sigh. "Aye, my friend. It's a shitty way to go."

2.

Anna arranged matters quite simply. The concierge at the hotel would ring a bell when Neumann returned and then arm himself with a crowbar. She had taken a room on the first floor, right across from the stairs. She would open the door and ask him in. If he tried to run, her man would shatter his shins on the way down. Anna had paid him enough to trust he'd do as he was told.

As it turned out, the crowbar proved redundant. She heard the bell downstairs and opened her door. Karel saw her the moment he had mounted the last step. He was dressed in a shirt that was two sizes too small for him, and sodden. His face and hands were filthy. He looked as if he'd been in a fight.

"In here," she said. "I've money. I will pay you for the truth."

He trundled in without hesitation: head bowed, shoulders hunched, reeking of booze. She yelled down to the concierge for coffee. He brought it holding his crowbar in his other hand. She wanted Karel to see it, but the big Czech barely raised his head.

Cigarettes got his attention. She lit his and passed it over with an outstretched arm. She did not wish to step too close to him.

"You are supposed to be in Russia."

A weak smile, the rest of his face hiding behind a puff of smoke. "I have returned."

"Talk, you bastard. They saw you being arrested. In a bar; the night we went to the morgue. Two men in leather coats. Frisch showed me the witness statements. But it's all lies, isn't it?"

Karel winced, looked over, scraped blood out of a swollen ear. "Ah, my arrest. I heard about it quite by chance. Much later, in a drunk tank, in Graz. They'd found me passed out in a church pew." He opened wide his arms, as if to say, *The things we do when we get tipsy.*

She didn't do him the favour of smiling.

"Well, the copper there read it out to me. I thought it was a warrant at first; thought my goose was cooked. But what it said was 'Notification.' From Vienna, Police Headquarters. To all stations in the land, et cetera. The language they use for those things! He had to read it twice before either of us understood. 'Suspected in Soviet custody; sought for interview by Vienna police'; 'Sightings to be reported to responsible unit, see paragraph four.'" Karel shook his head and shrugged. "Once he had made some sense of it, he was all for sending me back to Vienna, under guard. He even made a phone call to someone, puffing out his chest and reporting that 'a subject answering to the description of so-and-so is in custody in X, awaiting trans-portation'—all sorts of phrases like that, all the time winking at me while I sat handcuffed to my chair. But they told him to forward the 'relevant paperwork' first, for 'assessment.' Well, that took the enthusiasm right out of my little constable. Paperwork wasn't his métier. Before long, I'd convinced him to let matters drop. For a fee, naturally. Sometimes I think the whole world is corrupt."

He sighed, mock-weary. "The truth is, I went drinking. After our trip to the morgue. At the bar I chanced on some acquaintances of mine. Army buddies, fallen on hard times, living on their wits. Crooks, if you will. They told me they were heading to the British zone, to Graz. Laxer rules, allegedly, easy ration cards. Plus they had stolen some jewellery. They thought I might know a fence. As matter of fact, I did. So I went with them. I meant to let you know, but then it sort of slipped my mind. I was embarrassed, I suppose. The thing is, I made up a little story about Beer and the Russkies, but once Sophie started making phone calls, it took on a life of its own. It seemed like a good moment to leave."

Anna listened to all this in silence, then shook her head. "It all sounds plausible, I suppose. You got cold feet and ran. Only, you're skipping over what got you so rattled." She paused, found her legs grown weak, dropped into a chair. "You know, I only figured it out tonight. The way you looked at Anton's corpse. Shocked and surprised. Total disbelief. I might have had my suspicions but for that look. It was so real." She lit another cigarette, ignored his entreaty to pass him the pack. "But it wasn't the body that shocked you. It was the eye. You hadn't known about the eye. Which means you can't have spent very much time with him. Not very much time at all.

"But how well you improvised! You said, 'It's his eye, but not his body.' Clever. You figured the police would know about the eye. Somebody else would have seen it. Or it would be in his files. You might even have thought that we were testing you: for all you knew, he'd had that eye since before the war. So you came up with a solution: his eye, not his body. And ran away as quickly as you could.

"It's almost funny. I talked to Kis tonight. You'll remember him, you two had a little heart-to-heart. Well, Kis recognized the body at a glance, a constellation of moles, for Christ's sake, on the back of Anton's shoulder. But even he didn't notice the eye." She shook her head. "It's too well made."

She tried to take another puff, found her hand shaking, ashes spilling on her lap. "Do you know what I think, Karel? You killed him. You killed my husband and then covered it up."

Karel did not answer. He looked behind himself. He might have been gauging the distance to the door.

"Just tell me," she said. It almost sounded like a plea. "You can cut and run afterwards. There's an ashtray on the table over there. You can use it to beat my skull in and jump out the window. It's isn't ten feet to the pavement. You'll be gone in no time."

Her eyes brimmed up. She wiped at them, furious, almost blinding herself with the cigarette.

"What did he ever do to you?"

Karel settled back into his seat.

"Nothing," he said. "Nothing at all."

3.

They sat smoking. When the pack ran out, she stood up, walked past Karel, shouted down to the concierge to bring up another. Karel talked. He only paused when the door opened, then resumed, mid-sentence, as soon as the concierge had left. For the first time since Anna had met him, all traces of the buffoon had left him. It was as though she were listening to another man entirely.

"I served in the Sixth Army, infantry. 'Flag-Junker-Exempted.' A shitty rank; one white V on my sleeve, and my breeches full of crabs. The only man in the unit with a made-to-measure uniform: I did not run to standard size.

"I was taken prisoner at Stalingrad. They marched us eastward, then loaded us on a train. A succession of camps, first near Uglich, then Smolensk, then all the way out to Turinsk. At Camp 221, I got diphtheria and almost died. A guard broke my ribs in 197 and locked me in an unheated closet for three days. And in 314, in Asbest, I fucked a Russian nurse and paid her with a plate of gruel. She was starving too. In April 1948, I finally got word I would be freed. But it took another six weeks. We had a lovely spring out in the Urals; a bloom of wildflowers, as far as the eye could see.

"I met Beer on the transport home. We were shut up in the same compartment, sitting on the same dirty floor. He had a friend with him; they had done years at the same camp. A fellow doctor, from Hamburg, judging by the accent, his hair as red as a flame. They were talking through half the night. I knew not a soul in the compartment and spent my time listening in.

"The thing is, I had heard of Beer before. There were stories going around about an Austrian doctor who had made friends with his camp commander. His personal physician, people said, for ailments of the soul. Head-shrinker stuff. There were some who said it was a little more saucy than that." He flicked ash. "Prison wouldn't be prison without stories of bum-fucking making the rounds.

"In any case, they talked, Beer and his Hamburg friend. About the camp, about home. He talked about you, and he talked about Lieschen. 'A crippled girl,' he said, 'a little darling.' He'd looked after her in '39. Then the system took her in its care. Beer had sworn to find her. His friend wished him good luck.

"At the border they got separated. Hamburg went north, Beer headed south. Beer made his friend memorize his address. I memorized it too: ——gasse 19. We rode the train together all the way to Vienna and never once exchanged so much as a word.

"When I got here, I forgot all about the good doctor. I was busy getting drunk. Girls, too. Four whole years, Frau Beer. It's a long time to go without.

"One afternoon, I ran out of money. Needless to say I was still drunk. I remembered Beer's address, walked through the front door of the building, slipped on the stairs, and banged the back of my head against the wall. There was a good bit of blood. I passed out on the landing.

"Next thing I know, Beer is there, looking down at me. He'd just come home, had a sheaf of letters in his hand. 'Comrade,' I say, 'we were on the same train, we shat in the same bucket.' He got me to my feet and took me into his flat.

"We sat in his study. I chose the floor: I was too dirty for his chairs. My head was bleeding. It bled on the wallpaper. Comrade Beer was too busy reading his letters to notice. He had changed since I'd last seen him, and not for the better. There'd been a sense of peace to him back on the train. Now his nerves were frayed. I recognized the symptoms. It's tough leaving the camp. A city full of people. And that strange sense of freedom: decisions waiting to be made. He told me you were coming back to him.

"That was later, though. First, he got excited about a letter. 'Lieschen,' he said. 'Finally, I found a trace.' She'd changed her name, apparently. 'Eva Frey.' He said it like it answered everything. A smile on his face, rushing to the larder to locate a bottle. 'Here,' he said, handing me a glass. 'We must celebrate.' It was then he noticed I was bleeding.

"He turned into a doctor. A dab of iodine and a bandage; he patched me up in minutes. 'Can I kip here for a night?' I asked. He thought about it. 'One night,' he said. 'My wife's coming back tomorrow. She wouldn't understand.' I thanked him like a good boy and asked did he have some food. We drank and ate until we ran out. He was quite drunk by then. 'Let's go out,' I said. 'Make a night of it.' I did not mention I hadn't any money.

"We hit the bars. You wouldn't believe how many bars there are. People starving, scrapping over ration cards, but at every corner someone will sell you apple brandy, or some vodka they've concocted from some rotten spuds. In any case, we got good and rat-arsed. Worked our way outwards, to the working-class districts, where the booze was cheaper. Beer paid for everything. 'Brother,' he called me. 'You're as big as a house.' We got chased by a Frenchy when he saw us pissing on his jeep. Then the drizzle turned into a proper storm. We ran down a street, hid in a gateway. A door was standing open, and inside was a gutted shop, undergoing renovation. Holes in the plaster, the smell of blocked sewage. But dry. I plonked down on the ground and was soon fast asleep.

"When I woke, Beer's hand was in my hair. He had a gentle touch. There was very little light: just the glow of the city seeping through the broken windows. All I could see clearly was one eye. And the look in that eye: cold, mechanical, fixed on my own. That, and he was stroking my hair. It scared the living daylights out of me.

"It took me days until I realized what he was doing. The wound on my head: he was tending the wound. The bandage had slipped with the rain. I found blood all down my neck later on. At the time, all that came to me were the rumours from the camp. His face so close, I felt his breath in my mouth.

"You know, it's funny. There was a lot of that sort of thing in the camps. Men loving men, it's as common as dirt. I got propositioned once or twice—subtle, mind; a hand on my shoulder, a questioning glance—and said no without raising a stink. But this, it scared me, my guts ran cold. All I wanted was to get away from him.

"I shoved him hard. He fell on his back, his wind knocked right out of him. I leapt up, scared and angry, looked at him in the gloom. If he had said something, or closed his eyes, made a gesture of apology—But all I saw of him was that look, that cold, dispassionate, somehow questioning look, one eye only, the other in shadow. So I kicked him, wishing to knock that look right out of him, kicked him hard in the belly, a soft sound, like kicking a football that is short on air. He rolled, tumbled over, came to rest on his back, the eye unmoved, unmoving, staring up at me with something close to glee. God, how I hated that look. I didn't know the eye was made of glass.

"I went on kicking him. I kicked him mechanically, my head empty of thought. It was only afterwards that I understood that I was angry.

Have you ever been angry like that? Something takes over, it's almost like joy. You forget yourself. All there was, was action: the fact of my kicking him. I kicked him good and proper. Stamped on him too, stamped on his face, the hands, the ankles, wanting them to break. I only stopped when nausea took over. I was drunk after all. I went outside to vomit. The rain drenched me. I went back inside and saw what I had done.

"He wasn't moving; lay on his belly, legs spread, one foot turned against its ankle, pointing up into the room. I thought for sure that he was dead.

"Shame hit me. Not regret, mind, nothing as complex as that, just hot, raw shame, the sort I knew from childhood, when you've peed in your bed. I had no thought of running away. What I needed to do was hide him. Nobody must know.

"I bustled about for some minutes, trying to come up with a plan. There was a yard full of rubble outside. And there was a cellar. I dragged him by the turned-up foot; heard his head bounce on the stairs. The cellar was black as a cave. I dragged him into what felt like a room, dropped him. When I was already back at the stairs, he made a sound. Not a cry; something like a sigh. An exhalation: the rustle of leaves. I jumped and ran.

"Out in the yard, going into the gateway, I saw his keys and wallet. They'd dropped out while I was dragging him. I scooped them up without thinking. Hiding the evidence. I ran until I found a patch of grass out by the edge of town. I passed out, woke to a goat eating the soles off my shoes and a boy running, arms spread into wings, making noises like a Stuka. He watched me vomit in a ditch and shot a salvo after me when I picked myself up and walked back into town.

"As soon as I passed a bakery, I remembered the wallet. I discarded it, everything apart from the money; threw it in a gutter. God, that cup of coffee tasted good; ersatz of course, but even so. I had five rolls and bought some schnapps from a *Tabak*. By lunchtime, I felt right as rain. It was only when evening rolled around that I started thinking about Beer. That final rustle of his breath. If it hadn't been for that, I could have buried the whole affair. As it was, it sat on my conscience. No, not my conscience, exactly. I just carried it around. It grew heavier with every hour.

"All that night I wandered around town. Aimless, drinking, muttering to myself. You see, I wasn't sure what to do. Even if I'd wanted to, I'd never have found that yard again. Still, the thought persisted. *Perhaps he wasn't dead.* Wasn't it possible, perhaps, that I had overestimated the state of his injuries? That he had woken after a few hours and gathered himself up. With a broken leg, to be sure, and a head like a wasps' nest, but alive. He was a doctor, after all; he would know what to do. I had visions of him with a little bandage around his leg: sitting in his easy chair, stuffing a pipe. So what if he'd tried to kiss me, stroked my hair? Who was to say the two of us could not be friends?

"By the time the next night rolled around, I couldn't stand it any-more. I returned to the neighbourhood of Beer's flat. I thought I would just take a peek. From outside, I could tell which windows were his. A light was on. God, if you could only imagine how happy I was about that light. I was sure we had turned it off when we left. I remembered it distinctly. The thing I forgot about, though, was that you were expected home. I drank myself stupid, plucking up my courage, then made it up the stairs.

"Out on the landing, doubt snuck back into my heart. 'What if he's angry?' I thought. 'For all you know, he's after revenge.' So I bypassed the bell. Dug his keys out of my pocket, opened the door. Better not give him time to prepare. I would walk in and tell him I was sorry. Of course, it took me time to fit the fucking key. You'd think I was trying to thread a needle: stood hunched over, eye at the lock, swaying and jamming the key into the knob.

"You know the rest. I rolled in, you were sleeping on the couch. I was well in the bag already; the shock of it gave me the rest. Come morning I had made my peace with it. I'd got used to the weight, or thrown it. A flexible conscience, mine. You questioned me, and it made sense all of a sudden. Beer was a queer. You had left him over an affair of his. Then

Sophie entered the picture, and you both showered me in money. I had no reason to move on. Not until they found the body."

He paused, seemed about to say something else, then fell silent, his head dropping into his hands, more from tiredness than remorse. Anna watched all this and smoked her cigarette down to the butt.

"You are lying," she said. She said it coolly, without pathos, as though testing a theory out loud. It was too early yet for her to assess what she felt about Karel's revelation. "You went out with him, lured him to a quiet yard, and killed him for his money. Then you came back to rob the flat."

Karel did not answer her, sat without moving, no emotion showing on his face. After some time she found the need to speak again.

"And tonight?" she asked, her eyes on his blood- and mud-stained hands, the bruises rising on his head and face. "Did you go out and murder someone else?"

He winced, started shaking. It took her some seconds to realize she had hit the mark. Her shock was genuine.

"You did, didn't you?"

He shook his head, though not in denial. "I went back to that yard," he said. "The strange thing is, I did not recognize it until tonight. I picked it out because the cellar door had no lock. Other than that, a yard like a hundred others. Mud and war rubble, and an old air-raid shelter underneath the main building. It never even crossed my mind that it might be the same.

"But when I was crouching there, behind the cellar door, it came back to me. I even heard something down in the darkness below me. The rustle of a man's breathing. Anton Beer come back to haunt me. And yet I sat and waited, despite his breathing at my back. Almost like a brave man.

"I should have waited longer after he'd dropped off the parcel; long enough to make sure he was gone. But the breathing got to me at last. I needed air." He shrugged: enormous shoulders heaving under the weight of fate.

"Whom did you—" she began asking, confused by his account, then stopped herself. She had no intention of administering justice. Let each bury their own.

"He wore a red scarf, Beer did, the night we went carousing. I laughed at him, but he said he'd caught a chill. A soldier's coat, dyed, and a red scarf worn like a muffler. 'I've been cold since '41,' he said. He hid his face and went boozing with me." Karel looked up, puzzled and worn out. "You know, all that night, I really thought he was my friend."

4.

They smoked their way through the second pack of cigarettes. She sat there, picking through his story; pictured it—Anton's fingers in Karel's hair—got Kis entangled in the thought, and herself too, the brittle memory of Anton holding her, stroking her head in the tender minutes after consummation.

"Do you hate them?" She forced the word. "Queers."

He waved it away. "Not especially. I got angry. That's all."

She nodded sombrely and considered the thought that she had lost her husband without reason. Just like all those other widows of the war.

Karel stirred. He rose slowly, not wishing to startle her. They had been talking by the light of a table lamp, and the single light source, shining upwards, emphasized the crude ridges of his cheekbones and brow.

"What do I do now?" he asked.

She did not hesitate. "Go. I never want to see you again."

"You won't call the police."

"There is no point."

Still he hesitated. "I have Eva here with me." He gestured behind. "What do I tell her?"

Anna winced at his appeal and refused an answer. He carried on all the same.

"Maybe she'll want to go back. To Robert. He doesn't know that—It was his brother whom I—"

She surprised herself with the force of her response. "Take her away. The boy deserves better."

Karel seemed relieved by this assessment. When he opened the door, he found Eva halfway down the corridor. She looked at him blandly, her face composed.

"The night porter said you had returned."

It was impossible to tell whether she had been approaching the door or retreating from it. She did not seem to notice the figure of Anna sitting behind him; at any rate she did not acknowledge her presence.

"Do you have the money?"

"Some of it," he said, and pulled from his pocket the soiled wad of bills. "But we have to run."

"Good," she said. "I'm sick of waiting."

He tried to place a hand on her shoulder as they climbed the stairs, but she shook him off.

She had never liked for anyone to touch her hump.

Part Three

When the Würzburg opthamologist Heinrich Adelmann first contacted Lud-wig Müller-Uri, the young glass-blower was barely twenty-one. This was in 1832. It was a doll that prompted Adelmann's letter, of Sonneberg manu-factory, that had curiously lifelike eyes. Eye prosthetics were primitive devices then, and French. A select number of Paris artisans manufactured them as painted shells made of thin-walled, lead-darkened glass. These eyes were tran-sitory objects: once inserted, the lacrimal fluid corroded the lead, roughening their surface; after a matter of months—sometimes mere weeks—the prosthet-ics caused such irritation they could no longer be worn.

Müller-Uri devoted many years to the task of manufacturing the perfect artificial eye. He replaced the lead first with milk glass then with cryolite, producing a more durable prosthetic whose subtle shade imitated the spongy white texture of the sclera. Not content with the look of a painted iris, he designed a way of producing its star-shaped, crystalline structures from tiny rods of coloured glass that were woven into the eye's surface. A specially de-signed melting process permitted him to suggest a soft, bleeding transition of sclera and cornea. It was left to his nephew, Friedrich Adolf Müller-Uri, to design the "reform" eye, a prosthetic shape much bulkier than the traditional "shell" or "bowl" eye, looking like a thick-walled, scooped-out semi-sphere, designed to fill the socket in patients where the entire eyeball had been lost.

Demand for all types of prosthetics spiked in the aftermath of the two world wars, though the political and material vagaries of those years left their mark on this, as on any other, industry. The Otto Bock Company, for instance, based in Duderstadt but manufacturing most of its wares in the medieval Thuringian market town of Königsee, provided a score of Great War veterans with leg and arm prostheses but saw its factory and materials confiscated by the Soviet occupational authorities, disrupting production for a number of years. Many World War II amputees flocked to Giessen, where two companies, under the names of Bergler & Rieder and Thöt & Co., sold a variety of made-to-measure prosthetic products. Müller-Uri's factory in Lauscha, meanwhile, continues to produce cryolite eyes to this very day; and a nearby toy manufacturer still sews looks of demure devotion into the faces of its dolls and teddies and stuffed dogs.

One

1.

Frisch came to Anna Beer's door early the next morning. He brought the news that her husband was dead. She opened the door but did not let him in.

"I know," she said, fetched the autopsy file from the kitchen table, and handed it over.

"You came to my flat last night," he said. "Trudi says you were looking for me."

Her answer was blunt. "I was. But now I don't need you anymore."

She closed the door and watched, through the spy hole, how Frisch slipped off his glasses and stood polishing their lenses, his face blank, his eyes blinking as though stinging from the cold.

2.

Robert came two days later. She had hardly left the flat. He was tired, hollow-eyed, inexperienced in grief. She made him tea and listened to his story; omitted to mention that she'd allowed Karel to leave. Robert sat, head bowed, weeping quietly into his cup. After an hour of this she took him lightly by the hand and led him to her bedroom. He only resisted her once, very briefly, when she lifted the shirt she had only half unbuttoned over his head. Afterwards he slept, one hand stretched across the top of her pillow, entangled with her hair. She lay next to him, taking in his smell, and found it reassured her. When he woke towards nightfall, she was pleased to see he was not ashamed.

"There's the funeral to see to," he said from the door, still doing up his trousers.

She nodded gravely, saw him out, then went through her wardrobe in search of her black suit.

3.

Robert returned the next morning, and the morning after that. After a week of this he stayed the nights too, went home only to change his clothes. They talked very little, spent most of the time in bed. Anna found it was good to be held.

"I have to go see the solicitor today," he announced one morning. "The factory is being written over to my name. Mother has agreed."

She nodded, considered what he was trying to tell her. "What exactly does it make?" she asked. "That factory of yours?"

He hesitated. "Some part you need for building radios."

"You don't know?"

Robert smiled sheepishly, picked up the phone, and called his lawyer, trying to find out.

4.

Nine weeks after Wolfgang's funeral, Robert proposed.

"I can't," she said.

He looked hurt.

"No, really," she said. "I don't have a death certificate."

"It can be arranged," he said.

She had noticed this in him: a new sense of certainty. It must come from being rich.

"Will you marry me?" he asked again.

"I am too old," she said, and took him back to bed.

5.

She often sat, stroking his face, his eye, thinking of Anton.

"Tell me about your tussle," she said.

"It was a boy from Vienna," he told her. "His father was a Socialist. He said he'd heard about my father. The detective. He said that he was nothing but a Nazi goon."

She smiled. "So you fought to defend his honour."

"No. I fought because I feared that it was true. I threw a chair at his head. He ran my face into the wall. For months you could see the stain."

"You got angry," she said. "It was almost like a kind of joy."

"Yes," he answered, looking at her in surprise. "How do you know?"

"A friend told me that that's how it feels."

6.

In February that year Poldi gave birth to her child. There were some minor complications, necessitating a week's stay at the hospital. Robert took Anna along when he went to visit her bedside.

"Look," said Poldi, pointing at the baby as though she could not believe it. "It's a boy. Don't he look just like his father?"

Anna stroked his chin and affirmed that he did. She wondered absently whether Herr Seidel had carried that same look of pride and expectation when afforded the first glimpse of his son and heir.

7.

Robert proposed again in May. The death certificate had just come through. It came in the post, without explanation, a single sheet of paper, signed and stamped. Robert had arranged it. She did not know how.

"It's stupid," she brushed off his proposal. "An infatuation. You lost your lover and now you think you must have a wife.

"I am too old," she said. That, and her uncle's maxim, voiced to her cousin when he first came home with a bride: "You don't have to buy the whole cow if you want a drink of milk."

"Will you?" he pressed her.

In time it became tiresome to demur.

"Your mother won't like it," she objected, her last line of defence.

"Mother can go to hell."

She did not ask what would happen if Eva chose to return.

8.

They were married in September. Robert's mother and Poldi were the only guests. From their excitement and laughter you would have thought they enjoyed themselves.

"Our life's a comedy," Anna said, as they made their excuses after the wedding repast and withdrew to bed. "It started badly and ends in a wedding."

He laughed and did his best to get her with child.

9.

He got stuck on the thought from time to time.

"How can it be?" he'd ask, and shift in his seat as though confessing a sin. "I thought I loved her."

"And now you love me."

He nodded.

"So you changed your mind. It happens every day." She could see the words frightened him. "I loved him too. My Anton. Even after."

"After what?"

"After I learned he slept with men." It felt good to say it. Robert seemed shocked at the revelation, then puzzled.

"How does it work?" he asked with a blush. "Sleeping with men?"

She laughed, and a minute later found herself explaining the mechanics as she imagined them. She found she had worked them out long ago, had made an inventory of all the possibilities.

"You're disgusted," she said, studying his face.

Indeed he had gone pale. But a minute later he confided, "What I was thinking: a man and a woman could do this."

"You filthy schoolboy," she chided him, but her hand reached out and squeezed her husband's, grateful for his words.

10.

When they packed up her flat, she took down the photo hanging over her bed, of a young woman with short hair. Robert had asked her about it many times.

"Who is she?"

She quoted what Eva had told her, the day they had talked in Anna's bedroom: "We will never understand all that has happened. We weren't here."

In the Seidel house she insisted on hanging the picture on the dining room wall. "It does us good," she said. "Debris from the past."

When strangers asked, she made her out to be a distant cousin, and called her Eva Frey.

11.

Two months after the wedding they found Frau Seidel crumpled on her bedroom floor, a frothy vomit on her lips. They brought her to hospital, assuming a stroke, and learned that she had ingested rat poison. Robert went home and threw out her entire collection of pharmaceuticals. It was assumed it was a mix-up, the result of frayed nerves. There was no reason to believe she had attempted suicide.

Detoxification was hard on her. On the advice of her doctor Robert had his mother committed to a private sanatorium at the edge of the city, where she was treated for morphine addiction. By silent agreement between her son and her physicians, she remained there even after the symptoms of withdrawal had subsided. Robert visited her once a week. They played cards and read the paper. Anna could not tell whether he was punishing his mother with her exile or was motivated by a sincere concern for her health. She did not ask. The house was brighter without her. Frau Seidel and Anna had never got on.

12.

Poldi's son was christened Gotthelf. Neither Anna nor Robert understood how she had decided on that name. As the boy grew into a toddler then a young child, Anna expected Poldi to leave. It wasn't lack of money that kept her. Robert had written part of the factory over to her; she received a yearly dividend of its profits. But Poldi gave no indication that she was planning to leave; she had never moved out of the room she'd lived in with Wolfgang, and spent much of her time there, listening to records and leafing through magazines. Once Robert's mother had left, she ventured forth more frequently and gradually took over many of the daily tasks of running the household. She cleaned, did laundry, took her turn at the stove. They lived side by side like strangers: cordially, that is, without friction. The only time she and Anna had a fight was when Anna suggested they hire a maid.

13.

They talked about Wolfgang only once. It was hard to say how it came about. Poldi's boy had slipped playing in the garden, cut open his knee.

Robert was away working. The two women sat together and tended to the howling boy. He ceased crying at last, curled up on the sofa with a toy.

"A tipple?" Anna asked, glad to be relieved from his noise.

"Don't mind if I do."

They had more than one. Halfway through the bottle Anna looked over at Poldi; her lean and sallow face.

"So did he do it? Wolfgang?"

Poldi returned her gaze, surprised. "Of course he did."

"Tell me."

The younger woman shrugged. "They were fighting, you know. Every day a little worse."

"About money?"

"Nah. About me."

"And?"

"It's just how you think it was. He got drunk, they had a fight, and he threw him out the window. He showed me how." She made a movement as though throwing a cat off the sofa, by the scruff of its neck. "He came to me after, ran in the room, put on his hat. 'I did him in,' he said. 'To hell with the bastard.' He was really calm, mind, only he forgot his shoes. I stood shoutin' after him, 'Take yer shoes!' but it was too late. The maid heard something or other and pretended to Frau Seidel that she'd seen for herself. Those two, they hated each other like spiders, they did. God knows why." Her eyes brimmed up a little, from booze and sympathy for her husband's ordeal. "I keep thinking he must've walked straight past him, lyin' there in the grass, bleeding like, and him wearin' only his socks."

"That's all?"

Poldi blew her nose. "What did you expect?"

"Don't tell Robert," said Anna. "It's better that he doesn't know."

14.

In the spring of '51 Sophie wrote from New York with belated congratulations. She did not explain how she had heard about the wedding. Two months on, Anna received a card announcing Sophie's own engagement; a year later, a similarly formal card announced the birth of a child. That was all they heard from the little journalist.

On none of the three occasions did Anna feel moved to respond.

15.

It was more than five years before Anna saw Frisch again. They ran into each other in the street. He was on his way home and invited her up for a coffee. She accepted and sat in his study, playing with her wedding ring.

"How extraordinary," she said, pointing at the top of his bookshelf. "What is it, exactly?"

"Police evidence," he said, fetching down the stuffed crow. "It's got some sort of infestation. And the beak has fallen off. I suppose he couldn't get the right chemicals after all." He told her the story of interrogating a Russian chemist in connection with her husband's murder.

Anna listened politely but showed no sign of real interest.

"It's all in the past for you, Frau Seidel, isn't it?"

"Yes," she said, "all in the past." Then added, "One thing, though, that I'd like to know. How did Robert's father die? The real one, the detective. We never found out the truth."

She expected Frisch to plead ignorance, but he answered her at once.

"He fell out a window," he said, and looked baffled when she started to laugh.

"It's almost a pattern," she said.

Frisch smiled his phlegmatic smile. "No, no, nothing like that. There was no suspicion of foul play. Teuben was drunk and slipped. He went to a party and attempted to urinate out of a window."

Again he had to wait until she finished laughing.

"Will you tell—the young Herr Seidel?" He had almost said "the boy."

"No," she decided. "He has quite enough on his plate thinking his father was a Nazi swine."

"Well," said Frisch, straightening his shirt front. "He was that too."

It was a morning full of mirth.

16.

On her way down from Frisch's flat Anna surprised two teenagers kissing on one of the landings. They jumped apart, embarrassed. Anna recognized the boy as the witness in the trial all those years ago. The girl was Trudi Frisch.

"What are you looking at?" Trudi barked.

"You've never liked me." Anna smiled, then looked at the boy. He was sixteen or thereabouts, something soft and trusting to his lean and girlish features. "Just like Robert used to be," she muttered to herself, and bestowed on him a smile.

The boy returned it at once.

"A handsome lad," she said to Trudi, then went on down, put an extra something to the swaying of her hips. When she reached the bottom of the stairs, she could hear the two youths enter into argument. She pressed the front door gently shut behind her.

17.

In the summer of 1959 a woman rang the doorbell of the Seidel villa. She was young, smartly dressed, and evidently well-to-do

"How do you do?" she said in English. "My German, I'm afraid, is very bad."

When Robert asked her to state her business, she blushed and gave her name.

"I am Judith Rothmann. I believe—Well, you see, my uncle used to live here."

Robert froze. Anna, standing in the corridor behind Robert, spoke past his shoulder.

"We owe you money," she said.

She said it quickly. She could not bear the thought that Robert's hesitation had roots in something other than his surprise.

The woman, meanwhile, looked from Anna to Robert, trying to establish if she was his mother, or his wife.

Two

1.

Eva and Karel left Vienna that same night. They woke up the forger, paid what they owed on the travel documents they'd commissioned, and headed north, then crossed the border into Germany on foot. By the new year they had made their way to Den Haag and spent most of their money on two berths to Boston.

All through their slow journey north, Karel was troubled by the thought that Eva had eavesdropped on his conversation with Anna Beer. He watched her closely for signs and caught her looking about herself from time to time, scanning the faces of strangers.

"No more guardian angel, eh?"

"No," she said, anger rising in her voice. "Now I've got you."

He expected to wake one morning to the sight of Eva holding a bucket of boiling water over his face.

2.

The boat had a two-week delay. It would have been wiser to leave her, but he found he did not wish to. The police must be after them, and as a couple they were easy to identify. Also, Eva herself was a risk. He could not fathom her emotions. She hardly spoke to him, shouted him down whenever he brought up Vienna, Robert, his killing of Wolfgang. All the same she stuck around, seemed reluctant to let him out of her sight.

When he went drinking, he found her insisting on coming along.

"You are making them nervous," he told her, pointing at the patrons at the bar. "You don't look like a working girl, and nobody comes here to drink with his wife."

"You're ashamed of me," she flared up, quietly, but with venom in each word. He started to deny it, but a look from her shut him up. "Leave, if you like. I can do without you."

There seemed to be no bottom to her spite.

3.

Two days into the crossing Eva fell sick. She was running a high fever. Concerned, the ship's doctor insisted on quarantine. Karel pleaded to share her isolation, arguing that, whatever it was, he was sure to be infected. He had not cared for anyone like this since his mother had died, more than a decade before: swaddling Eva, changing her sheets and nightdress, forcing beef broth down her swollen throat. In the early hours of the morning she grew lucid and stared at him in surprise. He thought she did not recognize him and attempted to soothe her with his voice.

"I'm here," he said gently. "Karel. Your friend. The Czech buffoon."

She frowned and grabbed his hand. Sometimes she looked as though she were crying.

4.

As she began to convalesce, he found himself plotting for hours, just to conjure her smile.

5.

Two weeks after they arrived in Boston, he climbed into her bed. He did so neither shyly nor forcefully but simply climbed in, still wet from a bath.

He was not even drunk. She did not fight him, lay still, expectant: from curiosity, perhaps, or because she was reconciled to the inevitability of the event.

Afterwards she caught his look. "You don't need to worry," she said, winter in her voice. "I won't get pregnant. They sterilized orphans as a matter of course."

It seemed to surprise her when he shook his head.

"It's not that," he said, dabbed with his finger at a spot of blood upon her thigh. "You should have told me. I thought you had—At the orphanage, or as a maid. Or the boy, for Christ's sake. You liked him. You said you shared a bed."

"I was saving myself," she told him coldly, turned over in bed.

He was amazed when, the very next night, she lifted her blanket and invited him back. Over the weeks and months that followed, she seemed to discover some pleasure in the act. She confided one morning, not without a smile in her voice, that it helped her fall asleep.

6.

They drifted, from Boston to Chicago, and from Chicago to Toronto, then westward, to the coast. Neither of them spoke the language. Learning it proved arduous. He worked as a day labourer, on farms in summer, in factories in winter. There always seemed to be enough work. Eva might have found work too, but within a month of disembarking it became evident she was pregnant. She gave birth in a hospital in Vancouver: twins, each with a back so straight it was a wonder to behold.

"I think I could not," she said to the nurse in her halting English.

The nurse, misinterpreting her tone, tried to reassure her. "I'll teach you about contraception," she said. "There is no need to go through this again."

She had been dismayed to learn that Eva wasn't married.

7.

Karel found work as a night porter at a hotel near the harbour. The owner, a Moravian in his sixties, took to him: he was starved of compatriots. Every evening, at the start of Karel's shift, he would join him behind the reception desk, drink beer and play chess. Within six months Karel was given the day shift, then was promoted to manager when the old one got caught with his hand in the till. His salary increased, and before long he took a loan on a house, with the old man's word as collateral. Eva watched his transformation from tramp to respectable citizen with quiet bemusement. She was attending night school and had expressed the wish to go to university once the children were in school.

At night she would sit by the children's bedside, running her fingertips up the beeline of their spines, Karel standing in the doorway, watching her smile.

8.

Blanka and Antonín. She had insisted on Czech names. "Nothing that sounds German," she said. They might have chosen Canadian names, but Jack and Jill sat too alien in their throats. At home she spoke English with Karel—accented, brisk, imperative: to her it was a language of commands. Only to the twins did he catch her whispering German, telling stories, the gentle singsong of Vienna alive in every word. He pretended to sleep sometimes, and listened to these melodies from home.

9.

She studied, earned a degree, found a job as a librarian. Now it was his turn to watch her change: the glasses, the tailored suits designed to minimize the hump, the expanding bookshelves of their house. She nagged at him. The fence needed painting, the hedges pruning, he left his dirty clothing on the floor. He grew angry, they argued, he in German, she in

English, to signal her contempt. Afterwards he made it up with flowers, with chocolates, with little funny stories that he adapted from the papers. It never ceased to bother him: how his irritation should swim topmost, undissolved within the ocean of his love.

10.

He never confessed Beer's murder to Eva. At first he was afraid. Then the fear gave way to something else, more akin to a contract.

"Did you hear—" he asked her one day, meaning the news of the day, that Stalin was dead. She didn't let him finish.

"Don't ever ask me that question," she shouted.

It took him days to figure out the nature of their miscommunication.

11.

In the early 1960s a letter arrived for Eva from Vienna. Karel did not have to read it to know it was from Robert. She took it without comment and only mentioned it once, over dinner, ladling soup out for the twins.

"He married Anna Beer, but she can't have any children."

"You still love him," he whispered, and was at a loss how to interpret her frown.

It was only later that it occurred to him that, in her own way, she had told him she was happy with her life.

Three

"Stalin's dead."

"So they say. Do you believe it?"

"No."

"How long have you been here, brother?"

"Five years in all. Two in this camp, two other camps before."

They spoke while cutting down trees. It was April: snow still on the ground, but a hint of spring in the warm air. Around them the woods of Siberia: birches, spruce, firs, and pine. The work left them little breath to speak. They left longer talk for later, lying side by side in narrow cots, searching their prison garb for fleas.

Vladimir was new to the camp. He was weak-chested, an *intelligent*. Until a year ago he had been a research neurologist at Leningrad University. He was still at the stage of imprisonment where he was adamant that a mistake had been made.

Aleksei let Vladimir speak before he shared the story of his arrest. There were rules of etiquette to this, and besides, they had plenty of time.

"I knew a neurologist once," he started, when it came to be his turn, "or rather a psychiatrist. He was my prisoner of war."

He built the story slowly, taking joy in the details, describing the camp, his rise to camp commander, then the sudden onset of depression. "It was like a trap door had opened under my feet. Darkness all around. I wrote to my wife, and all she did was send me socks. I thought, *Any day now I*

418

will take my life." He paused, more for effect than any need to collect his thoughts. "He noticed it. He hardly saw me at all, I was shut up in my barrack, avoiding the camp, but the few glimpses he had of me convinced him of my condition. His Russian was not bad. When I passed him, inspecting the condition of the sick bay in which we made him work, he said to me, 'It's like when a potato catches the blight. You break it in half, and all you find is rot. That's how it feels.' He said it quietly, so only I would hear. I stared at him and ran away as though he were the devil.

"Three days I waited until I sent for him. I really thought he was some kind of devil. I shut the door behind him, made him stand while I sat in an easy chair, polishing my handgun. I wanted him to know I could shoot him any time. But he already knew. It was myself whom I wished to remind.

"He waited in silence. A patient man, the sort that can fill you with rage. 'You are here,' I said at last, just to say something, 'to be punished for your insolence.'

"He nodded but did not reply.

"'Who do you think you are?' I yelled at him.

"'Anton Beer,' he said. Just that, no rank, not even 'Doctor.' Just his name.

"'You are a dog!' I raged at him now; you know how we learned it in the army. 'A filthy dog!'

"'Camp Commander,' he said to me, 'you are sick. Let me help you.'

"I roared at him and kicked him out. I was too upset even to order any punishment. 'Get him out of my sight,' I yelled at my orderly. The doctor followed him without another word.

"Naturally, I gave in. The very same night, I was plagued by thoughts of suicide. These weren't just idle thoughts, either. I was making plans, whether to use my gun or some other device, where to sit, whether to leave a letter, and if so what to write. It got to a point where I stood at the mirror, combing my hair, so I would look good, or at any rate decent, when they found me. What worried me most was working out when I had last eaten, and whether I had voided my bowels since then. The thought of killing myself was long familiar, but I was disturbed by the thought that I might shit my pants.

"So I called for him, had him brought to me in the middle of the night. He was cold and walked over to the stove, stood with his back to it, warming his ass.

"'Speak,' I said to him, 'make it quick.'

"'I am a psychiatrist,' he said. 'I have seen people in your condition before and have helped them. Without help,' he said, calmly, quietly, 'you will die.'

"I was taken aback. I had not considered my problem a medical issue. 'There is a drug?' I asked, hopeful, and immediately sought to dampen my hope. 'Of course, drugs are very difficult to obtain these days . . .'

"'No drug,' he said. 'It's a matter of talking.' He saw my puzzlement and hostility and quickly carried on. 'Your soul is clogged up. Constipated. Words have a way of unclogging it. Releasing the pressure. I know this is strange to you, Commander, and I am not putting it very well. But what do you have to lose?'

"I laughed at him, called him names, told him he wouldn't pull the wool over my eyes. I literally thought he must be some sort of spy, or an agitator perhaps, who was planning mischief. But he was right, of course: I was dying by inches, and had nothing to lose.

"I won't bore you with the therapy. I asked another doctor about it once, and he told me it was all humbug, and, worse, decadent, reactionary. Unpatriotic. Against the precepts of Marxist-Leninist science. There is no soul, and talk is just talk. For all I know, they are right and I recovered all by myself, the way one wakes from a funk sometimes, quite suddenly and without reason, and catches oneself laughing at it all. There can, after all, be no scientific measure for the effectiveness of talk.

"Nor was there anything very special about what he did. 'Start anywhere,' he said, me sitting in my chair, himself placed by one side of me, nearly turning his back. So I would, a little spitefully even, picking some topic that I knew was useless, how the cook had annoyed me the previous day, and how sick I was of bedbugs. He'd listen and ask questions about some detail. I would elaborate, and next thing I knew I was talking about my wife, or my father, some boyhood memory of trying on his uniform and getting in trouble for it, that sort of rot. At the end of each session I'd send him back, under guard naturally, and think to myself what a waste of time it all was. But I was no longer planning my own death.

"It went on for a few weeks. I got better. Not all at once, and not without setbacks, but slowly the dark cloud lifted from me. I wrote home and thanked my wife for the socks. Beer still came to me, four or five times every week. I knew the boys were talking all over the camp, but what could I do? I was afraid of slipping back into despair.

"In March that year he grew sick. Some sort of infection of the eye. He explained to me what it was, but of course I did not really understand him. There were some drugs that could have helped him, but despite my best attempts I was unable to procure them. The eye had to be removed. The camp surgeon did it. They fixed him up with a patch, a rag, really, just something to keep dirt out of his wound. I asked him did it bother him, and he told me there was an itch. The desire to rip the patch off, scratch inside the socket. The wound was still fresh.

"By then the talks had ceased. I felt quite healthy. It would have been best to disassociate myself from him, of course, ship him off somewhere, but I felt I owed him somehow. I had been unable to obtain the drugs needed to save his eye, but perhaps I could organize a prosthetic, something to replace the patch. I wrote letters and managed to obtain an eye from Moscow. It was so crude that one could barely recognize what it was meant to represent; when he wore it, it sucked all life out of his face. He soon returned to wearing his patch.

"There was a glass factory in the town not far from the camp. They were building scientific equipment of some sort and stayed operational all through the war. I had taken to drinking with its manager from time to time, and he had told me about one of his workers, a young man who—

421

on his own time, after hours—amused himself by blowing glass in the old manner, with a long sort of straw. He had learned it from his grandfather, he said, who had himself mastered it in some factory in Germany. The youth, the manager told me, was nothing short of a genius. He could mix colours of perfect radiance, and shape the most delicate of forms, cutting and polishing them with an astonishing level of detail. He showed me a figurine he had made, an animal half lion, half peacock. I could not believe the detail of the feathers. It would have fetched a fortune in the city.

"I had him brought to me, from curiosity more than anything. He was almost still a boy, a peasant type, with a broad face and thick blond hair. I described what I wanted. At first he showed little interest. After the wonders he had already produced, a coloured marble seemed to represent little challenge. But then he grew intrigued by the idea of fashioning an eye that would imitate the real thing down to the smallest of details. He insisted on meeting Beer. It was highly illegal, of course, taking a civilian into the camp, but I figured what the hell. We were a thousand miles from the front.

"The boy made no sketches, he just stared Beer in the eye. 'I must remember the precise shade,' he said. They stood right by a window, sunlight slanting in. There is an angle, when the sun hits the eye from the side and behind, where it will glow, really glow, and turn almost transparent. He stood an hour, memorizing the eye. Then he went home and made it.

"It took him several months. When he delivered it, it was gorgeous, a true work of art. I was tempted to keep it, as a souvenir, so to speak, but in the end my sense of indebtedness won out. I had Beer called to my quarters, presented him with the eye. The boy had used the earlier prosthetic as a guide for the eye's shape and size, and it was a good fit. When he wore it the next day, everyone stared. It was put around that he had somehow regrown the eye. 'It still itches,' he told me, 'but when I see myself in the mirror, I myself can't believe it. I close my good eye, to test whether I have sight.'

"Shortly after, I was transferred. A promotion, really: I was to run a camp much closer to home. I had stopped having anything to do with Beer by then. For some reason, seeing him with his new eye had become irritating to me. I left without saying goodbye and was demobilized a few months later. Before long, I was back home. Very soon I had forgotten about Anton Beer. Oh, sure, he had saved my life, and we had come to like one another, I suppose, insofar as that was possible, given our stations in life. But when I was home, the whole thing took on a somewhat different aspect. I felt sheepish about it, almost as if I had somehow been tricked. So I pushed it from my mind; went back to the 'business of living,' as they say. I had long before applied for a new apartment, and it finally came through. Then there were problems at work, a difficult superior, a secretary who made eyes at me. You know how it is. I was busy.

"When they arrested me, all I could think about was whether I had been denounced by someone at work. Oh, I was indignant! Ran through the names, looking for the one it could be. Maybe Stepan Stepanovich, the boozy swine! And then the interrogation started, and all they wanted to know about was the camp. They already knew everything. They even got hold of the eye! Tracked down Beer, the camp guards, some of his fellow prisoners. A whole folder full of statements. And the things they did to the doctor! They showed me pictures of his body. They picked him up abroad, they said. He was tortured like nothing you have ever seen. Confess, they said, Beer told us everything. I did, of course, but it was never enough. 'Swine,' they said. 'What else did you talk about?' 'Confess, you traitor. What state secrets did you pass on?' 'He tried to recruit you, didn't he? How was the information to be relayed?' Whole months of this, and beatings too, of course, until my every bone ached and my teeth hung loose in my gums. In the end they charged me with 'collaborating with the enemy.' I was fortunate I was not shot. Mother Russia needs loggers. I got twenty-five years. The price for survival, eh? But you know what, brother? I am glad to pay."

He paused, tired from his long story, then looked around. "I wonder about that boy, though. The glass-blower. He might have got arrested just for making that eye. Every time new prisoners come here, or I am moved to another camp, I look for him, my heart shrinking." He clenched a fist in front of his chest in illustration. "I should not have drawn him into it. But the truth is, he made a beautiful eye."

2.

The prisoner, Vladimir, listened to all this without comment and with a slight air of discomfiture. Perhaps he disliked the former camp commander and his veiled confession about his German lover. Or else he knew too much about prosthetics to believe in tales of magical eyes. He shook his head in any case and did his best to change the topic.

"Tell me, friend. Do you have a wife and children? You do? Tell me, what are they called? Anna and Yulia. Beautiful names. And how old— Ten! A good age, that. Go on, why don't you tell me about them."

Not far from them, in the bunk across a narrow strip of floor, sat a prisoner, hunched over, listening to them, cutting open a sparrow with the sharpened handle of his spoon, and slowly, carefully, pulling its delicate skin from off its flesh. Nobody knew his name. He spoke only to himself, called himself a ghost. Even the professional criminals, who served their time alongside the "politicals" and often exploited them without pity, avoided him. The right side of his face was caved in where his interrogators had beaten in his teeth, and one of his fingers had been broken so many times it stood up almost vertically from the back of his hand. When asked straight out what he had done to earn such treatment, he'd once whispered a story of how he'd "fought against God." There could be little doubt that he was mad.

Acknowledgements

When I set out to write *The Crooked Maid*, I had contracted the Balzacian bug: I wanted to write a world, not a book. All the same, a world must be assembled piece by piece. The train ride came to me early, as did the theme of parricide, both in conscious homage to Dostoevsky, whose books I love. Other, less conscious, Dostoevskianisms have crept in, further proof that books are dangerous things: you read them and they impose on you not just their words but a whole sensibility; not incidents but a mode of seeing reality.

Structurally, the book owes much to Dickens. I read *Our Mutual Friend* early into its writing, and took note of Dickens's daring in stacking incident upon incident (and coincidence upon coincidence); of his ability to connect characters high and low through crime, family scandal, and the brittle threads of chance; of his book's unstable tone that drifts from comedy to tragedy and back and is capable, despite its author's much-decried sentimentalism, of calling forth real emotion; and of his deft management of the book's vast cast (Dickens would have made a good film director).

The trial at the centre of *The Crooked Maid* owes much to Kay Boyle's wonderful 1950 *New Yorker* reportage on a Frankfurt war crimes trial. Many of its details are directly inspired by this report, which is a wonderful literary performance in its own right and (along with Boyle's other essays on postwar Germany) deserves to be rediscovered by a wider readership.

The Crooked Maid is set only two years after my first book, *Pavel & I* (albeit in a different city), but the postwar moment it depicts is quite distinct. If *Pavel & I* captures the catastrophe of deprivation at its lowest—and coldest—point, *The Crooked Maid* is interested in the social and moral flux that accompanied the early years of reconstruction. The year 1948, when the book is set, was a year of change. West Berlin had been cut off by the Soviets and had to be supplied by air; Czechoslovakia had gone Communist; and Vienna was rumoured to be riddled with spies: the Cold War had started in earnest. At the same time, identities were shifting, and an assertive type of Austrian nationalism that distanced itself from Germany, and was given licence by the Allies to describe Austria as the first victim of an expansionist Reich rather than its willing bride, was gaining ground. POWs were still returning home, displaced persons languished in camps, denazification was slowly being wound down. In Vienna itself—a city that combines aspects of the metropolis and the village—neighbours, work colleagues, and families faced each other across the chasm of their respective war experiences, a drama played out in the shadow of entire strata of society who had been murdered by the Nazi regime. I did not want to exploit the suffering that took place in this age of uncertainty but simply to understand it: so I started far from it, in a cozy train compartment, over a cup of sweet (yet bitter) tea.

Inevitably, the book contains inaccuracies. Some of these are conscious simplifications and anachronisms for the sake of brevity, suspense or poetic effect; others will have snuck in despite my best efforts. It is hoped that neither sabotage the larger truths at stake. I would like to extend my heartfelt thanks to those historians who continue to expand our knowledge about Austria under the Nazis; to Wolfgang Wieshaider, whose legal expertise helped me decode the things I saw while shadowing a number of present-day criminal trials in the Viennese courts; to Martin Herles and Žofia Mrázová, who are my first port of call for all questions Viennese; to Petra and Carolus Stiegler, for the generosity of their hospitality; to A. H. Merrills and J. Boyd White, for reading early versions of the manuscript and offering invaluable feedback; and to Joe Peschio and Elena Zakharova, for their linguistic insight and friendship.

I also wish to thank Jennifer Lambert, Jane Warren, Kathy Belden, and Helen Garnons-Williams at HarperCollins Canada and Bloomsbury for their enthusiasm, insight, and hard work, as well as Alex Schultz for the deftness of his editorial pen. To write a novel is to take risks: one follows one's impulse, against all reason. It is in the nature of the editing process to balk at risk and try to contain it; to err on the side of the conventional, safe, innocuous. I am grateful to be working with editors who are willing to defy this dynamic. They have helped me become a better writer every time I run the gauntlet of their criticism. My thanks also go to Simon Lipskar, my agent, who has been unwavering in his support, and to the team at Writers House.

Much of *The Crooked Maid* was written at a time of great personal sadness for me. I should not have finished it were it not for the support of my wife, Chantal.

This is her book also.

NOTE ON THE AUTHOR

Dan Vyleta is the son of Czech refugees who emigrated to Germany in the late 1960s.

He holds a PhD in History from the University of Cambridge. His first novel, *Pavel & I*, was published to international acclaim. His second novel, *The Quiet Twin*, was shortlisted for the Rogers Writers' Trust Fiction Prize. An inveterate migrant, Dan Vyleta calls Canada his home.

www.danvyleta.com

NOTE ON THE TYPE

The text of this book is set Adobe Garamond. It is one of several versions of Garamond based on the designs of Claude Garamond. It is thought that Garamond based his font on Bembo, cut in 1495 by Francesco Griffo in collaboration with the Italian printer Aldus Manutius. Garamond types were first used in books printed in Paris around 1532. Many of the present-day versions of this type are based on the *Typi Academiae* of Jean Jannon cut in Sedan in 1615.

Claude Garamond was born in Paris in 1480. He learned how to cut type from his father and by the age of fifteen he was able to fashion steel punches the size of a pica with great precision. At the age of sixty he was commissioned by King Francis I to design a Greek alphabet, for this he was given the honourable title of royal type founder. He died in 1561.